I Love the Way You Lie

You Lie

Arianna Fraser

Dedicated to Lynda and Erin, who prove that sisters are not always bound by blood, but by love, support, and the occasional snarky text.

Chapter 1

*In which we meet what must surely
be the most unfortunate girl in all
the Nine Realms. And her exceptionally horrid mother.*

The girl was staring up at the reverse sickle
moon, just as she always was when the
guards came for her. Smoothing down
her white dress, she gave the moon one last longing look. The girl turned around and walked
past the soldiers and through the door. She knew
what she was being called for, what the Queen of
the Dark Elves required, and she hated it. Hated
it with every cell in her body – the body that was
designed even before her birth to be a monster.
She was used to the looks and the whispers as she
walked down the hall. The girl refused to honor
any of them with a look.

"There she is, our little Executioner." Hearing the rasping croak of her mother's chief military advisor, her full lips tightened. She loathed General Gorum- tall with a vicious hooked nose and extensive facial scarring. He looked more like a vulture, feeding on carrion- looking for another bite of dead flesh. The girl passed without a glance. He wasn't important. She would do the terrible thing her mother would compel her to do, and if she was fortunate, she would be allowed to go back to her cell to stare at the moon again.

"You've kept me waiting..." her mother snarled, sitting tall and impossibly beautiful on the carved obsidian stone throne. The girl didn't apologize, but she bowed low enough to touch her mother's feet, standing again gracefully.

"What would you have me do, my queen?" The girl's voice was low, as if hoping not to be heard.

Three men were dragged before her, already beaten and bloody from several rounds with her mother's interrogators. The prisoners recognized her right away and began shrieking and pleading for mercy.

"One lies," Queen Alfhild, Her Majesty of Niflheim drawled. "The other two speak the truth. Tell me which is which, find my traitor."

The girl's eyes turned on them, a lavender shade. Unusual, compelling eyes, but for anyone in the Black Court, seeing her gaze turn to them was the most terrible thing that could happen. Because that meant that the victim's brain was about to be shredded into a thousand shrieking pieces, and their body along with it.

The slim white form walked down the granite steps, heading for the first man. He immediately began to shake, blood pouring from his nose and eventually, his eyes. The girl stepped back and shook her head. "He is not the one," she said, moving to the second man. He wailed and began flailing, fighting against the chains until the guards cruelly yanked his head back with a grip on his hair. His watery blue eyes were terrified as they were forced to meet hers. The prisoner could feel it already: black roots creeping through his mind, searing through his nerve endings. Greedy taloned fingers plunged in and pulling apart his memories, his thoughts, and fears- finding the treats they wanted and plucking them from his head. The pain was unspeakable, and he could feel the very structure of his sanity torn apart.

Suddenly, it seemed they were standing alone in that huge black room, she and he. "Why did you take it?" she asked sorrowfully. "What could have compelled you to defy the queen's rule?" He could only continue to shake his head, screaming louder and louder until he collapsed to the floor in a boneless heap. The girl stepped back and looked at her mother again. "Majesty, he is the one."

The woman leaned forward on her throne eagerly- her black eyes sparkling and ruby lips stretched into a savage grin. "Finish it here," Queen Alfhild purred. The girl's body was still, but there was a slight tremble to her mouth as she turned to do as her mother required. The traitor's body rose in the air, higher and higher, suspended over the greedy gaze of the Black Court. The Dökkálfar loved this sort of entertainment, watching the agony and suffering, hoping it would be prolonged for as long as possible. The unfortunate star of their little play of death began to spin, screams torn from his throat as blood began leaking from every pore in his body, black bile spurting from his mouth. Within moments, the body simply exploded, no longer containing enough within him to hold the traitor together. There was laughter and a light round of applause as if the courtiers had just seen a puppet show. No one noticed the girl's little body sway weakly, or if they did, it didn't matter. Trudging back up the steps to the queen, the girl watched as her mother's head tilted back, mouth open and eyes closed as if enjoying an orgasm, which she likely was. Without opening her eyes, Queen Alfhild murmured, "Debrief my advisers on what you've seen. Then you may return to your room." One ebony eye opened to stare at her offspring. "What, child? Nothing to say?" The girl folded her hands in front of her and shook her head, eyes respectfully lowered. But the Unseelie Queen was in the mood for more sport, so she fixed her eyes on her only child and spoke with the sweetness of a dessert laced with rat poison. "My dear..." her mother purred, "I feel certain you wish to speak."

The girl's pale hands gripped each other, fluttering like anxious birds.

"Do you not feel pride in your service to the Crown, daughter? Doesn't it fill you with joy to act as the Executioner of the Black Court?" Queen Alfhild noticed with cruel enjoyment that her daughter's teeth were gritted together as if to hold back the desperate truth flooding from her vocal cords.

"Well? Answer your queen," the odious General Gorum was there again, standing behind the throne, an expression of almost nauseating anticipation on his scarred face.

The girl's eyes darted back to her mother, watching the queen raise two black fingernails in a "come hither" gesture, and she broke. "I hate every moment of the evil you compel me to do. My very existence is a source of shame to me- to be used in such a monstrous way."

The huge black room was silent, eagerly awaiting the Dark Queen's response. "There now, my dear, dear daughter. Doesn't it feel so much better to speak your truth?" Taking her eyes from her trembling child, she spoke to Gorum. "After she's told you everything the traitor knew, give her 100 lashes for her ingratitude and insolence to the court."

"With pleasure, Your Grace," the general's voice shook with excitement.

The girl forced herself to bow gracefully to the monster on the throne and followed the disgusting Gorum and her guards from the throne room.

After enough time to be certain he'd pulled every scrap of information from the girl's memory, the general rose, wandering to the far side of the room and admiring his vast collection of whips and floggers. "It must be so difficult for you," Gorum mused in faux sympathy, "being forced to speak only the truth. No matter how unpleasant." Stretching his burly arms in his uniform jacket, he selected a nasty length of leather with sharp metal tips. "Certainly, princess, your unparalleled ability to find the truth in others is so very useful. It's the reason your mother hasn't gifted you to me," he leered, "yet." With his nod to the guards, the girl was dragged by her chains across the room to a set of manacles on the wall as the general raised his whip. "One..."

When the girl was released from her bonds and carried unconscious to her cell, General Gorum wiped the girl's golden blood from his hands and strolled to the queen's antechamber, where a beautiful young nobleman was feeding her slices of fruit in between kissing her feet. Waving her admirer out, she leaned forward. "What did you find?"

Gorum remained standing out of striking range. His monarch had a nasty habit of lashing out at whoever was closest when angry. "It is King Loki. He's behind everything- the recent raids wearing our borders, the slowing of the trade from the other realms-" The general ducked left as a heavy metal goblet shot past his head. "And he's been given a great deal of intelligence regarding troop movements and palace security."

"Filthy upstart!" The queen was angrily pacing the room. "That idiot Odin should have killed that devious little bastard before Loki killed *him*." She snorted inelegantly, "Sloppy sentiment! What else?"

"The traitor gave up everything he knew," the general shrugged, "the king trusts no one, he wouldn't have given his spy anything of use. But my theory... I would postulate that King Loki intends to bring Niflheim under his direct rule, as he has Vanaheim and Svartalfheim."

The Dark Queen angrily drank from her goblet, "I was this close to snaring the Dwarves, all the marvelous weapons they make..." Tapping her fingers on the table, she ordered, "You must find more of that bastard's informants. I'll make sure the girl pulls every scrap of intelligence from these spies." Gorum bowed and left, grateful that he'd escaped with his hide intact.

When the next set of guards came to relieve the ones at the girl's cell, one asked in a bored fashion, "Any changes? Orders from the queen?"

The two soldiers looked into the cell and chuckled. "The assassin will be no trouble tonight. She had quite a whipping at the queen's order."

His companion guard shuddered. "Ugly, foul thing. All the blood is an improvement." The four Dökkálfar laughed then, cruelly, as the first two left to get some rest.

Looking into the cells, one of the new guards said tersely, "You must make her ready for transport immediately." He was already opening the door and walking over to where the girl lay face-down on her cot.

The other guard was on his knees, hands knowledgeably running over the girl's lacerated back. "I can stabilize her, but not for long."

Shrugging, the man took a blanket from the cot, ready to wrap the still form in its warmth. "Do what you must, but do it quickly." Watching the spell sending a green mist over the girl's tortured body, he chafed with impatience. He would have assisted in the healing, but he needed his strength to transport all three of them past the castle enchantments and far enough away to get the girl out of the Black Court.

"She's ready, Sire."

The man frowned at the doubt in his companion's voice, but wrapped his bundle and held her close. Seconds later, the three winked out of the cell. The arrival elsewhere came with a jolt, and the poor girl moaned in agony before she could stop herself. "Hush, little monster," soothed a beautifully rich voice above her. "I must take you to safety before we are detected. You must be silent." Without even intending to, she looked up at the form towering above her and nodded obediently before slipping into blessed unconsciousness again.

When the girl opened her eyes again, she was on a diagnostic table and fuzzy forms in white robes were around her. The pain was still agonizing, dozens of cuts reopened by all the movement. Trying to find anyone or anything she could understand, her gaze finally landed on a face close to hers. Even coming from the Dökkálfar, where everyone boasted exceptional beauty, this face was extraordinary. High, sharp cheekbones, a firm, set mouth. Thick ebony hair tumbling over his shoulders, one glossy strand brushing her cheek. And his eyes- the girl nearly drowned in them, the gleaming emerald of the most perfect, translucent gem.

"Just rest, little one. These people are here to heal you. You are safe now; your mother can no longer hurt you."

The girl's voice was raw from the screams she'd held back during the whipping. "Who are you?" she barely managed to whisper, "Where am I?"

A grin stretched across the beautiful man's face then- one of such feral anticipation that she shivered. "You're at the palace here in Asgard, little one. And I am your Lord. I am King Loki."

He watched those lovely eyes widen in shock and fear before she was pulled back into that deep well, the dark dragging her under.

Chapter 2

In which King Loki's new acquisition learns about the concept "out of the frying pan and into the fire."

When the girl rose from the murky water in the well, she could hear that Voice again. Smooth, deep and eloquent, speaking authoritatively. "...Is she fertile?"

The girl's brow wrinkled. Fertile? Who was what?

"Yes, Majesty. Aside from her injuries- and there are many here, some quite old. But her reproductive capabilities are quite effective. In fact, the Princess is... ah... a... virgin."

There was laughter then, mocking laughter. "Untouched? Why, this becomes an even more delightful acquisition at every turn. Tell, would the injuries preclude...." The girl fell asleep again, too exhausted to try to understand who they were discussing.

The next time she opened her eyes was a revelation. There was an unexpected light in the room. Sitting up carefully, the girl realized she wasn't in the Healing Room any longer- trying to brace herself on her shaky arms, she looked around carefully. It was a huge, comfortable bed that held her, covered in rich velvet blankets and silk sheets in a darkly grand green. There were books - thousands of them - circling the bed in tall, tottering stacks and lining the floors, spilling out of bookshelves that covered the nearby wall. The girl's fingers twitched, longing to open one. She'd only been allowed free reign in the Royal Library at the Unseelie Court until her mother discovered how important it was to her. The first time the Queen tried to hold her daughter's access to the books as leverage over the unnatural role the girl was forced to assume, she never entered the library at her mother's Castle again. As exciting as all these literary treasures were, there was something more compelling. Not the reverse light of the sickle moon in Niflheim - nor the blacklight that shadowed her cell - had ever been this compelling. It was golden, almost searing, and the girl stumbled towards the source, a huge, open balcony that led to the outside of the room.

The girl was staring into the strange, enticing light when a muscled arm swept across her waist, making her gasp and freeze in place. "Easy, darling," the resonant voice from the night before purred into her ear, "you were about to plunge over my balcony. Despite your unique healing capabilities, that seems like an unnecessary challenge."

Even with her terror at being blocked, the lure of that blinding light was far more imperative. The girl carefully pulled away from that long arm. "May I... may I please walk outside?"

The king's brow furrowed as he looked her over carefully. "As you wish, little one."

She turned and wobbled like a newborn giraffe. When her feet crossed from the shade of the darkened room to the glorious golden sunlight, the girl gave a gasp, dropping to her knees. It hit her. Like a thousand blazing bonfires, the heat seared her and she welcomed it. Loki watched as her palms raised, open to the sun. A silver light danced playfully from one palm to another. "Aaaahhh..." she moaned, "I never dared dream of seeing the sun. Not in this lifetime." A glow infused her, surrounding the girl in searingly bright light, slowly fading until it disappeared. Loki's eye traveled over his prize. The interaction with the sun seemed to have helped her greatly- all the lash marks were gone from her back and arms. "Thank you, Sire," she breathed.

Looking out over the balcony, her eyes widened to see the peaks and spires of the golden city. There was a massive white stone wall that encircled it for as far as she could see, and the buildings glistened in the sun. She could smell the salt tang of the sea and turning to the east side of the terrace, the girl could see crystalline-blue waves rolling over the sand.

There were distant shouts and laughter, and her brows drew together. It sounded strange, alien almost until she realized what was missing: the screams of the tormented, the howls of her mother's savage dogs. The terrace she stood on was a mosaic of grey granite and a golden stone. Flowering vines curled along the pillars and a tiny waterfall came from seemingly nowhere to trickle through a portion of the stone and over the side. Absently nodding, the girl realized she was in the golden Palace of Asgard, where Odin had ruled for thousands of years and the beautiful gods - the Æsir - fought wars and created legends. And then the girl remembered who was King now- Loki.

She watched his face, her expression carefully impassive. Loki wanted something from her. Everyone always wanted something from her, so this was no different. She just needed to know what it was, and how she could escape. Even as cut off from the universe as she was, the girl knew how to listen. King Loki of Asgard was the most feared ruler in the Nine Realms. The god killed the Allfather and banished his strongest rival amongst the Gods- Thor- forever to live out his life on Midgard. He'd made it clear from the beginning that every ruler would bend a knee to him, or he'd simply take over their realm himself.

Loki walked around her in a slow circle. The girl looked much better, washed and dressed in a fresh green gown. "What is your name, darling?"

He was standing in front of her, and even as tall as the Dökkálfar were known to be, the king towered over her, surely over seven feet tall. Just as she'd thought last night, he was beautiful, but he was fearsome, too. King Loki was clad in leather armor so dark green that it was almost black, silver buckles and clasps, and the pauldron- heavy silver shielding covering his shoulders. Her new captor was deceptively lean, but she could tell his broad chest and those long legs were heavily banded with muscle. She'd heard about his savagery on the battlefield.

"I asked you a question."

The girl flushed, embarrassed to have been

caught staring. "I don't know, Your Majesty."

Loki's dark brow arched. The girl wasn't attempting to be rebellious; he knew from his spies that she was incapable of deceit or guile. "You don't know your name, or you don't have one?"

Her head dipped lower. "I may have been given a name at birth, My Lord, but I have never been called by one, so I do not know."

The king's estimation of the Dökkálfar Queen was rising. What kind of a diabolical bitch would refuse to name her own child? "Well, then," he soothed, "we shall find one for you now." He walked around her again, enjoying the obvious discomfort it gave her. As the terrifying, monstrous Executioner of the Black Court, she was likely used to everyone averting their eyes from her, turning away. No one wanted that deadly lavender gaze on them. But Loki found it very pleasant. "Hmmmm... ah. Ingrid, I think. Yes, quite fitting."

The girl simply stared back at him, confused. "Fitting? But Ingrid means 'beautiful goddess.' It could not be further from the truth. Unless perhaps you mean it ironically?"

Loki's fascination with this utterly curious creature grew. "You believe I mean to mock you by naming you after a beautiful goddess?" He knew the girl couldn't lie to him, so her comments were sincere.

"Why else?" she answered in a matter of fact tone, "I'm terribly ugly. I'm a monster."

Folding his arms across his broad chest, the king continued to watch her. Really, the pretty little elf was enthralling, like a strange species of life he'd never seen before. "You think you're repugnant?"

"I am grotesque," she answered, looking at Loki as if he were dim-witted. "Everyone says so."

Most men would race at that moment to assure this odd creature of her spectacular beauty. But the king was a god, not a man, and this little monster's ignorance of her appeal could only suit his purpose. So, he gave an elegant shrug and chided, "Nonetheless, your name is now Ingrid. Do you understand?"

Her brow wrinkled, but Ingrid nodded obediently. "As you wish, Sire."

Loki moved into the main chamber and seated himself in a huge and comfortable chair, pouring a glass of wine from the bottle next to the large platter loaded with food. Following him, Ingrid felt her stomach rumble, the noise humiliatingly loud in the quiet room. Her host's eyes glimmered and he gave her a smile. "Come here, Ingrid."

Reluctantly, she did as she was told, walking over and intending to perch on the far end of the long couch next to the king's chair. One of those damnably long arms snaked out and scooped her onto his lap. Ingrid froze, terrified. She couldn't remember ever being this close to another person or being touched in such a way. A strangled little moan slipped between her lips and Loki looked at her closely, feeling her heart rate accelerate to an alarming speed. Putting one long hand over her chest, he murmured, "Slowly. Slowly, now." Ingrid watched the green light pour from his fingertips into her skin. She could feel the organ slow its terrified gallop into a canter. Ingrid's shaking stopped, and she took in a deep breath, letting it out in a gasp.

Ingrid was suddenly aware that the king's hand hadn't left her, and in fact, was big enough to cover one breast as his rough fingertips were stroking the other. But his gaze hadn't left her face, watching the color return. "Ah- calmly, Ingrid!" Loki chided as she made another attempt to get off his lap. "You will remain right where you are, darling. Why did you respond so violently?"

"You- you're touching me," she shuddered.

Those long fingers tightened suddenly on her nipple, then released again at her yelp. "Yes, and I intend to touch you a great deal, little one, and in a far more intimate fashion." Loki said, "You're so frightened because you're a virgin? Is that the cause?"

"N-n-n-no!" Ingrid stuttered. Despite the Trickster's calming spell, her body was trembling again, legs desperate to bolt. "You're TOUCHING ME!"

Those calloused fingers continued idly stroking her silky skin as Loki pondered her utter terror. The Executioner of the Black Court, reducing to a shuddering mess? "Ah," he said abruptly, "are you telling me that no one touches you? Ever?" The last came out incredulously. Even for someone as cruel as he could be, Loki could always remember embraces from the goddesses, boorish hugs from Thor- the strokes and kisses of a thousand different lovers. "You mean to say that this is the first time you've been touched in your life?"

Ingrid could feel the calming balm from his magic sink back into her skin as she tried to answer him. "As far as I can remember- please, My Lord, please let me stand!"

The king's other arm came down heavily on her lap, pinning her in place. Moving slowly, he leaned close to her ear, speaking calmly in his slow, seductive voice. "Shhh... little one, be still. Move past your fear. Is this painful? Am I hurting you?"

Taking a shaky breath, Ingrid managed a small "No?"

"Good girl," he purred into her ear, enjoying the spray of goosebumps on her long neck from his breath, "such a good, good girl. Your lovely breasts..." Loki trailed off, still stroking the calming spell into her. "So luscious that I must kiss them." Before she could object, his dark head bent, so stark against her pale skin, to lay his lips on the swell of her breast. She could feel his lips part into a grin as she shuddered involuntarily. "Does this hurt? Have I harmed you, Ingrid?" The king hadn't moved from his comfortable position, so she could feel his lips move against her stiffening nipple as he questioned her. "Answer me."

"I am n-n-not used to this much sensation, Sire," Ingrid pleaded. "May I please move away? Please?"

The Trickster's mouth had moved on to her other nipple, his rough palm holding the weight of her breast gently. He pulled off the pink surface to answer, "No." Ingrid had no choice but to sit still, pinned by his heavy arm and those devious lips. The warmth of his spell spread through her wildly agitated nerves, and Loki grinned again as he felt her rigid body begin to slump into his. He'd pulled down her dress, resting in folds at her waist as he played with those delightfully silky breasts. When she finally gave out a moan as he pulled on a nipple with his mouth, he relented and sat up. Ingrid's arms came up to cover herself, but the king pushed them down again. Putting a glass of wine to her lips, he ordered, "Drink." Ingrid did, and he set the goblet down to put a slice of melon to her mouth.

"Eat."

Ingrid wasn't certain why she sat, nestled on his lap, obediently eating and drinking as he instructed while Loki idly stroked her breasts. But she did.

Chapter 3

*In which Ingrid learns things her
books had never taught her.*

O nce the two had eaten and drank their
fill, Ingrid's pulse began to speed again
from the speculative way her "host" was
watching her.

"How do you feel, my darling Ingrid?" he
asked, one hand smoothing over the soft flesh of
her belly.

"I'm better, Majesty, thank you?" His elf's anxiety over the shift in mood was obvious, and
Loki could see those sweet hips shift, longing to
leap from her resting place on his thighs. He was
unwilling to grant her release. He had already enjoyed the enchantment of the simple matters of
teaching her how to be touched, how to be still
and allow him access to her tender body. Not
that he was prepared to allow her the advantage
of knowing how very lovely she was.

Looking up to see her wary gaze, the king smiled and attempted to look reassuring. "You haven't eaten much in a very long time. I suspect you're quite weary. I'm going to carry you back to my bed and tuck you in. You will not struggle or fight me. Do you understand?"

Ingrid gazed up into his translucent green eyes. Why did he have to be so beautiful, so kind... she thought wistfully. But she knew it was merely a distraction while he gauged her strengths and weaknesses. "Yes, I understand." Ingrid forced herself to be still against her instinctive reaction to twist out of his grip as the Trickster stood easily, lifting her in his arms. He carried her back to the huge bed where she'd been roused before and put the girl back into the silky sheets.

"Despite your session with the sun, you need more sleep to recover," Loki said with false solicitude. "Do you feel like you can rest?"

Ingrid could easily read his lack of interest in her fragile physical state. He was attempting to bond with her as he pretended to care about her well-being. "I will be fine, Sire. Thank you for your kindness."

His terrifying eyes narrowed. Loki easily saw past her courtesies and Ingrid's attempt to smooth past the truth. "Why, darling. You sound so wary. I thought we'd reached past your initial... reluctance. Do you need more touching from me?"

He had his answer when her eyes widened in fear. "No! Ah, no. Thank you for your kindness?" Ingrid hesitated, would he accept her assurances and leave her alone? "I'm very tired..." Her excuses died off at the chill that swept over his beautiful face, turning it to white marble.

Loki stood up, his sudden movement making Ingrid curl into herself protectively. He made an elegant motion with one hand and was then covered only in loose silk lounge pants. Gently pulling up one sleeve and then the other, the King of Asgard - and by default - the Nine Realms, covered her breasts again, tucking them into the soft nightdress with careful fingers. "We'll lie together, pet." A long, slow, and vulpine smile crossed those lips. "I have a need to feel more of you, Ingrid."

Swallowing back her fears and protests, she stretched out on the lovely, soft mattress, tensing when one of those muscled arms dragged her back against her captor. "Shhh..." he soothed, "sleep now. I'll watch over you." Feeling the cool length of his body curl around hers, Ingrid set to puzzling those foreign words, "I'll watch over you." Why did the words make her feel so safe? Confused and tired, the elf gratefully submitted to a blissful dark.

Loki couldn't explain - even to himself - the dark anticipation he felt as he held the elf against him. The intelligence from his spies suggested a terrifying and powerful presence that tore apart flesh and seared minds with pleasure and impunity. Witnessing her reluctant performance and subsequent punishment yesterday at the Black Court decimated his theories of this weapon of flesh that Queen Alfhild wielded. That Ingrid was powerful, Loki had no doubt. But no one spoke of the elf's exquisite face and form, her shy nature or her innate and almost cellular resistance to the torture and death she cast upon the enemies of her queen. He had actually felt her suffering at forcing her cruel "gift" upon others as he stood disguised as a guard in her mother's court. To draw his new prize into a faithful bond where she could accept her role in "The Greater Good" could cement the unstoppable progress his ambition had blazed across the universe. The Crown Princess of the Black Court was the key. He knew it.

When Ingrid woke again, it was late evening or early morning. It was difficult for the girl to read the constellations and movement of the night sky in Niflheim, everything was reversed. "As it should be," her mother used to hiss, "the way it will be throughout the Nine Realms when I am victorious." The Queen of the Black Court was very fond of discussing the horrors the universe would face- the fire, blood, and death. Ingrid would do her best to remain perfectly still during these diatribes, attempting to make herself smaller and smaller until she would surely be invisible. But invariably, Alfhild's black eyes would land on her daughter. She would demand the guards drag out some random, howling prisoner, Ingrid would be required to rip them to shreds, hearing their screams echo through her. She gave a violent shudder. No matter what she had to do, she would never return to Niflheim.

Ingrid startled again as a blanket was placed around her shoulders. "You must be freezing, little one," purred the voice of her... host? Captor? "Are you looking for the moon?" Loki looked down as she nodded her head, trying to edge away from him without making it too apparent, and his thin lips twisted with amusement. Queens, slaves, noblewomen- even a Valkyrie or three had begged for his attention over the centuries, yet this curious creature with the body of a goddess and the mind of a monster couldn't bear to have him touch her. Nonetheless, he took her chin in one big hand and turned her face, pointing in the right direction. "Here in Asgard, you will find the moon near the constellation of the Seven Sisters just before dawn."

"Ooohhh..." Ingrid sighed, "it's full."

The king stood back and watched that curious phenomenon again, the silver light surrounding and embracing her little body.

Her eyes were the color of the violets in Frigg's gardens as she looked up to him. "Thank you," she said gravely.

"What do you thank me for?" Loki said curiously.

"For the sun," Ingrid answered as if it should be obvious, "and for the moon."

He had to throw back his dark head and laugh at that. "I fear I can take no credit for them, little one. But I'm pleased to see them heal you."

Watching his glittering eyes, she was surprised to see he was telling the truth. Of course, that was likely only because he wanted her at full strength for whatever... thing he wanted from her. The thought made Ingrid shiver again, and the king drew her back inside. "You're cold, darling. Come back to bed."

Covering her with silk blankets, Loki urged a half glass of wine to her lips to help Ingrid back to sleep. Hovering, but carefully not touching her, he used his most beautiful, persuasive tone.

"Tell me, little one, who taught you to look to the moon to regain your strength?"

It took a long moment for the princess to answer, almost tipped over the edge into sleep. "My father..." she finally whispered, almost too faint for Loki's sharp ears. "He would say... look to the moon, my Halfling. I will be there looking back...." Her lips stilled as Ingrid fell asleep, and to his surprise, the king's endlessly active mind slowed, and he did too.

Waking the next morning, Ingrid was shocked by two things: first, that the king's hand was cupping her breast in his sleep and that something hard was poking her in the back. Loki woke the instant he felt her stiffen, a slow, dark smile spread across his face as he realized what was causing her alarm. "Shhh- no, do not pull away," he ordered, voice even lower from sleep and with an edge of a growl. "Am I hurting you, darling Ingrid?"

"N-no?" her voice wavered, and he wondered if all their progress last night had disappeared.

"Then be still for a moment, and just feel. My hand is on your lovely breast- do you feel your nipple tighten?" His long fingers, heavily calloused from years of knife and swordplay were stroking her pink tips, enjoying her reaction.

"That feels good, doesn't it, little one?" He felt Ingrid nod and scolded her. "You must answer me."

"I'm... I'm not sure." she admitted, "I don't understand it."

"When I do this-" Ingrid yelped as the king plucked one nipple, "do you feel it elsewhere?"

"Like a shock?" she finally answered, "In my nerves?" Loki rolled her onto her back so the elf had to face him, still keeping one heavy hand on her breast. He pulled at the nipple again, enjoying her shiver.

He leaned down to place a kiss just under her ear, whispering in a filthy, luscious way. "Do you feel it here, little one?" Loki prodded as he slid his other hand down her stomach, touching her pelvis very gently. Ingrid's hands fluttered up like frantic birds, trying to push him away.

"Don't! I- it's-" She didn't know what she was asking, other than it was all so very... much.

The king's hand slid a little lower, a finger just hovering over her silk-clad slit. Pulling her nipple into his cool mouth, he carefully held it with his teeth, tickling the end with that unfairly dexterous tongue of his. One long finger reached down to deliberately tap Ingrid's clit.

"OH! Sire, PLEASE, please don't-" Ingrid was wiggling now, trying to move from the avalanche of sensation tearing down her nerve endings.

Loki spread her legs further and put his body between them, pressing his hardened cock against her in a most invasive way. He could feel her pulse speed up again, and carefully licked her frantically fluttering pulse on her neck. "Hush, darling. You're scaring yourself," he soothed, pushing another calming spell into her skin. "I won't cause you pain or take your innocence. I'm just showing you that touch can feel very," he ran the tip of his tongue all the way up her neck to her lips, "very good."

Pressing his lips against her warm, full ones, the king barely held back a groan. Gods, she was spectacular. Everything tasted and felt sweet and fresh on her- not at all like the Dökkálfar he'd fucked before. One hand moved up to hold her head still, and the spell was finally taking effect, Ingrid stilled and allowed him to kiss her, gently pulling her swollen lower lip between his teeth. As he slipped his tongue into her mouth, she tried to push him away again, but Loki sucked on her lower lip, distracting her. The heat he could feel between her legs told him she was not unaffected by his efforts, and the Trickster began gently pressing his stiffness down on her warmth, rotating slowly.

Ingrid was nearly in tears. It was all so much,

his huge body pressing down on hers- he was heavy and she couldn't move... but his tongue in her mouth was cool, slipping in and out in a slow, delicious way and that hard part of him kept pushing on her. The Dark Elf was inexperienced. But while untouched, she'd stood miserably at many of her mother's "dinners" that ended with everyone in the room mounting anything or anyone unfortunate enough to be in their path. But she had no idea that... part could be so large. Did he put that in other women? How could they like that? As if hearing her thoughts, Loki backed off slightly, the only contact was his mouth against hers as he hovered over her.

Between kisses, he instructed, "Put your arms around me, Ingrid." As she obeyed him, she was startled to feel his bare skin was cool. It was smooth, rippling over those thick bands of muscle she'd been certain were there, as he began to carefully move his hips against her again, her fingers tightened onto his back. Raising his head, he looked down at his lovely acquisition. Her cheeks were pink, breasts heaving rapidly as she tried to adjust to everything assaulting her senses all at once.

A slow, evil grin spread over his lips as Loki looked down. "You can dig your nails into me, darling," he teased, "it won't be the first time." As his hips gave an especially deep push against her pussy, Ingrid gasped and did just that, trying to hold on somehow. Still kissing her lips, her eyelids, cheekbones, tracing the contours of her face with lips and tongue, the king whispered, "Do you feel how wet you are? Can you feel those sweet juices trickling from your quim? That means you're enjoying this, darling. So rest your mind for a moment and pay attention to this wonderfully responsive body."

What was she supposed to do? Ingrid desperately tried to slink into Loki's mind, wishing to know what he expected from her- "Ah!"

He gave her inner thigh a sharp slap. Ingrid jumped and gasped in shock. "That was meant to hurt," he said sternly. "You do not attempt to enter my consciousness without my permission, you bad little girl. Answer me."

"I understand," Ingrid whispered, still focused on that thick thing between her legs, pressing insistently against her.

"If you try this again, I will punish you." Loki was no longer smiling, all movement stopped as he stared down at her coldly.

"Yes. I'm sorry." Ingrid didn't know what would take away that cold, angry expression from his face, but she was still very much on fire in her lower half. And for the first time, her fear of the outcome was being overruled by the decisive interest her body was showing in what happened next.

Loki's expression softened slightly, a teasing, cynical smirk touching his lips again. "Would you like to come, darling?" He knew she had no idea what he meant- usually, sexual fulfillment in the Black Court was related to death or agonizing pain. And while the king was very much looking forward to trying out a little pain on her sweet, soft body- this was not the time.

She shook her head. "I don't... I don't know what you want me to do."

Kissing her ear, Loki bit her lobe and assured her, "Nothing, sweetness. Just be still." He began to push more insistently against her wet pussy, making sure his stiff cock was still rubbing against her clit, his silk pants grinding against the thin fabric of her dress. His mouth dipped to one breast, suckling and nibbling at it as his hand stroked the other. Listening carefully to her breathing, Loki could tell how close she was. "Little one, I'm going to make you come now. You'll feel very wet and warm. This belongs to me, to your King. You will not have these without me. Do you understand?"

He could tell Ingrid was trying to answer him, but nothing came out but a shamefully loud whimper. "Please?" she groaned, "Please?"

Angling against her clitoris, Loki ordered, "You may come now." His dark head dipped to suck on a pink nipple- hard and she came. Shaking and shuddering uncontrollably as something was done to her that didn't hurt. For the first time, it didn't hurt. It was... wonderful.

Chapter 4

*In which Ingrid finally has the
courage to ask the hard questions.
And Loki is having none of it.*

I ngrid learned early on that survival at the Black Court meant being able to read people quickly. She was already alert to the fact that the intent, visual inspection Loki was currently conducting likely meant some kind of forced intimacy for her. They were just finishing breakfast in his council room.

After she'd recovered from the "coming" he'd given her, the king conjured a warm, wet cloth to clean her, enjoying her mortification as he did so. Then, he'd called in servants to dress her, giving her such a long look of filthy intent that even her attendants had to fan their flushed faces discreetly. "Attend to your new mistress," Loki drawled. "None of that ridiculous gilt and flouncing. Simple. My colors." He'd disappeared into the bathing chamber, leaving her alone with the three women staring at her.

Ingrid was miserably aware of how she looked with her crumpled dress and smelling of Loki. After an awkward silence, the elder attendant cleared her throat and stepped forward. "Good morning, Your Highness. I'm Hannah, these silly creatures are Gundrun and Elsa. We have the honor of attending to you. Do you have a preference of style for your hair?"

The girl knew her knee-length hair was likely not fashionable. "I... I do not. Perhaps I could depend on you to help me with Asgardian styles?" The two youngest lit up, chattering excitedly as if they were dressing a particularly expensive doll. Hannah shushed them and set to work. But as she held a dress to Ingrid's shoulders, her charge gasped and stumbled back, knocking awkwardly into the stone wall. Loki chose that moment to emerge from the other room, already dressed.

"What happened?" the king asked sharply, "Why is my lady distressed?" Seeing the blood drain from the faces of her attendants, Ingrid knew his legendary temper was no rumor.

"Nothing, Sire," she assured him hastily. "I just stumbled back into the wall. My clumsiness."

Eyeing her with that steely gaze, Loki knew

she was speaking the truth, yet still holding something back. Because he appreciated the slick nature of the maneuver, he let it go with a nod. "Bring Princess Ingrid to my council room when you are finished."

Grateful for the reprieve, Ingrid and her attendants exchanged relieved smiles. "Forgive me, Highness, I'm so-" Hannah was frantic to apologize, but the Dark Elf shook her head.

"No need, truly. I do not like to be touched; it is... upsetting to me. I would appreciate your patience."

"Well, Hannah did creep up on you," Gundrun volunteered helpfully. "So, it's her fault."

"Hannah's fault," agreed Elsa.

Ingrid smothered a smile at the older woman's look that promised retribution and directed them back to the task at hand. "Could you tell me a bit about Asgard and life at the palace?"

Fingers and lips flew as the ladies dressed her, and listening carefully, the girl knew getting the young maids to talk without Hannah's quelling frown would be more useful. But she stored every scrap of information away. When they were finished, they invited her to stand in front of the king's huge mirror. "I've never seen anyone more lovely grace this castle," Hannah said proudly, "except perhaps Queen Frigg."

Ingrid smiled blankly, seeing the same monster in the mirror as always. Silver-blonde hair piled on top of her head, broad cheekbones under those murderous eyes. Her body was slim, with a small waist- but with larger breasts than most of the sylph-like Black Court. Queen Alfhild liked to mock her daughter, telling her she had "teats of a peasant." In all, the same vile reflection Ingrid always viewed.

A little taken aback by the girl's disinterest in the finished product, the three guided her out to the echoing stone hallway and through an endless series of corridors until knocking on a gigantic door of blackened wood bound with iron.

The door was opened by a guard, stepping back to show the king in conversation with a woman wearing a Healer's robe. They both stared at Ingrid for a moment before Loki waved one elegant hand, dismissing everyone. "Come, darling. Break the fast with me."

And so here they were, the meal finished and that look - that terrifying, arousing expression - back on the god's face.

"May I ask a question, Sire?" Ingrid was desperate to avoid another round of the king's heavy body over hers.

Loki was circling her, enjoying those spectacular breasts displayed to modest advantage by her pale green gown. "You may," he nodded.

"What do you want from me?" Ingrid asked flatly.

Pausing in his visual inspection, the king towered over her ominously. "Why, Ingrid..." He drew her name out in a slow, clearly displeased fashion. "Is this how you thank your King? For rescuing you from brutal cruelty? At the risk of my own life? Caring for you as you recovered from your beating?"

For once, Ingrid refused to be quelled by Loki's intimidation. "I know what I am," she said quietly. "I am a monster, a weapon. There is no one in the Nine Realms who would wish to save me." Ingrid forced herself to look him in the eye, her gaze clear. "Thus, it can only be that you want something from me."

It was certain that King Loki, Allfather and His Majesty of Asgard and by extension the Nine Realms, had never been spoken to in such a way. Not for a very long time. The girl endured his slitted emerald gaze for as long as she could before dropping her own.

"At this time," he finally uttered, "I have absolutely no use for you, little girl. Other than keeping you from being wielded by your psychotic whore of a mother. And tell me, darling- who is Daddy? I can only imagine, given how you've turned out."

Ingrid's face was sheet-white and she stood, frozen, by the time Loki finished his taunt. Looking down, he recognized her stance as identical to the one she took in the Black Court. Feeling an unreasonable sense of rage at the girl shaking before him, the Trickster called angrily for the guards, telling them to return her to his rooms.

Ingrid dropped unsteadily to the huge chair where they'd shared dinner the night before. She'd expected to see the inside of a dungeon cell rather than his luxurious chambers. Certainly, this part of her curse was working perfectly. Her host-rescuer-captor had lied when he'd told her he had no intention to use her. Loki had very specific plans for her, no matter what he'd said. The elf's brow furrowed. It had been risky - throwing his hospitality in his face - hoping his anger would let his plans slip past that armored mind of his. She knew he wanted to utilize her curse for his own benefit- but there was something about "training" her? Too "reckless?" The last glimpse she'd caught from Loki was a vision of them standing together, and she was round with child. The image chilled Ingrid's heart, and with a low moan of fear, she wept silently, learning long ago that weeping out loud only invited punishment.

When the king finally returned to his chambers that night, he was tired, angry and a little drunk. His idiot generals insisted on bringing him bad news with no solutions to offer. Loki was the master of all he surveyed, but there were always challenges and treachery, particularly from Alfhild, that Black Court lunatic. A cruel smile tugged at his expressive mouth. The Trickster had made no secret of who spirited away her weapon, and from his intelligence reports, the Dark Queen's rage was simply incandescent at her loss.

The subject of his deliberations was curled up in his favorite chair, an untouched dinner tray and a towering stack of books to her left, several thick volumes piled on her right. Ingrid was clutching a huge book on potions and spells and fast asleep. The scene signaled desperation to Loki, remembering trying to read as much as he could before the books smuggled into his cell from Frigg were confiscated by Odin. He'd been imprisoned for an "Offense Against the Crown" numerous times, usually after cleaning up one of the Allfather's messes. He gritted his sharp teeth. The Allfather. The very title was offensive. Odin's parenting skills made that lunatic bitch who bore Ingrid seem positively maternal. Look how Thor and Balder turned out: everything stripped from them by their own arrogance and carelessness, thanks to their pompous sire.

Loki shrugged, pouring another glass of wine. Of course, he'd killed his father, King Laufey of Jötunnheim so really, it was all semantics at this point. Dropping carelessly to the seat adjoining Ingrid's he jolted it purposefully to wake her.

She did, with a start and jumping from the chair, still clutching the book in front of her like a shield. "Sire," she said, carefully gauging his mood. He was angry, she could see that, those perfect ebony locks in disarray and waving around his face. Frankly, Ingrid preferred it to his usual severe, slicked-back style.

"Hello, darling," he purred, "and how is my sweet acquisition this evening?"

Ingrid's heart dropped, but she tightened her mouth. At least the false solicitude was over. "I am well. Would you care for some food?"

His haughty eyes dropped to the delicious-looking plates, but Loki's face was cold. "I am hungering for something else. Since you have no other purpose..." he paused cruelly, "I think you should assist me."

She tried, she did. But Ingrid's heart started pounding wildly, her pulse fluttering beyond what she could control. Torture, she knew. Punishment, Ingrid understood, she could endure it. But this beautiful, heartless man was wildly capricious. Sometimes, a punishment was vicious words from his tongue, sometimes, that tongue was used for a purpose meant to bring wildly intense pleasure. Still, she'd never begged before- not since she was a little girl who missed her father- and she wouldn't start now. Ingrid's breath left her in an "oof!" as Loki slung her over his broad shoulder and continued into the bedroom. Throwing her in an inelegant fashion on to his bed, the king pushed up her skirts and latched his chilly mouth over the warmth of her center. This time, she did shriek. Ingrid had no understanding of what was happening to her- aside from the fact that the pain she'd been bracing for was instead a wildly arousing heat and eager rush of juices to her pelvis. Her hands went desperately to the king's thick, black hair and pulled, but he wouldn't stop, angrily sliding his arms under her knees and linking them in a grip that kept her from moving. That deliciously chilly tongue was darting all over her swollen center, biting, licking and tickling parts of her with the tip of Loki's unfairly talented muscle.

One arm left her spread legs, but as the girl tried to close them, chains sprang out from the bedposts, locking Ingrid in place with knees opened wide. His furious emerald gaze left her to look between her thighs with humiliating interest. "Why, darling," Loki purred, "your sweet little pussy is dripping wet... just like a common tavern whore. I begin to doubt your purity..."

To the Dark Elf's horror, two thick fingers began tunneling up her channel- a place that had never been touched- not ever in her lifetime. "Ow! Oh, please stop!" The plea fell from her lips without thought- she could feel the hard edges, the spread of his fingers pushing carelessly inside her. There was nothing she could do- Ingrid could tell her abilities were not something that could break the chains or release her from Loki's anger. Closing her eyes, she tried to relax- to make it hurt less- but pain, she understood. As the Dökkálfar Princess, she knew agony. So, as those long fingers kept pushing deeper inside her, Ingrid kept drifting deeper inside herself, pulling away from what was happening to her.

The burrowing assault stopped and that deep, growling voice spoke again, lips moving against her clit. "Oh, this won't do, little one. You are not allowed to withdraw from me." Another strangled shriek left her lips as those of her captor latched to her most sensitive bit and pulled sharply, at the moment his long fingers shoved deeper. "Ah, there it is..." Loki's voice purred, making her flush of humiliation even worse. "I doubted this bit of tissue, but you are untouched, aren't you, pet?" The king rose up, crawling over her generous breasts to stare down at his acquisition's overwhelmed gaze. Leaning close, he breathed into her ear, "I'm so going to enjoy tearing you, darling, feeling that tight little quim wrap around my cock, milking my come? I'm going to fuck you so deep inside your virginal cunt that your womb will have no choice but to take my seed. The next time I touch you, my precious elfin slut, I'm going to get a child on you. And I will so enjoy hearing you beg for it."

Ingrid never could have imagined that the growl of her captor's voice, those insistent fingers sliding in and out just outside her maidenhead and his terrifying promise could launch her screaming into an orgasm. It continued far beyond what was even pleasurable, those skilled lips forcing another orgasm, and then another whether she could bear them or not. And when Ingrid was finally exhausted and crying from her arousal, she felt her king kneel above her and spurt over her stomach. Shuddering from the last of her convulsions, the elf felt Loki's rough fingers rub his essence into the skin of her belly, long fingers playing with his come. And when he ordered, "Sleep, little one. You're going to need it," Ingrid mindlessly obeyed, falling into a dreamless sleep like a dive into a bottomless ocean.

Chapter 5

In which Loki tells the truth. Sort of.

After he'd successfully orgasm'd the girl into an exhausted sleep, Loki lay awake, plotting his next move. The Dökkálfar army had pulled in some of their forces, particularly around the areas where his troops tangled with theirs-and won. There has been no word or demand yet from the Black Court, but the king had no doubt it was coming. He was eager to put a child into Ingrid, something that would cement his hold on her. The main concern was whether taking her virginity would be so terrifying for the little elf that she might be driven to lash out. After seeing her literally tear that man apart at her mother's court, Loki was certain he didn't want to have to match powers against her. One dead princess and an exploded king were not in his plans. The subject of his thoughts turned over in bed, the silk coverings sliding down to her hips and showing the long line of her back. Loki's emerald gaze narrowed as he examined the markings the Healers had shown him that first night.

"Is it some kind of ritual scarring?" the king frowned, examining the long lines and marking peeking out from the brutal lash marks on the girl's back.

The healer shook her head. "We don't believe so, no. And it's not a tattoo. But there's clearly a physiological meaning for the pattern." Watching the readings from the runes she'd cast; the healer tapped her lip. "I'm going to do some research, my Lord. I'll see what I can find."

Loki's eyes dropped to the peaceful face of the Dark Elf. Unconscious and free from pain, she looked... like an angel.

Lying in bed beside her, Loki ran the lightest touch of his fingertips over the markings again. Really, they were beautiful, the intricate detail of feathers on graceful wings running the length of her back. The sweet lines were marred by a brutal chain detailing that punctured through both wings of the strange phenomenon on Ingrid's back. Her shoulder blades flexed a little as he continued tracing her lines, but not in a distressed way. More as if... her King's touch might actually be soothing. He found the waterfall of her silky hair to be the same- there was just so much of it, winding through his fingers, curling around his wrist... Loki finally fell asleep with his head resting against those pale locks, his cheek absently rubbing against her curls like an exceptionally silky pillow.

Waking and getting out of bed was the elf's sore reminder of the night before. Her nipples were still reddened, bite marks on her neck, bruises from the slow, sucking kisses the king had lavished on her breasts - but most immediate - the tenderness between her legs. Moving carefully, Ingrid made for the bathing chamber, only to see Loki leaning against the door and already dressed for the day in his dark green and silver armor. His most vulpine smile hovered on his lips, a pointed reminder of her disgraceful behavior the night before. Likened to- what did he call her? A tavern wench.

Deliberately looking over her bruises, the king purred, "A bit stiff this morning, little one?"

Barely concealing her glare, Ingrid dipped an exaggerated curtsy as she passed her tormentor to reach the bathing chamber. "Nothing of note, Your Majesty," she blinked up innocently before escaping into the room and gently shutting the door. She growled a little as she heard his mocking laughter as Loki left his chambers. Finally clean again, Ingrid gloomily examined the bruises again, hoping Hannah had something to cover them.

To their credit, all three kept completely straight faces as they draped and rearranged the cloth of her gown to cover most of the love bites and discreetly handed Ingrid a little makeup to conceal the rest. To her relief, they'd also brought a breakfast tray, so she wasn't facing a repeat of yesterday's experience. But when done, they stood. "The girls will take you to the Royal Library, Highness," said Hannah with a smile, "the king will meet you there." Ingrid's heart leaped at the prospect of all those lovely, lovely books- then plummeted again at hearing Loki would be lying in wait for her.

Entering the vast room- the girl held her hand to her heart worshipfully. It was five stories high, with narrow walkways and ladders to get to the incalculable number of books, manuscripts, scrolls, even a section of an arcane script on animal skins. At least she hoped they were animal skins. A small blaze burned in a fireplace large enough for her to stand in, the stone covered in hundreds of carvings of the Gods. "Beautiful..." Ingrid whispered reverently.

"I agree." The king was leaning against one of the huge wooden tables. He was gazing at her with that- with that look again! He ran his tongue along his lower lip to reinforce he'd not been speaking of the library. Straightening, Loki strolled over to her. "I gathered from that toppling mountain of my books you were racing through last night, that you find books as important as I do." He could feel her withdraw into herself again. If she spoke, she would be forced to tell the truth, thus giving him another weapon for compelling her to do whatever terrible thing he had planned for her.

"Ingrid." His big hand went to her chin, forcing her wary eyes to meet his. "I give you my oath as King that I will never deny you access to this library or any other. Frankly," Loki's wicked grin was back, "-there are so many more satisfying ways to punish you, little one." He savored the look of alarm in the girl's wide eyes before dropping his hand from her face.

"Why have you called me here, Sire?" Ingrid intended to handle this meeting with the king better than the last.

Instead of the anger she'd faced yesterday, Loki pulled out a seat for her, gesturing for her to sit. Eyeing the girl intently as he seated himself across from her, he suddenly gave a small chuckle. "I find myself in a bit of a quandary, darling. I am the God of Lies and Trickery. And yet I have acquired a princess that can only speak the truth. And more alarmingly, you can tear the truth from others, then rip them apart, down to the last cell." Pouring himself a glass of wine, he offered one to her. Ingrid declined politely. She couldn't tangle with this brilliant man without a clear head. Leaning back gracefully, Loki draped himself across his chair and eyed her over the rim of his wine glass. "Yes," he said suddenly, "I do want something from you. Actually," he purred, "there are many, many things I want from you, little one." The king leaned forward, those dark forest eyes gleaming, "And I intend to enjoy every. Single. One. Of. Them." Ingrid felt pinned, like a cobra's next meal unable to run from the spell of the snake's gaze. Another salacious smile crossed Loki's mobile lips before he leaned back, all business. "I was at the Black Court the day you were forced to interrogate and kill that spy. One of my best!" he said between clenched teeth. "I know your mother compelled you in your role. The blame is not yours."

Ingrid felt a horrified flush stain her cheeks. She was irrationally humiliated to know he'd witnessed her doing such a terrible thing.

"The blame is not yours," Loki repeated, "look at me." Forcing those lilac eyes upward, she tried to compose herself. "It is obvious that you did not wish to do those things. I could see your struggle. How does the Dark Queen compel you?"

Ingrid gazed evenly back, saying nothing. He

truly thought she would offer him a way to force her on a silver platter?

Loki impatiently waved one long hand. "This isn't an interrogation, little one. I'm simply trying to understand you."

Thinking for a moment, the girl decided to tell him what her mother drilled into her for years. "Queen Alfhild has told me that she is the only one in the universe who can compel me because she is-" Ingrid swallowed down her self-loathing, "-is my mother."

Loki raised one dark brow. "Then it should allay your fears that I could force you to use your considerable power."

He was lying. The girl knew it instantly. The king was certain he could find a way. What-what was that about her back?

He reached out one long arm and hauled Ingrid over the table before she could blink, throwing her over his lap and yanking her skirts up. The slap from his huge hand across her bottom was acutely painful. The girl yelped before she could stop herself, and the palm slapped the other cheek. Ingrid didn't cry out this time, keeping her teeth gritted. "What did I tell you last night when you attempted to enter my consciousness?" Loki accompanied the query with another slap over a reddened handprint.

"To not do it?" Ingrid replied, flinching as his hand came down again.

Loki spread his knees wider, jostling Ingrid. "And-" Slap! "what did I tell you-" Slap! "would happen if you disobeyed me?"

"That you would punish me?" The elf's hands tightened into fists. He couldn't break her through a beating. He must know that.

"You are a bad little girl!" Loki growled, "Apologize!"

"I am your captive!" Ingrid hissed, no longer able to hold her tongue. "For what should I apologize!" She gasped as one big hand seized her hair, tearing it from its elaborate style and wrapping it around his fist. Loki paused for a moment, appreciating how many rotations of his wrist that it took to immobilize Ingrid by that lovely, long tail of pale silk.

"Stupid, foolish girl!" the king hissed, slapping her bare bottom again, three times in rapid succession and enjoying the muffled whimpers and groans. "Did I violate YOUR privacy, little one? Did I attempt to steal your inner thoughts?"

"No, Sire!" Ingrid sobbed, humiliated to show this kind of emotion for what was really, a truly benign punishment based on her life in the Black Court. Even knowing the God of Lies was manipulating her, Ingrid sagged obediently against his lap, trying to stifle her sobs as he finished thirty swats in a spanking so aggressive it showed her how angry he was at her attempts to breach the walls guarding his thoughts.

"Ingrid, a child so unwanted that I had to name you-" Loki yanked her head upwards by his fistful of her hair, "have I ever attempted to violate your mind?"

"N-no, my King," she wept, suddenly ashamed of herself. Her body jerked as he spanked her twice more.

"Have I beaten you, shamed you?" Loki demanded, forcing her to look at him.

"N- not until now, Sire," Ingrid's eyes were streaming tears, and she was furious at herself. The night that horrible General Gorum whipped her within an inch of her life, she didn't shed a tear. But now? From a spanking? What was happening to her?

"Then do not dare - not ever - to breach my privacy again. Do you understand?" The tall god watched as her slim shoulders shook as she cried face down on his lap.

"Yes." Ingrid managed to speak it out loud.

"Yes, what?" Loki continued, inexorably.

Wiping her nose and trying to stop crying like a child, Ingrid gasped out, "I will never attempt to enter your mind without permission."

"Without permission, my King." His voice was cold, but Ingrid could feel that his terribly long fingers were making an exploratory circuit along her center - without real intent - as if simply exploring for the day.

"W- without permission, my King?" Ingrid pleaded, trying to regain her composure.

Those lovely, rough fingers paused for a moment, then continued stroking the juices from her channel along the path to her tender clitoris. "We are more alike than you think, my sweet truth-teller," Loki mused. "Neither of us wants to be forced to do the bidding of another. Both of us have had to. Despite what you think, little one, I have no wish to force you to commit more atrocities."

"You're lying!" sobbed Ingrid, "You want to use me- you think I need training! You-you want to breed me!" Her terror and distress were so obvious that the king regretfully pulled his hand from her center and sat her upright on his lap. The heat of her spanked ass against his leather trousers was arousing, but he tried to stay on task. Unwinding her hair from his fist, Loki smoothed it down, stroking it and rocking the girl's shaking form, murmuring soothing nonsense. Finally feeling the shudders stop, he raised her chin to look at him, his thumb wiping away the last of the tears.

Shaking his head, Loki mused, "I remain constantly amazed that despite the lifetime of horrors you faced at the Black Court, you find me more terrifying."

Ingrid whispered, "I knew what was expected of me there. I knew what would happen, no matter how unspeakable." She felt the soft rumble of the king chuckling.

"Is spending time with me truly so terrible, little one?"

"It is the uncertainty of what you intend for me to do, my King."

Loki smoothly angled Ingrid to sit more on one hip, taking the pressure off the heated, uncomfortable flesh of her spanked bottom. This, unfortunately, put her directly on his crotch. "What I intend," he emphasized the word, "is to teach you how to manage your gift so you don't have to create the atrocities your mother craved."

Ingrid stared at him. She so wished she could believe his kindness. But even nestled on his lap, the girl knew that for the God of Lies, it all simply served a purpose.

Chapter 6

In which Ingrid learns something utterly wonderful. And Loki proves that the best lies are filled with half-truths.

"**W**ould you like me to show you?"

Ingrid blinked. "Show me?"

Loki was unusually patient. "I can always spot a lie; you always discern the truth. Our thought process is quite similar. But you've never been taught how to temper your gift."

The girl surprised the unsurprisable Loki by violently struggling to her feet and pushing away from him. "What I do is no gift!" she spat, "It is a curse, an utterly monstrous thing! When I first understood what I was, I ran away to keep my mother from using me. The second time I tried to return to the moon."

He frowned. The phrase "return to the moon" meant the voluntary end of life for a near-immortal elf. It was unheard of. "What did the Dark Queen do then?"

Ingrid smiled bitterly. "After a four-day beating with an iron whip-" The king felt a chill run up his spine. Iron affected an elf the same way acid would damage a human. "Mother told me she would kill a thousand children if I ever tried again."

Loki was stunned, despite his calm expression. As monstrous as he knew Queen Alfhild to be, this was beyond comprehension.

Finally gathering his wits, he stood, towering his seven-foot body over hers. "I understand your horror and loathing now. But what if you could redeem the role of Executioner by taking on the mantle of Protector? It would certainly suit you."

Ingrid held herself back from him warily. "How?"

A flash of anticipation went through his eyes, and the girl nearly pulled away before he took her hand and led her to a cushioned window seat. The afternoon sun was gleaming, and Loki impulsively opened the giant stained-glass window, admiring how the sunshine surrounded the elf and poured through her. Then it clicked. "Your father- he must have been a Light Elf." Ingrid shook her head, confused. "Think, darling. You could not draw strength from the sun's rays if you were full-blooded Dark Elf."

Those huge lilac eyes looked up to him, shocked. "I... I remember my father, just a little. He would call me his 'Little Halfling'."

Loki swallowed both her hands in his big one. "This should be further proof to you, little one."

"Of what?" She was still staring up at him with those luminous eyes.

The king leaned in, squeezing her hands. "That you are also of the Ljósálfar. You are no monster."

"Let us begin." Loki stood from the remains of their afternoon meal, taken on the window seat to allow the Elf to enjoy the sun.

Ingrid reluctantly stood too, rubbing her anxious hands on her pretty green dress. Strolling through the stacks, the king selected a few volumes and led her to a deep, cozy daybed. Handing her a random book, he cautioned, "You must remember to not use your gift as a sledgehammer. Only a gentle poke is needed here, do you understand?"

"I'll try," the girl sighed, "but I have never not hurt anyone I've read."

The look he gave her then was filled with filthy promise. "Do you not remember writhing in that big chair the night before last, wanting desperately to find release?" Ingrid flushed and looked down. "Now, don't be shy- my point is that you merely tickled around the edges of my mind, quite delicately, you greedy minx." Loki gave her a long, deliberate kiss. "Now then. Touch the book, feel the weight of it in your lap. What is it's subject?"

"Gardens- medicinal to be precise."

"Now, just touch along the edge of my consciousness- I give you leave. Tell me what you hear." Loki pulled a silvery curl behind her ear.

Ingrid bent her head, tilted slightly, and there he was. *The Narcissus plant is found at water's edge, drooping over the surface, much like the Midgardian myth-"*

"You see?" Loki interrupted.

"I did!" Ingrid gasped, excited. "I heard you reading the book, I could see you by the fire, just there!"

"Well done, darling!" The king kissed her again. Ingrid found herself absurdly pleased by his praise. "I'm only giving you simple experiences to read as you develop your skills." She flushed and nodded, knowing he was taking a tremendous risk with her terrifying ability. "Here, try this one," he took the book from her and handed her a little blue volume.

This time was completely different. Loki's voice was like a touch- silky, exquisite elocution. *'I bring you then to the grove, I lay you back against the grass, unlacing that cruel bodice to free your beautiful breasts- so pale and silken, stroking your pink tips to their stiffened peaks. I bite them, my love, enough that you gasp and arch, yet your lovely legs part wider, inviting my tongue to play inside you, feeling your slick making the way for me...'*

Ingrid was speechless, clutching the book in one hand, the other in the firm grip of her King.

'How shall I be, my angel? Soft and loving- we have been apart so long. Or shall I throw you on your back to take you roughly? Is the returning warrior half mad with lust and need? Spreading those thighs as I open just enough of my armor to plunge inside you? So blissfully tight after my long absence, wrapping around my spear like wet velvet... I take your thighs in my hands to rut against you, the sweet air filled with sweat and your slick, our parts joined and parted to plunge deep and join again... How many times has my shaft thrust into your sweet core? How many times did your legs part to welcome me?

Your heat and wet- how I long to remain inside you forever...'

Ingrid suddenly gathered enough of her scattered thoughts to find herself flat on her back with Loki's long body over hers, pressing his hard cock insistently against the thin fabric protecting her center. She found her hands gripping his thick hair, that dark head against her pale breast, licking and sucking the nipple. "Your Majesty!" Ingrid nearly shrieked, so shocked and embarrassed by what had happened.

Loki looked up, releasing her nipple with a teasing "pop!" *"The Love Journals of King Eir The Conqueror to Queen Astrid."*

Swallowing against her dry throat, Ingrid managed a weak, "The... the what?"

He gently pulled her upright and began putting her breasts back into her gown, lacing it closed with suspiciously practiced fingers. "The book, darling. The passage from *'The Journals of the King'*?"

"You! That- that was no exercise! Oooooh! You tricked me!" Ingrid was spluttering with rage.

Eyeing the enraged girl with wounded innocence, the God of Lies pulled her to her feet. "I might have enjoyed this exercise a bit more than

I needed to," he agreed shamelessly, "but you still read my thoughts perfectly, did you not?"

Her full lips parted in sheer outrage before Ingrid pressed them together in mortification and fury.

After graciously walking the girl back to his chambers and kissing her with such intensity that her knees buckled, the king suggested a nap after her "strenuous" afternoon and left after tucking her in. Then, the rage he'd been holding in swept over Loki as he strode angrily to the Healer's rooms. Ingrid was half fucking Light Elf! If he knew it, it was only a matter of time before the White Court in Alfheim discovered it. By law, they could come to stake a claim on her as family. Refusing them would start a break between the realms of disastrous proportions- the Ljósálfar were Asgard's most loyal allies. But he would not give the girl up. Clenching those huge fists, he decided tonight was the night he would tear her, and his magnificent sperm would place a child inside that warm little belly.

"Are you insane or incompetent!" Loki roared at the Head Healer as the others scattered.

"Your Majesty- I- I- was just about to report to you-" the woman stammered, "please, Sire! Allow me to-"

"Your report would have been far more useful

yesterday!" Loki snarled. Angrily waving away the rest of the staff, he waited until the room was clear. "Tell me what you've found." His voice was deadly quiet, which signaled the worst of all times to be in his orbit.

Shaking, the healer brought him to her charts and pushed the buttons for images. "Her Highness is only half Dark Elf; on the maternal side-" she began before stepping back from the tall god leaning in menacingly.

"Tell me something I do not know," he snarled.

"S- s- she also holds genetic material from the Light Elves..." Loki made an impatient 'get on with it' gesture, and the healer nodded anxiously. "But that isn't all. The girl has Fairie blood."

There was dead silence in the room, broken only by the buzz from the scrying fields.

"That's impossible," Loki said flatly, "the last of the Fairies stepped sideways from the sun centuries past, disappearing from the universe."

Sweat was beading on the healer's forehead, but she stood her ground. "There is no mistake." Showing him the molecular and genetic structure from the girl's blood, Loki could see the elegant spiral of her DNA. She brought him an old book, open to an illustration that looked like the markings on Ingrid's back. "These patterns are not random, Your Grace- they are the remnants of the wings gifted to the Old Ones. Whatever her connection is to the Fairies, it's an ancient one."

Walking slowly through gardens of the late Queen Frigg, Loki's tried to process the profound significance of Ingrid's true origins. Her viperous mother had to know - by the Nornir - the Dark Queen's black talon likely stirred this magical genetic mix. But Fairie blood? How?

Loki thought of those lovely wings marking her back- and now the significance of the image of the chain cruelly binding them made sense. The illustrations the healer showed him sparked his memory of several other books he'd read about the dwindling Fairie culture. He'd been fascinated with them for centuries until the other gods caught his interest and mocked him relentlessly for it. Fairies? It had been millennia.

Since the beginning of time, Fairie was synonymous with power and magic until their ability to fly diminished, their wings disappeared. Then, the entire race began to lose their fertility- to bear children. The centuries passed as the magnificent race dwindled, until one perfect afternoon all the Fairie remaining raised their beautiful faces to the sun and simply... disappeared. Thousands of years of speculation finally concurred what was left of the legend-ary and powerful culture found somewhere else-some universe or dimension that allowed them to continue.

To add the fitting cap to the afternoon, a trembling delegate met Loki as he entered the palace. "Your Majesty- there is word from Alf-heim. King Leafstred says he wishes to speak to you regarding your recent, ah, visitor. He re-quests an audience tomorrow."

To the man's relief, Loki simply stared at him with that terrifying, cold face as he waved the poor delegate away. Clasping his hands behind him and booted feet spread, the King of Asgard stared out at his kingdom. He didn't manage to kill the Allfather, exile the other gods and take control of the Nine Realms by being a fool.

Ingrid woke from her nap to see Loki beside her, reading a book on one bent knee as his hand idly stroked through her hair. "Ah, there you are," he was smiling down at her, "do you feel better?"

The girl sat up, shifting a little, unnerved by his tenderness. "I'm well, Sire, thank you." He was looking at her in that intent appraisal again, though it didn't feel sexual this time.

"Good," the king rose, offering his hand to her. "You must be famished, come."

They ate on the huge terrace off his bedroom, the sweet scent of flowers planted by Queen Frigg drifting up in the warm evening air. Finally, Ingrid put down her fork. "You have something to tell me."

Loki leaned back in his chair, folding his hands. "Hiding anything from you is going to be a problem, isn't it?" Fighting an irrational pleasure at his hint of a future, the girl flushed and smiled. The king waved his hand and the remains of the meal disappeared. He placed a book in front of her. "What do you know of the Fairies, darling?"

Ingrid leaned forward, smiling in memory. "I loved to read about them until- at any rate, I find them utterly fascinating." Loki watched the dreamy smile spread across those full lips. "Imagine a time when the skies were filled with the winged Fairie. They fought in the Titan Wars and turned the tide against the end, it's said. And their art, and music..."

The king couldn't help the smile that curved his mouth. Her excitement was so similar to his own- as a child, he coldly reminded himself. "I used to read every book I could find about the Fairie," he said reflectively. "But I never imagined that I would meet one in my lifetime."

The elf smiled at him, a bit confused. "Such a thing will never happen, I suppose."

Loki leaned out one long finger and tapped the book. "Open the book to the illustration."

Still uncertain but smiling, she did so, pausing at the beautiful painting of the wings. Running a finger over the page, Ingrid marveled, "So real. They seem as if they might fly off the page."

He was still smiling at her in that curious way. "When is the last time you saw a reflection of your back?"

"Is this more of your teasing, my King?" Ingrid asked, uncertain.

"Not this time," Loki chuckled. "Come."

Smiling, but anxious, Ingrid rose and took his hand. Pulling her to his huge mirror, the king turned her, his nimble fingers beginning to unlace the back of her dress. Putting defensive hands over her bodice, she tried to move away. "What? Is this another trick?"

His emerald eyes met hers gravely. "Not this time." Turning her back to the mirror, he handed her another one. "Look at your back. What do you see?"

It wasn't as if Ingrid had never seen her back- just not often. She hated seeing the lash marks from her nearly constant beatings. Her uncertain gaze went back to Loki's expression- it was intent, eager. "I see... my back? The scars..."

He opened the book to the illustration. "Look again." Loki watched her expression dissolve from confusion to shock. Her disbelieving lavender gaze went from the book to her back, to him, then back again. "There is no mistake," he said. "You are part Fairie."

"H- how did you discover this?" Ingrid gasped.

"The Healer who cared for your wounds when you arrived here found something beautiful and unexpected in your DNA," Loki said, emphasizing the word beautiful. "She approached me today with the wonderful news, she took some time to research her findings to be sure. It is my honor to be able to tell you." The king chose his words carefully, he knew Ingrid viewed her creation with nothing but disgust and horror. He had to change her beliefs before getting her with child. The girl was still staring at her reflection, rapt. Loki bent and put his chin on her shoulder, gently stroking the tips of his fingers along the markings. He felt the elf's involuntary shiver and smiled, knowing she could see him as well. "Exquisite," he praised his voice almost a growl.

Ingrid shivered again, embarrassed he could make her knees weak with only the sound of his voice. And then she felt it- regret? Uncertainty? From someone as utterly certain from the king? "There's bad news," she said flatly, swinging back to careful and withdrawn. The girl tried to pull away from him and regain some self-control, but he stopped her. Those cool fingers traced the small of her back.

"Do you see these markings, Ingrid?"

She nodded sadly. The chains were hideous, tearing through the delicacy of the wings. "Yes, there's certainly nothing like those on a real Fairie."

"Do not say that!" Loki snapped, "You will not degrade your rare and unique heritage!" He softened his tone, looking at her troubled face. "This is a dark seidr," he bent again, tracing the mark of the chain. "This is how the Black Queen compels you. If we can find a way to remove it, you would be forever free from her cruel influence."

Ingrid's eyes were huge with an appeal as she looked up to him. "Is such a thing... do you really think such a thing is possible?"

Loki smiled down at her fondly, hand cupping her cheek. "I will read every book- consult every mage in the Nine Realms if I must," he said with complete honesty. "I will find a way to break her seidr on you."

The hopeful light in those violet eyes died again. "There's more. What are you not telling me?"

Loki took his hand away with the last thumb stroke over her smooth cheek. Turning her to the mirror, he rapidly re-laced her dress. Looking over her shoulder to her apprehensive reflection, he stared at her gravely. "The Elven Court knows you are here," he said it quietly, so he heard Ingrid's horrified gasp. He found himself hating how the blood drained from her face, leaving her sheet-white and trembling, and he let her see his unhappiness with seeing her this way. "They have sent a politely worded demand to see you. Tomorrow."

He almost felt a completely unfamiliar stab of guilt as Ingrid backed away, shaking her head frantically. "NO! No! I will NOT go back there! I'll- I'll leave, right now. Let me go, Sire, please! I have ways to hide, they'll never find me!"

The king held up his hands slowly as if trying to not spook a deer. "Ingrid," he said calmly, "you must listen to me, darling. You must know that Asgard and my protection is the only thing keeping you from being captured. Your moth- The Black Queen's trackers are legendary. The

Unseelie Court has the right to demand your return. But I would never allow it."

The elf sat on the window seat abruptly, as if all the strength had left her legs. "You know it is inevitable that the Dökkálfar will raise a protest. Surtur's Demons, perhaps the Dwarves would support them. There will be a battle, lives lost because of me..."

Loki walked over with measured steps; her downcast gaze saw his black boots standing in front of her before he bent those long legs to kneel in front of her. Taking her shaking hands in his big, cool ones, he angled his dark head to meet her eyes. "This is a way that no one can demand or force your return. You would be free from them."

Ingrid despised herself for the surge of hope within her. "How? What is this?"

Squeezing her hands a little tighter, Loki gave her his longest, most alluring smile, comfort radiating off him in great waves.

"Marry me."

Chapter 7

*In which lust can be lies and sex
can be a weapon.*

K ing Loki the Allfather, His Majesty of Asgard woke late the following morning
with a dark grin he couldn't seem to
wipe off his face. Ingrid was sleeping next to
him- quite deeply, given her exhaustion from
the night's activities. Loki had expected how
wildly erotic it would be, tearing away the elf's
virginity. But he'd been more than pleasantly
surprised at her responsiveness.

"Come here, darling." Loki's voice was calm,
reassuring as he held out one broad hand, expecting her to take it. Ingrid shyly did, a little unsteady on her feet. The king pressed two
glasses of wine on her earlier, promising that it
made the act easier. She felt his long, clever fingers undoing the dozens of tiny buttons on her

dress, whispering in her ear with that dark, resonant voice of his- how very beautiful she was, how satiny her skin. Ingrid could actually feel his voice sink into her, those sweet, persuasive words trickling down her spine, stiffening her nipples and making that secret part of her tingle. She was naked before her eyes even opened to see Loki standing over her, still dressed in his dark armor. The elf uncomfortably crossed her arms over herself, but his strong hands pulled them away, enjoying a leisurely look up and down her with those knowing jade eyes.

"You must never hide yourself from me, sweet Ingrid. Not your body, not your pleasure, not all those utterly arousing little moans and whimpers you make. These all belong to your King. And I will have them from you." He chuckled then and swept the wildly blushing girl into his arms, carrying her to the bed. His hard leather armor and rough silver plating chafed against her, but Loki's mouth was over hers, running his tongue between her full lips, sucking on the bottom one, drawing her tongue into his cool mouth. Putting her on the bed, the king stood at the foot, carelessly stripping off his armor, then his boots, shirt and finally the leather pants. He was amused to see the girl's mouth drop open- even if it was from anxiety, rather than admiration.

Ingrid was nearly paralyzed, watching the

god on his hands and knees, crawling up the vast expanse of velvet coverings to reach her. He was radiating the strangest things at her- she could feel lust, desire, anticipation. She didn't have to dare pry to feel it. But... there was also admiration, appreciation, even as Loki looked at her. How could he feel those things, looking at someone as ugly as she knew herself to be? He'd picked up one foot, then the other, kissing them - a king! - kissing her feet! His eyes never left hers, watching her lovely face as his lips and tongue ran a line up her calf and knee, then tracing that pointed tongue up the sensitive skin of her inner thigh, to- Her hand shot down, trying to shield her center from him.

"Y- your Highness!"

"I've told you, darling. You hide nothing from me, nothing." Then Loki's cool lips were sucking her pink nether ones into his mouth as that damnable tongue started tickling along her slit, ending up at-

"OH! Oh, you have to stop! Oh, by all the Gods, that is- OW! Are you biting me?" The last protest came out in a squeal as Ingrid tried to scramble away from the feeling of his teeth carefully holding her clitoris between them. A heavy arm, hard with muscle slammed down over the girl's hips, holding her in place.

'Ah-ah, little one.' The elf could hear him, even though those sharp white teeth were still locked on her tender bit of flesh. Her eyes widened; it was the first time Loki ever skated the surface of her thoughts to communicate. Then his tongue came to tickle the swelling clitoris held captive in the king's teeth and the shock of it made her back arch wildly as her hands grabbed his shoulders, currently between her thighs and blocking them apart. Worse, Ingrid felt them shake as her diabolical lover laughed soundlessly, then putting that hyper-aroused bud between his chilly lips to suck on it. This started off another round of shuddering and gasping, her silver-blonde hair flying everywhere.

Gently sucking Ingrid through her second orgasm, Loki placed a finger at the entrance of her channel, feeling the wetness making its way out. Pulling off her, he gave her a smile that was pure filth. "So delicious, darling. I could feast from this delectable quim all night." One long finger was swirling her slick up and down between her lips, making the girl shudder.

"It's not like this at the Black Court." Her voice was small, still panting through the last of the aftershocks.

The king's brows drew together angrily. He

knew she'd been forced to stand behind her mother's chair, holding still and silent as an orgy would rage around her, eyes fixed on some point in the distance. He'd caught a glimpse of it once as she'd come against his cock rubbing her clothed center. But Loki forced himself to keep his voice light. "How so, little one?"

He admired those delightful breasts heaving as the girl tried to breathe again. "There was... there was blood and screaming. Agony." Her light voice was calm, but he could feel the horror behind it. Sliding up her body and drifting kisses as he did so, Loki hovered above her, turning her chin to look at him.

"The corruption and filth of the Black Court will never have a place in our bed," he promised. It wasn't a lie. Even for someone with perverse appetites and centuries to enjoy them, Loki was always repelled by the vicious carnality of the, and it took a great deal of effort to disgust the God. He kissed along the line of her jaw, her lips, her high cheekbones. Even as he was comforting his tasty little virgin, the Trickster was pondering the easiest way to take her innocence. Innocence and Dark Elf was never a combination he'd encountered, which was shocking to a god with over a thousand years of experience. "There is pain, Pet. When I first take you. But this juicy quim... it will take all of me in and each time will become more pleasurable, I assure you." Playing with those satiny breasts that fascinated him, Loki placed the broad head of his cock at her entrance, idly swirling his hips to slide himself against her.

"Is it- is it supposed to be this large?"

Loki nearly bit a hole in his lip to keep from laughing at her anxious little question. "I can promise you, sweetness, that you will come to appreciate that aspect." Bending his head to a nipple, Loki sucked on it pleasurably, and then on the other, waiting for her tight thighs to loosen around his hips. Bracing his feet, the king began pushing inside her, just a bit of thick, hard flesh at a time until he felt that little barrier. He shoved through the tissue, enjoying the feeling of tearing her open as he made a sharp bite against her nipple. The pain of one was meant to distract from the agony of the other but tears spurted from those startled purple eyes. One big hand holding her hips still, he kept pushing into her excruciatingly tight pussy. Loki's eyes clenched shut, trying to keep the erotic sight of Ingrid's tear-filled eyes and the clenching of his thighs to drive deeper into her to keep him from embarrassing himself by coming like a boy into his first quim.

Ingrid was shaking underneath him, her fingernails unknowingly sinking into his arms. It was even more painful than she'd feared. She was used to pain. It had been a near-daily part of her life for as long as she could remember. She could bear it without sound or expression most of the time. But this! It burned, this thick thing invading inside her, his cool, heavy body sliding against hers as he finally reached the top of her. Ingrid could hear her soft sobs and his kisses against her trembling lips, whispering soothing words, gentle hushes as he drank down her pain.

When the elf calmed enough to withdraw her nails from his biceps, Loki's hips began moving back and forth again, feeling his cock rubbing against the ragged remains of her virtue. The intensity of his arousal made that eloquent, expressive voice of his deeper and slightly slurred, pleasuring Ingrid through his speech and the steady flow of praise for her body. "If I'd even imagined the feeling of your exquisite, grasping channel, I couldn't have stopped from seducing you the moment you'd recovered. The feel of you wrapped around me...."

Ingrid could feel two rough fingertips slide to her filled center, bracketing his cock, feeling her opening stretched tightly against him, filled to bursting. The god above her groaned, seemingly undone by a loathsome murderess like her. She could feel those long fingers spread the silky proof of her helpless arousal dripping from her body's tight seal around his shaft, sliding up to wet her clitoris and gently tug on the sensitive little button between his slippery fingers. His other hand hitched her thighs higher on his hips. "Cross your ankles around my waist," Loki urged, and Ingrid moaned at the change in angle, that thick, invasive cock rubbing against her from the inside and outside, all at once. "Aaah..." he growled, "there's my good, good girl..." The gentle, persistent rubbing of her over-sensitive clit, the movement of his lips on her mouth, her nipples, her neck- and the sheer stretch of her King's cock shoving and pulling through her channel... Ingrid was putty, boneless and moaning, begging the god above her to stop - but then to never stop - needy and shaking in a way that made her utterly helpless.

Fortunately, Loki seemed to know what she wanted, because he played with her tender clitoris, licked those hard little nipples and praised her with a stream of utterly filthy compliments in her ear as that hard piece of him shoved in and out of her, forcing Ingrid's consciousness into a tight focus of pleasure and pain as the god above her dragged her kicking and screaming into her third orgasm with that driving cock and Loki's whisper of, "Come for me now, little temptress, tighten around my cock while I spurt into you. Your pleasure is mine to own. Give it to me now." One rough hand slipped under the small of her back, caressing her and pushing her up hard against that driving piece of meat.

And with a sudden fuzz that blanked out everything but the cock inside her, the fingers playing and touching on her body and those treacherous, silky words, Ingrid obeyed him, screaming her pleasure in a way that she'd never expressed in her existence. And as he praised and kissed her, the girl felt safe enough for the first time in her life to fall asleep as he cleaned the blood from her thighs and his cock, Loki rubbing his come back up inside her, pressing gently with those long fingers to make sure her channel received it all.

The king groaned silently to find the memories of their first, second and third coupling the night before were already hardening him again. Exquisite little Ingrid was his, utterly. He'd never mentioned which Elven Court requested her audience, counting on her terror to distract her from his omission. He'd never mentioned that taking her virginity and claiming her transferred the link on that cruel chain binding her wings from that Black Court bitch to him. And the King of Asgard never told the girl that despite her fears of creating a monster, he'd already placed his seed within her and started a new life- a combination of Jötunn, Ljósálfar, Dökkálfar, and Fairie.

The king who'd killed the two men he'd called "Father" and "friend" could barely wait to find out what he'd sired in the body of the sweet girl sleeping beside him.

Chapter 8

In which Ingrid is convinced.
And impregnated.

The delegates from Asgard arrived promptly in Alfheim the following morning, bowing deeply to an impatient King Leafstred. "Your Majesty," began the lead delegate, "we bring greetings from King Loki the Allfather, His Majesty of Asgard, His Royal Highness of Jotunheim. He thanks you for your interest in his new guest, but fears he cannot honor your request. At this time."

The Asgardian was reminded of the Light Elves' ruthlessness in battle, where their forces would simply tear their enemies to pieces, their perfect faces expressionless. King Leafstred was wearing an expression that came uncomfortably close. "The White Court holds familial claim to the girl. We believed she'd been murdered with her father."

The delegate could feel his colon slam shut in terror as the White Court guards began making their way closer. "Your Highness!" he said desperately, "King Loki and Queen Ingrid are on their honeymoon, with strict orders to spend it in seclusion- you understand- but a post-wedding celebration and coronation to introduce the new queen to the Nine Realms is already being prepared for their return."

If the sweating delegate hoped the news would mollify the Light Elf King, he was sorely disappointed. The entire room fell silent- making the grinding noise of Leafstred crushing his steel goblet quite clear. "Loki has taken the girl in marriage? As his queen? AFTER A MERE THREE DAYS OF HER ACQUAINTANCE?"

Indeed, the devious Loki had convinced the terrified girl this was the best course. Still kneeling before her on his stone terrace the night before, he gazed into that expressive, lovely face. "I know we do not know each other well, darling," he said calmly. "But as Royal matches go, ours is a promising one." The king kissed one shaking hand, then the other. "I will never let that Black Court bitch hurt you again, no one will compel you to do evil."

Ingrid stood, pacing frantically. "I- I cannot, I

WILL NOT bear children! I will not condemn an innocent child to bear this curse! Marriage is impossible!"

Loki stood, waving his hand and opening the back of her dress, smoothing his cool fingertips along her wing markings. His other arm wrapped securely around the girl's waist, not quite pinning her against him. "Sweetness, my precious girl, you are the last known descendant of Fairie in our universe. We do not yet know how your mother combined your origin, but I assure you, you are rare and beautiful-"

"No! No! I am a monster! And I cannot create anything other than the same!" Ingrid put her shaking hands over her face.

"Do you find me to be a monster?" Loki's voice was genuinely sorrowful. It was a tone she'd never heard from the supremely self-assured god, sadness and even a little uncertainty. One of his big hands reached up to take hers away from where they covered her face.

As Ingrid looked down, she realized the hand holding both of hers was blue. Cobalt, to be precise.

Loki watched her expression intently. He knew he was taking a wildly dangerous risk, showing her his true self. Whatever he might have expected, it wasn't the smile of happiness as she looked up at his carefully expressionless face.

You are Jötunn!" Ingrid gasped, "I had forgotten your origin - it is not often spoken of - I have always wished to meet a Frost Giant. They would never associate with the Unseelie Court. I've read so much about them..." She was lost in delicately tracing the whorls and raised markings along Loki's arm to the spreading cobalt shade that traveled up his neck to his face. The king closed his eyes. This was the true test, no matter what Ingrid said. Frost Giants were the stuff of nightmares for most of the Nine Realms, the stories mothers told their children to terrify them into good behavior. The gigantic, savage blue race that was said to eat the flesh of man, to slaughter entire villages of innocents for entertainment. The monstrous Jötunn hidden in their frozen, isolated realm and rarely seen outside of it- other than allegedly set to unleash death and terror. When her warm little hand gently traced over those sharp, cruel cheekbones, Loki opened his eyes - slitted black pupils and red irises - the fiery color of Hel. Lavender eyes met red, and then the girl smiled in sincere pleasure.

"My king. You are... you are beautiful."

Loki stared back at Ingrid, the Princess who could only speak the truth. Hands around her waist, he abruptly raised her level with his full Frost Giant height and kissed her until she was breathless, little feet dangling somewhere above his knees.

From there, it was a matter of summoning the High Priest to the castle and letting Ingrid's silly gaggle of women spirit her away to be dressed. "Your Majesty, this is most unusual!" spluttered the holy man. Loki was letting his servant adjust the rest of his ceremonial armor before dismissing him with a wave.

Swinging his forest green cape over his shoulders with a practiced flair, the king stared down that elegant nose of his to the flustered priest. "Time is of the essence, Her Highness's safety is at risk. No one," a muscle ticked in Loki's jaw, "no one would dare lay claim to what is mine."

The priest and the king took their places, Loki lounging on his majestic throne. Ingrid was a vision, a sheer white overdress embroidered with emeralds and silver threading. Her gown was a simple sleeveless dress that managed to subtly play up two of her features that the king enjoyed most. At his specific request, her waterfall of hair tumbled to her knees, wound with strings of pearls. Subtle, unfussy, elegant. His Ingrid. He felt such a surge of possessiveness that the elf's step faltered. The Throne. That expression.

The Black Court's hideous images began running through her mind, and she almost turned back. In a moment, Loki was before her, kissing her hand gently. Leaning in close, he whispered, "If you believe that I am beautiful, sweetness, then you must accept my belief that you are simply incandescent. Exquisite. Lovely, without and within. Can you try?"

Looking into his translucent emerald eyes, Ingrid almost believed it was possible. She shyly took the hand he offered her and they knelt before the priest.

So, while the poor Asgardian delegation was hoping to escape the clearly displeased King of the White Court with all their limbs intact, Ingrid was stirring from sleep, every muscle in her body making itself known. Letting out a little groan, she tried to remember the night before. Loki's courage to show himself to her and his vow of protection. Raising her left hand, she stared open-mouthed at her exquisite wedding ring, a huge diamond that flashed blue like a cloudless sky, then again, the palest green like the Vanaheim ocean, then back to a vivid azure.

"Good morning, darling girl," purred a lovely, deep voice to her left. "You've slept so long I'd begun to think of waking you, but..." a calloused hand slid down her hip, "I imagined you needed the rest." The wicked chuckle into her neck from the god wrapped around her echoed through Ingrid's already hypersensitive nervous system.

"I'm sorry for sleeping in, Sire?" It came out as a question, really, the new Queen of Asgard too shy to look her husband in the eye.

"Mmmmmm..." Loki moaned pleasurably, nuzzling his face into her wild profusion of curls, one rough hand sliding up to cup her breasts, idly teasing her nipples. "Aren't you..." he rolled her over, settling between her thighs, "the most erotic surprise?"

"My King..." she gasped in embarrassment. As Loki ground against her center, she couldn't suppress a moan of pain.

"Little one," he soothed, "still sore? I can help you with that."

He stood and made his way to the bathing chamber; Ingrid could hear the water running. Hitching the sheet higher around her breasts, she looked around the beautiful room. She could vaguely hear the roar of the surf outside, suddenly remembering they were in his summer estate by the sea. Ingrid remembered the ceremony, his beautiful words that forced her to offer the same trust about their origins - monstrous or not - and repeat the ancient phrases that bound them. Looking down at her ring, she marveled again at its beauty.

"It belonged to Frigg," Loki said suddenly, walking in from the bathing area. "It's not her wedding ring from Odin," he said with a sneer, "but the ring she chose to celebrate her role as the Allmother. It was held in the treasure vaults along with all the Royal Jewels at the Palace. I chose it for you. I do not think you would like the gaudy and ostentatious wedding ring she was forced to wear."

Ingrid nodded with a smile, careful to avoid discussion of the god Loki killed to hold his throne. "It's beautiful, Sire, thank you."

The feral smile that always unnerved her crept across that perfect face. "Now, darling Ingrid," he purred, crawling across the bed in a repeat of last night. "I believe allowing me access into your sweet quim and smearing our juices all over each other as we came-" Loki chuckled at her painful flush, "I believe we are acquainted well enough for you to address me as Loki, or at the least, husband."

"Yes, my... oh!" the girl gasped as her new husband nipped her shoulder, "Ah, Loki?"

Carefully pulling those white teeth out of her skin, the king lifted his wife and carried her into the bathing chamber, with a gigantic granite tub big enough to fit half a dozen people. Given the rumors of her new husband's legendary appetite, the elf suspected he'd filled it to capacity more than once. He seemed to sense her emotions because Loki gave her a tender kiss. "Let me take care of you, little one." She gasped in spite of her efforts to be silent as he lifted her onto his lap in the warm water and began to soap every inch of her, soothing over the bite marks, teasingly stroking her breasts and idly circling her nipples.

Loki grunted, enjoying the way her pink nipples tightened instantly against his long, exploring fingers. As he pinched both nipples at the same time, rolling them between his chilly fingers, Ingrid let out a loud, startled yelp. She slapped her hand over her mouth, and he immediately pulled her hand away from her mouth. "You will NOT hide from me, darling. Every cry, every whimper, and moan belong to your Lord. I've told you this once." Those long, knowing fingers slid down to her pussy, two bracketing her clit and none-too-gently giving it a tug.

"Ah! My husband, it's so..."

"Rough?" Loki whispered into her ear, "Uncomfortable? Or both, but still so good you don't want me to stop?" He continued to play with her for a bit, enjoying all the desperate little sounds he dragged out of her. Easily lifting his wife and settling her on his long thighs, the king pushed back the wet strands of her hair before taking her hips to lift her over his cock. He was genuinely shocked at how hard this uneducated virgin made him, how intense it felt, spurting himself inside her. Her whimpers, then teeth burning against her lower lip to silence herself brought him back to the present. "Oh, little one..." Loki's voice was sin. "Is your sweet quim still tender? I'll make you feel so very good... soon you'll beg to fit me inside you, sore or not." Ignoring Ingrid's pained gasp, Loki pushed himself back into the sleek, tight sheath that now belonged to him. The channel that would soon give him his child. He chuckled darkly, adjusting his bride to ride him more easily. But first, he would enjoy the unspeakable pleasure of this painfully tight cunt and the silky, beautiful perfection that surrounded it. The perfection he owned.

Still moving her hips up and down on that thick piece of meat, Ingrid couldn't reconcile the change in her body. She understood pain. Thanks to her new husband, she also understood pleasure, almost more than she could bear. But both? Together - coupled with Loki's sweet words and stroking hands - it was so much. It was, it was... so much. And as Ingrid heard the pleased chuckle in her ear, she came against him. She simply didn't know how to respond to her husband's teasing and utterly obscene encouragement, still rubbing her clit against the hairy base of his thick cock. Loki's big hand was pushing hard against her spine - making her skin there tingle madly as she came - the feeling was a nagging, prodding insistence of something vitally important that she couldn't seem to make herself remember.

"It's time for you to come again. I want to feel your delicious quim ripple against me as I coat the clutching walls inside you with my essence... making you so wet." Loki's cool lips were against her ear, nearly growling with his need to come inside her. Ingrid's back arched, feeling and hearing the greedy tone of her husband surround her. "Open your mouth, little one. All your cries and moans are mine. And I will have them now." Without hesitation, the Dark Elf gave a gasping moan and arched her back, clinging to whatever part of Loki she could grasp as that invading cock of his pushed into her hard- painfully hard as his knees spread and his big hands pulled and squeezed on the girl's ass, forcing the orgasm her sore pussy never thought she could endure as Loki shoved her down hard, on his spurting cock.

Chapter 9

In which Ingrid learns about "aural orgasms" and Loki finds out that just because he wants something, doesn't mean he's going to get it. He reacts to this much as you might expect. Badly.

It was Ingrid who woke her husband this time when the afternoon sun was just beginning to shine into their bedroom. They'd both fallen asleep again after their morning round of vigorous and rather acrobatic sex. A slow smile crept across Loki's face as he felt a small hand begin to stroke his burgeoning cock. For a moment, he thought he was back in the palace with a particularly talented whore. But Loki didn't allow women to sleep in his bed after fucking them, and he grinned, gloating that he was married to the lovely owner of that stroking hand and also on his honeymoon. Turning his head to whisper into his wife's ear, Loki purred, "Why, darling. Ready again? Our marriage becomes a better decision by the moment."

He lifted Ingrid's head, forcing her shy gaze to his amused eyes. She flushed a little, but smiled and kissed his jaw. "Good afternoon, my King, ah, Loki." The girl's hand was still stroking his thick erection until the King grinned devilishly.

"Is there something you'd like from me, pet?" Loki put his hand over hers, wrapping his long fingers and showing his bride how to stroke him, tighter, slower... until they were both breathing heavily.

Ingrid suddenly felt anxious- what if he thought her behavior wanton? "It- you- you were already, um, quite solid so I didn't think you'd mind if I just..."

Loki was listening - but his long legs were tensing and feet braced on the bed - so close to coming that he groaned and yanked her hand off his cock. He attempted to smile reassuringly at her anxious query, "Did I do it in the wrong way? I could-"

"Gods, no, little one!" Loki quickly turned Ingrid and put her on her hands and knees, rough fingers slipping to her pussy to make sure she was ready for him. To his triumph, his lovely little wife was, indeed. Sliding into her as slowly as he could stand, the king idly played with her breasts as he watched the glistening length of him slide in and out of Ingrid's tender channel. Passing one big palm over the small of her back, he enjoyed the feeling of the slightest tug of the chain marking against his touch.

The slight tug made the elf stiffen suddenly, clamping down so hard against Loki's cock that it paused his thrusting. "What? I..." Ingrid's attempt to recall something important died off as her husband swiftly went back on his haunches, pulling her back to his chest and roughly pulling her knees wider.

"Look down, my lovely wife." Loki's voice was sin. Sin and promise with a guttural edge that sent goosebumps up and down Ingrid's arms. "Look at your perfect, pink quim, clutching on to me so greedily." He smiled against her long neck as a little gasp left the girl's lips. His long fingers slid down her abdomen to bracket her lips, pulling them wider to show his lengthy shaft pierce her repeatedly. The new angle pushed him hard against those tender nerves inside Ingrid, as those fingers squeezed her clit between them. "Ah, ah- no looking away," he admonished when her head fell back against his shoulder. "You must see what a terrible temptation you are to me, darling. Every second out of this snug little pussy is torture. Now, how am I to rule Asgard when all I can think of is sliding back into you..." Loki's was deepened into more of a silky growl, lips moving against his bride's sensitive ear. "I do believe my sweet, shy Ingrid enjoys it when I speak in such a filthy way." He shifted his legs, pulling her knees wider and on the outside of his. "Mmmmm..."

The elf shuddered this time, feeling his pleased rumble snake down her spine. "You want to let go, don't you, pet? All this sweet slick... smearing all over my cock." Loki took a fistful of her hair, pulling it sharply, serving to arch her back and pushing his driving cock harder against all those sensitive, delicate places within her. His other huge palm pressed against her flat stomach as he chuckled darkly. "Why, my delicious wife, I can feel myself moving inside you..." This loosed a desperate whine from the poor girl, mouth slack and unable to form words to respond. Her cruel husband kept up his loving stream of obscenities into her ear, making her certain she could come simply by the sound of that guttural, knowing tone. "Wouldn't you like to come, little one?" Loki licked a line up Ingrid's neck to her ear, biting on her earlobe. He could feel her nod desperately, unable to form a coherent sentence. "Won't you feel ever so much better, darling? That lush kitty is simply gushing sweetness, it's rubbing all over our thighs," he delivered the ruthless finish, "you've dripped on my sac, darling, would you like to feel it?" His hand on her abdomen grasped her wrist and wrapped her shaking fingers around his slick scrotum. "You will come for your King, little one." Loki's tone took on a harder edge. "I will have it from you. Now."

With a grateful moan, Ingrid did as she was told, back arched into a frantic bow and clenching so desperately against his swelling cock that it catapulted Loki into his own finish. He found himself growling and spurting violently into her, squeezing her against him. As his wife went limp inside the cage of his arms, it took the king a moment to realize she'd actually fainted. His self-satisfied growl rumbled through his broad chest as he pulled himself from her and put her on her side, curling behind her protectively. Putting a hand on Ingrid's flat belly, he stroked the soft skin, thinking about the child he'd placed there.

Finally, Loki rose to clean himself and fetch a cloth for his little bride, cleaning her thighs and pussy after playing with her slippery lips for a moment. Then, putting his dark head to Ingrid's abdomen, he ran his fingers over her skin, green feelers slipping from his fingertips into her, looking for the tiny, beating heart of his progeny. Black brows drew together as his spell moved over and over her womb, searching for the child he was certain he'd placed there. Finding nothing, Loki angrily rose and poured himself a glass of wine, stalking back and forth across their bedroom, naked and sipping from his drink. How was the stubborn creature defying him?

Staring down at Ingrid's innocent, sleeping face, he remembered soothing her before their wedding, assuring her they would not bring children into the world before she was ready. Loki's promise melted the last of the elf's opposition and she'd kissed him gratefully. Of course, he thought irritably, as her husband and King, he would be the one to decide when she was ready. And that would have been the first time he pushed his cock into her. How could his magnificent sperm not yet have taken root?

Stalking to the mansion's library, Loki went through his reference books until a vague passage reminded him of something he'd learned long ago. Elves - Light or Dark - could not be impregnated without their consent. As his wife began to stir in their bedroom, Loki's crystal goblet smashed against the library wall, trailing a long stream of red wine down the surface, like blood against an enemy's cooling body.

Chapter 10

*In which The God of Lies does
what he does best.*

To say the "honeymoon was over," was an understatement. The King of Asgard and his new Queen finished the day and slept that night at the beautiful mansion by the sea, but Loki didn't touch Ingrid again. Half of him could barely keep himself from tying his wife down and fucking her stubborn body into submission. The other side just wanted to strangle her for managing to elude his wishes. It all made Loki clench those huge fists and leave the room.

The next day, the terrible news came, and the royal couple returned with haste to Asgard. "How did this happen?" Loki hissed between clenched teeth. "Where was our border intelligence?" In what could only be in alliance with the Black Court, the Demon King Surtur sent troops into Vanaheim, destroying several villages and killing hundreds.

"My King," Ingrid spoke calmly and respectfully, aware of the generals of Asgard's military surrounding him. "I have watched the Dark Queen's strategy for years, if you allow me, perhaps I could offer-"

"Go to our chambers," her husband said shortly, eyes not lifting from the map spread before him.

"But Sire, I-"

"GO TO OUR ROOMS!" The furious gaze looked nothing like the indulgent and loving god who'd wooed her these past days, and Ingrid bowed her head and left, lips pressed tightly together to keep from trembling.

Loki slipped into their bed that night after Ingrid had fallen asleep waiting for him. He coldly looked over her beautiful face, a limp hand still holding a book open on her lap. Shedding his clothes, the king flicked his fingers at the light, sending the room into darkness as his hands spread his wife's legs. Ingrid came awake with a start to find her husband feasting on her sore but eagerly moistening pussy. As her hands slid into his thick hair, Loki took one of her swollen lower lips between his teeth, biting down and making her yelp, then going after the other one. Once the girl was shaking and wet, he moved swiftly up her body, plunging his heavy cock inside her, not seeming to hear Ingrid's gasp of pain as he moved within her immediately.

Ingrid almost felt as if she was being ravished by a stranger. Her dazed mind was trying to catch up with this unfamiliar assault, even though her hands clutching to his shoulders knew them- recognized the pull and tug of the muscle underneath. "Loki?" Ingrid whispered, trying to hear the comfort of his voice.

"Shhhh..." the king said, but nothing more as he finished inside her. Pulling from her body, Loki went into the bathing chamber, not returning with a cloth to clean his wife as before. Curling on her side, Ingrid wrapped her arms around herself and pictured making herself smaller and smaller until she fell asleep.

Her husband was gone when she woke the next morning, and Ingrid rubbed her aching head as she politely tried to answer her younger maid's questions about their trip. Hannah shrewdly watched her new Queen for a moment, then shooed the girls out on errands. "Your Majesty," she said kindly, "allow me to draw you a warm bath. Perhaps you'd like to relax for a moment, then I'll bring your breakfast to you?" The elf's look of relief and gratitude told her everything she needed to know. In no time, Ingrid was resting her sore body in the water, examining fingerprint-shaped bruises on her arms and thighs.

Ingrid felt rootless, drifting from her reality. She didn't even have a name until Loki rescued/kidnapped her from the Black Court and her murderous mother. But now, she was a wife and a queen, and she had no idea how to help her new husband. Trying to make notes on the Dökkálfar military strategy from before, she sent the information via courtier to the room where her husband was sequestered. Restlessly returning from a walk in Queen Frigg's gardens that evening, the girl wrung her hands, frustrated that she could not offer more help. To Ingrid's surprise, Loki was already there in their chambers. "I'm sorry I've abandoned you, my darling." His voice and expression were sincere- she could see that easily with her gift.

Ingrid was still for a moment. "I am so very sorry my mother's influence caused so much death and pain," she said gravely.

Her husband shook his head, rising to take her fine-boned face in those big, cool palms of his. "None of this - *none* - is your fault, my angel. I am sorry for taking my anger and concern out on you." Those reassuring hands slipped from her as her husband turned in shame. "How could I have not known that bitch's plan?" Loki said, as if to himself. "This is my responsibility, little one, not yours."

Ingrid watched her tall, proud husband slump on a chair. Going to her knees, the girl took his hands in hers, looking hopefully at his downcast face. "I was a risk. I am truly sorry that it added to your burden, dear husband. I know you care for your people. I do. I will do anything I can to help."

She softly nuzzled his hands until Loki looked up and at her. "Then love me, sweet girl. Help me to forget for tonight, at least." Ingrid could have wept with gratitude. There was nothing she wouldn't do for this beautiful man. She gently pushed him back on their bed.

Remembering how he'd played with her center, the queen placed her lips on his cock, enjoying the sudden hiss as her warm mouth met the tip of his swollen shaft. Gathering her courage, she raised her lavender eyes to his heated emerald ones. "Will you show me what pleases you?" Ingrid asked with a shy smile. His big hand came down to stroke her cheek.

"You feel perfect, my darling. Could you fit more of me inside that warm mouth of yours?" Opening wider and arching her neck as her king directed, Ingrid found that she could, enjoying the strange power of his helpless thrusts against her throat and his stream of compliments. His hand came down to gently stroke along her cheek. "Put your other hand on my sac, like you did the other afternoon."

Keeping one hand on the base of his cock, the girl did as she was told, playing with the heavy skin, rolling the testicles inside it. Ingrid was careful, his hip movements told her this prompted some decisive attention from the king. His long fingers drifted through her silver-blonde curls until he groaned and pulled her mouth off him.

"Come, darling," Loki purred, "sit on my lap." He lifted his wife easily, spreading her legs to angle over his crossed legs. Ingrid sucked in a gulp of air as she felt the uncomfortable stretch of her thighs over his, but her husband's persuasive kisses distracted her long enough for him to position her as he liked. Drawing her arms behind her back, Loki looked down, appreciating the thrust it offered those lovely breasts he enjoyed so much. His dark head bent to kiss and suck on those pink tips, enjoying how quickly her nipples hardened for him. Putting his lips to her ear, Loki whispered, "Since the moment I viewed your perfect breasts, I've dreamt how it would be to see our child suckle from you."

Ingrid shuddered- her husband's voice was his deepest and most persuasive, purring along her nerve endings. His hand gently grasped her wrists, holding them together with his strong fingers. They rested just against the base of the girl's spine, against the cruel chain markings. "I still remember your beautiful face," he whispered, making goosebumps sprout where his cool lips moved, "the first time you obeyed your King and gave me your orgasm. Mmmm..." Loki groaned, moving his wife over his cock. "Your exquisite lavender eyes, so wide in astonishment." Sliding her down his thick shaft, he waited for that little moan Ingrid gave when he was fully seated within her. His fingers holding her wrists stroked over that sensitive marking, feeling the pull of the binding again. Green light spread from his fingertips against her skin, soothing and calming her tight muscles as her thighs spread wider to accommodate him. "Do you feel me inside you? How we fit together so perfectly?"

"Yes..." Ingrid stuttered, so overcome by his cool, thick shaft inside her and his dark voice coiling into her ear. "You feel so good, my King!" She gasped as Loki thrust a little harder. "The way you stretch me? I did not know- ah!" Her husband's talented hips were thrusting again, moving his cock deeper inside her. "How can it- it hurt? Ah! But feel so wonderful..." The elf's voice died off in a gasp. What Loki did to, and for, her was nothing like her understanding of sex from the Black Court, where everything was pain, misery, and degradation.

As if he could hear her thoughts, Loki whispered, "You should never be afraid of me- of what we do together. I will always keep you safe. Anything I do that hurts you will give you as much pleasure, if not more. My beautiful, elegant girl..." He was thrusting into her then, and it was difficult to think of anything more than the drive and pull of his cock in her. Her thoughts were so clouded, for some reason- confused. "Loki... oh, my King!" Ingrid moaned, touched that this god came to save her from her hell, made her feel such things, gave her a home. "I- I love you, my husband... mmmm..."

An unholy grin lit up her husband's face, hidden in her thick waves of silvered hair. "My darling," he purred approvingly, "the perfect words from my little one. I want our daughter to have your sweet nature, perhaps my dark hair, so lovely, don't you think?"

Still focused on the erotic stretch and pull of his cock inside her, Ingrid nodded mindlessly, her back arching further to take more of Loki inside her.

"Or," the king mused as he began to thrust harder, "a son. A boy with silver-blonde hair and green eyes, wise and courageous like his mother? How beautiful our children will be..." He could hear his wife's gasps as she drew closer to her finish, and his fingers tightened on her wrist slightly as he pushed his spell through the bindings and up her nervous system. "Don't you think so, darling?" Loki prompted, "Can you imagine how brave they'll be, the magnificent things they will do for the Nine Realms?"

Ingrid's head was lolling, until a particularly sharp thrust from her husband sent her upright. As his other hand went to her clitoris, rubbing it firmly, she knew she was supposed to be listening, she was supposed to answer her King...

"Don't you, my wife? Say yes, and then you may come for me." Loki's voice was steel, the girl would have shrunk from it if she was in her right mind, but love, gratitude, her impending orgasm were all too much. "Yes! Yes, our children will be perfect!" Ingrid moaned blissfully.

"Yes?" Loki asked again, feeling his come boiling up through his cock and ready to explode into his wife.

"YES!" Ingrid cried out joyfully at his last brutal thrust that sent the head of his shaft through her cervix and into her womb. As Loki released her hands, she leaned against him, shaking and clutching to his shoulders as his cool essence poured through her, the elf luxuriated in Loki's loving compliments and tender words, how his hands stroked down her arms and back, soothing her. After she fell asleep, the king played with the come seeping from her center, still swollen from the rigorous ride he'd given it. Pushing it back inside her, he smiled malevolently.

Finally rising, he shrugged into a robe and poured a drink. Walking out onto his balcony Loki stood where he could see both his sleeping wife and the garden the late Queen Frigg planted centuries ago. Showing such weakness - remorse - was loathsome. He hadn't lied to Ingrid; she would have known. But to bare such vulnerability was utterly disgusting to him. Despite having gained his throne through murder, Loki was a good king. The Nine Realms were never in better condition than under his rule, no war, no famine. But he knew the emotion would drive his wife to want to please him, comfort him in any way. It was the simplest thing then to push the spell through her, not giving her a moment to question or disagree. Finally stripping and sliding back into bed with his wife, Loki ran one hand over her stomach. He could feel it then- it? Him? Whatever form it took, his child was inside his queen.

Chapter 11

In which Ingrid's life suddenly looks a lot like Dorothy's in "The Wizard of Oz." As in, "Surrender Dorothy!" But with a lot more blood and entrails.

T he morning brought more bad news for the King of Asgard. Two bloodied scouts returned from the borders of Vanaheim. Angrily taking their report of the devastation from the combined forces from Surtur and the Dark Elves, he gritted his teeth in rage. "Is there anything more you can tell me?" Loki asked evenly. The two men looked at each other, then handed him a scroll made of what he knew to be human skin.

In bold, vicious strokes, it read simply: "Return the Girl." Loki's jaw flexed so tightly that he nearly cracked a molar.

Waiting until their king regained control of his rage - making him less likely to gut one of them with his wickedly sharp blade - one general spoke. "The good news here, Sire, is that the Demons and the Dark Elves failed to bring Nidavellir to their side." Loki's face was still white with fury, making general wonder if he'd waited long enough.

"Send healers to the injured there, all the supplies they need. But no troops." their king said suddenly. "The Dwarves are strong fighters with superb weapons. Send your spies out through the border regions with Nidavellir and Vanaheim." Standing, Loki angrily threw the grisly message onto the stone floor and exploded it into green flame with a furious gesture. Cursing the Black Queen for accelerating his plans, he irritably rubbed his eyes. "Send messages to King Leafstred and the Jötunn Regent. We must formulate a plan to rid ourselves of that Black Court bitch."

Ingrid woke with a pleasantly sore feeling; one she'd become accustomed to since pulled into Loki's orbit. The god in question was seated on the terrace, book in his lap, staring out at the magnificent city. Hearing the sheets rustle, his sharp green gaze turned to his wife. "Good morning, my lovely queen." The elf could feel immense satisfaction radiating off her husband, and she gave him a little smile as she raised her blonde head for his kiss.

"And to you, my husband," Ingrid's greeting was shy, it was both alien and rather lovely to call the feared King of Asgard "husband." Rising as Loki pulled her from the bed, the girl was swept up in another greedy kiss, feet dangling as he lifted her to his mouth.

Giving her a rather curious smile, Loki stroked her cheek. "I'm sending those cackling hens in to make you ready. I'm going to take you on a ride."

Ingrid smiled eagerly. She'd always loved horses, though she'd never been allowed to ride one. So she'd rushed the girls through her toilette to be ready in record time. Loki placed a possessive arm around her waist as they left the palace and entered the courtyard. She'd seen very little of the Palace and its huge population, and the avid stares made her uncomfortable. "You! Stable boy!" Loki barked, "Make my horse ready and a gentle mount for the Queen."

The man shoveling horse dung raised his head, and Ingrid stifled a gasp. Even with his filthy face, anyone could recognize the (formerly) dashing Freyer, God and twin to the Goddess of Love, Freya. But how could such a hero be working in the Royal Stables? Bowing brittlely to the king, Freyer turned to go into the barn.

They could still hear him from where they stood as he shouted, "Tyr! A gentle mare for the new queen." The angry rumble that answered him sent a malevolent smile over Loki's lips.

Wisely keeping her questions to herself, Ingrid nodded and thanked the huge, bearded man who brought a pretty golden mare to her. "Your Majesty?" The God Tyr was missing his left hand, but his right hand grasped the stub and leaned over to give her a lift on to the horse.

"Show some respect, stable boy!" Loki's voice cracked like a whip behind her. Ingrid turned to see he was already astride a huge black stallion, looming over them. "Give the Queen a proper mount." The elf bit her lip as the large god went clumsily to his hands and knees, presenting his back as a step. Ingrid's gloved tightened, all the horrible memories of the cruelty and degradation she'd been raised with making her stem a tide of nausea. Looking at the man before her, she knew her husband's ire would be even greater if she refused it. Taking the lightest possible step from his back to her saddle, Ingrid murmured "Thank you, Warrior Tyr." The burly god looked up at her in surprise before Loki's cold voice cut in. "You do not address a stable boy with honor, my dear. In fact, he has no name at all." The queen tried to show her apology with a small smile to Tyr before nodding to her cold husband. Following after him and out the gates of the palace, the old stories about the king's ruthlessness rose from her memory.

Crossing quickly through the city, Loki led her into the countryside and into a lush green forest dotted with lakes, teeming with wildlife. "They do not fear us?" Ingrid asked curiously as two huge deer and their fawns remained seated in the brush as the riders passed them.

"Not here," her husband shook his head, "this is the Royal Family's land. Queen Frigg wanted a place free from violence. She was adamant that the Gods had seen all too much of war and brutality." There was a slight, reminiscent smile on Loki's face, and it made his wife smile too.

"She sounds utterly magnificent, the All-mother," Ingrid ventured. "The servants speak of her in near worship."

Loki's smile was gone as he glanced over. "She was," he answered shortly. He spurred his horse, and there was no more conversation.

Finally stopping in a clearing surrounding a crystalline blue pond, the king made a rather dashing dismount. Running his gloved hand up one of her legs much higher than what could be considered proper, he gave his wife a leer. "You ride very well, darling. Perhaps we'll find you something else to mount."

Flushing and aware his words were audible to his personal guard, Ingrid put her hands on his armored shoulders as Loki's arms wrapped around her waist to take her from the saddle. She felt his chest shake with a silent chuckle as she slowly slid against his hard body until her feet touched the grass. Still amused, the king kissed the top of her silvery blonde head. Waving to the men to stay behind them, he walked Ingrid closer to the pond. "We used to swim here a great deal when I was younger," he mused. "Thor would try to beat me across the pond. He won for the first century or so, but never after. He'd become enraged and try to dunk me." Loki chuckled mirthlessly, "However, I have huge lungs and can stay underwater for a very long time. A very long time indeed."

"It sounds as if there was quite a competition between the two of you- more than any of the other gods," ventured Ingrid. Her cold husband never offered personal details, and she was extremely quiet, hoping he'd continue.

Loki's eyes were narrowed from the glare off the water. "If the oaf had stopped swinging Mjöl-nir long enough to listen, perhaps his banishment wouldn't have been necessary." His gaze turned suddenly to Ingrid. "You've heard all the stories, I'm certain. Elves are terrible gossips."

An inappropriate bubble of laughter nearly popped out of the girl, but she smothered it in time. How to explain to someone as arrogant as the king how she would crouch at the door of her cell to hear the guards. How desperate she was for any scrap of information from outside her mother's realm? Instead, Ingrid shrugged. "I'm an attentive listener. And as you say," she smiled, "the Dökkálfar are terrible gossips."

Loki shrugged, his handsome face set in cold lines again. "Then you know the worst," he said indifferently, "and it is most likely true. But as long as you are loyal to me, darling, you have nothing to fear." One corner of his thin mouth turned up as his hand went to her chin. "But you are my good, good girl, aren't you little one?" His voice had dropped to that luscious purr, feeling like a cat's rough tongue along her nerve endings. Loki laughed as his wife gave an involuntary shiver at the sound. "Sit with me," he held up a hand to help Ingrid sit at the edge of the deck with him. She shook her head. "What was that, darling?"

His queen flushed a little. "I cannot understand how you can move so gracefully under the bulk of all that armor."

Loki's smile wasn't a pleasant one. "Centuries of trusting no one but myself to guard my safety." Ingrid impulsively took his hand and squeezed it, wanting somehow to show her support. He kissed her hand, playing with her slim fingers idly. "There is something we must discuss."

Ingrid's heart sank at the change in his tone and her mind leaped to his from habit, trying to pry an edge loose to look inside. In an instant, the girl was over his lap again and she bit into her hand to keep from shrieking from that first, thunderous slap. She could feel the silk tear as her husband ripped her undergarments off, spanking each cheek four more times. The girl was shaking with silent sobs, unprepared for the galactic shift in the moment.

When Loki spoke, his voice was low and deadly quiet. "Did you have my permission to read my mind?"

Still shaking from her silent tears, Ingrid said, "No, my King."

"And yet you attempted to." His hand was heavy on the small of her back, keeping her in place.

"I am s- so very sorry," Ingrid sniffled. "It is a habit, s- self-preservation, you see. I will not do it again."

Loki's cool hand smoothed over her blistered

bottom. "What do you mean by 'self-preservation'?"

"It was h- how I could prepare myself to face terrible things." Ingrid surreptitiously wiped her nose, "I would learn of it first and be ready, no matter how bad it could become."

His wide palm continued to absently stroke her rosy flesh. "I see. But I do not intend to ambush you with cruelties. You must learn to stop. We are not the Black Court. You are my wife and Queen of Asgard. Do you understand?" Loki watched her blonde head nod and smothered a smirk. "You need to use your words, little one."

"Yes, I understand, my king," she whispered.

"Very good, darling," he soothed. Drawing her upright, Loki straightened her skirts as she blushed, looking back to see if his guards were watching them. "The Dökkálfar troops have attacked more outlying villages in Vanaheim, and even ambushing the Dwarves," Loki said, watching her carefully. "I fear our wedding celebration will also be a council of war. We cannot allow your mother to continue this murderous trend. Do you understand?"

Ingrid shrugged, the wedding celebration meant little to her, though she was very happy to be married to this god. But her common sense told her the bloodshed was due to her kidnapping. "It's because of me, isn't it?" she asked flatly.

Loki grunted as he stood, lifting her as well. "Your mother is a psychotic, bloodthirsty bitch. Do you truly think she'd change her ways simply because you were returned to her... ah... tender care?" He lifted Ingrid's drooping head again to look her in the eye. "You are my wife. You will never return to Niflheim." Smiling in the warmest way he could force, Loki added, "The Light Elves have heard of your rescue, and King Leafstred is ecstatic. He knew your father and is eager to make your acquaintance." He watched closely as the look of apprehension crossed the girl's face. She was picking up on his conflicted emotions. "The White Court is our strongest ally," her husband continued carefully. "But your precious origins - no one must know about your Fairie heritage until we know who to trust - who might help us understand more. Can you keep this a private matter between us?"

Wide eyes blinked up to his trustingly. "Of course. I understand, Sire."

His pleasure at so easily managing this sweet girl sent another filthy grin across Loki's beautiful face. "What is my name, little one?"

"My King..." she whispered.

"What was that?" He leaned closer, his scent surrounding her and making his little queen dizzy.

"My... Loki..." Ingrid managed as he closed his lips over hers.

They rode back together, sharing secret smiles as he told her more about Asgardian history. Ingrid almost didn't mind how painful the long ride was on her red and blistered bottom.

Chapter 12

*In which Ingrid gets the best orgasm
ever, but the worst sort of discovery.*

L oki told himself it was a reward for behaving with such delightful obedience
that day- but whatever the reason, he
pampered his wife relentlessly that evening.
First was a lengthy bath, where he scrupulously
washed every inch of Ingrid, murmuring utterly
profane compliments and suggestions so unnatural that the girl only understood half of them.
Then, laying her in front of the fire as the cool
night air seeped in from the open balcony doors.
Ingrid relaxed in a state of disbelief that the
King of Asgard- and more or less monarch of all
the Nine Realms, would be tenderly massaging
her with a fragrant oil, smoothing his hands
down long limbs and silky skin. She was, however, jolted from her half-doze by Loki's wickedly long fingers, suddenly resting casually on
her mound and spreading the oil to the anxious

little pucker of her anus.

"M- my King?" Ingrid tried to whisper, but it came out more like a squawk.

"Ssshhhh..." he soothed. "We have played with your mouth and this tight little quim, but surely you would not wish to deny me your tender bottom? It is a right only a husband should experience," he soothed, kissing her shoulder. "Something very private that should be reserved for your King?"

Despite her best efforts to forget, Ingrid knew many women - and men - were taken like barnyard animals from behind on the sumptuous marble floors of her mother's loathsome court. But it never occurred to her that normal relations between man and wife included such a thing. Trying to keep her voice from wavering, the elf responded, "You said the filth of the Black Court had no place in our bed?"

Her husband's broad chest jolted against her as he chuckled. "Pet, though your mother's court sought to profane everything erotic and sexual, it is a husband's right to claim everything from his wife. Everything." Those treacherous fingers paused for a moment before gathering more oil and idly circling her bottom again. Shifting to move over her, Loki took her hips in his big, cool hands and stroked them soothingly. "Just as it is the responsibility of any good husband to make certain his sweet wife is ready to receive him." The fingers were back again, holding his thick cock, stroking it up and down her slit. "Tonight, we'll just... play, darling. There is nothing to fear. I won't hurt you." He could see his queen's slim hands grip a pillow with white knuckles, but Ingrid issued no complaint. Pulling her hips higher, Loki began to slide his uncomfortably swollen shaft inside her, head drooping backward as he enjoyed her pussy's resistance. He'd had virgins before, certainly. But there was something so unspeakably erotic about being the only man who had ever - or would ever - be inside the sweetly grasping walls of his wife. The wild surge of possessiveness that drove his cock hard back into Ingrid's body surprised even Loki. No one else would ever touch his wife. Not ever.

The elf's eyes fluttered shut against the wild surge of emotion from her husband. Coupled with the deep push of his shaft inside her, it was overwhelming. But she felt a strange kind of safety too, as his thick arm crossed between her breasts and held her to his chest. Loki was biting into her shoulder, and the girl could hear the mindless chant of *'Mine, mine, mine, mine...'* from his unguarded thoughts as he shoved that wonderful, painful, delicious cock back and forth inside her. She suddenly stiffened as his sharp index finger began sliding carefully into her bottom with the same rhythm of his spearing of her pussy. "L- Loki." Ingrid tried to form words with her suddenly numb lips, "you s- said, you s- said-"

"Just playing, sweetness," he kissed her ear, "just... exploring. Can you feel me? I'm inside you, darling, from both directions." Loki grinned against her neck, feeling his wife freeze as he stroked his finger against his cock, separated by such a small partition of tissue. "I can feel your little quim straining to hold my cock, your pucker stretching to fit my finger. You feel-" Loki thrust with a grunt, "-unspeakably tight around me." His thrusts became faster as one sharp finger idly stroked inside her anus, "Those tight, silky walls clinging to me..." His chuckle was on the edge of terrifying, "I could pull you inside out, couldn't I, darling?" His broad hand ran up the length of her spine and wrapped Ingrid's long flow of silver-blonde hair around his fist, arching her back and putting her ear next to his treacherous mouth. "I can feel you shake, little one, writhing against my fingers and cock. Your breath's coming faster and faster now, and you and I both know how very close you are to coming." He watched the coil of markings that held her wings begin to twist slightly with his movements, and it was too much. "You will come when I command it, my very good girl. Come NOW!" Loki enjoyed Ingrid's answering wail as her passage tightened down on his spurting shaft is a pleasantly painful way. "I can- uh! I can feel the pulses of my cock inside your wet little quim with my finger in your back passage- I don't think I've felt you come this hard before, sweetness." He enjoyed his wife's moan as he ran his chilly tongue up her neck. "I do believe you enjoy my finger right where it is, my darling." The king bit her neck when his wife stubbornly shook her head. Turning them to the side, he gently pulled himself from both channels and stroked her, enjoying Ingrid shuddering through the last of her orgasm. "Such a good, good girl..." he soothed, triumphant.

Ingrid was roused abruptly from bed the following morning by the chattering of her attendants, who were busy laying dresses out on every flat surface in the dressing room. "What's all this?" she yawned, tying the sash of her robe.

"The king has ordered new gowns for you, Majesty," Hannah explained as she adjusted the sleeve on another green dress. "It's fortunate," she added tactfully, that green is such a lovely color on you."

A small, wry giggle came from the elf. "Indeed, since this appears to be the only hue in my wardrobe." Just then, Loki swept in regally, eyeing the array of gowns before spotting his wife. And there it was, Ingrid thought while flushing, that look of his, knowing, seductive, and of course, deeply pleased with himself.

"Good morning, my lovely queen," Loki practically purred with satisfaction, "how are you feeling?" He gallantly kissed both her hands. "No ill effect, pet?" He could see her simply writhe with embarrassment as her attendants made themselves busy on the far end of the room. "Sit on my lap, we'll choose your gowns." Ingrid could feel the king's lips curve into a malicious grin as he pulled her briskly on to his lap, startling a painful squeak from her mouth over the condition of her bottom, still sore from being spanked and the thick intrusion of his finger.

There had to have been at least thirty dresses there- all in the king's colors. Loki began rapidly choosing between them without bothering to ask Ingrid's opinion. A bubble of irritation rose in her chest, shouldn't she be selecting her wardrobe? When her hand rose to point at a lovely sage green gown with silver detailing, her husband merely waved his hand dismissively and it was gone. "I thought it was very pretty," she protested quietly.

He made an indulgent shake his dark head. "It is not what I wish for you." Sensing her frustration, Loki ran through the rest of the gowns rapidly, leaving six out of the original thirty.

"Now, darling," he ordered, "you'll model these for me." Gently pushing Ingrid up and off his lap, he steepled his long fingers and smiled at her indulgently.

"All- all right," his wife agreed, "if you'll wait in the main room, I'll change and-"

Loki laughed, but it was humorless. "I've no inclination to move, darling. Take off your robe and have your girls dress you."

Ingrid's eyes went wide, then narrowed in frustration. Why was he playing this game? Of course, she'd been naked before her husband, many times. And while her attendants kept their eyes politely averted when helping her bathe and dress, the elf knew they'd seen her unclothed as well. It was the humiliation of the two combined, Loki watching as she stood bare, being dressed by her maids like a doll... or a plaything.

"Remove your robe, darling." Loki's voice was steel, unyielding. Ingrid could feel the discomfort from Hannah and the girls, but they scurried to obey, taking her robe and trying to quickly put her into the dress. She pressed her full lips together and kept her gaze from her husband. The dressing room was dead silent, save for the rustle of the silk as they fastened the dress around her. Looking up, she could see the lustful emerald eyes of the king looking her over. She stood uncomfortably until he nodded. "This will do." Loki smiled at his wife lecherously. "Next."

By the sixth dress, Ingrid's fingernails were digging into her palms, remaining outwardly composed. "Does this please you, Sire?" She was proud her voice remained even as his knowing smile made her grit her teeth.

"It will do." Loki stood, his towering form looming over her. He stared down until his wife was forced to raise her eyes to his. Only then did he glance at her silent attendants. "The third dress for the afternoon, the fifth for this evening." He turned and swept away, his dark armor and silver fastenings glistening as he moved.

Turning to look at the elaborate, full-length mirror, Ingrid could see her face was pale, with a red, angry flush on her cheeks. Soft hands lifted her hair to remove the current dress she was wearing, and suddenly the elf raised her hand. The vision of her husband gleefully winding her endless flow of hair in his fist last night made her jaw tighten. Ugly memories from her mother's court rose in her mind, and she impulsively turned to the others. "I'll need some scissors, please." They all looked at each other, puzzled, but found the shears she requested. Pulling her hair out as far as her arm could stretch, Ingrid took the blades and began sawing through the thick strands as she could hear the protests suddenly rise.

"Your Majesty! Your beautiful hair!"

"Please- could we help you-"

Angrily, stubbornly, the queen finished her task and threw the long handful of hair into the fire. Watching it burn, she bitterly said, "One should never leave hair out to be found. It is used in quite terrible spells." She turned to see the three women staring at her in silence. For the first time in Asgard, she could see the fear in their eyes.

Finally, it was Gundrun who came forward with a nod. "Your beautiful hair... it will be so easy to style now." Ingrid gave her a grateful smile and let the girl pile her now waist-length hair on top of her head.

Entering Loki's private study, the elf watched as her dark husband looked her up and down. The dark green gown was almost black, like Loki's armor, with silver jewelry. With her pale hair and purple eyes, Ingrid was heart-stoppingly beautiful. "My Queen," he kissed her lingeringly. "Exquisite. Perfect." Looking over his shoulder, he called, "Lady Runa, take the queen to the antechamber. I'll join you shortly."

Loki stood aside long enough for Ingrid to see

a lovely brunette glaring back at her. Wiping the expression of hate from her face, the woman curtseyed. "Majesty, allow me to take you to where you need to go." Ingrid glanced back to her husband, but he was already looking over some maps and speaking with an advisor. Raising her chin, the elf followed the hostile woman from the room.

Walking down one of the cavernous marble halls, Ingrid gritted her teeth. Loki had put her into the care of his mistress - his former mistress - she hoped. "Lady Runa, how do you know my husband?" She was practicing now, using the delicate skills her husband taught her to edge around the corners of the woman's brain, rather than slashing through it.

It wasn't difficult- Loki's mistress was practically shrieking her thoughts. *'Pathetic whore,'* it burned from the woman beside her, *'how could my Master tolerate this weak bitch?'* She could see it now, the two of them fucking, her husband pounding viciously into this yowling strumpet, her hands yanking at chains around her wrists, Runa's back bloody from a strapping, from the lash still gripped in her lover's hands. Loki's hands.

Chapter 13

In which Ingrid discovers there are harder things to handle than just Loki.

Back straight and face carefully composed, Ingrid followed her husband's mistress into a small antechamber that the queen knew led to the Great Hall. Apparently, they were making an Appearance. Lady Runa swung to face her, all condescending smiles and airs. "The king wanted me to bring you here, Majesty, to give you a bit of advice about fitting in here at court."

"Fitting in?" Ingrid wanted to laugh; she'd never fit in anywhere, not with her curse. But she remained composed as she would in front of any enemy. "How kind of you, Lady Runa." The queen's lips twisted into a bit of a giggle, and the other woman saw it, her face flushing angrily.

"Well, since your marriage is in name only, and meant to bring about an heir-"

Ingrid's brow raised; the mistress was going for the jugular.

"-His Majesty wanted me to instruct you on how to behave, how to survive the challenges of the Asgardian Court."

Ingrid couldn't help it. She burst into nearly uproarious laughter, the first in her life. It felt wonderfully cleansing, the elf realized. A sunken part of her flared into life, and she smiled pityingly on the startled Runa. "Survive? My dear, you have. No. Idea. What kind of Court I have survived." She found herself drawing closer to her husband's mistress, enjoying the step back the woman took.

Runa's powers were nothing compared to Loki's, but she could command a spell when needed. She tried pushing fear and insecurity into her enemy as she hissed, "You'll find it is a mistake to not seek my friendship. I am a formidable enemy, and I hold the King's heart."

Ingrid didn't even bother being clever, she briskly sorted through the twisted thoughts of the witch in front of her to find what she needed. "Begging the King to sodomize you while beating you bloody does not mean you hold any part of him. My husband could have found the same with any tavern whore. You think I fear you?" Suddenly, Ingrid's chest was blazing, fists clenched as she stepped closer again, Runa stepping backward. "My mother is Queen to the Black Court. Do you think there is anything you could possibly do that could terrify me after a life with her?"

"My, my. Such discord." The cool and amused tone of Loki infuriated Ingrid, but she turned with a serene and innocent smile.

"Hello, my husband. The Lady Runa was attempting to give me advice about, ah, what was it? 'Fitting in' here at court."

It had just occurred to the king at that moment that he'd sent his new bride off in the malicious hands of one of his whores. Well... perhaps mistress was a more accurate term since Runa handled many of the events and celebrations at the palace. To Loki's heartless amusement, he realized her hostess duties currently included his wedding celebration. No wonder the witch was out of sorts. Cold emerald gaze turning to the suddenly anxious Runa, he smiled thinly. "Any education required by the new queen will come from me." Loki cruelly caressed his wife's soft cheek. "And you are such a very quick study, aren't you darling?"

Ingrid's lashes lowered away from Lady Runa's obvious humiliation. While she was proud - and to be honest, quite surprised - at her ability to defend herself against the jealous witch, it didn't include enjoying the brutal set down the woman was enduring. "Y- your Majesty," the words came between Runa's gritted teeth, but Loki stopped his mistress mid-sentence.

"I'm sure you have last-minute details to attend to, Lady Runa. That is all."

"But SIRE-" Runa was shaking with rage.

Flicking his long fingers in elegant dismissal, Loki spared her one glance that drained the blood from the angry witch's face. "Surely, you wouldn't be so foolish as to have me repeat myself. Leave. Now." The King and Queen of Asgard kept their gaze on each other as the shaking woman sketched a quick curtsey and left the room. Pulling a loose curl behind Ingrid's ear, he continued as if there'd been no interruption. "Such a very quick study, my good, good little girl."

His bride stared levelly back; her beautiful face expressionless. While her mother would never allow any transfer of power by actually taking a husband, the Dark Queen enjoyed a series of Regents that she used as lovers and for court duty. Ingrid was well acquainted with the practice of taking lovers outside the marriage, but it hadn't occurred to her until that moment that this would be something she would be forced to accept. She could see by Loki's taunting smile that he knew very well what she was thinking and that he didn't intend to discuss it. Instead, the elf schooled her expression into one of courteous inquiry and asked, "What is expected of me tonight, Sire?"

Loki could feel the girl's spirit pull away from his in an almost visceral way, and his dark brows drew together. His mouth opened to retort but heard their titles being announced and the excited buzz from the crowd. Taking her unresponsive hand and placing it on his arm, he said sharply, "Mingle, smile, remember who you're introduced to and reveal nothing. Do you understand, darling?"

"Of course," was her chilly answer as the tall doors opened to the Great Hall.

The jumble of light and noise hit Ingrid fullbore, and she kept a lovely smile on her face as she tried to focus on something specific to regain her equilibrium. That happened to be King Leafstred, as the Light Elf stepped forward with his queen to be introduced first. "My dear," the Ljósálfar King's voice was resonant with emotion, kind. "We believed you died with your father. It is a miracle to see you alive, and- well?" The last came out as a question as Leafstred glanced for the briefest of moments at the imposing figure of her husband, who was watching the exchange closely.

The elf remembered to bow her head in return before asking hopefully, "You knew my father? I- I know nothing about him, I would love-"

Loki interrupted so smoothly that it ended the conversation seamlessly. "We are so very eager to learn more of my wife's parentage, my friend," he purred, smiling at the Light Elf, "may we meet later for a private moment after the banquet?"

Leafstred bowed his head regally, "Nothing would give us more pleasure, thank you."

Ingrid's head was spinning as she smiled, nodded and stored away names and details for later study as the endless reception line snaked along the head table before the meal could begin. Vanaheim's unmarried king gave her hand a long, lingering kiss before smiling at her wistfully. "How is it, My Lord, that you always capture the hearts of the fairest in the Nine Realms?"

As his wife flinched just slightly at the word "capture," Loki's lips stretched back into a savage grin. "Fortune favors the bold, Lorstin." The Vanir monarch raised a brow at the taunt but nodded politely to them both as he left for his table. Looking out over the huge hall, filled with everyone of importance come to pay homage to his rule, the King of Asgard raised his long arms and bellowed, "Welcome, honored guests! The beautiful Queen Ingrid and I thank you for join ing us to welcome the beginning of a new period of prosperity for us all. Now please, eat, drink, and enjoy." The music came up as he finished and sat to thunderous applause. Loki looked down to see the elf gazing at him with a small smile from his commanding presence over these nobles. A corner of his mouth twitched. Lean-ing so close to her ear that Ingrid could feel his lips brush against her sensitive lobe, "Why, dar-ling- such a sweet smile. I can almost believe you mean it." Chuckling as he felt the girl stiffen against him, Loki kissed her neck and soothed, "We'll speak of everything that concerns you later, yes?" Feeling her nod against his jaw, he drew back and reached for his wine.

The White Queen leaned in close to her hus-band's ear. "It almost seems as if they care for each other. Is it actually possible the king means this as a true match?"

King Leafstred's silver-blue gaze was nar-rowed in thought as he watched the Royal table. "To the Assassin of the Black Court? I suppose stranger things have happened, but I doubt it. He means to cement his hold on the girl." Seeing Loki's malevolent gaze turn to them, the Ljósál-far abandoned their whispered conversation for something more socially appropriate.

But the new Queen of Asgard was having trouble eating anything. A thousand inquisitive feelers poured in from throughout the Great Hall, and filtering them was drowning her. Ingrid had gone from a life where every face and thought turned away from her, lest they be the latest victims of the horrors she could bring down so easily. But all these-

"THIS is the Black Court Murderess? She's a child-"

"I've never seen such a lavish presentation, King Loki must be very pleased with his new acquisition-"

"-but she's so lovely, this is the executioner everyone feared?"

"I wonder why he married her so quickly-"

"-the gall of the king, having his mistress and his wife at the same table!"

Looking to her left, Ingrid realized the gossip was correct, Lady Runa was seated halfway down the table, still obviously seething from the king's treatment. Looking around the room to the seating closest to them, the new queen could see the avid faces staring back, and suddenly sorting through the thoughts, found several examining her with resentment and jealousy.

"What does that meek little thing have that I don't? She can't know more than to open her legs-"

"-at least that witch Runa's not set aside, that means the king intends still to fuck us."

Dismally, Ingrid wondered how many women here her husband had taken to his bed. As her stomach churned, she wondered how many more he planned to use. An unfamiliar feeling seared through her spine, stiffening it and making her look cold and regal. Perhaps Loki didn't intend to take women outside their vows. And more intriguingly, the thought surfaced, *'Maybe I don't have to allow it...'* The sudden burst of jealousy and anger was new to the elf, but she didn't push it away, examining the swirling emotions as she mechanically smiled, laughed at the right times and applauded at the end of several speeches congratulating the new couple. When the lavish meal was finally finished and the music became louder and more boisterous, her husband rose and held out one huge hand.

"My lovely Queen, dance with me."

Ingrid eyed the proffering hand and forced down a shiver of anxiety. She'd never danced before, but standing behind her mother's chair at countless events had shown her how. Lips in a polite smile, the elf placed her hand in her husband's and let him guide her to the floor. Blinking against the searing flood of thoughts, she tried to focus on the cool sensation of Loki's hand, his wintry scent and the clear signals of desire building from them both. Sliding his other palm against her narrow waist, her dark husband leaned down. "Just follow my lead, my pet. You're so graceful, you'll dance beautifully."

Strangely gratified that he'd sensed her uncertainty, the queen smiled and fixed her lavender gaze on his, taking a deep breath. The music began, and the sweet strains of the harp and dulcimer made it easy for her to feel the music and move with her husband. Loki kept his gaze on hers the entire song, effectively blocking out the deluge of thoughts around them. They moved through the crowds, everyone standing back respectfully to allow the King of Asgard and his new Queen the first dance. As Loki bent his wife over one arm as the last of the tune faded, others eagerly joined them as the next song began. Ingrid found that she loved dancing, at least with Loki, who moved with his usual sinuous grace on the floor as he did everywhere else. His strong arms easily led her from one step to another, making it appear as if she'd done this all her life. A bubble of gratitude rose in Ingrid's chest for his curious kindness. The dances were not necessary, but he'd continued as long as she smiled and laughed, almost involuntarily, delighted that there was something- anything that she could do that did not involve death and suffering.

As the crowds dispersed and the Royal couple finished their farewells to the most important guests, Loki took his wife's hand. "I know you are weary, darling. But we did agree to meet with King Leafstred. Can you do this and not reveal any secrets we hold between us?"

Ingrid barely stopped herself from rolling her eyes. Years of holding her tongue in her mother's hellish court made her count each word carefully before releasing it from her full lips. But she smiled instead and nodded. "I understand the importance of the counsel we keep, husband. You will not be disappointed."

Eyeing her curiously, Loki smiled suddenly and kissed her. "I have no doubt of that, darling."

Seeing the King and Queen of the Seelie Court again made the elf's heart rate begin to speed up wildly. Ingrid could feel her husband sending soothing green waves into her nervous system, trying to calm her, but all she could think of was that these people had known her father, that they perhaps knew anything about how she came to be. Loki broke the awkward silence between the two couples by seating the women and offering wine. When they'd all settled in the king's cozy personal study, Leafstred was the first to speak. "My dear Ingrid, what do you remember of your childhood, of your father?"

She regretfully shook her head. "Next to nothing, I'm afraid. I remember... I remember his touch, the warmth. The only understanding I had of love before was from that feeling. I was so small. I remember only that one day my father was there, and the next he was gone. My mother would have me beaten when I asked about him, so I stopped." Ingrid was so deep in her memories that she missed the expressions of shock and pity from the Light Elves. Looking up, she asked hopefully, "What can you tell me about my father?"

King Leafstred leaned forward. "He... Ulbricht was my brother. He was second in line to the throne. You are the Crown Princess of the White Court."

Ingrid could dimly feel Loki's hand convulsing against the small of her back as she processed the words. She wasn't just a monster, finding refuge in the arms of her dark and beautiful captor. She had a family.

Chapter 14

In which Ingrid's crushed little soul decides to go through puberty. All at once.

L oki could barely tamp down his rage and frustration fast enough to keep his bride from feeling it. The Light Elf's *brother?* Gods, could this get any more complicated? He vaguely remembered the death of young Ulbricht- a hunting accident, it was said. No one paid much notice to the second in line for the throne when the ruler was likely to live ten thousand years or more. But as his furious emerald gaze watched the King and Queen of the White Court clasp his wife's hands, he was pleased, knowing the long-married couple did not have heirs of their own. His sweet, innocent Ingrid was indeed the Crown Princess. A dark glee swirled in his chest as he thought, 'Gaining hold over the Ljósálfar is going to be far easier than I'd expected.'

Loki looked up in time to see Ingrid turn to

him with a happy smile. "What do you think, my husband?"

"Forgive me," he said smoothly, "I fear I was still lost in the surprise of your parentage, my darling. What did you ask?"

King Leafstred spoke, "We'd hoped to take the Queen on a visit to Alfheim, to have her meet more of her kin, learn more about her father?"

That black rage boiled up in Loki's chest again. Curse his wife for her exceptional pedigree! The king swept his most regal expression across his pale face. "I fear there are far more serious threats that must be countered first. It is the reason I requested your counsel so quickly."

If King Leafstred had not been seasoned by of ruling the Ljósálfar- so well and so regally for countless millennia, he would have given a deeply cynical laugh. 'Counsel,' he thought with wry amusement, 'as if the Great Trickster ever listened to anyone but himself.' Nonetheless, the Light Elf bowed his head in agreement.

"After all," Loki said in his silkiest tone, "you have another family member to protect, and I have my precious bride." He caught Ingrid staring at him with an incredulous expression, but she quickly smoothed it over. Loki, however, was never one to leave a lesson unlearned, even if it was in front of newly discovered relatives.

Taking his wife's hand, the king leaned closer dropping a kiss on her palm, then raking his teeth over her knuckles. One of the many secrets he'd uncovered from the elf's lovely body is the sweet hitch in her breath when he bit her. "Since the moment I rescued Ingrid from the Black Court-" Loki smiled, placing the emphasis on the word 'rescue,' "-I have been struck by her beauty and courage, surviving that filth and wondering if anyone would come to save her..." The last was a direct hit on Leafstred's inability to find the truth about his niece. Loki could feel his wife stiffen next to him.

"I- I expected no rescue," Ingrid protested lamely, "I am a monster, an executioner-"

Her husband cut off her protest with a hard, lingering kiss, gently biting down on her full lower lip. Ingrid was acutely aware that Leafstred and his queen were shifting uncomfortably at Loki's salacious display. "This sweet girl didn't even have a name! A base cruelty that only that Black Court bitch could be capable of..."

Flushing with humiliation at the gasps of pity from the Light Elves, Ingrid shook her head, "These things, surely they do not matter now-" Loki cut her off with a tender kiss to her cheek, then sliding over to bite her earlobe out of view of the Ljósálfar Royalty, enjoying her little yelp.

"Who- ah, who gave you your name then, my dear?" The Alfheim Queen was valiantly attempting to clear the uncomfortably erotic atmosphere.

"My husband," Ingrid answered in a small voice, still trying to control the shudders started by the king's sharp, white teeth.

"Beautiful goddess, I believe that's the meaning," Queen Soren answered encouragingly, "it certainly fits, my dear."

Leafstred could stand no more and graciously encouraged his wife to take Ingrid and leave the room. "There is much to discuss to protect both the realm and your queen. Would you two prefer to retire and relax before taking your rest this evening?"

Ingrid was struck again with frustration by being shut out of crucial discussions about her mother's war tactics, where surely, she could offer insight. But a pre-emptive goodnight kiss from her husband, with another subtle nibble on her tongue, ended the discussion. Reluctantly bowing her head to both kings, the elf allowed herself to be drawn away by Queen Soren. As the woman walked down the huge hall flanked by their ladies in waiting, a gasp alerted them to the arrival of a delegation of Frost Giants. While some of the women shrunk back in fear, Ingrid stopped and nodded respectfully. "I am the new Queen of Asgard. It is my honor to welcome you, gentlemen. I hope we may speak later about Jötunnheim, but in the meantime, please allow my hostess-" the elf nodded to a terrified-looking Lady Runa, "to know if there's anything you need. Welcome to Asgard. We honor your loyalty." The entire contingent stopped dead in the hall as Ingrid addressed them, and after a short, stunned silence, the head of the group bowed respectfully in return.

"We thank you, Your Majesty." The tallest Jötunn spoke, his voice was raspy, as if from disuse, but Ingrid was thrilled to recognize the same growl she'd heard from her husband in his most unguarded moments. He paused, his blood-red eyes looking her over carefully, so tall that the light behind him was blocked and casting her in his shadow. The blue warriors were all dressed in leather kilts, armor, and little else. "We are... unused to such a welcome, but we honor your kindness."

Ingrid nodded and smiled in return. "I hope on your next visit; your families will accompany you. I would like to build a friendship between us." The head Jötunn's brow rose, but he bowed and the group walked on to meet with Loki and Leafstred.

Ingrid turned to see her attendants staring

at her, open-mouthed. Even the Light Queen seemed surprised. "Such courage, my dear! The Jötunn terrify most."

"Oh, I've always admired them," beamed Ingrid. "Courageous, refusing to do what is against their code. I've never met a Frost Giant before, they would not come to the Black Court, no matter how many times my mother would summon them."

"You admire their principles," ventured Queen Soren as they continued their walk.

"Very much so," Ingrid agreed. "They're a fierce and certainly harsh culture, but there's something so intriguing about them." She caught Gundrun's shudder out of the corner of her eye. "Why do you fear them?" She turned to the girl, who looked deeply alarmed to be the focus of the group.

"Th- they are terrifying!" she stuttered, "the Jötunn leave babies out to die in the cold and they eat-"

"Nonsense!" Ingrid interrupted sharply. "They may look different and perhaps frightening, but that doesn't make them monsters!" She gazed bleakly at her reflection in a tall window. "Monsters often look just like us."

It was quite late when Loki finally returned to their rooms, well past midnight. His wife was still awake and staring into the fire. Her time with Queen Soren simply returned her to that dismal space where she was an abomination and everyone wanted something from her. The Light Elf was kind and subtle, but she questioned Ingrid repeatedly about her heritage, how her skills came to be. Ingrid suspected Soren was prying for information about her Fairie blood. Everyone wanted something. So, when her husband pulled her to her feet to kiss her, Ingrid pulled back as quickly as she could.

Loki's brow rose. "Not the greeting I expect from my beautiful bride," he chastised, pulling her back a little faster, causing the elf to bump into his wide chest. Her hand rose to push against his armor to distance herself, but her husband's arm went around Ingrid's waist like a bar of iron, refusing to let her move. "Now, what's this, little one?"

Ingrid childishly looked away, refusing to meet that intent gaze. "Nothing." Even to her own ears, her tone couldn't have been sulkier. Why did everyone wanting to use her now make her angry and resentful? She bore it calmly in her mother's cruel court, but here, Ingrid felt cross, put-upon.

Her husband's tone changed instantly, pulling the elf out of her pout. "You sound like a spoiled brat, little girl. Do you know what happens to spoiled brats?" One hand went under her chin, lifting Ingrid's sullen face to his. "I will give you one chance to apologize to your King." Loki's long hair brushed against her cheek as he leaned in closer. "I suggest you take it."

Suddenly thinking of his mistress Runa and all those jealous women tonight, Ingrid's violet gaze narrowed back. "It is for you to apol-"

Loki cut his wife off mid-sentence and seated himself, throwing her over his lap and making her heavy gown disappear. Ingrid was laid bare in her transparent silk shift, angrily wiggling like a trout on a riverbank. He gave a cold grin as he held the furious Elf down. Loki could have easily magicked away her undergarments too, but he enjoyed the satisfying sound of tearing them off Ingrid's lovely body, which then made the girl yelp in response.

Her dark husband's brow rose with interest as the Queen angrily kicked her legs and hammered at his lean thigh with her fists. It hurt. While Loki was fascinated with this sudden bout of ferocity from his usually quiet and compliant bride- her behavior would not go unchecked. Yanking both hands behind her back and up in an uncomfortable hold, Loki brought his other palm down on Ingrid's ass with a resounding slap that echoed through the vast room, along with her outraged shriek. "Spoiled brat behavior is not tolerated here, little girl, and certainly not. From. You!" Loki reinforced the last three words with the harshest blows he'd ever used on his wife's bottom. Admiring the red, raised handprints on the elf's shapely ass, he ran those treacherous fingers between her cheeks and stroked them along her lips. Shaking his head, he lamented, "Dry as a bone, what a shame. I must remedy this." While Ingrid continued to angrily fight his hold, the king delivered fifteen more thunderous strikes to her ass and thighs, occasionally pausing to slide a finger inside her, or stroke her clitoris. When she managed to bite his leg hard enough to draw blood, Loki kicked her legs open and slapped her center. To his cynical delight, his wife was now quite wet, which added to the sting. As Ingrid cried out from the burn in her softest parts, she angrily went to bite him again. Loki grabbed her hair to hold her teeth off his long legs as he warned, "Ah, ah, no biting! Such a bad girl- What happened to your hair?"

Ingrid stilled, remembering her husband had not been aware of her impromptu moment with the scissors. She knew Loki loved to play with her waterfall of silver-blonde locks and suspected he wasn't going to applaud her decision. "I cut it this morning," she hissed defiantly.

Her announcement was greeted with another sharp slap to her vulnerable, wet lips- which was then greeted with another furious howl. Loki pulled her hair to force her to look at him. "You will do nothing to change your appearance without my express permission! How dare you!"

"It's my hair!" Ingrid spat back. Suddenly, she was on the floor with her enraged husband hovering over her.

"No, darling, that is incorrect." Loki roughly pulled her thighs apart and pressed his hips between them to block his wife from moving. His hand squeezed harder in her silvery curls before letting go with a shake. "This belongs to me." Seizing a soft breast, he snarled, "this belongs to me!" Ingrid shrieked as that rough hand cupped her stinging nether lips and Loki laughed with a hard, ugly undertone. "And this- this sweet little quim quite definitely belongs to your King. You are mine, little monster, and you'd best not forget that again!"

Ingrid was frozen, staring up at the terrifying face and cruel eyes that didn't even resemble the beautiful god who'd seduced her with sweet words and kisses. This was the face of the king-who had killed two powerful Monarchs he'd called friend and father to gain his throne. It felt like ice water was dumped down her back as the elf's gaze wavered. This was the face of the God of Lies who would do or take anything he wished and no one could stop him. And that, she realized, included her. Ingrid was jolted out of her frightened thoughts as three fingers pushed into her. Gasping, she tried to pull loose.

"No, darling," Loki purred, "you will stay right where you are. Your King has a use for your body." He punctuated the warning with a hard press of fingers against her silky channel, pushing in and out without giving his wife a moment to breathe.

Gritting her teeth against the feeling of his sharp, probing fingers Ingrid protested, "I am your queen, not your whore!"

The king's laugh was as unsympathetic as the broad head of his cock, pressing hard against her opening. "But little one, I believe you were terribly-" Loki pulled his fingers from her and thrust that hard, invasive shaft deep inside his wife, grinning at her trembling lip. "-terribly displeased to meet some of my whores at our wedding celebration, were you not?"

His thrusts were jolting Ingrid against the cold floor and she couldn't get a second to accommodate him. Loki kept pushing roughly through her tight channel, with or without her help. As he bent to kiss and bite at her breasts, the elf realized that wasn't completely true. She was wet- wildly so- even as his hard pelvis stung against her sore center and her searingly painful bottom was being rubbed against the stone beneath her. Still, she was wet!

Some dark part of Ingrid stirred like a snake, coiling and sliding through her nervous system. She'd witnessed the expressions of those torn between agony and uncontrollable pleasure, standing at attention in the Black Court. The elf's breath started coming faster as that twisted nature crept forward, pushing her to rise up against Loki, locking her legs around his narrow waist and blindly sink her nails into her husband's shoulders, trying somehow to orient herself again.

Loki felt the change in his wife, looking down to see the conflicting emotions warring for control of her expression, that luscious body wound tight. Hoisting her hips higher, he went up to his knees and back on his heels, yanking Ingrid closer. She moaned at the change in position, her king's thick cock rubbing harder inside her at this angle, her back arched and pressing down on him. The elf's pale hands flew to her own hair, pulling and gripping her scalp. What was happening to her?

His hips kept hammering into hers, but Loki's cool hand slid up her heaving stomach to her throat, wrapping those long fingers around it, pressing down on her racing pulse. "Who do you belong to, little monster?" Her husband's voice was sin, and Ingrid could feel the murky part of her surge to him. She yelped at an extremely rough thrust. "Who, little monster?"

"Don't call me that," Ingrid managed to moan, terrified by her body's response to her husband's cruel pounding. His hand tightened around her throat, while the other slid to her traitorous clit.

"Behaving like a spoiled little monster? I will indeed call you that." Loki perversely shoved harder, knowing he was already pressed painfully against his wife's cervix with nowhere left to go, but grinding his hips down anyway, wanting more, wanting deeper inside this beautiful, infuriating monster with the face of an angel and a body- well, a body that was responding like a whore. He had to pull his greedy gaze away from where his driving cock split Ingrid's body, forcing her to yield. Loosening his grip on her long neck, he asked harshly, "Who do you belong to?"

Humiliated by the wanton, helpless moan that came from her sore throat, Ingrid managed a weak, "Y- You."

The king's calloused fingers slid along his

wife's sensitive clit, grasping it between two of his digits and pulling it. "Louder, little monster, I didn't hear you." He could see Ingrid try to go away into herself, her eyes turning from him. "You will look at me, wife!" He yanked her upwards, bouncing her on his cock with his face inches from hers.

"Who. Do. You. Belong. To."

He punctuated each word with a thrust, and Ingrid's dam broke. "YOU! Oh, by the Nornir, you, m- my King! I am yours!" She grasped at his shoulders, slippery with sweat. She could feel his low, triumphant chuckle as he purred into her ear.

"You may come."

With a grateful, drawn-out wail, his little monster did just that, clamping down so tightly on his cock that he spurted with her, his huge hands on her ass and pressing Ingrid tightly against him, relishing every shudder and twitch from her clutching passage.

Chapter 15

In which lessons are learned.
Some, the hard way.

When the King of Asgard (and by default all the Nine Realms) taught a lesson, he taught it thoroughly. Loki woke his exhausted wife twice more that night to make certain she'd retained his instruction. The second time was simply rolling Ingrid on her back and checking to make sure she was still wet enough to receive him. Those huge lavender eyes startled open as he thrust, but she kept her gaze on him as her King ordered. The feel of her warm, sleepy body under his brought him to a finish much sooner than he'd planned, but Loki's dexterous fingers finished off his moaning wife in time.

Shrugging on a robe, he poured a drink and sat in the seat that had become a habit- positioned to see his sweetly sleeping bride on one side, and keeping an eye on his kingdom from his gigantic stone balcony on the other. After the first time Loki had ravished Ingrid, he lifted her limp form and put her into bed, wiping away their finish from her sticky thighs and bringing a glass of water to her lips.

Uncharacteristically for a creature as selfish as Loki, he never lazily demanded his wife get up and tidy them, he'd become accustomed to attending to Ingrid's aftercare, soothing bites, and scratches, healing anything damaged during their rougher moments. When she fell asleep, he'd often comb her hair, laying the silver-blonde ribbon of silk across his lap and smoothing it gently. Loki found the act calming, forcing his restless mind to stop darting to and fro- allowing him to curl around his bride and sleep. Perhaps that was the cause of his rage when he found she'd hacked off more than half of those lovely curls. He ran his thumb over his mouth, watching Ingrid sleep. He actually understood her suddenly rebellious behavior. In many ways, his wife was a child- stunted from birth from learning to grow and develop independence. The king chuckled and took another mouthful of "Scotch," an excellent beverage he'd found on Midgard. In essence, Ingrid was going through adolescence. So now, his delightful and deadly wife required a careful mix of small moments of independence, without ever forgetting who was truly in charge.

The third time Loki woke his bride, it was with the sweet kisses and gentle words with which he'd wooed her into marriage. Ingrid could feel the faint hum from his fingers against her bruised skin as her husband healed the worst of her scrapes and marks. He'd pause to kiss and stroke her as he went. Chuckling as she shivered under his lips, Loki ran his cool palm down her thigh. "Such a good girl," he purred, "my sweet, good girl..."

Ingrid shyly stroked his hair, loving the soft thickness as it pulled through her fingers. She was absurdly pleased to be her King's good girl again. So, when he knelt over her with that heavy cock in his hand, she sat up without prompting to put it in her mouth. Loki's head dropped back in pleasure. Ingrid was timid and inexperienced, but her mouth was like molten lava, searingly hot and so good against his frigid shaft. He wrapped his sac in her silky hair and cupped it, feeling the smooth slip and slide as she embraced him between those full lips. "Such a very good girl," he groaned, hiding a grin as his wife happily redoubled her efforts. An apt student indeed.

Ingrid could feel her husband draw closer- those narrow hips thrusting upward, the muscles in his thighs tightening into iron- but Loki regretfully pulled his cock from her mouth.

"My beautiful, sweet wife," he crooned, "you are far too talented with that warm mouth of yours." She smiled up shyly, still so happy that she'd pleased him that she'd forgotten his treatment from the night before. When his hands went to her waist and urged her upwards, Ingrid looked up in confusion. "My King?"

Slipping smoothly under her, Loki gently lifted her and straddled her over his lap. The elf shivered, feeling the erotic slip and slide of his hardness between her legs. "Ride me, my lovely Ingrid, my precious girl."

"How- what do I-?" Ingrid was nervous, looking down at his beautiful, seductive smile.

"Rise up on your knees," he encouraged, "good- now, slide down me. This is at your pace, love." The blazing heat of her passage surrounded him, Loki groaning as he split through her. "So good - like that - darling. I can feel you pull and spread for me; you are exquisite." Finding that Ingrid moved up and down faster when he spoke to her, Loki stroked her pink flesh, idly circling her clit with no real pressure. "You look so beautiful above me, taking your pleasure in such a wanton way... mmmm... I can feel your hips circling, darling. Are you trying to find that sweet spot inside you? Try this..." His rough hands pushed on the small of his wife's back, arching it and angling her pelvis to feel the full pressure of his cock against those nerves inside her.

"Oh! I feel you..." Ingrid's startled gasp suddenly made him harder, and his thumb began circling with real intent. Emboldened by her husband's seductive smile, his sweet elf moved up and down faster, circling her hips at the same time. No matter how much she'd loved feeling Loki inside her all these times, moving on her own, finding the places that felt so agonizingly good, was wildly empowering. Ingrid knew she was pleasing her practiced and jaded King, but pleasing herself on his amazing shaft- at her pace- it was unimaginably erotic.

"There's my good, good girl," Loki groaned. "Your quim is wrapped around me like a warm, wet scrap of silk." He moved his strong hands to her hips to move the elf up and down faster on his cock. What a delightful student his Ingrid had become. "There you are..." He was pushing the base of her spine again, rubbing her clit against the hairy base of his cock. "Who is this brazen creature?" Loki teased gently, "this delicious temptress..." His flattery was not false, his wife's head was back, pink mouth open and breasts pushed forward by the graceful arch in her back. "Are you ready?" Loki whispered, knowing Ingrid's keen hearing could very well absorb his lecherous praise as she moved to their completion. "You take your pleasure, darling. I'm ready to come with you."

It was all she needed, and the young Queen of Asgard came with a soundless gasp, overwhelmed by it all. And as she fell to her husband's broad chest, he was there to welcome her, wrapping his arms around her and kissing the top of her head. Ingrid fell asleep with Loki's beautiful voice in her ear. "My good, good girl..."

When Ingrid woke late the next morning, it was to an empty bed, but holding a note with more of the same praises in her husband's bold handwriting. With a blush, she realized he'd included some powders for her bath to relieve the intensely sore lower part of her that was making itself known. Pulling on a robe, the queen greeted her attendants, too tired to pay attention until Hannah exclaimed, "Majesty! Your hair- how is this possible?"

Looking up and to the mirror, Ingrid realized her hair was once again to her knees. Lips thinning, she answered bleakly, "The king, of course."

Stubbornly, Ingrid hacked off her hair again that morning, then met with her husband and the royalty from the White Court for a farewell luncheon. She knew Loki wouldn't let her go with them for the proposed visit, but couldn't find it in herself to be angry. She was a target of the Black Court. Better to be here and not put

I Love the Way You Lie

others at risk until the issue could be settled. Still, standing and waving goodbye to the Light Elves at the Rainbow Bridge was bittersweet. Ingrid was desperate to know more about her heritage, but part of her knew they were equally desirous to know the truth about her.

As the brilliant flash closed the gate, the queen nodded her head to Heimdall, who gravely nodded back. Loki wasn't with her, still deep in discussion with the Jötunn, and the elf was restless. Turning to her guards and attendants, she announced, "I would like to visit the city." The security detail eyed each other dubiously, but she was the queen, and there was no direct order from the king to countermand her decision. Walking through the streets, Ingrid felt her spirits lift. She'd never been allowed to walk around freely in Niflheim, and this was really her first independent outing here in Asgard. Relishing the moment, she allowed her younger attendants to drag her from one market stall to another, tasting figs from the country, cheese from a local dairy and exclaiming over bolts of embroidered silk from Vanaheim. The late afternoon sun glinted off the golden stone that paved the streets, sending a warm glow over the city. There was a profusion of flowers and greenery, every shopkeeper proudly displaying baskets and window flower boxes filled with every kind and color. Looking around her, Ingrid could

169

see that the populace was well-dressed, there seemed to be no beggars. Children darted back and forth through the open-air market giggling and chasing each other. The pleasant moment was shattered by shrill screaming and a crash from a nearby building. Instantly the guards snapped to attention and surrounded Ingrid. "Captain!" she called angrily, "Go find the disturbance, surely someone needs help!"

The man shook his head. Captain Asgeir was a long-time commander in Loki's army and knew his duty. The world could explode and he wouldn't leave the queen's side. "I beg your pardon, Majesty. But your safety is our only priority."

Just then, the doors to the building crashed open and two men came stumbling out- clearly drunk and both beaten bloody. A furious woman kicked one in the ass, hastening his departure. She shouted, "And never come back!" to the cheers of the scantily-dressed ladies on the balcony, straining their heads to see the brouhaha. The woman looked up for a moment, blue eyes connecting with Ingrid's. They widened in recognition, then narrowed in anger as she turned and walked into the structure again, slamming the doors shut.

"What was that about?" Ingrid asked Gundrun.

"Oh, that's a whorehouse," the girl said dismissively, before looking at her mistress anxiously. "Am I allowed to say-" Ingrid made an encouraging motion with her hand, nodding her head to get the girl moving again. "The woman who threw those horrid men out- that's the Goddess Freya - I mean, the former - rather, the..."

Hannah stepped forward and hustled Ingrid in the opposite direction. "What is the legendary Goddess Freya doing in a whor- in a House of Ill Repute?" asked Ingrid, mystified by the whole affair. Her attendant refused to say anything further, and watching the frightened expression on the woman's face, the elf did not pursue it until they were alone in the king's quarters again. "Tell me, Hannah. Why was the goddess there in such a place?"

The older woman sighed, mopping her brow. "Majesty, this is not fit conversation for one of your stature-"

"I am your Queen!" Ingrid interrupted. "Tell me Hannah, I will never speak of it to anyone. You know that."

"The Lady Freya was... she was placed there by the king."

Ingrid's brow wrinkled. "I don't understand."

Her attendant sighed, absently folding clothing and moving about the room, too nervous to sit. "When Prince Thor was exiled to Midgard, some of the other gods were punished for supporting him."

The elf nodded, rising as well to pace alongside Hannah. "I've seen two of them! Freyr and Tyr saddled my mount the other day. This is how they were punished? Where is Balder?"

"He works an iron forge at the Royal Blacksmith's, Majesty."

Rubbing her forehead, Ingrid ventured, "Freya, she is not- ah, she is not one-"

"No! No, she is not a whore." Hannah sighed bleakly. "She is their scullery maid"

The queen's stomach dropped to her feet. Loyalty to Thor was enough to make Loki sentence Asgard's greatest Gods and heroes to a lifetime of Hel?

"Darling..." purred a beautiful voice. "I'm so pleased you've returned. What were you ladies chatting about?"

Ingrid's blood turned to ice. Her husband had entered the room.

Chapter 16

In which even the God of Lies can't keep his mouth shut when there's an orgasm at stake.

Ingrid squared her shoulders and turned to her husband, putting a smile on her face. It wasn't difficult. After all the relentless pleasure he'd lavished on her the night before, the elf was feeling dangerously soft toward her husband. Nodding to send her terrified servant away, she walked to the king, hopefully raising her chin for a kiss, which he graciously gave.

"We were speaking of the Goddess Freya," she answered in the only way she could, truthfully.

Loki's brows drew together. "And where, my darling wife, would you have seen this woman?" He was idly kissing one of her soft hands, nibbling gently along the knuckles. It took Ingrid a moment to remember what they were talking about.

"I- I wanted to take a walk through the market in Asgard. There was a disturbance from a nearby building and the Goddess-"

"Do NOT call her Goddess." Loki interrupted coldly. Seeing the alarmed expression on his wife's mobile face, he smiled, walking around to kiss her neck from behind, gently massaging her shoulders with those strong hands.

"W- what was her crime, my husband, to be condemned as a scullery maid in a whore- in a House of Ill Repute?" Ingrid struggled to focus on their dangerous conversation as his cool lips slid down her throat.

Loki's voice vibrated down his wife's spine as he whispered in her ear. "Treason to the Crown."

"Is... is that why there are gods who work in your stables?" Ingrid gritted her teeth, trying to focus as his long, treacherous hands rose up the front of her dress to cup her breasts. Her breath hitched- they could both hear it- but it was from discomfort, rather than arousal. Loki seemed to know the difference and held her sensitive chest more carefully.

Lightly stroking her nipples, he rumbled, "Yes. It was a merciful act. Their fate should have been death." The king smiled against her shudder. "Tell me, darling- what happens to traitors in the Black Court?"

Ingrid stiffened against him. "They would be tortured." Her answer was flat and bleak. "For centuries, if possible. And then finished. Likely by me."

Those rough fingers against her silky nipples paused for a moment, their owner having forgotten the memories such a question would bring. "Then you see that their punishment was a merciful one." Loki turned his bride to look at him. "I am capable of mercy, my sweet girl."

She looked up into his beautiful eyes, lost for a moment in the swirl of green and blue. "How did they commit treason to the Crown?" Ingrid flinched as her husband's fingers tightened reflexively against her sensitive breasts before they withdrew, pulling the bodice of her gown into place.

"When I took my rightful place of King of Asgard - and of the Nine Realms - I gave Thor one chance to bow before me and swear his loyalty. He did not. So I took Mjölnir from the oaf and banished him to Midgard."

Ingrid's eyes widened in shock. "You- you took Mjölnir?"

Loki's expression turned cold, speculative as he looked down at his wife. "I was the rightful

King of Asgard," he sneered. "I do not need the ridiculous relic to hold my kingdom. But that does not mean I don't control it." Those emerald eyes narrowed as he grasped his wife's wrist. "Would you like to see it, darling? A bit of a tourist attraction?"

"It's not really necess-" the elf began, but Loki was already dragging her out of their chambers and down the huge hallway, Ingrid miserably aware of soldiers snapping to attention and following their strange procession. Throwing open the huge doors of the throne room with a wave of his hand, Loki pulled her to the center of the room and just to the right of his massive throne. There was a towering granite stand she'd not seen before, with a glass dome that covered the top. Inside rested the legendary hammer, lifeless within its elaborate cage. The soaring room was silent and dark, and Ingrid could hear the echoing footsteps of her husband as he walked around the stand holding Thor's weapon, then walking to pause behind her again.

"Thor was a fool to challenge me. Of all the Æsir, the oaf knew my power best." Those cool hands slipped up Ingrid's shoulders to stroke her neck again. "He was distraught, I suppose, over the death of Odin. The dolt! He attempted to contest my rule, and those who labor in my stables and Freya- that lovesick idiot- stood behind him."

Perhaps it was a lifetime of brutal Dark Elf machinations, but Ingrid couldn't find it in her to condemn him. "I see," she said thoughtfully. "You did what you had to do to secure your throne." She sighed as the hard hands behind her softened to stroke her silky skin. "In my mother's court, their sentence would have been unspeakable." His chuckle sent another shot of ice down her spine, but Ingrid carefully leaned into her dark husband. "Why didn't you kill them?"

There was a pause, and she wondered if she'd gone too far.

Those long fingers slid down her arms and cuffed her wrists. Stepping in front of her again, the tall figure of her dark husband looked down at her. "Because they could be useful."

Uncertain but nodding, Ingrid allowed Loki to lead her to the gold and white veined granite steps to his throne. Walking up to the imposing seat at the apex, she wondered why he was being so honest with her. Seating himself on the obsidian dais, the King of Asgard slouched arrogantly, looking down at her with his legs spread wide. His green-black armor glowed in the lighting, making Loki look beautiful. Pale, unearthly, almost mythical as he lounged, looking down his nose at her.

The moment was still as Ingrid looked at the king who'd stolen her away from her monstrous parent, married her and now gazed down at her with all the haughtiness of a god who knew he owned everything. Including her. One light brow finally arched, and the elf ascended the final steps to draw even with her husband. "There is only one throne here," she said coolly.

A flicker of surprise passed over his stunning face so quickly Ingrid wasn't sure she'd seen it before Loki spoke. "You think you deserve to sit beside me, little one?"

She smiled then, ducking her head. "You took me, my husband, knowing that I can only speak the truth, I can only find truth in others..." Ingrid circled behind him, one light fingertip stroking across his broad shoulders as she walked. "I am certain you had other reasons-" the words choked her, knowing that her foolish, romantic dreams of the god she married were not returned. "-but a king needs a queen by his side. You must have known I could be this for you." The elf was in front of him now, looking into those crystalline, speculative eyes. Her own stare was unflinching. Though Loki sat as she stood, he was so tall their gaze was still even.

There was the slightest softening in his pale face as she watched him, her beautiful, confusing god. Loki's huge hands slid along her waist, slowly feeling the curve of her, still staring into Ingrid's eyes. Inside, his mind was raging. How could the God of Lies know the truth when he heard it? But the king knew without a doubt his Ingrid stood there in her courageous way, stubbornly telling nothing but the stark truth of the thing without embellishment. Suddenly lifting his bride onto his lap, his hand roughly stroked through all that silver-blonde silk again, pulling her hair from its elaborate style. Watching it fall to her waist, a sly smile stretched his secretive lips. "Stubborn minx," Loki purred into Ingrid's ear. "You cut it again?"

His lips were so close to her, Ingrid thought feverishly, that she could feel him form the words against the sensitive skin of her neck. "You own me, my King," she whispered into his mouth. "But it is my hair." As she expected, her dark husband angrily growled and grabbed the mass of curls falling down her back, snapping her neck to the side and biting down on the thin skin there.

"All of you is mine," Loki hissed, before clenching those sharp teeth down almost hard enough to draw blood, enjoying the heave of his bride's breasts against his armor. Ripping down the front of her elaborate gown to gain better access to her curves and secretive hollows, the king bent his head to kiss along her body as his fingers slipped to her pussy, stroking along her lips as they swelled, enjoying how quickly his little one's body became wet for him. Feeling her slim and determined fingers trying to at least release enough of his armor at the waist to find his rapidly swelling cock, Loki yanked her up with a growl, long enough to wave his hand and remove the leather coverings on his body. Ingrid's tattered remains of her exquisite gown chosen by her husband just days before hung off her arms as she was lifted, then pulled down over that thick, beautiful staff that made coherent thought leave her mind, the absence giving room to the driving need to rise and fall on her King's hard flesh, cool as well water inside the heat and coil of her channel.

"Oh..." it was a half gasp, half moan as Ingrid tried to adjust to the stretch and pull of her husband inside of her. His persuasive hands were busy, one stroking her clit gently as the other held to her hip, guiding her up and down on his shaft. She dropped her head onto his hard shoulder, already shining with a sheen of sweat as his sinuous hips slid and yanked along her sweetly tightening passage.

"My Queen." His beautiful, resonate voice made Ingrid want to give him anything he asked for. Anything.

"Yes, my beloved?" Ingrid asked shyly.

There was a pause in Loki's thrusts, hand still on her hip as he absorbed what his wife had said. "Do I truly own your heart, little one?"

Ingrid forced herself to look into her husband's keen eyes, forehead resting against his. "Of course," she answered slowly. "You gave me safety, a home. Marriage and your... oh! Oh, gods! Your-"

She could feel him laughing, the movement jostling him deeper into her. "My cock? My invading shaft inside that grasping, wet cunt of yours?" Ingrid's head dropped back as his angle changed and forced her hips harder against his. "I can feel you..." Damn the knowing, speechcraft of his deep, resonate voice whispering into her ear! "I'm in you, love. To the hilt. All of you shaking and fluttering around me like a flock of frightened birds. And you so love it, darling. Don't you? Knowing you can't stop my fucking up into you until I'm spent?"

"My- my King..." Ingrid moaned, clutching harder to his silky black hair and his shoulder. She could feel it, his thick chunk of blood and muscle inside her, driving up with such a terribly intimate knowledge of her body, of what would make her twitch, or moan, or even shriek.

He was driving into her faster now, one rough thumb still stroking along that slippery clitoris and the hand gripping her hip already leaving bruises from holding her so tightly. "You do not fear the monster you married, little one?" Loki punctuated the question with an especially hard thrust.

Even feeling the spongy tip of him push at the painfully sensitive circle of her cervix, the elf shuddered and moaned, "I am the monster, my King. And yet you still embraced me. How could I do less to someone as beautiful as you?"

The cold chuckle from his muscled chest rumbled against hers, but Loki was bringing her up and down on his shaft so quickly that her strong thighs were beginning to shake and Ingrid could do nothing but moan. With a final, harsh surge, the king shoved that prodigious cock of his all the way through his bride, grinning at her confused moans, a mixture of pain and comple- tion. Groaning, his hips thrust helplessly as the King of Asgard and all the Nine Realms came inside his wife so hard that they both arched against the painful clench of her satiny walls against him. Dropping that dark head to her shaking shoulder, he groaned, "My wife, my lit- tle one... my pregnant queen. Our children will rule the universe." So satisfied from their mutual release, Loki never even felt the suddenly rigid stillness of his Ingrid. The dark room echoed with his harsh gasps and her sudden whimpers as their blended flesh held and slicked along each other.

Chapter 17

In which Ingrid finally shows her claws.

"**W**hat did you say?"

His wife's high, horrified voice broke into Loki's pleasant afterglow, still panting and inside her warmth. It took him a moment to hear Ingrid's questions and a moment more to realize he'd slipped and revealed her condition. Running his hands soothingly up and down her back, the king leaned in to kiss her neck, attempting to calm her. "Now, darling..."

Ingrid struggled loose, pulling his cock from her as she wrapped the tatters of her dress around her and got to her feet, backing away from the throne. "You said I was with child. Why would you say that? This cannot be!"

Groaning, Loki waved his hand, armor assembling over flesh as he stood as well. "Darling, I know this is a shock to you. But yes, you are carrying my child."

Her hands flew to her stomach, unconsciously seeking the life there. Still backing away from him, Ingrid stuttered "I- I- I cannot be pregnant! Elves must give consent-"

"You did," interrupted Loki, "and you are." Grabbing her arm as she nearly toppled backward down the stairs in her retreat, he urged, "You must be calm, wife. This is-"

"No!" Ingrid shouted, the loudest he'd ever heard her. Somewhere behind them, a window shattered, and Loki growled.

"Little girl, stop this now. You must listen to-"

"I do not have to listen!" She was shaking with rage now, "What have you done to me! You promised me- you gave me your word!" Loki's head whipped to the right as a brutal cracking sound came from the stand holding Mjölnir. A jagged fracture ran through the impenetrable glass around the weapon.

The king could feel the dark energy begin radiating off his wife, her fury and terror swirling through the power that was beginning to rumble the granite dais. "INGRID!" Loki amplified his voice to stop the girl's hysteria. Her head snapped back to look at him, eyes glowing. He thrust two fingers at her harshly. "You will stop. You will be calm. Do this now."

To her horror, Ingrid involuntarily stumbled forward a step or two. The strange, insistent tug from the small of her back was familiar, she had felt it many times before when her moth- "You have control over me," she whispered, dropping to her knees, hands still pressed against her abdomen. "You found the way to take my mother's hold and make it your own. You betrayed me."

Loki knelt in front of his horrified wife, who instantly crab-walked backward to keep away from him. "My wife, you must stop this and listen. Stop!" Ingrid's body obediently froze in midmotion and she began to sob. "Your sovereign hold transferred to me when I took your virginity." He reached out and grabbed her ankle, pulling her back as the weeping elf began moving away again. "I used a compulsion spell to get you to agree to a child during your passion." The God of Lies knew Ingrid would know if he wasn't honest, but it was still so jarring to be speaking the truth. Loki couched every thought and word in half-truths and diversions, simply by habit. She was shaking her head over and over, trying to dislodge this cruel new reality.

"How could you?" Ingrid's voice was small, like a child's. Her utter despair made even her cold husband feel a painful twinge in the location of where a heart might reside.

"Darling..." his exquisite voice was at its most persuasive, and Loki's hand tightened on his wife's ankle as she tried to pull away again. "Darling, I did what had to do. As my wife and carrying my child, no one can challenge my claim to you. Not even your viperous mother. It was the best way to stop any conflict before it began. I know you are frightened of bearing children. But our sons and daughters will be magnificent. Not monsters."

Ingrid's eyes raised to his, a Byzantine shade from her tears. "You are a monster. I will never forgive you."

Loki continued to speak to her, using his sonorous voice and sweet words, trying to lift the shock that crushed the elf. But Ingrid's face turned from him. She was utterly still, tears sliding unnoticed down her face. Finally, at a loss, he angrily waved a hand and transported her back to their bedroom, putting his unresponsive wife to bed.

When the king woke the next morning, it was to an empty space where his wife should have been. Rising, he walked naked into the great room, where a startled Elsa dropped the breakfast tray she was carrying with a gasp and a clattering of broken dishes. Loki growled irritably and looked to Hannah as the only sensible creature in the room. "Where is my- where is your mistress?"

Hannah quickly composed herself into a curtsey, head bowed. "We believed her to still be in bed, Sire."

Loki's teeth gritted in a snarl, angrily dressing as he picked up Ingrid's hairbrush. Using the pale strands left in the bristles for a spell, he found her in his mother's garden. Transporting behind her, the king watched her still form for a moment, another twinge spiking in that unused portion of his chest.

Ingrid was still in her nightgown, a shawl pulled around her shoulders. She was pregnant. The enormity of that single statement was more horrifying than anything her murderous mother could ever have threatened. Ingrid's monstrous heritage was now embedded in another- an innocent. And combined with that of the God of Lies! How could this poor child be anything but a curse? For a fleeting moment, the queen considering making her way to the Bifrost and throwing herself into the Void. Almost instantly Ingrid was furious with her despairing thoughts. Her hand slid up slowly to cover her abdomen protectively. *'For shame!'* she scolded herself, *'no matter how this child came to be, he or she is here. The only thing that matters is protecting her from the greed of others. Perhaps I can save her...'*

The elf jumped with a gasp as Loki spoke just behind her. "Darling, you shouldn't be out here so early. You could become ill. You don't want to have anything happen to our child, do you?"

"The worst of things have already happened to our child," Ingrid said flatly. She stood slowly, stiff from having sat in the damp and chill for too long. "She has a liar and a thief for a father and a murderess for a mother." It was then Loki realized his wife had hacked off her silvery waterfall of hair, cropped close to the scalp. The discarded curls lay in a pile at her feet, and glancing at it sharply, Ingrid set it ablaze. His Queen moved past him without a glance, returning to the palace.

The day did not improve from there for Loki. He was accosted by a group of his military intelligence the moment he entered his reception room. Irritably waving his hand to seal the room from sound, the king slumped in his seat, legs spread. "Tell me what you found in Niflheim."

The group exchanged uneasy glances. "Sire, the Black Queen has changed strategies from killing to taking hostages." The agent who spoke shuddered visibly. The man had worked deep intelligence for his king for over a decade, but he'd never seen anything like the carnage he witnessed this week. Queen Alfhild's rage over losing her daughter spread across the borders for Vanaheim, Svartalfheim, even venturing into Jötunnheim as retaliation. "She sends a thrall ahead to our troops as the Dark Elves take their captives. The thrall delivers her message and then..." The spy shuddered again. "They... they melt, Majesty, there is no other way to describe it."

"How many hostages?" Loki's voice was cold and composed, but his fists on the tabletop gave him away.

Another spy sighed and rubbed his forehead. "Thousands, Sire. Including the King of Vanaheim."

It seemed as if the stone walls surrounding them began to shake along with Loki's growl through gritted teeth. Everyone gratefully fled the room at his furious gesture, almost stumbling over each other in their haste.

Had theirs been a normal marriage, Loki and Ingrid might have bridged their differences to seek solace and advice from each other. But both were used to a lifetime of bearing their burdens alone, and the cold silence stayed between them that night. The queen was back in the big chair with a pile of books next to her when the weary and angry Loki entered their rooms. Ingrid was asleep, one hand placed over her still-flat stomach and the other supporting her drooping head. Loki eyed her resentfully as he stripped off his armor. Why couldn't the stupid girl grasp the importance of this? The most powerful ruler in the Nine Realms had honored her with marriage, a title, and most importantly: his child. The stubborn little fool should be grateful! Roughly pulling her from the chair, the king strode to the bedchamber and dropped his startled wife on the bed. When the suddenly awake and furious elf tried to leave it, he stopped her with a glare. "You will do nothing to endanger the health of my child. Sleep in this bed. Eat. Do everything possible to care for this baby."

"As if I need your instruction," Ingrid hissed mockingly. "You need not tell me how to care for my child. I am the only one here to protect him."

With a growl, Loki was on her, flattening his wife against the mattress and yanking her arms above her head. "Why do you insist on provoking me, darling? You will obey me without complaint!"

His Queen huffed out a furious laugh, "You've made certain of that by taking control over me through treachery and lies. But you cannot control my tongue!"

Her dark husband paused over her, looking

down with a cold, thoughtful expression. "Shall we put that to the test?" To Ingrid's helpless fury, her nightgown disappeared and Loki's hands were sliding down her suddenly sensitive skin. She tried to push him away and bolt from the bed, but found herself helpless, unable to move. "Whether you are Ljósálfar or Dökkálfar, you need me." He paused and laughed at her furious hiss. "You're not that ignorant. Haven't you wondered why these-" one big hand slid up to hold a breast, "-are suddenly so sensitive? Why you come against me, writhing and screaming? You won't be able to think of anything save me fucking you for the next several months." Running one long finger up her suddenly damp center, he laughed unkindly. "Certainly, your precious little cunt can't resist me, darling. Have you forgotten the heat an elf enters during pregnancy?"

'Oh, by the Nornir...' Ingrid suddenly remembered her beloved books and how they described the sexual madness an elfin female entered after conception. She moaned, tossing her head angrily and trying to distract herself from her suddenly needy lower half.

"It's all right," soothed her diabolical spouse, "tonight I won't test you. Soon, you'll have to plead for my cock, but as of now..." His wife shrieked as Loki's considerable shaft pushed through her wet channel, sliding in and out with infuriating ease with a quim desperately ready for him, no matter how Ingrid tried to control her rebellious body. The shriek died into a moan as he moved against her, long, luxurious strokes that rubbed enticingly against and inside the elf's writhing form. With infuriating ease, Loki brought Ingrid to an explosive finish as she arched against him. Afterward, she lay shuddering, still holding him with arms and legs wound around her husband's muscled body as he found his own orgasm inside her. She bit back a moan as he whispered in her ear, cool lips moving against the thin skin of the elf's neck. "You will crave this moment soon. Every night. And I will graciously give it to you, my darling wife." Loki chuckled, pulling out of her warm little body with a groan. "After you beg me, of course."

Ingrid was stiff and still beside him until the king fell asleep, a smug smile still pasted on those thin lips. Rising with a wince at sore and twinging muscles, she carefully made her way to the bathing chamber to clean herself. Finally dressed in a fresh gown, she wandered out on the terrace, unconsciously selecting the chair her husband used to keep watch over everything that mattered to him. With a deep sigh, Ingrid looked up into the silent face of the moon, wishing for the trillionth time that her father was here. The moonbeams began to gently dance along her skin, and she raised both hands to the sky before pausing, placing one palm back against her abdomen. "Little one," Ingrid whispered, "I do not know if you're a boy or girl, only that you are mine. I will love you and protect you. It is all I can offer, but I will be certain that it is enough." She smiled softly as the silver strands of energy began seeping through her palms and over her body. Keeping one hand over her belly, she whispered, "This is the moon, my sweet one. It nurtures us. Here... doesn't that feel lovely? Your mother loves you, little one. Always."

Loki watched his wife from the shadows, suddenly jealous of his child as her hand curved tenderly over her stomach, the moon's rays gently seeping into her skin and through the tiny body of his progeny.

Chapter 18

In which Ingrid and Loki discover that victory over each other can be quite hollow, indeed. Plus, Runa is a total bitch. And a witch. Both of those.

When Ingrid woke the next morning, her husband was already gone. With a sigh, she rose to stretch her still-tender body and walk out to the terrace. There was more activity than usual in the courtyard, couriers coming and going and soldiers mounting up and riding in battalions to the Bifrost to be transported to far away borders. Her eye caught that of Freyr, who looked up briefly from saddling a horse to give the queen a polite nod. She nodded back with a smile and made an impulsive decision. Having the girls dress her in riding gear, Ingrid left her chambers, only to have four men from her security detail immediately close ranks behind her. 'Does Loki think I'll try to run away?' she thought sarcastically.

"Your Majesty," Captain Asgeir bowed, "how may we assist you?"

"I wish to go riding," the queen answered, heading in the direction of the stables and leaving the men no option but to follow.

Tyr was busy shoeing a horse when the group arrived, and he looked up in surprise. "Majesty," he nodded courteously, "would you like the same mare as before?"

Ingrid smiled with relief; happy the man didn't hate her for Loki's cruel antics at their last meeting. "Yes, please. She was lovely." Looking over her shoulder, the queen could see her soldiers were busy getting their own mounts ready. "How- how are you, Sir Tyr? I see so much military activity here- will you and Sir Freyr be joining them?"

The man's brows drew together furiously until he realized the elf was being sincere. "No, Majesty, our services have not been... eh... utilized in such a way since... well..."

Ingrid nodded sadly. "I know, since Prince Thor's banishment. Times like these- when your skills would be so helpful- you must be very aggrieved to be tethered here, so to speak."

Tyr stroked his scruffy beard, eyeing the new queen closely. He knew her reputation and knew she couldn't lie, but could she be acting as a spy for the king? "Forgive my insolence, Majesty, but why do you ask?"

Ingrid's hand paused from stroking the mare's silky mane. "I am not gathering information, Sir Tyr. It is difficult to see your gifts and those of the others wasted." She suddenly smiled, an almost childlike expression. "I've heard so many stories of your heroics over the years-" sobering suddenly, Ingrid met his gaze. "I know what it's like to be compelled to that which is against your nature."

The huge god before her suddenly bowed low. "I thank you, My Queen."

The captain and the rest of her security detail were mounted on their horses and ready to go, so Ingrid accepted a hand from her new friend and settled easily into her saddle. As the group left in a cloud of dust, Freyr came out of the stables and stood with his friend. "What was that about? Is the new queen spying for that blue bastard?"

"No," Tyr said slowly. "The queen is incapable of lying. Her concern...it was for us." The two stood and stared thoughtfully at the dust left by Ingrid's departure.

The king's rage over not finding his wife still

in their chambers terrified Ingrid's maids, and they scattered after explaining their mistress had gone for a ride. Striding down to the stables, Loki kicked aside the harness Balder was repairing. "Where is Queen Ingrid?" he snarled, not giving the god a moment to rise.

"I do not know, Sire," Balder answered slowly. "She wished to take a ride. But her security detail was with her."

Dismissing him with a wave of his hand, Loki's brow furrowed. 'The lake. It's the only place she knows.'

When he galloped into the serene space around the water, the king found he was correct. His wife had peeled off her riding boots and stockings, cooling her feet in the still water as the soldiers stood respectfully away to give her some privacy. Loki glared at the soldiers as he dismounted. "What," he hissed, "is Queen Ingrid doing out of the city with the danger surrounding her?"

The men were battle-hardened, long in the king's service. But his rage was terrifying to behold. "You gave no order regarding letting the queen enter the Royal reserve," ventured the captain. Stepping back as Loki actually growled at them, they watched as he strode angrily over to his wife.

"What are you playing at, my darling wife?" Loki purred maliciously, knowing he was sending a bolt of ice down the elf's spine.

To his expectation, Ingrid stiffened and rose quickly. "I just... wished for some quiet," she answered honestly. He was towering above her, those emerald eyes watching her expression carefully.

"Do you think leaving the protection of the city was wise when the Black Court's efforts to kidnap you are a very real threat?" Loki's voice was sharp but not as cruel as before. He watched as she tiredly rubbed a hand over her forehead.

"I suppose not," Ingrid managed, "I'll return immediately."

"See that you do," he answered coldly. "We have another banquet tonight, a delegation from the Dwarves and the Jötunn are here."

"I met the Jötunn regents," she answered to his surprise, "I will be happy to do anything I can-"

"No need," Loki cut her off cruelly, "Lady Runa is perfectly capable of handling the event." He looked her up and down, insultingly. "Just be pretty and..." he leaned in closer, enjoying his wife's sudden angry flush. "...show up." Mounting his stallion, he rode off without a backward glance.

Ingrid furiously allowed her trio of assistants to flutter around her for longer than she could bear that night, fussing with her exquisite gown, stringing her- once again- knee-length hair with jeweled clips and delicately painting her face for the grand evening. Finally escorted into the Grand Hall by a courtier, she found Loki deep in conversation with the Jötunn regent as the smug Runa hovered around them both like a malevolent bee. Forcing her expression into composed lines, Ingrid joined them. To her pleasure, the Frost Giant turned and bowed to her immediately. "Your Majesty. We are pleased to see you. Your notes about your- the Black Queen's military strategy was very helpful today."

Ignoring Loki's suddenly sour expression, the elf nodded graciously in return. "I am so pleased that those millennia of watching my mother's movements could be of some *small* assistance."

The feast did not improve the atmosphere between the King and Queen of Asgard. Though they sat next to each other, the two never spoke, instead attending to guests and trying to keep from strangling each other. To Ingrid's rising fury, Runa continuously dipped over her husband's shoulder to whisper in his ear- ostensibly on matters related to the evening. But no one missed the witch's hand on the king's muscled arm or his warmer than appropriate smiles back. Ingrid knew this was her punishment for her rage and accusations of betrayal, but she stubbornly ignored their behavior and the hatefully intrusive thoughts that poured in from every direction.

"My, my- perhaps the elf doesn't have such a hold over our Loki after all-"

"-why is the queen allowing that bitch to make a fool of her? Doesn't she know-"

"Hmmm... maybe the king is realizing his little Dark Elf pet isn't worth all this trouble after all-"

Ingrid could feel that familiar fire rising in her blood, forcing herself to take deep, calming breaths to hold it back. She would not be provoked to harm or kill. Not ever again. Not even for those loathsome gossips or the witch currently fawning over her husband- and the father of her child, she suddenly realized. When the long feast was finally, blessedly over and she felt she'd attended to the important guests, Ingrid withdrew from the dais with a politely murmured "good night" to anyone who was paying attention. Refusing to look back, the elf missed a viciously triumphant look from Runa that might have changed her mind about her vow to never kill again.

"My sweet little one..." the guttural purr of Loki's voice rumbled up Ingrid's tender spine as her husband turned her over, running his tongue up her neck and sliding through her lips as the king settled between her thighs late that night, waking her from an exhausted sleep. "You handled the Jötunn beautifully. I am very pleased with you... so I'm going to reward you, darling."

Decisively interested in being inside his wife, Loki missed her furiously clenched fists and slack form, waving away their clothing to feel her warm little body. In fact, the God of Lies' desire was so intense for his pregnant bride that it took halfway through thrusting into Ingrid to see she wasn't responding. Hovering over her with a haughty, raised brow, Loki scolded her. "Now, little one. This childish behavior is unbecoming. Your King is inside you. Make me welcome." Her narrowed eyes were slits of rage, and Loki began to thrust into her sharply, ignoring her hiss of discomfort as he pushed inside her narrow channel. His sweet little slut wasn't wet and ready for him as usual, Loki realized in irritation. Placing his calloused thumb against her clit and pausing with his cock pressed deep against Ingrid's cervix, he gazed down sternly into her eyes, which were refusing to meet his.

"Look at me."

His fury radiated through the simple sentence, and Ingrid shuddered in spite of herself, meeting that cold gaze.

"Have you forgotten who you belong to, little one?" Loki gave an especially hard push as he questioned her, enjoying her pained gasp. He began to chuckle, the vibration grating on the elf's nerves as he began to shove that huge shaft of his inside her carelessly, in and out again. "Do you truly think I will allow such a pouting child at my court? You will-" the god smiled coldly, hearing the moan from his wife as he began a brutal rhythm on her smaller form, "-learn to behave. You will obey me without complaint, my stubborn little slut." Loki was spitefully pleased, knowing the stretch and bite of his pistoning cock would build her arousal along with his insistent finger against her clit, but then pull her away from any pleasure gathered in the act.

But Ingrid went past her pain and the cruel tugs of arousal in her sparking center to stare into his dark eyes, pleased that she could remain expressionless under his assault.

Loki tried to break down his bride's walls, using force, then a soft and smooth whisper, then a furious dominating pattern that finally sent him into an explosive orgasm over Ingrid's still form. Growling, he yanked his cock from her, rising off the bed to stride into the bathing chamber, leaving an exhausted and suddenly wet-eyed girl to huddle under the covers. Suddenly, Ingrid thought as she wiped away those stubborn tears leaking from her eyes, her victory didn't seem as satisfying as she'd expected.

She'd cried herself quietly to sleep by the time Loki emerged from the bath, and he stood over his wife, still outraged at her defiance, her sheer ingratitude for his generosity. He wanted to wake Ingrid and pound into her with fingers and cock until she screamed her orgasms over and over- until his little one begged for mercy. He almost reached for her until he glimpsed one pale hand draped protectively over her pregnant belly. Stalking from their chambers, Loki headed aimlessly for his private study until halted from his thoughts by a scantily-dressed form blocking his way.

"My King..." crooned the Lady Runa, barely dressed in her gown. Loki watched as one hand came from behind her back, holding his whip. "Allow me to help you rest from your cares..."

Without a word, Loki yanked her by one arm into his study, slamming the heavy oak door shut.

Chapter 19

In which Loki discovers that his perverse appetites and centuries to enjoy them aren't nearly as interesting as a pissed-off elf in heat.

Some nagging sensation woke Ingrid later that night, an irritable prodding from that shrunken part of her that had suddenly bloomed during her tangle with the witch Runa. If Ingrid had been raised with the slightest sense of normalcy, she would have recognized it as self-esteem. She tried to roll over and return to the oblivion of sleep, but that angry twitch inside refused to allow it, coupled with a fretful push from her pregnant body, cross at the orgasm denied it. Sitting up, the queen sighed and pulled on her dressing gown, stumbling a little as she made her way into the main room. The fire was burning low, showing enough light to know her husband was not in their chambers. Running a hand through her endless length of hair, Ingrid absently resolved to cut it again in the morning. Something drove the elf to walk down the halls, thinking Loki would be in his study- perhaps if they talked-

With another stinging 'crack!' Loki drew the lash down over the writhing witch's back, watching the red stripe across her back well with blood. Suddenly disgusted, his hand went slack, dropping the whip. Runa was moaning and writhing with a theatrical flourish, enjoying his brutality. What was he doing? Her head lifted from where she was tied across his desk. "Why-why did you stop?" Runa gasped, breasts heaving as she pushed her crotch against the wood, trying to find relief.

"This is done." Loki flicked an elegant gesture at the witch's bonds to release them and turned away.

"W-what do you mean, Master?" Runa was trying to recover from her orgasm and comprehend why her King's loving attention had stopped. She could feel the blood trickling down her back, proof that Loki loved her- needed her.

"I mean that we are finished!" Loki snapped irritably. "I no longer desire you. I no longer desire this."

The witch gasped, "You do! Look at me!" Runa angrily raised her fingers, red with her blood from the lash, concrete proof to her of her King's devotion.

Emerald eyes rolling in irritation, Loki turned from her. "This was a mistake. Go to the Healers. Have them restore you."

"Mistake?" The witch's voice rose to a scream. "The mistake was wedding that Elfin whore! You love me!"

In an instant, the king's hand was around her throat, cutting off further howls of rage. "Beating you bloody to satisfy your need for pain and then fucking you to satisfy mine does not mean love-" he hissed contemptuously, "it means we fucked. And I am done."

Runa clawed at his leather pants, trying to release his cock. "You don't mean it, my King! Just- just fuck me and you'll-" In an instant, the witch winked out of sight, Loki whirling to look around his study. In the doorway, he found his furious and silent bride.

"Darling..." he drawled, "did you do something to the Lady Runa?"

Ingrid shrugged, walking further into the room and shutting the door. "She is unharmed."

Loki's eyes narrowed at this utterly unprecedented behavior from his meek little wife. "Then where-" The king's query was cut off by a sharp slap across his face- almost a fist, really, based on the amount of force behind it. Rubbing his cheek, he looked at Ingrid with new respect. "Now, how did you manage that, darling? I hold your bonds."

"How DARE you!" Ingrid was seething with rage, hands shaking as she forced herself to stay focused. A shattering window by Loki's desk showed her she wasn't altogether successful.

"Ingrid..." Loki's growl couldn't be more terrifying as he advanced on her slowly, hands out as if to catch a stray pup. The cautious gesture wasn't necessary, as his wife launched herself at him, knocking the king back against his own desk. Climbing his long legs like a tree, the girl wrapped her own around his waist, tightening her thighs when her husband attempted to shake her off.

"You," she panted furiously, "are mine. My husband. And you will not lay with another!"

Very little still stunned the King of Asgard. Over two thousand years of life, a delightfully sordid imagination, and the resources to explore it left him with very few surprises. But the dove he'd married digging her talons into him like an enraged falcon was a genuine shock, so it took him a moment to respond. "I am your KING-"

"And I am your wife and the mother of your child!" Ingrid shouted back. She leaned into Loki, gripping his armor's silver detailing on his shoulders. "You did this to me- I- I need your care to carry this child- I feel like my spine is on fire..."

The paradigm shifted again and a slow grin crept across Loki's face. "Now, little one," he soothed, "I suspect being left unsatisfied earlier has made you cross. Shall I take care of this for you?" Ingrid didn't know how to answer her arrogant and grinning husband, so she simply bit him on the neck. Hard. It was the last thing Loki expected, and after yelping in surprise, he started laughing. "Oh, you're going to pay for that, little girl," he growled. Turning her towards his desk, the king attempted to place his wife on the wooden surface. Ingrid's strong legs clamped down around his waist and she clung like a limpet to his tall body.

"No!" She shook her head before burying it in his neck. "Not there."

Loki's eyes rolled and he turned, mildly irritated at himself. Even a god as indifferent to the emotions of others as he was, knew that placing his wife on the piece of furniture used to beat his mistress was a tad outré. Placing Ingrid in a big armchair, he swiftly pulled one leg over the arm of the chair, then the other leg on its twin. His wife's hands fluttered down, trying to cover herself, but the king briskly slapped them away and dove in.

Ingrid could feel her husband's chuckles vibrate through her pussy and up her spine, but she couldn't bring herself to care about the wanton display he'd made of her, once that cool tongue joined his chilly lips, attacking her.

Loki put his forearms over her twitching thighs, keeping her immobilized as he ran the tip of that pointy tongue through her swelling lips and up the sensitive cleft between them, pausing to delve into her channel, enjoying the moan that forced itself from his wife's mouth, her back arching helplessly. His thumbs slid down to hold those swelling petals open and give him room to work- the king mauled his bride's pussy with unashamed relish, enjoying how quickly he could break down her defenses. Her long fingers slid through his hair, stroking his thick strands and scratching his sensitive scalp with her fingernails. Loki groaned and pushed his head into her hands like an impatient cat, still enjoying the taste of her, the sweetness and how it glistened against her clitoris, where his lips fastened down, sucking slightly harder than was comfortable. Ingrid's hips went up, then slammed back down by his forearms. Loki slid one thumb inside her channel, and the other inside her ass, grinning against her spasming quim as the elf erupted with a shriek. As she was still shaking from the abrupt series of orgasms her diabolical spouse pulled from her, his cool body was suddenly over hers and that lovely, thick cock was sliding through her channel, pausing every now and then as another aftershock tightened her to immobility for his shaft.

"Now, now," Loki soothed, "relax, darling. We have so much more to do tonight." He began pushing his way back into her with a deft twist of his hips, and Ingrid moaned at the exquisite pressure.

"To- to do?" she managed, still gasping from the force of his mouth on her.

Loki began pumping in and out of his wife, pulling her legs wide at the knee, enjoying the sight of his magnificent cock splitting into her sweet channel. "Yes, little one. Tell me. How many times did you find release with my mouth?" He gave an especially hard thrust, enjoying her rapturous groan.

"Th- th- oh! OH! Three..." Her voice died off into a whimper as her husband did that swivel with his hips again.

"I see," he mused, still thrusting vigorously

into Ingrid. "Then I believe... hmmm..." Loki's head fell back as she clenched down on him again, involuntarily. "Seven more will do?"

"Seven!" Ingrid gasped, "More?"

The beautiful face of her dark King leaned close to hers, eyes glittering pale like new leaves. "At least." With another strong push and her nipple in his mouth, he checked two more orgasms off the elf's delicious "to do" list.

"It must be the baby," Ingrid thought, as she pulled against Loki's broad shoulder, trying to force her husband to turn and take her again. It was their fifth time that night, not counting the chilly reception he'd initially found with her. Her husband came awake slowly, nuzzling her warm skin as his hands moved like a blind man's, following the familiar topography of Ingrid's sleek form. Slipping inside her again, Loki gave an unsympathetic grin at her moan of pain, even as those long legs of hers wrapped around him again. He'd even tried to stop her when they'd reached his "goal" of ten orgasms for his pregnant bride. But the elf whimpered so delightfully, pleading in that sweet, shy voice of hers as she boldly grasped his swelling cock like an accomplished harlot.

"It must be the baby," Loki mused, rolling her

on top so that he could play with those sensitive breasts. "I'm going to keep you with child for the next two thousand years."

Late the next morning, the Queen of Asgard woke and sleepily stretched before stopping with a miserable yelp. All the memories of the night before flooded her awareness and the surge of embarrassment she felt threatened to swamp her. But Ingrid couldn't regret a moment, remembering how desperately her body needed her husband inside of her. She'd kissed Loki's hand in gratitude more than once for at least banking the fire raging in her skin, even if they couldn't seem to douse it. Hearing the door open, the elf pulled the blankets up over her bare breasts, expecting her maids. Instead, her husband entered, dressed in loose lounging pants. "I turned away your cackling hens this morning," he was grinning in that filthy, knowing way he had as Loki examined the way her hips shifted restlessly, trying to find a comfortable perch on that well-worn quim of hers. "You're going to need the kind of care today that they will not understand." Barely refraining from a smug chuckle at his little one's gasp as he picked her up, Loki carried her into the bath filled with warm water and simmering with oils and herbs. Seating her on his lap, he carefully washed his wife's body, enjoying the fact that she was too exhausted to insist on bathing herself.

"Will it always..." Ingrid was searching for how to ask, "when does my body leave this heat?" The king's eyes looked up from where he was spreading suds over those delightful breasts.

"When you give birth," he answered, unsympathetic to her pitiful little gasp. Loki relented when tears simmering made her upturned eyes violet. "Now, now," he soothed, "no tears, little one. This delicate quim of yours will adjust-" he patted it gently, "and we will learn how to pace your heat." Kissing her trembling lower lip, Loki smiled down at her, almost kindly. "I will take care of you."

Perhaps it was those reassuring words or the gentle way Loki bathed her, but Ingrid finally relaxed, that tight knot in her chest beginning to loosen. After he dried her with many kisses and compliments, the king carried his wife out into their terrace, wrapped in a huge towel. Seating her on his lap, Loki raised his face to the brilliant azure sky of Asgard. "You need the sun, darling. It will help you heal." Ingrid nodded and tried to rise, but her husband's arm stayed wrapped around her waist. She could feel the sun's rays begin to filter through her skin as he placed his big hand over hers on her abdomen. "May I take the sun with you?" Loki asked. For the first time ever, Ingrid saw an expression of uncertainty on her husband's face. Nodding with a small smile, she relaxed back against his broad chest and took his other hand, raising it palm up to the sky like hers.

"By the Nornir..." he said, astounded at the play of light entering her cells, dancing to his and back again. Loki could feel her heart beating inside his chest, saw her smile with his amazed grin. And for one perfect, searingly clear moment, he was inside the body of his child, and then- they both stiffened together, feeling their souls dance into another tiny form inside her abdomen, feeling the flutter of recognition from the fragile life of one, and then the other of their children.

Gasping, then laughing together, Ingrid and Loki ran their hands over the sunlight dancing across their skin, urging the rays to spread to their babies. "Twins..." Ingrid marveled, shaking her head. Children were rare and treasured in the Elfin races, and twins were nearly unheard of. The hand of her husband suddenly turned her face to his for a long kiss, breaking only to smile down into her glowing face. They sat together in silence, basking in the moment until a cloud covered the sun and they stiffly rose, making their way back inside to dress.

Loki was lacing his pregnant bride into a pretty green dress when his fingers paused for a moment. "Oh..." he said, suddenly recalling the evening before. "What did you do with the witch?"

Ingrid shrugged as she walked away, braiding her - once again - knee-length curls. "She is unharmed," she assured him. "The guards should find her soon."

It was actually closer to sunset when the Royal guards on duty finally heard the enraged howls of the Lady Runa, wrapped in her own whip and dangling naked and upside down from the highest tower of the palace.

Chapter 20

In which Loki "tempers" Ingrid's heat and the Queen of the Black Court becomes impatient.

"**I**n the past, the Dark Queen preferred to strike and withdraw quickly, utilizing the shock and fear..." Ingrid's sweet voice was calmly reciting the horrors of the Unseelie Court's battle strategy under her mother's rule. "...given the new focus on hostages, I believe she is creating a subspace to hold her captives. They remain in stasis, and she is not required to feed or house them..." Loki was attempting to pay attention, but his wife's sleek form and the barest hint of a swell on her abdomen was making it nearly impossible. His children were within her. His twins. Loki had children, of course. No god with 2,000 years of carnal knowledge escaped fatherhood. But none that he'd planned, that he'd intended. Loki would find out about them after the fact, finding that he was used for his DNA or the potential to blackmail Odin for power or wealth. None were really in his form, after all, a serpent or horse, or the terrifying ruler of Hel. The king had always perversely enjoyed his monstrous offspring- his self-loathing made manifest. But these innocent creatures nestled within the elf- he'd felt their perfection, their power. His. His children.

The emerald eyes of the Trickster looked up to see his council gazing at him expectantly, including his queen. Loki had been amused earlier when she'd insistently followed him into his private meeting with his generals. With a twist of that mobile mouth, he'd allowed it, enjoying Ingrid's stubborn glare as she'd refused to back down. She had valuable intelligence, he had to admit it. But a Dark Elf in the war council? The new queen or not, Ingrid was from a race they'd fought against - lost countless warriors in endless battles. After seeing his commanders shocked and offended by her presence, Loki capriciously pushed her forward, asking her thoughts and including her in on the discussions. By the end of the day, all his men were won over to his Queen's wisdom. Still, sensing Ingrid's weariness, Loki called an end to the meeting and transported her to their rooms.

The elf smiled as she felt her husband pulling her dress from her, kissing her lips, her neck as he put her back against the soft silks and linens on their bed. "Mmmmm..." Ingrid sighed in gratitude, hearing Loki's approving purr in her ear. The depth and darkness of that exquisite voice made her shudder- feeling the power of his long, thick body encasing hers.

"My sweet Valkyrie," he teased, kissing and licking along her jaw, those full lips and then down to capture a pink nipple. "Commanding such attention from my generals. If only they knew..." Loki's mouth moved lower to the gentle swell of her stomach. "If only they knew the treasures inside you, how sweet your welcoming quim feels, the taste of this nipple..." Ingrid groaned as his lips bit and pulled to prove his point. She could feel that fire start blazing up her spine again, yanking Loki up to kiss him, opening her thighs in silent invitation. "Ah, ah!" he chided, "not just yet-" he grinned at his wife's protesting moan as his fingers slid down to her pussy. "There is an order here, Pet."

Still kissing his firm mouth and enjoying the feeling of her King shaping his words against her lips, Ingrid managed "Or- order? I don't- Mmmmm..." her query died off as those long fingers slid into her still-sore passage, stroking against her G-spot and encouraging the hopeful flow of moisture making her slick. "Oh! Oh, Gods!" Ingrid's back arched against her first orgasm of the night. Loki had pulled her aside twice that day to pleasure her, once with his fingers, and the second time simply ordering his military advisors out of the room and lifting the elf on the table, thrusting into her with a hand over her mouth.

Loki laughed, "Only one god, darling, your King." As his wife gratefully came from his finger's knowing movements, he kissed her again, enjoying her warring expressions of relief and pleasure. "There's one..." he purred and slid down Ingrid's shaking body to place those cool lips on her heated ones.

"You pig! You imbecile!" General Gorum dodged another heavy goblet as the Dark Queen screamed at him. "What do these thousand hostages mean if there is no response from Asgard! Do you know how much effort it takes to maintain the stasis? I should have you gutted!"

The general sketched a shaky bow in return, "There is no response yet, my Queen, not yet. Our intelligence shows that King Lo-"

"Don't call him a King, that filthy little upstart!"

"-that Loki was enraged beyond measure at the reports. He is likely trying to craft a response first. But he must negotiate. All the Nine Realms would protest if he allowed a thousand people to die, along with the Vanir King and the noblemen from nearly all the Nine Realms." Gorum was the master of soothing his Queen, but her fury at being denied her daughter was making her dangerously unstable.

Angrily flicking her black-tipped nails, the Dark Queen snarled, "Send him the heads of a dozen of the Dwarf noblemen. Be certain word makes it back to Nidavellir of their demise because that swine on the throne of Asgard cares nothing for the fate of the Nine Realms."

As her general bowed and made a hasty retreat, Queen Alfhild slumped back on her throne. The girl must be returned to her- she must. The Unseelie Court's future depended on it. Hesitant footsteps echoed in the nearly empty hall and she looked up, angry at the intrusion. "What is this?" the queen snarled.

The Dark Elves before her bowed, as one stated quickly, "Majesty, we were gathering intelligence in Asgard when we found a source for you. An insider."

Talons tapping on the obsidian arm of her massive chair, she hissed, "I'm waiting!"

"A source within the Palace, my Queen. A traitor who claims to be able to deliver your daughter to us."

A slow, vulpine grin stretched the thin black lips of the Dark Elf. "Tell me more."

Long after his wife fell into an exhausted sleep, Loki stayed awake next to her, absently smoothing her hair as it grew back down to knee-length. He was sitting up with a book in one hand and Ingrid's head in his lap. His nimble brain was revisiting the weaknesses in the Black Court's strategy while admiring the princess he'd stolen from them. One big hand slid from her golden strands to run idly along her bare arm, then resting on her stomach. No one could have known by looking at Ingrid that she was pregnant, but as an avid student of his wife's body, Loki could see that swell that proved his children were there. The book fell unnoticed to the floor and his other hand began stroking her breasts. A smile curved his thin lips as the girl stirred slightly, her mouth opening as the king's calloused fingers slid over her newly sensitive nipples.

Perhaps it was never being around the creatures who bore his other children, but Loki was amazed at the changes in his wife's body- some small, barely noticeable, but of constant fascination to him. Long fingers ran along Ingrid's stomach, the curve of her waist- he chuckled as she twitched a bit in her sleep from the tickling sensation. Sliding back down to that lovely, tight quim, Loki stroked over her sore lips and channel, green energy drifting from his fingertips to heal her. Just feeling the slick and the warmth of her made him groan, and he rose over his wife, intending to take her again. His thick cock was painfully swollen from the sight and feel of his Queen's pregnant body- but seeing Ingrid's serene face as she slept peacefully made him pause. With a grunt, the King of Asgard - and by default all the Nine Realms - for the first time exercised concern for the comfort of his bedmate over his own. He pleasured himself and shot his orgasm over his wife's smooth abdomen, rubbing his essence into her skin like lotion before scenting her appreciatively and falling asleep.

Ingrid was dreaming, trembling at the horror of the images forced into her subconscious. *Her cruel mother stood nearly waist-deep in bodies- innocent souls brutally murdered by Niflheim's foul troops. The Dark Queen's eyes were closed as she dreamily licked the blood from her fingers, humming her pleasure at the carnage before her. As if sensing her daughter's presence, Alfhild's head snapped to the right, black eyes open and glaring at Ingrid. "This is your crime, little bitch. Their blood is on your hands. But it is NOTHING!" The Queen of the Black Court screamed, "NOTHING compared to what will happen if you do not return to where you belong! You WILL come back!" A horrid smile spread the mottled lips wide, "Or I'll come to find you..."* Her mother's words trailed off into a childish sing-song voice, giggling with insane glee. Ingrid bolted upright and nearly fell off the bed, crawling for the open doors to the balcony, desperately searching for the moon. She shrieked as hands lifted her suddenly from the stone terrace.

"Hush- little one, hush." Loki's beautiful voice soothed her seared nerve endings as he lifted her and carried her to a chair, seating her on his lap. "You were dreaming, that's all. Only a dream." Her King's sonorous whisper stilled Ingrid's shuddering body and she instinctively tucked her head under his chin, hands going to cover her stomach. He shifted her briefly and pointed to the horizon. "There's your moon, darling." Lifting a shaking hand, Ingrid nodded gratefully, still too terrified to speak- knowing the first thing out of her mouth would be a scream.

Chapter 21

*In which Ingrid finds she is not as good
or as honest as she thought.*

"**G**ood morning, Sir Balder." Ingrid gave
a shy smile to the quietest of the
gods imprisoned in Loki's stables,
currently bent over a blacksmith forge with
a horseshoe. He rose immediately, giving the
Queen a respectful nod.

"And to you, Your Grace. Tyr is otherwise occupied; may I saddle your horse?"

"If you would be so kind," Ingrid smiled again,
drawing on her riding gloves. It has become rou-
tine for her to visit the stables each morning,
taking her mare for a ride with her Royal guard
not quite breathing down her neck. Loki was too
busy with military challenges to accompany
her, but he encouraged her riding, knowing it
pleased his wife. His wife was also pleased to not
be joined by her husband and his cruel taunts to

the gods he'd placed there. "Is Sir Tyr near?" Ingrid proffered a full basket, "I brought some hot breakfast- the day is so chilly..."

As if his olfactory senses were as powerful as his sword arm, the aforementioned god came from the stables. "What do I smell? Ah, Majesty!" He bowed, giving the giggling queen an elaborate obeisance. "You are here to rescue me from near starvation! My savior!"

Balder rolled his eyes. As if the gigantic meal Ingrid had sent down last night from the feast was not enough.

The Royal Guard watched from a distance, disinterested in their Queen's banter with the disgraced gods as long as it didn't violate some mandate from Loki. As Balder finished saddling Ingrid's horse, Freyr and Freya came around the corner, stopping short as they spotted the queen. Ingrid watched as Freya's beautiful face creased into a sneer, then a scowl as she made some minute effort to remember she was sneering at the Queen of Asgard. She hadn't believed it when her three closest friends told her of their tentative friendship with Loki's bride. "She's a spy," the goddess had snarled, "you're really that easily swayed by a pretty face?" But watching her friends' easy banter with the girl made her wonder.

"Freya!" Her twin was gesturing at her. "Come meet the new Queen." Glaring at him, Freya made her way over as slowly as she dared without being called out for disrespect from the watching Guards.

"Your Grace," Freya managed stiffly, attempting something resembling a bow.

"Lady Freya," Ingrid answered graciously, "I watched some of your handiwork the other day- as you booted those two horrid men from the broth- from the house? I am glad the girls have someone to look out for them."

Blue eyes still glaring, Freya attempted a smile. "Thank you, Your Grace." The words dragged out of her like a gargle, and even her three friends looked at her, brows raised.

Seeing the tension, Ingrid chose to withdraw. "A pleasure, Lady Freya. I hope you enjoy your breakfast, gentlemen?"

Tyr stopped chewing. "I must share with these oafs? I didn't know I would have to share!" The Queen laughed over her shoulder as she galloped off.

"You fools!" hissed Freya. Can't you see what she's doing?"

Her fellow gods all looked at the enraged

blonde with mixed expressions of confusion. "And what would that be?" queried Balder.

"She's- she's obviously- well, it's clear that Elf is just here to spy!" Freya floundered, feeling a little foolish at her intense hostility to the Queen but unable to control it.

Freyr leaned back, a sly smile crossing his face. "Well, as the King's "stable boys" he drawled mockingly, "I can't see that we would have much to offer, other than the occasional tale of an old battle when the Queen asks for one. Your dislike wouldn't be due to Loki rescuing her from the Black Court and marrying her... now, would it?"

"What are you saying!" Freya was gasping with rage and red-faced, not quite knowing why. Balder and Tyr were carefully looking elsewhere, but Freyr could never resist baiting his twin.

He gave an elaborate shrug, "Perhaps because of your ill-advised past with Lok-"

"Don't even SAY IT!" Freya advanced on a grinning Freyr who put up his hands to defend himself. She cuffed him angrily on the ear and stalked away, the three gods desperately trying not to laugh.

"You shouldn't taunt the wench," scolded Tyr. "You know her past romps embarrass her."

Freyr rolled his eyes, turning back to the

stables. "Not enough to stop."

"All the same," Balder reminded him, "you know she dreamt of being named Queen and Thor's wife one day."

Freyr's handsome face sobered. "Thor. I wish we had any word of him." Deflated, the three returned to the menial tasks they were condemned to by the King.

Ingrid pondered the hostility from Freya as she trotted along. She knew, of course, precisely why the goddess resented her. It was hardly difficult to read the shame and arousal radiating off Freya- that she'd lain with her husband while yearning for Thor. The Queen's brow wrinkled, what did they call this at the Black Court? "Ah, yes. Hate-fuck." Ingrid didn't realize she'd said it aloud until hearing the captain begin to laugh and hastily turn it into a cough. Flushing miserably, the Elf spurred her horse to a gallop, hoping to leave her embarrassment and the uncomfortable subject behind.

But in fact, it was getting harder and harder to drown out the hundreds of mental slings and arrows from her husband's endless round of conquests. Walking back into the castle, Ingrid nodded politely to a group of noblewomen deep into their curtsey to her. But as she passed, the

Queen could feel the hate prickle along her spine from a redhead in the group. *"Stupid little virgin, what could she possibly offer the King after I've taken his whole cock down my-"* With a screech, the woman fell over as a heavy vase crashed down against her shoulders. Ingrid continued on her way, refusing to listen to the woman's dramatic wails. 'I didn't do that! I didn't!' she thought, ashamed to see she was trying to lie to herself- the Princess who could only speak the truth.

"Hannah?"

"Yes, my Lady?" Ingrid's servant entered the room, carrying a huge dinner tray.

"Where are the scissors?" The Queen was looking through the panoply of grooming items Loki insisted on procuring for her.

Setting down the tray, the older woman sighed, "you're cutting your hair again, my Lady? How many times-"

"As many times as is necessary to gain some control over my own body!" Ingrid snapped, furious that they were going through the same tired ritual. "It's my hair!"

Hannah stepped back so hastily she nearly stumbled; eyes wide. "Forgive me, Your Grace- I- I will find another pair immediately."

"No, Hannah, I am-" The Queen sighed as she realized her maid had left the room.

When her husband returned to their chamber that night, he was a little drunk and clearly in a good mood. Ingrid was soaking in their huge bath, staring blankly ahead of her as he entered. "...Darling?"

The Elf startled, sending a wave of water over the edge of the granite bath and dousing Loki's boots. "I- I am so very sorry!" Ingrid gasped, feeling near tears and hating herself for it, "I must have been half asleep-"

"Hush." The lovely, resonant voice of her King soothed her as he undressed with a flick of his wrist and stepped into the water with her. "Boots can dry, Pet. I am not angry." Loki looked down as Ingrid's silvery head dipped against his chest. "You're crying, darling. Has someone offended you?"

The Elf could feel the frost creeping into his tone and shook her head quickly. "No!" She tried to calm herself, feeling his suspicion. "No, my King. I... I don't know. I just feel..." Loki could feel himself thaw as his wife tried to stifle her sad little sobs.

"Darling," he soothed, feeling rather proud of himself, "I believe your lovely Elven hormones are playing havoc with your mood."

Loki was a bit startled at how quickly Ingrid's head shot up, her wet violet eyes seeking his. "Do you think so?" she whispered. His brow creased as he watched her full lower lip tremble, a feeling of mild concern rising. His Queen was notoriously stoic, even when ripping men to shreds at the behest of her mother.

"Yes, sweetness," he soothed, "this is to be expected. Perhaps you should speak with a midwife. It might help ease your fears." Ingrid nodded rapidly, grateful for advice from a living person, not just the pages of her beloved books.

"Thank you, Loki," she sighed, "that- that would be good."

The King's molars ground together, watching his wife's relief sweep across her expressive face. "This means I'll have to ask a favor from Leafstred- and worse, revealing Ingrid is with child," he thought sourly, knowing he needed someone more specialized in Elven pregnancy than Asgard could offer. Still, feeling Ingrid's arms slide around his shoulders to hug him, Loki couldn't stop his own muscled ones from surrounding his wife protectively, helping her rise up and slide down on the cock he didn't even know was already hard and eagerly seeking her warmth. "I'll take care of you," he whispered, enjoying the shudder from Ingrid as her pussy tightened in response on his swollen shaft, both of them groaning together.

Chapter 22

In which Loki and Ingrid discover the hidden depths of the other.

"**S**he is WHAT?" Thundered the King of the White Court. "By the Nornir! You've been wed for DAYS, Loki!"

"By the last count, three months," snarled the King of Asgard. "I do not need your outrage. If you truly care for the daughter of your lost brother, help her now." Loki grinned inwardly to hear the unflappable Light Elf growl with fury. Through the scrying mirror that the Kings used to communicate, he could see Leafstred struggle to control himself.

"We will send two of our best midwives immediately," the Light Elf managed. As the connection faded, he added ominously, "And we will be joining them." The connection went dark before Loki could retort, and with a growl, he angrily waved the mirror dark again. As if that psychotic bitch from the Black Court was not enough trouble. "Elves," he hissed irritably.

"Elves?" Hearing the sweet voice of his wife, the King pasted an affable expression on his face. "What about them, my dear husband?"

Loki smiled sincerely this time as he watched his pregnant wife make her way to him, her lilac eyes shining with the simple pleasure of seeing him. She was always so easy to please, he mused, running one big hand through her (once again) shortened locks. She never whined for jewelry, for a retinue of courtiers, elaborate displays and festivals. 'The advantage of a wife kept captive her entire life,' Loki thought callously, 'she doesn't even know what to ask for.'

"Good news, my angel," Loki soothed, "King Leafstred and his wife will join the midwives coming to us from Alfheim. Perhaps we can learn more about your father." He watched curiously as excitement, then discontent crossed his wife's guileless face. "You are not pleased?"

Ingrid forced a smile and shook her head. "I would so like to know more, but... so would they."

Loki frowned, pulling the Elf onto his lap. "How so?"

Her troubled eyes met his emerald ones as

Ingrid confessed, "the Queen, she- she was very kind that night you sent us from the War Council, but quite insistent. They know something about my Fairie heritage, I'm certain of it. The Ljósálfar questioned me over and over about my birth." She could see her husband's shrewd expression melt into something blander and reassuring.

"All the more reason to keep our own counsel until we know who acts in our interests, correct?"

'MY interests...' Ingrid heard briefly before Loki's thoughts closed to her.

She forced a smile. "I'll just... speak with the Palace Steward about the dinner tonight and leave you to your work." Ingrid tried to rise from his lap, but the King pulled her down again.

"Not just yet, darling. First, I must take care of your... delightful side effects." Loki's grin was filthy and unrepentant as he pulled Ingrid's skirts up and hoisted her unceremoniously onto his girth, enjoying her rapturous little shudder as her pussy clutched greedily to him as she slid down, her pelvis meeting his. He let her stretch inside for a moment, circling her hips and becoming used to him again- from the two enthusiastic poundings he'd given the Elf that morning. 'Really,' thought the King as he began sliding Ingrid up and down his length, 'it's a miracle this little quim ever has time enough to close.'

Finally set free by her lecherous spouse, glowing and walking a little unsteadily, the young Queen tidied herself and finished her duties preparing the palace staff for the big evening. The witch Runa's ignominious ousting from the palace left a gap that Ingrid was more than happy to fill. Even though she had limited experience in overseeing such things, the palace steward and his fleet of housekeepers and cooks were more than happy to assist. There'd been a muffled celebration the night the still-naked witch was escorted from the halls of Asgard, ending her relentless bullying of anyone lower in power than she. Pushing errant curls from her face, Ingrid raised her face to the wind circling the huge courtyard. Followed by her ever-watchful Royal Guard, she made her way to the stables. Balder rose from his forge to greet her.

"My Queen," he bowed respectfully. "Did you wish to ride- again?"

Ingrid flushed, it was true that she's already taken her ride that morning, stubbornly exploring part of the coastline with her damp and irritable soldiers. "No... no, I just..." She sat abruptly on a bale of hay, a humble perch that the god was certain no Queen of Asgard had taken before.

The quietest of the Gods of Asgard cautiously began working at his forge again, as Ingrid's guard shifted uneasily, waiting at a distance to see what their eccentric charge would do next. The Elf cautiously took in a deep breath and let it out again.

Finally, Balder spoke, his tone kind. "Why do you come here, Your Grace?"

Silvery-blonde head leaned tiredly against the fencing, Ingrid admitted, "It's... restful here. You do not think ugly things." Her gaze rose to meet his, warily awaiting a mocking response, but Balder's brown eyes were understanding.

"Court life is always surging with speculation and intrigue," he agreed, laying down a red-hot horseshoe and picking up another. "I imagine the Black Court was more of the same?"

The Elf shuddered involuntarily. "Indeed. But there, at least- every face, every thought turned from me, terrified they would be next. But here- it is a flood. A deluge..."

Balder was silent, still working the metal through the flame as he listened. "Lo- the King was helping me manage my curse, but he is so busy nowadays, thanks to my mother." Ingrid looked down at her clasped hands, embarrassed to speak so frankly.

"It can be most overwhelming, my Queen," the god answered slowly. Putting down his tools, he drew a hay bale opposite that of Ingrid's. "In my training, I was taught to clear my mind and block out everything but battle. Shall I show you?" The gaze that met his effectively crushed any doubts the god had about his Queen. Her loneliness and desperation were obvious. Seeing her nod, Balder urged, "Close your eyes... good. Now, picture a place of great stillness and calm." Her fair brows drew together. She didn't have such a place, not here and definitely not at the Black Court. Finally settling on the lake on the Royal Family's land, she nodded. "Now, picture being in the center of this place. Nothing can touch you. Nothing can harm you. Everything outside the borders of this place can rage around you, but you are untouched. Can you see it?"

Her plump lips smiled in gratitude; eyes still closed. "Yes... I can."

'Good!" Balder praised her. "Simply picture yourself there when all eyes, all thoughts are upon you. You are still focused, still aware, but-'

"Your Grace!" The sharp one of her captain startled Ingrid's eyes open. "We should return to the Palace; the Light Elf delegation should be arriving soon." His face was cold, and dark with suspicion as he gazed between the disgraced god and his Queen.

Ingrid nodded, getting quickly to her feet, smoothing her gown self-consciously. "Of course. Sir Balder, thank you for- well, thank you." The quiet god nodded with a quick smile and bent over his forge again.

"My dear," King Leafstred's smile was open and kind and he gently kissed the cheek of his niece. "Are you well?"

Aware that he meant her pregnancy, and equally aware of the avid stares around them, Ingrid smiled innocently. "Quite well, Your Grace, thank you." The Light Elf looked at her closely, Ingrid was glowing, happy and lit from within in a way she hadn't been before. Squeezing her hand, Leafstred nodded. "We shall speak later."

The banquet was excellent- food and ale flowing freely, their myriad of guests laughing and enjoying themselves. Loki looked down at Ingrid, conferring quietly with the steward before returning to the conversation at the table. Leaning close, the Trickster whispered, "You've done well, little one." Flushing with happiness at praise from her spouse, Ingrid was about to reply when four of the guests rose woodenly from their tables far down the hall and walked toward the Royal table. Guards sprang to stop them, but Loki's eyes narrowed, allowing the four to approach, surrounded by the guards.

He felt Ingrid's terrified gasp as she whispered, "These creatures are from the Black Court!" Holding up an imperious hand, the king stopped all sound in the vast hall.

"King of Asgard." Everyone shuddered to hear the voice that issued from all four gaping mouths, a nauseating harmonic of screams and growls shaped into speech. "Her Most Vengeful Majesty of Niflheim, Queen Alfhild sends her greetings." A pile of severed heads suddenly clattered to the floor in front of the flesh puppets. Ignoring the screams, the four continued, "The Nine Realms will cry for mercy as their pleas are ignored by the King who would rule them. A thousand heads more will grace your gates in a week if you do not return Queen Alfhild's stolen child." And as his scouts had reported to Loki, he watched as the four drones simply melted into a pile of quivering flesh, trickling around the gaping skulls of their victims. Ingrid sat frozen, watching the delegation from Nidavellir, the dwarves recognizing their loved ones among the carnage. This was her fault.

"The fault is not yours." The Ljósálfar Queen

was holding Ingrid's cold hands, trying to massage some feeling back into her limp grasp.

Ingrid's laugh was bleak. "Who else could be to blame but me?"

"Stop." The Light Elf's grasp was firm, and one hand pushed Ingrid's quivering chin up. "I have lived these last five thousand years to see the misery and death inflicted from the Black Court under your mother's cruel reign. It will continue- with or without you until she is stopped. You have something more important to defend now than just yourself."

"I- I would have found a way to return to the-" Ingrid tried to swallow her nausea, "-to my mother's rule to stop this, but..." One hand automatically went to cover her stomach protectively.

Her newly discovered aunt closed her hand over Ingrid's. "This child may be the key to peace," Queen Soren smiled. "A miracle, truly. The baby needs your strength now,"'

The young Queen of Asgard wet her lips. "Two miracles."

Soren laughed with joy. "Twins?" she whispered, mindful of the courtiers nearby. "The White Court has not welcomed a double gift for over three thousand years!" Placing a kiss on Ingrid's forehead, she murmured, "You are a blessing, Ingrid. Not a curse."

Finally returning to their rooms later that night, Loki irritably rubbed his throbbing head. How did that Black Court bitch get her flesh puppets past his guards? Entering their main room, he stopped to see a fire burning in the huge fireplace and a tray of fragrant desserts and sweets next to his favorite chair. Arching an eyebrow, he looked to his wife, smiling hopefully from the door to their bath- the king could see she'd already filled it, the steam rising in the air. "Wife-this is not the night," Loki managed to keep most of his impatience from his tone. "There is much for me to do-"

Ingrid steeled herself and walked to him, chin up and meeting his irritable gaze. "The work will still be there in the morning, Loki, whether you face it exhausted or rested and restored is up to you."

The king eyed the firm expression on his queen's lovely face and smothered a smile. His dove was showing her talons, again. Trying to curb the automatic dismissal rising to those cruel lips, he said, "And what would you suggest, darling?" The relieved and joyful smile Ingrid gave him was nearly worth the night of battle strategy he was giving up.

"First, a bath." Pulling Loki into the bathing area, Ingrid dropped her robe, knowing his agreement would be guaranteed. Enjoying the sight of his wife's skin glowing in the candlelight and the soft swell of the stomach that held his children, Loki instantly magicked away his armor. Ingrid hummed lightly as she cradled her husband's lean body in front of her, washing him by hand, enjoying the sleek bulk of muscle under his marble-perfect skin. "Head back," the elf's soft command sent Loki's head resting neatly between her breasts as she washed his hair, scratching his scalp as he groaned pleasurably. Feeling his hands begin to restlessly move over her skin, Ingrid pulled back with a smile, swimming a bit in the deep tub to circle in front of her King. Loki watched her uncharacteristic boldness with interest. "Do you remember at the lake, telling me that the Jötunn have very large lungs that allow them to stay underwater for a very long time?"

Her husband eyed her, nodding slowly. "Yes, but that has that to do with-"

Ingrid's lavender eyes sparkled as she leaned forward as if to share a secret. "Dark Elves are equally gifted." As she disappeared under the surface, Loki jerked as that hot little mouth of hers latched onto his cock, lips and fluttering tongue making his head drop back with a thud against the bath.

"Where did you learn to do such a delightfully audacious thing, darling?" Loki was sitting comfortably in his chair, being hand-fed the little desserts from his wife.

"From you," she admitted, cheeks flushed red. "You do that to me, and I wanted to-"

With a grunt, the king kissed her, tasting himself on her tongue. "Very well, then how did you know I favor the chocolate confections?"

Ingrid laughed. "They are the first you select after dinner. You only allow yourself one in front of guests, so as not to show weakness. But you will have several when we're alone."

"Mmmmm..." Loki was still savoring the truffle she'd popped into his mouth. Taking the wine glass she offered him, he gave Ingrid a speculative grin, filled with all manner of carnal promise. "And now, my lovely, observant wife?"

This time, Ingrid's smile was uncertain. Handing him the book he'd been reading the night before, she asked, "I hoped you would read to me while I combed your hair?"

"My hair?" The king was genuinely perplexed, then shrugged. "You really want to smooth my hair while I read to you of Midgardian battle strategy?" Laughing at her enthusiastic nod, Loki shrugged and opened the book. "*The Art of War, penned by Sun Tzu.*" Ingrid listened quietly while brushing her husband's thick, black hair, gently tying in small braids at his temple and behind his ears to hold the heavy locks from tumbling into his face.

Loki never knew how many nights she'd laid awake, perfectly still as he'd combed her hair, humming snatches of old songs, murmuring poetry or sitting in silence as those rough hands smoothed her hair with a gentleness never seen in the Ruler of the Nine Realms. She mouthed soundlessly, "I love you, my King."

The fire crackled as Loki turned a page, his deep, resonant voice continuing, "*Chapter Six: The Substantial and The Insubstantial. Thus, a great warrior takes control of others and does not let others control him. By holding out temptation, he can make the enemy approach...*"

Chapter 23

In which Loki and Ingrid find the darkness is not so easy to dismiss.

Ingrid's hands were shaking slightly, she couldn't tell with anticipation or anxiety when she met with the Ljósálfar midwives the next day. Despite the elf's efforts to shoo away Loki, ("This is a woman's matter, Your Grace!") he ignored them and leaned against the wall, watching the examination with interest.

"Open your robe, please." The head midwife was a no-nonsense Light Elf who was clearly experienced with anxious new mothers. Gently running her hands along Ingrid's smooth bump, she questioned, "Have you had any pain?"

"No," the queen shook her head, "nor nausea."

"Very good," complimented the midwife. "And your heat? How are you managing it?"

A choked laugh from her husband made Ingrid

blush furiously, but she managed to answer. "My husband has been very kind and... ah... accommodating," she refused to look at a still chuckling Loki, but the midwife gave him a brief glare.

"This is a positive beginning, Majesty, but I would suggest some breathing practices to help you when the king is not available."

A cold bolt shot up Ingrid's spine as she looked up. Loki gone? She couldn't do this without him! "I- I cannot bear the heat without my husband," she managed, soothed as she felt him take her hand.

"I have no intention of leaving you in distress, darling," Loki soothed, "but the Lady Mistral is correct. In case there is some event that calls me away, you must have other methods." Ingrid shook her head, suddenly overwhelmed. How could she do this without him?

Midwife Mistral was gently examining her breasts, and Ingrid finally backed away, closing her robe. "Not- not now. I'm tired, I- I want to go to our chambers." The Ljósálfar woman looked at her, standing to take her hands.

"The examinations - the bearing of children - it can all be very overwhelming. I understand from the king you've not been touched before coming to Asgard." Ingrid's startled eyes darted to the guarded ones of Loki. He'd spoken to the midwife first?

"I only explained some of the challenges you faced in the Black Court," he soothed, cupping her cheek in one cool hand.

The midwife angrily shook her head. "To have never taken the sun!" she hissed, "Abominable!" Smiling back at the queen, she continued, "Any problems taking the sun and moon, then sharing them with the babies?"

The first true smile spread across Ingrid's face. "It has been simply wonderful. We can feel them respond."

The midwife's brow arched. "We?" she queried, looking at the Royal couple.

"My wife has gifted me with sharing the sun with her and our children," Loki explained smoothly, "we felt our babies respond."

Midwife Mistral leaned forward, perplexed. "You were able to take the sun, Majesty?"

"Certainly," he agreed, "the light passed from Ingrid to me, then to our children and back again."

The midwife stood, eyeing him more closely. "I have never heard of a non-Elf being able to share such a sacred thing before. Most unusual."

Loki escorted his silent wife back to their rooms, looking down now and again at her blank expression. With the huge oak doors finally shut between them and the world, he pulled Ingrid on to his lap. "Was it being touched?" Loki asked, "Why are you so upset?"

Ingrid was ashamed of the sheer neediness and desperation of the words that tumbled out. "You wouldn't leave me alone, would you? I cannot bear this heat without you! I- it would hurt the babies somehow because I couldn't control the fire in my skin, it would burn us and-" Ingrid knew no Queen of Asgard would beg her spouse in such a pitiful way, but she was terrified after a lifetime of never being touched to going back to the same. Loki's hands were the only ones she could bear on her for other than the briefest of touches.

"Hush, darling, hush..." Loki kissed her eyelids, her cheeks, cupping his wife's heated face in his chilly palms. "I will never let you suffer. But we have many months left before you deliver our children and war may call me away-" he kissed her lips as a sob erupted from the elf. "-but we will make certain you have other means if we must be separated. I can teach you to bank the fire." The king's words halted as his shy wife climbed him to grasp his shoulder and the back of his neck, desperately kissing him and fluttering that little pink tongue of hers through his lips. "Now, little girl- you can't- you can't just rub against me to stop a discussion that frightens you- I am not done-" But he was wrong, as Ingrid's clever little fingers had already unleashed his traitorous cock and was squeezing it encouragingly as it hardened. Laying her on her back and rising over her, Loki growled, "We'll finish that talk later, you bad little girl." He tried to sound threatening, but the pull of her hand leading his shaft inside her finished the sentence with a groan.

That strange dark began rising through Ingrid's blood as her husband pounded into her, more roughly than usual, especially since she'd become with child. Her sharp nails began creasing red half-moons into his arms and shoulder until her husband flipped her onto her hands and knees with a growl. "Hold your claws, little cat!" Loki snapped as his wife flailed behind her, trying to grasp his thigh to ground herself as he began shoving in and out of her again. Loki gazed down to see his beautiful cock shining with his wife's juices, pouring from her cunt and slicking down their thighs. "My delicious little slut," he growled into her ear, "my wanton whore. You're practically leaking. Shall we put these juices to a purpose?" Ingrid was too far gone to notice

Loki's broad shaft sliding from her pussy and down to her second opening, wetting her with her own liquid. She moaned loudly in protest as her dark husband pulled himself from her channel and rose up slightly.

"What- Loki?" As the wide head of his cock pushed through the tight ring of her ass, Ingrid's head flew back, hitting his shoulder. Her breath was knocked from her in shock, so the queen simply wheezed helplessly as her entire body stiffened. Her lungs drew air back in with a gasp and a shriek as Loki slapped her bottom. Hard.

He knew he was being rough- that he didn't prepare his wife with fingers and stretching before taking the last of her virginity, but the same dark coil spiraling through Ingrid's raging bloodstream resonated with the cruel, cold core of his own shadow. So, Loki simply bit the back of her neck viciously, keeping her still as he continued to push up her tight canal, enjoying the feeling of forcing the tissue to part for him. The rigid stillness of his wife's body reminded him of the shewolves he'd seen taken by their mates, and the Trickster growled helplessly, remembering the savagery again of being in his wolf form.

Ingrid felt his growling vibrate down her spine and circle through the passage her husband was violating. Even though he'd toyed with her ass with a teasing finger or two, she'd never imagined... this. But while the pain was nearly debilitating, she perversely began to enjoy it, that dark blood strumming through her veins and setting her nerves on fire. Loki roughly yanked on her hips, pulling her up and on to his cock harder, ignoring her scream.

Shoving his fingers into her pussy, he chuckled into her ear, "Sweet, succulent whore, you needed this, didn't you?" Loki grinned at her moan as he gave an especially hard push into her ass. "Such a dirty little girl, you want your King to fuck you everywhere, don't you?" Slapping her clitoris sharply, he hissed, "Answer me!"

Her husband had never spoken to her so harshly before, with such ugly words, but Ingrid was shuddering with the flood of black lust tearing through her, and if they'd been facing each other as Loki fucked her, he would have seen the translucent violet of her eyes slowly turn obsidian. She could only answer by reaching up to claw into his hair swinging over her shoulder and yanking on it viciously. "More!" the Dark Elf gasped, "More!"

Loki lay awake that night, watching Ingrid sleep as he stroked her hair, his seidr drawing it back to its full length again. After they'd come, growling and grunting more like animals than husband and wife, she'd fallen asleep before he'd even finished her aftercare. He'd been angry with himself to find blood from their coupling, healing her and soothing the bite he'd left on the back of her neck. Surprising too was the bites and scratches from her that he'd not noticed during their vicious coupling- along with a chunk of his long black hair still clenched in her fist. Ingrid was on her stomach, face turned away from him, rather than curling into his side and under his arm as they always slept together. Frowning, the king fell into an uneasy sleep, dreaming that he was lying under the Black Queen as poison dripped from her charred talons into his mouth. His nightmare was so vivid he didn't hear Ingrid moan, twisting miserably and one hand flailed in front of her as if to fight off an attacker, the other pressed desperately against her vulnerable belly.

When Loki woke the next morning, he noticed the breeze flowing freely through the chilly room. Rising to close the huge doors to the terrace, he found the glass panels shattered, lying in shards on the stone floor.

Chapter 24

In which Ingrid finds her inner Dark Elf is pushing front and center. Plus, a highly alarming surprise.

By the time Ingrid opened her weary eyes, the shattered glass was gone from their bedroom, and the doors repaired with Loki's magic. He'd resolved not to discuss it with her, not wanting to upset his wife. Curling on her side and holding her belly protectively, she tried to push away the last of the poisoned images from her dream. "Just a dream," she whispered, "just a dream. Nothing to concern you, my little ones."

"What was that, darling?" Loki entered the room, head cocked to hear Ingrid's whisper.

Sitting up and carefully angling onto one hip to protect her raw bottom, Ingrid shook her head. "Nothing of note, my husband. I was- I was talking to the babies."

A surprisingly warm smile crossed her spouse's lips as he leaned down to kiss her, then her belly. "And have they answered back?" Loki's tone was low, intimate as he teased her, and she smiled back.

"Not yet. But it is only a matter of time." Her eyes sparkled up at him, and Loki felt a curious twist in his gut. There was a tug there- like a line drawn between him and her belly- as if his children were pulling at him.

Dropping another kiss on Ingrid's lips, he stood, pulling on the rest of his ceremonial armor. "I must meet with the rest of the war council. I want you to meet us for a luncheon- the Jötunn delegation wishes to see you. If I didn't know better, I would think you had enchanted them, darling."

She nodded and smiled, but as Loki left, a sudden fury swept through her, her fists clenched into the silken sheets, tearing them. "For a luncheon? How dare he!" Ingrid raged, "I should be there now, talking about troop movements and strategy. And he thinks my only value is entertainment at a meal? Arrogant, stupid-" A huge vase holding lilies on the center table in the room shattered, spraying shards of porcelain and flower petals everywhere.

Hannah hurried into the room, flanked by her

younger shadows. "Majesty, are you-"

"I am quite well," Ingrid said, stepping around the wreckage. "I merely..." she paused, trying to think of an excuse, but her honest tongue blocked them all. "Could you clear that up for me, please? I wish to take a bath."

With a worried frown creasing her round face, Hannah nodded, bending to begin picking up the pieces as she nodded to Gundrun to assist their Queen.

Despite her flare of resentment, Ingrid enjoyed meeting with the military delegation from Jötunnheim. She shamelessly begged for stories about life in their frozen world, aware that her husband was listening as well- but pretending disinterest in the conversation. The Jötunn weren't used to speaking much- and even less about their secretive, frigid rock. But the queen's sincere interest thawed them enough to share a few tales from home. "And how do you decide then, on who you marry? Is the spouse chosen by your parents, as before, or-?"

"Darling, forgive me," Loki interrupted smoothly, "it is time for us to return to our council. Gentlemen?" He watched her full lips tighten, then Ingrid nodded respectfully.

"Of course. It was a pleasure, thank you all." She forced a smile as the Jötunn placed their forks down on their half-eaten plates and rose politely to follow the king, even though the meal was not anywhere near its finish. Confused servants bringing in the next course froze as the Frost Giants stalked past them.

"Majesty?" Her head of staff approached her, "Shall I... clear?" His head was lowered respectfully, but Ingrid felt his compassion, which embarrassed her.

"Please do. Have the desserts sent to the king's council rooms." Making her lips shape into a smile, the elf nodded to the palace steward and rose to leave. Stalking along the massive marble hall, Ingrid looked up at the four-story height, the frescoes of ancient kings, queens, and heroes seeming to mock her. Dismissed. Dismissed just like the luncheon Loki wanted her to host.

When her guards or a courtier would attempt to join her, Ingrid would angrily wave them away. So, when she heard the urgent hiss of "Your Majesty! Please!" she turned to lash out at the annoyance.

"Sir Freyr?" She was surprised, she'd never seen one of the disgraced gods inside the castle walls.

The blonde man loped over to her, looking around with a certain anxiety. "My Queen, please- I beg you to come with me. It is very important."

Ingrid frowned, "Is someone hurt? Balder, or-"

"Please!" Freyr pressed urgently, "You know I would not presume to bother you if it were not a matter of life or death."

"Of course, lead the way," she nodded, lifting her skirts to move faster. Ingrid could feel the suspicion and anxiety rise within her as she followed the agitated man to the stables. Something was very wrong, and Freyr knew what he was doing was treason. *'But what?'* she thought in confusion, *'What could he possibly-'*

Tyr met them at the stable door, ushering her inside urgently, shutting and locking the heavy panel behind them. It was darker inside, cool and redolent with the smell of hay. "Were you followed?" he asked the blond god, who shook his head.

"No, her security detail was not with her, praise the Nornir."

Ingrid broke in. "What is happening? Why are you being so secretive?"

A huge form stepped from the shadows. "It is

because of me, Your Majesty."

Ingrid whirled to stare at the gigantic man before her, his keen blue eyes clouded, long blonde hair indifferently clubbed back into a braid. "This cannot be," she gasped, horrified, "you cannot *be* here, Thor!"

Chapter 25

In which Ingrid is bold and resourceful, Thor is risking the lives of everyone who loves him, and Loki is uncharacteristically wonderful... at first.

T hor stepped closer to the horrified elf, reaching one big paw out in supplication. "My Queen- I do not wish to alarm you-"

"Alarm me?" Ingrid gasped, "Are you all mad? This is an act of the highest treason! Prince Thor- why would you do such a thing?"

Ingrid felt rather than saw the other gods make an uneasy circle around her. She didn't feel threatened, just... corralled. Her mood was not improved when Freya stepped into the light as well. "I told you she wouldn't help Thor," she snarled to the four men, ignoring her.

Ingrid's eyes narrowed as she finally lost her patience. "You will speak to me with respect, and face to face, Freya," she snarled, no longer bothering with the honorary "lady" before the goddess's name.

The blonde was obviously taken aback by the sudden chill from the elf but Tyr stepped between them. "Hush, Freya! Let Thor speak." Turning to Ingrid, the bearded man put up his hands placatingly. "Please, My Queen, I beg you-please allow Thor to explain."

Ingrid suddenly wished she was still back in bed, wanting to start this day over again. "Prince Thor, this is madness. Please tell me why you have broken your exile! This act is punishable by death!"

The God of Thunder's face turned dark and bitter, "And the one I called my brother would be delighted to send me to ashes. But please, will you hear me?"

Sitting abruptly on a bale of hay, she nodded and sighed. "This must be something of grave importance for you to risk so many lives."

His big hand passed over his exhausted face, and Thor nodded. "It is for the life of my beloved. For Sif."

Sitting on her bale as the others gathered round protectively, Ingrid could feel her heart squeeze painfully in sympathy as the huge man stumbled through the story, choking back tears at one point. "She is dying, Queen Ingrid. Without help from Loki, I cannot save her."

Feeling suffocated, Ingrid stood, walking back and forth as she thought. "But... Sif is a goddess- how has a mortal disease affected her so?"

"A demi-goddess," Thor bleakly corrected. "The exile and ravages of mortal life have weakened her severely. As Gods, we can stay young and strong for millennia without aid from the Goddess Idunn's Golden Apples. But for one such a Sif..."

"You have consulted all the experts on Midgard?" Ingrid rubbed her forehead, "There is nothing they can do?"

Wringing one rough palm over the other, Thor shook his head. "There is nothing. Sif will not live another fortnight without a miracle."

Ingrid bent to look at his lowered face, tickling along the edges of his consciousness. Thor was telling the truth- his wife Sif was deathly ill, nearly unheard of for a goddess- even a minor one- of Asgard. The picture of Sif's pale, waxen face held in Thor's mind like a scrap of a love letter sent tears to her eyes. "Thor..." she said helplessly, "I cannot imagine a way I can convince my husband to grant your wish. I am not certain I could keep him from executing you for breaking your exile." Beginning her pacing again, Ingrid nodded. "There is only one thing to do."

Thor looked up suddenly, his dim blue eyes clearing for the first time. "What, my Queen? What do you suggest?"

Squaring her shoulders, Ingrid looked at them all calmly. "I must be the one to obtain the Golden Apple from Idunn."

Returning to the palace, the queen was flooded with both agitation and exhaustion. How had this day turned sideways so quickly? Thor- the former heir to the throne of Asgard, and now desperate enough to risk death? And the disgraced gods- surely, they knew this was treason? Were they willing to face torture and death as well? And now, their secret was kept from the King of Asgard by his wife- his Queen! Ingrid was ashamed of her petulance at the meal- pouting and sulking because Loki didn't respect her military knowledge? What did it matter in the face of this dilemma?

Loki returned from the war council to find his bride sitting on the terrace, staring out at the city with a book forgotten on her lap. Leaning against the door, he folded his arms over his chest and enjoyed the vision of Ingrid's beauty. She was glowing slightly, one hand on her still-flat stomach as she finished sharing the sun with his children. "What a pity," he purred, coming forward to kiss the elf's lips, then her forehead. "I had hoped to join you in time to take the sun together."

Her lashes fluttered closed as Ingrid enjoyed the cool press of her husband's lips on hers. "I am sorry to have missed that as well. How was the meeting?"

Loki shook his dark head, pressing more kisses down her neck. "Let us speak of more interesting subjects, for instance, removing this completely unnecessary dress from your lovely body..." He stepped back as Ingrid rose from her chair, pushing her - once again shortened - curls behind one ear, her agitation obvious. "What is wrong, darling? Where is the smile you always have for me?"

Ingrid turned and buried her face into the chest plate of his armor. "I am sorry, my dear husband! I am happy to see you... it's just..."

Loki's glossy black hair brushed her cheek as he bent his head to her. "What, little one? What troubles you?"

Looking up into his concerned emerald gaze, Ingrid could not have felt worse. "Why-" she sighed, "why will you no longer allow me into the war councils? You found my experience helpful before? I finally felt like I could be of use..."

Sitting down in her vacated chair and sweeping his wife on to his lap, Loki wound his long arms around her and held her securely. One big palm slid down to seat itself over her abdomen. The comforting chill radiating from his hand sank into Ingrid, calming her frustration. "My darling, it has nothing to do with your intelligence or your value. You were enormously helpful in teaching us how to track the Dökkálfar troop movements. But this is bitter and evil work. I cannot risk your health or that of our children." Thinking of the shattered doors from the night before, he rubbed her stomach and continued, "The stress that it can spark in you- I will not take this chance. I still consult with you, do I not?" Dipping her head on to her husband's broad shoulder, Ingrid had to agree. Loki did return from war council with questions for her many times that week. "Do you understand, little one?"

Ingrid sighed, burying her head under Loki's chin. "I do. Thank you for listening to me."

Kissing her fragrant silvery hair and absently setting a seidr to re-grow it overnight, he soothed, "I know I have not been as available to you. Allow me to make it up to you." Closing her eyes as she felt those long, clever fingers loosen her bodice, Ingrid felt the twisted knot in her stomach relax. Her husband still valued her. He still craved her. Loki was vaguely aware his luscious wife's mind was restless, but he was too focused on the need to get inside her. A grunt escaped him as his hands covered her breasts- so beautifully swollen and tender from her pregnancy. "Your breasts- these lovely, full breasts- they fit my hands perfectly now, darling as if they were meant to shape to my fingers." Grinning at her little moan as he gently pinched her nipples, Loki stripped them both bare before lifting Ingrid and carrying her to their bed. "Now darling," he purred, "we must stay on schedule."

"No! Oh, please, Loki! I can't bear-"

His dark chuckle vibrated against her sensitive nipples as he laughed into her generous cleavage. "What kind of husband would I be if I didn't ease your discomfort, my precious little one? Let me take care of you. I think twelve orgasms will do for tonight." Ingrid's attempt to whine was stifled into a yelp as Loki's wonderfully chilly mouth latched on to her sensitive clitoris, worrying it gently with his tongue before drawing the tip of it up and down her slit. "No protests now, darling. I can already feel these sweet lips swell, and so delightfully juicy..." Feeling her hands slip into his hair, Loki growled. "There we are. You may come." And with a desperate thrust of her hips, she did. Twice. "Ten more..." her diabolical lover soothed as he flipped her on to her hands and knees.

Ingrid was grateful for Loki's extremely talented attentions that night, because she was desperate for him, her elfin hormones ignoring the stress and drama of the day for something more elemental. And the constant edging into orgasm kept her secret thoughts buried deep, just where they needed to be. Gasping as Loki's thick cock slid into her again, Ingrid's focus narrowed into the feel of him inside her, those rough hands gripping her hips and moving her easily- back and forth, circling to press up against her sensitive walls. Loki was watching the slide of his thick shaft in and out of Ingrid's body. Leaning close, he whispered to her in his beautiful voice, the cultured elocution slurred with his lascivious gloating. "How could any cunt ever be this sweet, little one?" Putting his long fingers to her temple, Loki forced her to see what he did- the vision of her juices greasing along his cock, shining and squelching in the most delightfully obscene way. "Can you see how well your little quim takes me?" He waited for her whimper that vaguely affirmed his question before continuing, yanking her upright and grinning at her little shriek as it drove him deeper inside her. "Your slick is wetting my thighs and yours, how needy you are, precious.

Shall I take my cock away? Perhaps coming twice was enough..."

"No!" Ingrid gasped, "No, no nononono... please, my King! I need more of you... mmmmm..." Her protests died off as Loki began shoving in and out of her clutching pussy, crassly, greedily and taking her like a common tavern whore.

Loki's eyes glowed fire, reading her fantasy. "Oh, darling... have I made a mistake, treating you so gently?" Ingrid stifled a painful wail as he roughly adjusted her again on his shaft, driving into her harder. "Does this depraved and wanting cunt crave harsher treatment?" Sliding two fingers to clasp her clitoris between them, the king chuckled cruelly when they slipped off easily. "Oh, my precious slut, too wet to even hold your pearl... Imagine me bending you over a table at a tavern in the city - rough wood stinking of spilled ale - wetting your bare tits as they slide across the surface? Flipping your skirts up to find a whore like you does not wear her silks, leaving that bare cunt on display? Chairs scraping as the men draw closer to see me fuck up into you, so wanton and desperate that you care not who sees you on display?"

"Oh! Loki, please..." Ingrid felt herself fall into the helpless convulsions of another orgasm, and yet another.

"Why, you bad, bad little girl." Her dark husband's voice was cold now, disapproving. "You did not ask permission." A huge hand gave a thunderous slap to one cheek, then the other as Ingrid thrashed against him. "You forget your manners, my greedy little Queen." To her shock, Ingrid came again- twice as her ass tingled and stung. She began crying in pleasure and frustration as Loki leaned close to her ear, hips still thrusting relentlessly. "Twice? Such a good slut. Only eight more, little one. Then I'll allow you to rest. Back to that tavern, my sweet whore... you push back on me..."

Loki didn't finish until he'd dragged the other eight from his wife with his cock, fingers, and tongue. On his third release, he came so hard himself inside her sweet grasp that he stopped breathing for a moment, every cell in his body attuned to the explosion between them. "Thank you," Ingrid managed to moan, "I love you, my beautiful husband... thank you..."

Trying to draw a full breath, Loki clasped her breasts in one hand and her pussy in the other. "Your King is going to keep you full with children forever. I will seed you and get you with child, again and again, watching this lovely body swell." He held her until he felt his exhausted bride fall asleep, rising then to gather materials to clean and heal her. Kissing the faintest bump on that smooth abdomen, he whispered "Good-night, my children," before curling around Ingrid and falling asleep himself.

To her surprise and happiness, Loki's face was the first thing she saw the following morning, his gaze intent on her as he ran his hands over her warm skin, enjoying the contrast against his chilly palms. "Good... morning," Ingrid managed, still feeling loose-limbed and pleasantly sore. She turned her face into his thigh where he was seated beside her, nuzzling him gratefully. He smelled of snow, the sharp scent of pine, and of her. Putting her head in his lap, Ingrid purred when Loki began smoothing her (once again) knee-length hair. "I thought you would be gone to the war council already," she yawned, feeling the hard muscles in his leg shift.

"I should be," the king agreed, "but I seem to unable to leave my beautiful wife."

Ingrid giggled a little. "It is very nice to wake up with you." Luxuriating as he stroked her cheek with calloused fingers, she sleepily wrapped her arms around his leg.

"Do you intend to hold me down and keep me captive?" Loki's voice was amused, but without the cynical bite it usually carried.

Squeezing his long leg more tightly, his Queen purred. "Perhaps."

Rolling her over onto her back, he slipped down, pausing to kiss her abdomen before settling between her legs. "Then I shall make the most of my captivity," Loki said, those knowing emerald eyes glittering at her as his lovely, cool mouth landed on her suddenly heated center.

Dressing in plain riding gear and an enveloping cloak, Ingrid walked from their rooms in a rather unsteady fashion. She tried to shove down the crippling guilt she was feeling. Her cold husband had never been sweeter and more attentive, treating her almost as if he loved... Shaking her head, the elf walked faster. She must do this for Thor. She could be in the Sacred Forest and out again without her husband knowing. Thor could have the Golden Apple; Sif would live forever, as she was meant to. And one day, Thor and Loki would be as close as brothers again. She was sure of it.

Hannah knocked on the bedroom door, listening for her mistress. "Your Majesty? The King told us to bring your breakfast. Shall I draw you a bath?"

A sleepy Ingrid answered. "I'm still exhausted, Hannah, I'm going to stay in bed and rest longer. Why don't you and the girls take the morning for yourself."

"As you wish," her maid answered, "sleep well."

The pale shadow of the queen shimmering under the covers in Loki's huge bed was not a strong projection- and her husband could have spotted the ruse in an instant. But Ingrid was counting on not being disturbed, and she prayed she'd be back before Loki sent for her. Taking a back stairway to the stables, she'd managed to avoid any direct encounters. Freyr and Tyr were waiting for her, holding her horse. "Where is he?" Ingrid asked.

Opening the stable door, Balder drew her inside. Thor moved to greet her, putting his large mitts on her shoulders, nearly knocking the sturdy elf over. "Ingrid, are you sure you must do this? Perhaps there is another way..."

Shaking her head, Ingrid patted his hands, stepping back to get his heavy arms off of her. "There is no other way. I will be back with your apple."

Thor shook his blond head, brow wrinkled. "My Queen, why are you doing this? You do not even know me. If Loki is to discover..." he sighed, and she could see his resolve was wavering.

Ingrid looked him in the eye, forcing him to

pay attention. "I am not doing this for you," she said clearly. "I am doing this for my husband. If you were to be destroyed by this, he will never have a chance to reconcile with you. I know he loves you. And you clearly love him."

Thor stared down in amazement, then took her hand to kiss it. "I do not know how the Trickster was fortunate enough to find you, but you will be the saving of him."

Ingrid smiled serenely. "Loki saved me first."

Galloping through the private Royal reserve, the elf went over and over the plan in her head. It had to work. It must. Pausing before a particularly lush grove of trees, she paused, eyeing it carefully. The two warriors flanked her. "This is the spot, Majesty?" Tyr was staring into the darkness, trying to see what Ingrid was staring at so fixedly.

"It is," she answered distractedly. "You must stay here."

Freyr spluttered. "We gave our word to keep you safe, my Queen. We cannot leave-"

"Men are not allowed in the grove," Ingrid interrupted. She'd spent most of the previous afternoon reading Frigg's personal journals.

She'd had a feeling Loki would have kept them since he had so few reminders of the Allmother left. Finding the passages about the Golden Apples confirmed her theory about the Goddess Idunn. Idunn cared for the sacred tree holding the Golden Apples that created or extended immortality and youth. The Valkyries from Valhalla were her only companions. It must be a woman to request the apples, and the task fell to the Allmother for centuries. Holding up her wedding ring handed down from Queen Frigg to Loki, the elf clearly uttered the command to open. Walking through the glowing portal that opened before her, she clenched her fists. This must work. She felt the unnatural pull of the grove to her- a longing to stay that was visceral. Taking a deep breath, she said, "You are so very near to Valhalla, it compels you," she counseled herself. "You must ignore this."

"This chattering..." a musical voice sighed, "always the chatter. Why cannot these gods keep silent?" Ingrid stilled. She had found the Goddess Idunn.

Dropping deeply into the most gracious curtsy she could manage, the Queen of Asgard bowed her head in respect. "Most holy of the Goddesses, I bring greetings from the Æsir."

"You may rise, elf." Looking up, she could barely view the form of the goddess, so glowing, nearly incandescent in her beauty. Looking her over, Idunn walked in a circle. "I do not know you. Where is Queen Frigg?"

Ingrid's brow rose. The goddess didn't know of the Allmother's passing? Was her isolation here that complete? "I am deeply sorry to tell you that the Queen Frigg has entered the gates of Valhalla. She... went into a decline after the passing of the Allfather." Tears turned her eyes byzantine at the thought of Loki's grief, knowing his actions caused Frigg's torment and decline.

"And you are?" Idunn was still examining her carefully as if she'd discovered an exotic looking insect.

"I am King Loki's wife, Ingrid. I have taken over the responsibility to gather the Golden Apples from you, my Goddess." As Idunn moved to her right, Ingrid could finally see the Tree of Life- a thing of astonishing beauty, with thick, glossy green leaves, beautifully burled wood on the trunk and the apples - the magical source of immortality - gleaming with a richness so exquisite that they were nearly painful to look at. Even the vibration of power from the earth around the Tree moved uncomfortably through the soles of Ingrid's feet.

"And who receives this Golden Apple?" Idunn hadn't moved, still gazing at the new Allmother.

"The Golden Apple goes to Thor, my Goddess," Ingrid answered, still truthful enough to allow her to speak. To her profound gratitude, the goddess nodded without questioning her, taking her left hand instead to gaze the wedding ring.

"This is Frigg's, I recognize it. But not her wedding ring. I am surprised it opened the portal for you."

"My husband wanted to use the ring that the Allmother wore to celebrate her family," Ingrid smiled, "and she viewed Loki as such." Looking down as her ring flashed a brilliant viridian shade of green, she cringed a little. Queen Frigg had loved Loki dearly. Before... She looked up to see the goddess watching her intently.

"Very well, Queen Ingrid. And where is my gift?" The blood drained from the elf's face. A gift? Frigg's journals had not mentioned a gift!

"I- I beg your pardon, I was not aware- May I return with your gift, my Goddess? It would be my honor."

Idunn flicked a finger to shape a bed of moss into a soft throne. "Very well. And then you will have your apple."

Ingrid's heart was pounding. Just to create her illusion spell, hide from Heimdall's golden eyes and find her way through the portal had drained her. Whenever her "gift" required destruction or death, it barely registered. But this new magic was overwhelming. As her frantic eyes rose to the goddess's, Ingrid suddenly tilted her head. "Your hair, Holy One. It is so lovely, a waterfall of ebony- I've never seen a color quite like it."

Even a goddess has vanity, and Idunn preened as she toyed with the ends of her long braid. "But what has this to do with my hair?" Ingrid look around the timeless garden, everything frozen in space as if the grove was captured in a drop of amber.

"Well..." the elf began to casually wander, careful not to step too close to the goddess or the sacred Tree. "As a woman, it can be pleasant to have a change every now and then, do you not agree?" Idunn's brow rose, but she was listening. Carefully unbinding her elaborate braids, Ingrid shook out her hair- Loki must have been especially insistent last night because her silver-blonde hair tumbled to her feet. With a wry smile, she admitted, "King Loki is fond of my hair- he was not pleased to find I'd cut it one day. It will continue to grow back, no matter what I do. May I offer my hair as your gift? A trifle, perhaps to amuse you? It will always grow back, no matter what you do with it."

"If I take it," Idunn mused, "you would not be able to grow your hair back, no matter how powerful the seidr."

A grin stretched across Ingrid's face. "That, my Goddess, would be your gift to me." The two eyed each other, and Idunn began to laugh, the elf gratefully joining in.

When the portal opened again with the stench of burning ozone and a blue-white glare that seared the corneas, Freyr and Tyr saw the queen clear the tear in space before it closed in on itself. She looked surprisingly cheerful and not at all battered as they'd expected. "My Queen, are you well?" Tyr asked, "Did the quest go as hoped?" The one-handed warrior swung off his horse, moving to Ingrid to help her on to her mare.

Patting the small silk bag at her waist, she nodded. "Now, let's return to Thor. And quickly. It's only a matter of time before he's discovered." The three galloped as fast as they could push their horses, heading into the stable paddock to dismount behind the huge Royal Stables. "Tyr," urged Ingrid, "please find Thor. We must do this now."

"No need." It felt like her entire spine had turned to ice as Ingrid turned slowly. The little side yard was instantly filled with guards, several holding weapons on the bound and battered Thor, Freya, and Balder all on their knees

in chains. And her husband, arms behind his armored back and legs spread wide. "It seems you
have much to explain, my dear, dear Queen."

Chapter 26

In which Loki does exactly what you would expect in the face of betrayal- he is a complete asshole.

"**M**y- my King..." Ingrid could do no more than a whisper, watching as Loki walked closer. His white face could have been carved from marble, it was so rigid, with a thin compressed mouth and eyes blazing so furiously that the elf felt like he was setting her on fire just from his gaze. After glancing down at her, the king strode past as if she didn't exist.

"Take the queen to our rooms. No one is allowed inside." Loki paused for a moment, his back still to the stunned group. Huge fists suddenly clenching, he added, "The rest go to the dungeons. the lowest level." There a shocked gasp behind her, but Ingrid couldn't move, couldn't turn long enough to look as her friends were dragged away. Her terrified gaze was focused on the broad back of the god walking away from her. When Loki slowed for a moment, Ingrid's heart started beating again, allowing her hope. He turned, walking back to her. Those blazing eyes slowly traveled down her body, pausing for a moment at her abdomen. His hand reached out and tore the silk bag from her waist before walking away again, carrying the Golden Apple with him.

Pacing back and forth in their room, Ingrid's thoughts refused to stop circling long enough for her to focus on anything properly. Thor's beloved Sif was dying. Thor was in the dungeon. Her friends were in the dungeon. After she gave birth, she could very well be in the dungeon, if not dead. And yet all that the elf could picture was her husband's open, loving expression that morning. He'd taken her slowly, lazily as he kissed her face, neck, and breasts, whispering how beautiful she was, how lovely their children would be. Feeling the droplets splash on her dress, Ingrid realized she was weeping. Loki would never forgive her. Never. To her husband, this was surely the worst kind of betrayal.

Loki didn't return to their bed that night, and Ingrid endured a broken sleep plagued with dreams of her mother laughing at her failure. "He'll send you back to me, now," the Dark Queen hissed, "worthless girl! Faithless bitch..."

Her laughter echoed in Ingrid's ears as she shot up in bed, staggering out to the terrace, looking for the moon. Finding the sliver of the new moon in the sky, she tried to concentrate on bringing its rays to her children. Perhaps her hands were shaking too much, or the lunar rays weren't strong enough, but the elf huddled in the chair, sobbing in despair.

Thor heard the measured footsteps of the god he'd once called "brother" long before Loki strolled into view. With a mirthless chuckle, he said, "You always did enjoy making a dramatic appearance, Loki," as the king rounded the corner of his cell and stood before him. The God of Lies seemed even colder, more sculpted into a fearsome countenance in his silver and green armor. "Is Queen Ingrid well? I've never known you to hurt a woman before- well, at least other than in play."

"My wife's welfare is not your concern, *brother.*" Loki emphasized the last mockingly. "I should think you'd be far more concerned for your own. How did you get the queen to betray me? Promises of power? Rule over Asgard?"

The God of Thunder chuckled mirthlessly, "None of those. I was trying to save the life of Sif- my Queen. Do you know why *your* queen was helping me, brother?"

"Do enlighten me," Loki drawled infuriatingly. "It won't save you from execution, but by all means..."

Thor walked closer, nearly against the force field holding him within the metal cell- a powerful energy that would fry him to a crisp if he tried to breach it. "She told me, 'I'm not doing this for you. I'm doing it for my husband. If you were to be destroyed by this, he will never have a chance to reconcile with you. I know he loves you. And you clearly love him'." Slumping heavily into a chair, the God of Thunder chuckled bitterly. "I told her that she would be the saving of you. And she said- 'he saved me first'." Hopeful blue eyes looked up to Loki's impassive gaze, and Thor shook his head. "Please do not punish her for that."

"Still attempting to give me orders, you fool?" Loki snarled. "You are nothing here, Thor! You denied your loyalty and left Asgard without a look back because you would not accept the truth of my rule. What did you think would happen? Sif was a mere demi-goddess- of course she became a mortal on Midgard!" Loki leaned forward, nearly roaring in his rage, "These pathetic creatures- they are like mayflies to us! How dare you!"

"Her life is being stolen from her," Thor answered steadily, though his voice was choking in grief. "My beloved Sif has so much more to offer the Nine Realms, not just Midgard. I hoped to plead for you to allow her to be healed here-"

"And instead sent my pregnant wife to face Idunn for a Golden Apple? Putting my unborn children in danger?" Loki's rage was incandescent- unable to bear his idiot friend's dismantling of all he held dear in less than a day. Proving that Loki was the fool- believing in Ingrid's loyalty and devotion to him.

Thor's shocked face cleared into a grin. "Queen Ingrid is with child? Twins? Brother- congratulations! Elfin children, what a rare thing!"

"Spare me your felicitations, you idiot!" snarled Loki, "Do not even speak of my progeny! You endangered them today - what if Idunn destroyed my - the queen for attempting this ridiculous quest for you?"

Thor leaned closer, nearly a hair's-breadth from the deadly field that held him. "And you would not do the same if your Ingrid lay dying?"

There was a furious hiss of breath before Loki regained control. "All of this for love, Thor?" The king smiled mockingly. "You love your Sif this much- to risk your life and those of the others disgraced to save her, much less the life of my- of the queen?"

Loki couldn't remember a time in these many centuries when he'd seen tears in Thor's eyes, but there they were, streaming down the god's cheeks. "I would gladly give my life for Sif's. If there were only a way, I would have done it already."

Thor should have expected nothing else, but now a cruel smile spread across the King's pale face. "Really..."

Ingrid had barely managed to sink into a restless doze in the chair overlooking the gardens when her maids entered the bedroom. "Majesty," Hannah said softly, "we are here to prepare you."

Rising stiffly from her seat, Ingrid said, "For what?" All three attendants couldn't look at her, their pale faces attempting to remain composed. Sighing, she shook her head. "It matters not. I am ready." As the women fluttered around her, dressing her for the day in some of her finest garments and jewelry, Ingrid's thoughts circled restlessly.

She knew without a doubt that her husband wouldn't kill her- not yet, at any rate, not before she'd given birth to the only thing she had of value- his offspring. But hearing the bustle and furor of the palace, she knew he was planning a spectacle- one that could only include the God of Thunder and the others. 'Perhaps he'll spare Freya,' she thought bitterly, 'I'm sure he would enjoy taking her as he forced me to watch.' Her heart and her belly twisted painfully at the thought, and Ingrid covered her stomach. Being escorted briskly from their chambers by her formerly protective military detail, she knew now their swords were more likely to prod her cruelly to keep her moving.

The walk to the Bifrost was long when not on horseback, but Ingrid refused to slow her pace, keeping her head high and ignoring the staring crowds, whispering and speculating openly about the spectacle. Before her, the heavily chained Balder, Tyr, Freya, and Freyr shuffled along as best they could with the chains hobbling each step. And before them- Thor was attempting to do the same, nearly dragged on a rope behind the huge black stallion the Loki was riding. Finally, the shimmering pathway was before them- Heimdall at his post next to the elaborate opening to the Bifrost. When Ingrid gratefully halted, she saw a large crowd of noblemen, military leaders, high-ranking delegates from the other realms. *'All here,'* she thought bitterly, *'to see the mighty King Loki make an example of those who oppose him. Even the god he called his brother.'*

Loki elegantly situated himself as he waited for the chatter and noise to die down, sweeping a cold jade gaze over the crowd. "Most of you know, I imagine, that Thor- firstborn to King Odin and Queen Frigg- chose to relinquish his loyalty to the throne as I ascended after the All-father's passing." He smiled benignly, knowing not a soul would dare to look up at that outrageous statement. "In my compassion, I sent Thor - he who I saw as a brother - to Midgard to live out his long life, with perhaps a short, blissful time with his now-mortal Sif, whom he seems to love so deeply."

The majestic expression on his face fooled many. "How noble!" sighed one.

"How romantic!" tittered two noblemen's wives, unused to any show of affection from their elderly spouses.

Ingrid gritted her teeth but remained silent.

"But this man has renounced his claim to the throne," Loki uttered coldly, perfectly clear in his deep voice that rang through the crowd. "He gave up Mjölnir, the sacred hammer gifted from King Odin. He gave up all of you!" A low grumbling went through the assembled nobles as they shifted, beginning to be drawn into Loki's web. "But how," mused the king in faux distress, "how can I order the death of my beloved brother, even though he has so flagrantly violated his exile? Recklessly risking the lives of those who still cared for him?" Looking around, Ingrid knew she wasn't the only one desperately gritting her teeth to remain silent. Thor's shackled hands dripped blood from clenching those brutish fists. "But what to do?" Loki's voice was softer now, more regretful as he clasped his hands behind him, pacing regally before the throng.

"His crime is great indeed," he pronounced, suddenly pulling something from a pocket and holding it aloft. "A theft of unimaginable magnitude from the Tree of Life the Goddess Idunn guards- a sacred Golden Apple!" Another shocked and angry rustle went through the king's audience at the sheer effrontery of such an act. With a pained, and noble sigh, Loki gazed upon the crowd. "Let it not be said that the King of Asgard is not without mercy." His benign smile was sending pulses of anxiety to Ingrid's body, crawling up her brain stem like red ants. "I shall return the god I see as my brother to Midgard, to live out his eternity there."

The elf sucked in a breath, finally understanding her husband's cruelty. Thor would be forced to watch Sif - the love of his life - die, helpless to save her. And he would be then condemned to live for many millennia until his broken soul finally traveled to Valhalla. Her attention snapped back when her husband spoke again, that expression of false sorrow still gracing his noble brow. "As for Balder, Tyr, Freyr and Thor's occasional lover, Freya-" a scandalized hiss sounded from the courtiers, the statement mocking Thor's supposed devotion to Sif. "As for these traitors, I must no longer allow mercy to guide me. They will live out their lives in the deepest circle of Asgard's dungeons until they rot and their life's spark expires."

Ingrid swallowed against the lump in her throat. Everyone was being punished in the cruelest possible way. What would be her punishment? But her husband's eyes fell on her and two fingers imperiously gestured her closer. Obeying with numb feet, the queen stood silent at his side as Loki leaned close to Thor. "All this for an insect," he hissed, "for a mortal." Pulling the Golden Apple from some hidden pocket in his armor, the God of Lies slowly, tauntingly waved it in front of Thor's face. "She will die. And you will watch, knowing that I hold the one thing that could have saved her. Enjoy your exile. I shall make certain you never leave that pitiful rock again."

Ingrid stared at Thor, tears in her eyes at his utter desolation. All the tales she'd heard of the magnificent God of Thunder were reduced to this huge, broken man before her. The god's blond head suddenly raised resolutely, nodding bravely to his friends, and then to Loki and Ingrid, standing before him. "Then this is goodbye," he said steadily. "Goodbye, Queen Ingrid." She nodded, tears beginning to drip from those byzantine eyes, "And farewell, brother. I- I wish we had more time." Pushed toward the vortex the grim Heimdall had already created, Thor straightened his huge shoulders and backed closer to the searing light, pushed by the swords of Loki's Royal Guards. The God of Lies smiled cruelly, holding up the Golden Apple - Thor's last hope - mockingly as he was pulled backward by the force of the planet's pull. It was then, that Ingrid found it was easy to sidestep her King's commands. To use the power of the gravitational pull to suddenly free the gift of Immortality from Loki's grasp and send it into the vortex along with Thor, safe from the furious command of Loki to return. And just before the painfully shimmering lights faded, the elf managed to glimpse the joy on Thor's face as he caught the one thing that would bring his love from the brink of death to nearly eternal life to share with the God of Thunder.

'I cannot stop shaking,' Ingrid noted absently as she was put back into their rooms, the luxurious prison that held her now. Even her maids couldn't look at her, quietly finishing their work

and leaving her dinner on a tray before speedily showing themselves out. To her shame, the elf's despair was transferring into the pained stimulus from her greedy center- throbbing impatiently as if her body had no idea the anguish her soul was suffering. Ingrid worked to control it- deep breathing, walking restlessly through their extravagantly spacious rooms, circling the endless stacks of books dotting their stone floors. She sang, moving to scraps of melody from the dances Loki had shared with her. When that became too painful, the girl drew an ice-cold bath and sat in it as long as she could endure, blue and shuddering before forcing herself to leave the water, concerned she might affect her children. Falling into another miserable sleep, Ingrid dreamt again of her mother, laughing and mocking her only child for her stupidity in thinking anyone could love her. Small things began to break through the soaring rooms- a vase, an elegant stained-glass window, then Loki's huge mirror. When the massive slabs of the stone floor began shifting and shuddering, a cool hand suddenly landed on the sweating forehead of the moaning queen.

"Hush now... hush, little one." Ingrid stilled as that blessedly chilly hand stroked her hot face and neck. "There's nothing to fear. You will never return to that Black Court bitch. Your babies are safe. No harm will come to them." The soothing, almost disembodied voice never specified that she was safe, but hearing the assurances about the tiny forms inside her drew the tear-stained elf back to sleep.

The next day was more of the same. Ingrid's silent handmaidens brought her meals, drew her bath and dressed her without a word, eyes averted. It took a few attempts at conversation for the Elf to realize they'd been ordered to not speak to her. Placing one small hand against the thick oak and iron-bound doors, she could feel the grim contingent of guards outside the entrance, more flanking the terrace. 'At least Loki is allowing me to take the sun for our children,' Ingrid thought bleakly, raising her hand to the skies. The shimmering energy helped put the anxious little souls inside her to rest again, but their mother couldn't stop pacing. Defiant, she tried three times to pleasure herself, desperate to relieve the ache searing along her center to her breasts. Everything hurt- even her clothing was too stimulating against her skin. After the last failed attempt, Ingrid burst into a flood of childish tears as she remembered that first night when Loki touched her- his words that suddenly carried more weight.

"Little one, I'm going to make you come now. You'll feel very wet and warm. This belongs to me, to your King. You will not have these without me. Do you understand?"

In despair, Ingrid realized his seidr was powerful enough to rule her even now. The third morning found the elf crying into her pillow as her body mindlessly rubbed against the silky sheets. This was going to be how her husband would kill her- by driving her mad with desperation and lust, until the only thing left was the shell needed to bear his children until they could be safely taken from her.

Chapter 27

In which Ingrid finally gets some action, Loki gets a talking-to, but no one really gets what they actually long for. Because life on Asgard is sometimes like that.

"**A**nd how is your sleep?"

The Ljósálfar midwife Mistral had returned from Alfheim to check on the queen. She was gently pressing on Ingrid's stomach while measuring the increase in the infants' size.

Ingrid looked up tiredly. "It is fine."

The midwife fixed her with a speculative glance before continuing, "Any special food cravings, or sudden, powerful emotional swings?"

Ingrid silently shook her head, painfully aware of Loki's cold glare and simply wanting this miserable examination to be over. She already felt like nothing but a brood mare to her husband, and to have him sitting in his favorite chair, legs splayed wide as always made it worse. He was watching every moment of the poking and prodding with intense interest.

Stepping back, the midwife nodded to Ingrid to close her robe. The queen clutched the edges of her silk covering gratefully. It was utter misery to stand in front of her husband, nearly nude and knowing he'd never touch her again. She couldn't even look at him, terrified that she'd see the disgust in those piercing eyes. "Majesty, the mood swings are important to track, because the conflict between Dark Elf genes and Light Elf- well, we are not certain of the hormones that might drive you during this time." Mistral's brow furrowed as she watched as the pale, silent girl secured her robe. The first time she'd examined the new queen, she was flushed and happy, even in her shyness. But this washed out version of the girl she'd seen before was deeply concerning. "And how are your sexual activities," the midwife tried to continue, "are they regulating your heat?"

Ingrid's head dropped again. "They are fine."

Regarding her with a deep frown, the Ljósálfar patted her hands. "Why don't you go relax, your Royal Highness? I believe your servants just brought in lunch." Ingrid nodded and rose without another word, passing her husband and leaving the room. As the king rose to go, the midwife stepped closer. "A word, Your Majesty?"

Loki made an imperious "get on with it" movement with his hand, but the midwife waited until she had his full attention. "Your banishment of Prince Thor kept the palace buzzing with speculation these last four days. While the queen was not directly implicated, there are rumors of course."

Fixing her with a glare, Loki snarled, "I have a kingdom to rule, healer. Are you holding me here to discuss gossip?"

But the Ljósálfar glared right back. "I know you care for your infants, but their health will soon be impacted if their mother is not given the attention and kindness she needs." Waiting as he gave her another sneer, the elf continued on. "She must be guided through her heats. The lack of congress between the two of you is obvious. She clearly isn't sleeping, and her weight has dropped."

Now Loki leaned in with concern. "Has this affected the twins?"

"No," she said sourly, "as of now they are simply utilizing the queen's body to get their nutrition. But this will continue to drain her strength until she has nothing left to give. Whatever the discord between you, if you do not resume the role of a caring husband, I cannot guarantee a healthy pregnancy."

Ingrid was pacing their huge terrace that night, looking to the sky and awaiting the rise of the moon. Other than plodding back and forth with one hand always resting on the slight swell on her stomach, she couldn't seem to focus on anything. Surges of her Dark Elf heritage would surface to hiss words of hate and revenge on Loki, the Light Elf side seeming to have nothing to offer but tears. Finally seeing her lunar opportunity, Ingrid tiredly sat down, eager to find some small relief in sharing the moment with her babies.

Loki watched the moment, despite his rage and the pain he would never admit to, he loved watching his wife's gentle hand over their children inside her, how the glow of the moon lit her face with ethereal beauty. When the moment was finished, he strolled forward from their bedroom. "Always a lovely sight, darling, watching you take the moon." Ingrid bolted upright, trying to gauge his intent from his expressionless face.

"My King-" she tried, "I am so very sorry that

my actions disappointed you so-"

Looming over her in the dark, his beautiful face cast in shadow, the queen could only see his eyes- a fathomless forest green tonight and gleaming coldly. His gaze went to their bed and Loki nodded to it. "Get on the bed."

Doing as he ordered, Ingrid scooted back until she was resting against the cushions, one held in front of her like a shield. Walking around the bed to see her more closely, Loki's lips twisted to see her pitiful, feather-filled defense. "Close your eyes, darling." Letting out a shaky sigh, she did, putting her head against the pillows. The elf stiffened as the mattress dipped, one knee then the other as he crawled toward her. Cool lips suddenly pressed against her eyes, each cheek-bone and trailing down her neck, then trailing across her collarbones. "Poor, lovely girl," Loki purred, "these last few days must have been tor-ture. Tell me, darling. Did you pleasure your-self?"

"You know very well I cannot," Ingrid man-aged, trying not to moan in a too needy fashion when those chilly fingers loosened her stays, let-ting her breasts spill out.

"Ah. That's correct," Loki chuckled without the slightest shred of sympathy, enjoying how his wife shuddered as the vibrations went down her spine to her eagerly wet center. "I did tell you that your pleasure was reserved for me, your King." Gently squeezing each breast before fastening a refreshingly chilly mouth on her heated nipple, he praised her, "These lovely breasts, so full and sensitive. I can imagine them filled with milk." Ingrid moaned and tried to slide her fingers into his ebony locks, but he stopped her. "Put your arms over your head and do not move them." Obeying his suddenly icy voice, the elf felt a flush of shame when he chuckled. "So eager. Perhaps I should put a gag and blindfold on you, too?"

Shaking her head and sending silvery-blonde curls flying everywhere, Ingrid pleaded, "Please, Loki! I'll be good-"

"You will not address me so!" he interrupted her, "You may address me as Majesty." Choking back her sobs, Ingrid nodded, not trusting her voice to speak. Deft hands stripped her of her heavy ceremonial gown and threw it aside. She could felt the cool skin of her husband lean closer to her heated center, and gulped, hips angling up sharply as her tender lips and clitoris were suddenly attacked by his lips and tongue.

It was mere moments before she gasped, "Please, may I come?"

"You may."

Groaning with relief and pleasure, Ingrid had to bite back a shriek as two icy fingers slid into her burning channel, forcing her to beg for release again, and again shortly after when he refused to leave off. As her hands mindlessly came down to run her fingers over his shoulders, those strong arms, Loki made an irritated noise. Flicking an elegant hand, gold chains shot out from the two head posts to wind around the elf's wrists, holding her immobile. She felt his rough hands take her hips and pull her down, pulling her arms taut in their bindings as he looped her legs over his elbows. Feeling his shaft begin it's sinuous slide into her channel, Ingrid gasped, then moaned. "Thank you, Lo- ah, Majesty!" Without speaking, he began to move slowly in and out, a twist of his hips that made the push and pull of his more than generous cock reach places inside her that the girl never knew existed. It took only moments more for her to beg him again for her release, and then again. Ingrid felt him rise to his knees, yanking her higher and wrapping her long legs around his waist as he began pushing harder- snapping his hips against the soft swell of her spread thighs.

Looking down at the beautiful, treacherous creature he'd married, Loki began slamming into her, one hand pinching her nipples while the other flicked her clitoris back and forth. Grinning at the sudden arch in her back, he slowed down again. "What do you need, darling?" the Trickster purred.

"Please," moaned Ingrid, "please may I come again?"

His hips had paused, the broad head of his cock just inside her desperately clenching cunt as he looked down into her sweetly flushed face, her eyes still obediently closed as the thick fan of her lashes shadowed her cheekbones. *'Still so beautiful,'* he thought resentfully, *'the lying bitch.'* Aloud, he said tauntingly, "You may. As many as you can manage darling. You may begin." With a brutal snap of his hips, Loki was back up inside her, slamming back and forth and enjoying her moans, then her shrieks and finally a scream that finished her. The sudden, violent clamping down on his cock forced the Trickster to his finish too, as powerful an orgasm as he could remember.

When her shaking finally stilled, Loki pulled from her, enjoying the sight of his seed spilling from her. "Open your eyes, darling."

The moment Ingrid looked up at the tall man over her, blocking the light from the moon, she gasped and stiffened.

"What is the matter, my ungrateful wife? Surely that was enough for the moment, even for a cunt as greedy as yours." The words were spoken from a chair to her right, and Ingrid's head snapped over to see Loki, pants still open as he stroked his cock, his fist covered with his come.

"Please- please make your shadow go away," Ingrid whispered, watching the clone leer down at her.

Loki's dark brow arched mockingly. "But why? Since the seed of the rightful King of Asgard is no longer necessary to get a child on you, my double will do just as well to satisfy your heat." Wiping his hand on her dress, the king stood and fastened his leathers again. "You will obey him as you do me. Of course, given the events of this week, I would expect you to do much better in your obedience."

As he walked for the door, he could hear his double begin to suckle his wife's breasts and the sound of her weeping. Ignoring the feeling that a knife was tearing through his stomach, Loki straightened his armor and left the room.

Ingrid lay on her side, knees drawn tight to her chest and trying to make herself as small as possible. As the shadow of her husband began toying with her again, she knew she couldn't control her desperate heat from rising to meet him. So, she did the next best thing to being free of him: curling into her mind and going far, far away from where her desperate orgasms and his silky, filthy praise could no longer touch her. As her faux Loki performed her aftercare, he dropped a kiss on her forehead, ignoring her shudder and walked whistling from the room.

Putting both hands over the swell on her belly, Ingrid soothed her tiny souls, singing a song to them she'd heard the maids hum as they cleaned the royal chambers. "It will be all right," she whispered. "It will, I promise." Loki, still in his chair but invisible, gritted his teeth as he heard her whisper. He sat still for most of the night, watching his exhausted wife sleep with bitterness and grief.

Chapter 28

In which Ingrid has had enough.

Ingrid woke the next morning consumed with an almost blistering rage. It was like nothing she'd ever felt before, and it seeped through her bones like an oily black sludge. She was silent as her maids dressed her, suddenly bitter that they so eagerly followed Loki's orders. Why should she bother to attempt a smile or engage them in conversation? They were his creatures. They were nothing to her. Ingrid ignored their nervous glances and tentative smiles, as she mechanically ate breakfast before leaving their chambers. When her Royal detail moved to stop her, she held up one hand, a resounding "crunch!" made the guards whirl to see a huge fracture in the stone wall opposite them. "I am taking a walk," she said coldly. "You may follow me at a distance or I can bury you under a ton of rock. It is your decision." Staring at their faces, the elf suddenly smiled. She'd seen frustration there before- exasperation, perhaps from having to look after the wayward queen. But, never fear. It was so pleasant to see it in their eyes now.

Walking through the courtyard near the Royal stables, Ingrid felt a sudden stab of grief, knowing that her only friends were no longer there. Had Loki really placed them in the lowest chambers of the dungeon? The guards would shudder when they spoke of it, calling it "The bowels of Hel." The sorrow nearly derailed her, making her knees weak as she paused for a moment. Feeling the men cluster behind her, Ingrid angrily waved them off. "Follow me if you must, but at five paces. You irritate me. You will find that it is not a wise thing to do." Smiling to herself as they hastily dropped back, she made for the gardens, humming happily. Ingrid walked quickly, enjoying the stretch and pull of slack muscles. Loki forbade horseback riding shortly after she became pregnant, and she realized how much she needed the exercise. Her hands were raised to cradle a wayward hummingbird when she heard the king behind her, telling her security detail to fall back.

"Petttttt..." In his rage, Loki drew out the despised name as he struggled for control. "How dare you disobey me, you little bitch! Do you think carrying my children protects you from punishment?"

Ingrid was still looking down at the tiny feathered body held in her hands. She knew perfectly well the captain of her security team would send for Loki immediately, even if he did not dare to challenge her himself. "We are the same, you and I," she barely whispered. "Buffeted on the winds of another's ambition."

"I. Asked. You. A. Question," Loki hissed between gritted teeth. Was this insane broodmare intent on making her impending discipline harsher? He could certainly accommodate her.

Raising her hands to release the tiny red and purple bird to the skies, Ingrid turned just in time to see a vicious thrust from Loki's hand, sending the little bundle of feathers smashing into a tree, falling bonelessly to the ground. "You monster!" she hissed, "You sick, cruel-" Ingrid was cut off abruptly with a furious gesture from Loki's elegant hand.

"It is now your time to listen," he hissed, drawing so close that she could feel the cool puffs of air from his furious breathing. "You dare threaten the Royal Guard?" The elf's eyes narrowed, glaring at him as her mouth moved soundlessly. "You think yourself clever enough to sidestep my commands? You *will* obey the Captain of the Guard. You will *not* threaten them again. You *will* do as you are told. Have I made myself clear, my faithless darling?" The last taunt set Ingrid on fire with rage, lips trying to force the words he'd stifled in her throat.

Breathing heavily, Loki tried to remind himself why he despised the girl before him. A liar and treacherous, just like everyone else, and- *'Ah,'* corrected the sane portion of his brain, *'but she did not lie to you. She cannot. She must believe what she told you.'* Trying to gather his thoughts, the king glanced at a terrified Hannah, Elsa and Gundrun literally hiding behind her skirts. "And you-" he hissed like a viper, "you will never let your queen walk free again on pain of death." Turning on one booted heel and walking away before he lost all control, Loki shouted over his shoulder, "Return the queen to our rooms. Immediately."

Loki as King of Asgard - and by default all the Nine Realms - knew his duties as Monarch. So he strode towards their shared chambers that night to provide "assistance" for his wife's heat. The fact that his strides could almost be characterized as "hasty" was not something he was willing to examine.

Ingrid heard the huge doors open, but she ignored them. Seated inside her dressing room, she was nearly buried in the rows of exquisite gowns in hues of forest green, peridot, emerald, and a dozen other shades of the king's colors. The soaring ceilings were softened by hanging silks, the tall windows open to the evening breeze. The queen's focus was on the bedraggled bundle of purple and red feathers cupped in her hands. "Rest now, little one," she whispered, "I must do battle with a demon." Hiding the tiny body in a box lined with soft wool, Ingrid rose and walked into the king's bedroom.

"What do you require, Majesty?" Loki turned to see his wife, clad in a sheer silk white robe, sleeves falling down to her fingertips and trailing behind her, long legs peeking out as she walked to him.

"It is what you require," he answered indifferently.

"Ah, yes." Ingrid drawled, untying her robe and letting it drop from her shoulders. "Thank you for your part in caring for our children's well-being. Where is your double?"

Loki's eye narrowed. "Do you think your behavior will not be corrected, darling?"

He didn't recognize the eyes that rose to meet his. Instead of the mesmerizing lavender that soothed him, they were a cold purple-gray. "Not as long as you care for the welfare of your future heirs," she hissed. "Please give me your shade and you are free to pursue your... kingly duties." Loki's glittering emerald gaze traveled down his wife's exquisite, nude body. Instead of the shy, blushing smile she always held for her husband, Ingrid merely looked weary, eager to receive her sustenance and to get it over with. Suddenly furious, he pushed sharply with one rigid hand and threw her on the bed. She didn't struggle, merely eyeing him with indifference. Loki ran a hand down his armor to remove it as his pale fingers traced over his body. Crawling on to their huge bed after her, they eyed each other like gladiators, eager to draw first blood and gauging the other's weaknesses. As he crawled up the bed after her, Ingrid couldn't control a shudder- he looked like the wolf she knew he could transform into. Dark, menacing, his eyes glowing with single-minded purpose. Grabbing one ankle, he yanked her sharply down the bed and under him.

"Such defiance," Loki snarled, "my fierce little wife is growing claws? What shall I do with you?"

Ingrid knew her retort was unwise, but at the moment, she simply hated the arrogant god above her, his vision of her as a possession or a toy to pull out to play with. "Whatever you will in bed- just leave me alone afterward!"

His grin stretched until the elf could see every one of his sharp, white teeth. "Then I will have whatever I want, darling." Leaning down, he pushed a hard kiss on her pillowy lips, enjoying the softness and the give as his tongue slipped into her mouth, tracing her teeth and sucking on her tongue. Closing her eyes, Ingrid could almost imagine this was the man who'd taken her virginity with soft words and tender touches meant to awaken her body. But the desperate surge of her heat and the cold voice of her Unseelie self forced her to harden her heart. Pushing up with her hips, the queen invited Loki to direct his notice downward, and he did. Slowly.

Ingrid watched as his silky black hair dragged lightly over her breasts, biting and nibbling, over her quickly increasing abdomen, and down to her center, where his strong hands roughly yanked her thighs apart. She was trying to be silent, biting her lip desperately and hands gripping the fine linen sheets. She would not beg. Not to him. As it turned out, it wasn't necessary. Loki was driven half-mad the night before after the second-hand responses from his shadow. It simply made him more desperate to conquer his stubborn wife with his own hands on her- no magic.

Running the tip of his nose down her sensitive clit and gently nudging it free from its little hood, he grinned in his devilish way as her hips canted up. "Ah, there you are, darling," he gloated, "and so utterly pink and delicious. Be still, now. Don't force me to restrain you."

Remembering the golden snakes wrapping around her wrists from the night before, Ingrid tried to keep her hands still. His cold tongue was Valhalla on her painfully heated center, and she gasped as he tugged her swollen lips between his teeth as one long finger slid inside her passage.

His glittering gaze turned up to see Ingrid's hands fly into her own hair, gripping it tightly as she tried to keep herself still as commanded. "So sweet," he soothed, "so very obedient..."

His Queen groaned as she tried to hold her composure, fighting back the urge to grip his head between her knees and mindlessly grind down to find that finish beckoning to her with every stroke of Loki's tongue. Finally, she could take no more and threw her head back. "May I come, Majesty?"

It felt odd and unwelcome to have his wife actually follow his orders and address him by the stilted formality, but Loki grunted and managed to say, "You may..." before diving back in. The god had always had a peculiar satisfaction in bringing a lover to one finish after another with his lips and tongue, but tonight after his wife found her first release, he surged up immediately to bury himself inside her. First, he slid inside her roughly, bouncing her up and down, and then transitioning to slow, long strokes that kept her on the edge without letting Ingrid fall over. "Be still," he crooned with a grin, "you do not have permission, darling. You must wait." It was only when his wife actually sounded like she was in pain, that Loki began pounding fiercely into her clutching wetness, enjoying the *"slap slap slap!"* sound of their combined arousal on her thighs as his hips slammed against them. Leaning close, he gloated, "Now, sweetness. You may come now. Let me feel you flood my cock. By the Nornir, you're so deliciously juicy..." Gently pulling her clitoris between two calloused fingers, he looked down to see the rapturous pleasure illuminate Ingrid's beautiful face as she wailed her release. Loki slowed for a moment, then began again after she caught her breath, beginning a gentle tap- tap- tapping on her clit to match the rhythm as his shaft plunged inside her. It was only a moment before she toppled over the edge again, and the process would begin anew. Loki forced himself with every ounce of centuries of self-control to not allow himself to finish before his sweating and exhausted wife had passed out from her fifth orgasm. Holding still inside her after flooding his Queen with come, he watched and waited for her to stir back into consciousness again. "There's my good girl," he said, stroking her cheek. After performing her aftercare and wrapping her securely in a fine wool blanket, Loki stroked her waist-length hair with some amusement. Imagine the cheek of enlisting the feared Goddess and Guardian of the Golden Apples to aid in her vendetta about her hair!

"Loki," she murmured, half asleep and not realizing she was not using his formal title, "Loki..."

"What, darling? What is it?" Still barely moving into consciousness, her small hand pulled his to her stomach, circling for a moment before the king felt a light, but determined tap against his palm. His jaw dropped, and Loki managed to gasp, "Is that - are not those - is it the babies?" A sleepy smile illuminated her face as if she was taking the sun, and Ingrid nodded.

"Our babies, my King."

"So delicate," he marveled, "like a butterfly's wing."

Ingrid giggled, still too sleepy to be self-conscious, "But quite persistent. Like their father."

For an ashamed moment, the sire of the tiny souls within his wife wondered if this was a sign of approval from his progeny. Were they pleased that their parents achieved some kind of a truce between them at last? Continuing to gently rub her belly until Ingrid fell back to sleep, Loki stared into the darkness, pride and fear warring within him against hope and a fierce kind of protectiveness for the three pure souls beside him in bed.

The Dark Queen was brooding, high above her cavernous hall as her two agents planted in Asgard came to kneel before her. "Your Majesty," one uttered respectfully. "Our spy within the palace now knows how to capture the Princess."

The fearsome ruler of the Unseelie Court looked a thousand years older, lines of stress and rage cruelly defining her rigid face. Leaning forward, she fixed those terrifying onyx eyes on her men. "Tell me."

Chapter 29

In which the Black Queen proves more cunning than anyone could imagine. And in which Loki might actually come to rely upon his wife. Maybe.

The smoke woke Loki first, his sensitive nose wrinkling in distaste at the oily, tarry stench filling the huge bedroom. Rising quickly, he strode to the terrace to see the sky over Asgard on fire. "Ingrid!" he called sharply, not taking his eyes from the horizon. "Get up and dressed immediately, have your guard bring you to my council room." His wife was already up and by his side, before he finished, and the elf gasped in horror as she watched the guards in the courtyard gagging and choking from the stench. Absently smoothing a big hand over the back of her hair, Loki linked to Heimdall, nodding as they communicated silently. "Hurry, wife. I need your counsel."

The king didn't miss the leap of joy in Ingrid's eyes, nor her smile. Giving her a hard kiss, Loki left the room, barking directions to the hastily assembled crew hovering outside his doors. She turned again to stare at the sky. "Mother," she whispered, "what have you done?"

It took longer than necessary to dress because Gundrun's hands were shaking as she tried to lace up the dress of her mistress. Ingrid bit back the instinct to snap at the little maid and took Gundrun's hands in hers. "My dear," she said kindly, "you must listen. No matter the sorcery that brought this fire, the king's power is far greater. Look at me - no, dear - look. I promise you, Asgard is protected." Chin trembling, the girl nodded and tried to hurry in her work. Looking around, Ingrid frowned, "Where is Hannah?"

As if on cue, the older woman came bustling through the door, laying out breakfast from a tray as quickly as possible. "Majesty, here's the sugar-water you asked for?" Hannah raised the little cup questioningly.

"Thank you, Hannah- don't bother with breakfast, please tell the cook to bring a large meal to the king's council room. If you ladies haven't dined yet, why don't you finish this food?" Taking the cup from the tray, Ingrid hastily made for the dressing room, bringing down the little box. She couldn't tell if the tiny bird was any better, but it did seem willing to take some of the mixture into its beak, so she sighed with relief. "Forgive me, little one," she murmured, smoothing the ruffled feathers. "I will be back to feed you later."

The war council was pandemonium. Arguments and questions flew back and forth as Loki sat still and thoughtful within the fray. Finally, irritated by the squawking, he snarled, "SILENCE!" Standing and beginning to pace, he glared at each of them in turn. "None of my most experienced agents have anything to offer? My generals have no way to explain how half of Alfheim, Asgard, and Vanaheim are ablaze? These billowing clouds of pitch?"

"I believe I can, my King." Ingrid didn't plan the dramatic entrance, and she was pink-cheeked and a little out of breath. Smoothing her gown and grasping for a more dignified entrance, the elf allowed Loki to seat her next to him- an honor that did not go unnoticed by those who had witnessed her fall from grace after Thor's return. Spreading her hands on the table, she tried to recall the exact battle in the past that her mother had won by this sorcery. "This is Den Evige Ild- the eternal fire. The Black Queen used this tactic during the Battle of Irrilund- against Svartalfheim? She attempted to annex the entire country under her own rule-"

"I remember!" interrupted one of the generals. "My father fought in that war! She-"

"Do you dare speak over the queen?" Loki's voice was low and cold, but it stopped the man in his tracks.

Turning instantly to Ingrid, the general bowed. "Forgive me, Majesty, I was encouraged and did not think."

She graciously shook her head. "I am grateful to see you encouraged, General Dartaan, we must all feel this way. The power of the fire only grows stronger as fear and hopelessness take over. We must all feel hope." Aware of her husband's smile, Ingrid confidently went on to explain the nature of the deadly seidr behind the blaze and how it could be contained. "But how was it set?" Ingrid asked, looking around the table, "There would have to be enemy troops inside the realm to carry in the Black Queen's curse."

"Which means our borders have weaknesses we were not aware of," mused Loki, "and why were the Dwarves not affected?"

"It could be that the Unseelie Court has finally reached an alliance with Svartalfheim," Ingrid frowned, "but the Black Queen could never accomplish it during my lifetime. Could it be meant to make us believe they had?"

Her eyes followed Loki's long finger as he ran it over his mouth. Unbidden, memories of what that finger had done to her clitoris the night before shocked and aroused her. Moaning inwardly at the eager rise of her heat, Ingrid tried to force herself to concentrate. "Contact our sources in Svartalfheim," Loki ordered, "let us see if the Realm is loyal to the Crown or not." Ingrid bit back a smile, the Dwarves had their own monarchy- trust her arrogant husband to already assume they were under his rule. "Send a request to the White Court to bring all their sorcerers who can perform Earth Magic here." Loki's smile would be considered gleeful if he weren't the most feared ruler in the Nine Realms. "And contact the Jötunn- I have need of them."

Everyone knew better than to question King Loki. He would tell them why when it pleased him or not at all. Rising quickly, the military heads went about their respective tasks, leaving the King and Queen of Asgard alone in the room.

"I can smell you," Loki said abruptly, "the scent of your arousal is so tantalizing that I was forced to clear the room before you reduced all my generals to drooling adolescents."

Ingrid's hands flew up to her painfully red cheeks. "Surely no one knew," she mumbled, "I- it could not have been noticeable!"

Loki laughed, but it was not unkind. "Darling, General Dartaan was seated at the end of the table and the man was already hard- did you not see him sweat?" One of his long arms reached over and dragged his embarrassed wife to him, seating her on the table before him. Placing her feet on the arms of his chair, he warned, "Do not move these little feet, or your spanking will not be one you enjoy, darling." Spreading her knees, Loki's eyes raised to her with the most lascivious grin. "Such a feast, sweetling! Such a shame I have only time-" his cool tongue ran a long, luxurious stripe from her clit to her channel, pausing to push his tongue inside as Ingrid's head dropped with a thud to the table. "-for just a bite." The king did so, earning a squeal from his wife before he dove in again, all chilly lips and tongue and teeth.

An hour later, Loki's lean hips were pounding forwards completion inside Ingrid's wildly spasming pussy. The table beneath her was wet, and he was looking forward to adding to the puddle when there was a timid knock on the door. "Y- your Majesty?" It was his ambassador to Alfheim, and the unlucky one shoved forward to disturb the king.

"WHAT!" Loki roared, pumping even faster, the force of his thrusts pushing a whimpering Ingrid up the table before he grabbed her thighs and yanked her down again. "YOU DARE DIS-TURB OUR-" he made the mistake of looking down and groaned at the sight of his glistening cock spearing into his wife, her pussy stretched tight around him. "-Our- Our STRATEGY MEET-ING?" The group outside looked at each other uncomfortably, knowing precisely what sort of strategy was being implemented.

"Forgive me. My King," the unlucky ambas-sador called through the thick door, "but the delegation from the Seelie Court has arrived."

There was a thud and a muffled moan from the room before Loki barked out, "Why didn't you tell us that immediately, you idiot? Escort them here with all due haste!" With a wave of his hand, the table was pristine again and Loki was pushing Ingrid's skirts back down. Steady-ing his weaving wife by taking her arm, he kissed her just under her ear. "Can you continue, little one?"

With an effort, Ingrid managed to focus on his smirking face. "Yes, of course... but you might have to help me sit down again."

Loki gave her a knowing grin, which made his wife yearn to slap him. He seated her next to him, pressing his fingers briefly against her sore center, healing her enough to be able to stay seated without writhing in overstimulated discomfort. "There, darling," he soothed, "all better now." Ingrid forced a polite smile as the delegates from the White Court entered the room. Damn her husband! How dare he look so calm and collected after what he'd just done to her! Even her pregnancy-induced heat was off, taking a nap somewhere.

The open door suddenly issued in the stink of the foulness of the air outside. Loki had sealed the room that morning, keeping the smoke from hindering their meeting. But the taint was an instant reminder of what the three Realms were enduring at this moment. Ingrid felt a stab of shame that they'd been pleasuring themselves while others were suffering. The delegates from Jötunnheim were close behind, and the Earth Sorcerers from Alfheim began complicated seidrs to combat the filth in the air- others sent to confront the fires at the source. With the queen's warning, everyone focused on blocking the fear of the flames tearing through the fragile land.

A gentle reminder from Loki sent Ingrid to their chambers to rest, grateful but embarrassed at her weakness. Despite satiating her greedy heat, her husband could do nothing about the clouds blocking the sun she needed to restore herself and care for the children inside her, the elf hoped some rest would help her. The mages had already set up a shield to block the worst of the smoke from the city- though nothing could be done about the oily pitch that darkened the sky. Lanterns were lit throughout the palace, but the shadows lingered in every corner. Any sleep the queen managed was restless: endless scraps of dreams where her mother would laugh and mock her. Sitting up abruptly, Ingrid shakily rubbed her forehead. She couldn't sleep, so she needed to be useful. Sending for the palace steward, she discussed sending face masks out into the city to protect those most at risk. His wide, honest face beamed in relief, grateful to able to do something- anything to help.

Dinner that night was a strained affair. Even with the addition of the Jötunn contingent, Ingrid found it difficult to encourage conversation between the visiting dignitaries. Everyone was focused on what might be happening to their homes at this moment. After a low discussion with the now-familiar regent from Jötunnheim, the elf was excited to learn the visiting Frost Giants could bring storms from their realm to the others- howling winds and ice that could tear away the soot and murk from the suffering. Looking at her husband, deep in conversation with King Leafstred, Ingrid couldn't conceal her smile. Her husband. Her King. Such a brilliant, clever god. He caught her fond stare from the corner of his eye and turned to her. "And why is my bride smiling in such a tender fashion?" Loki whispered into her ear, "Certainly, there was nothing tender about what we did this afternoon." Enjoying the helpless flush that stained those smooth cheeks, he leaned in to kiss one, feeling the heat of it against his cool mouth.

"I admire you, my King, your cleverness- how you know how to help your people. That you do not retreat in the face of disaster. It is... it is new to me."

Loki studied her wide eyes, the sincerity there unsettling. He was used to praise, certainly. Ridiculously extravagant praise- far more lavish than what the elf could offer. But the Trickster knew her shy admission was the truth, and his surge of affection for her- even after betraying him with that idiot Thor- made his gut twist, his mind uncertain how to respond. Before he could decide, a grim-faced General Dartaan came to the table, waiting for Loki's impatient gesture to approach.

"Your Majesty. We are at war. The Demon army has breached all three borders at once."

Ingrid's chest felt compressed as if the weight of a thousand wailing souls fell upon it. It was her Mother. She intended to kill every last one of them.

Chapter 30

In which Loki teaches Ingrid how to be "self-sufficient."

Ingrid stood on their terrace, searching for the moon in the soot-filled sky. She knew it would be obscured, but the increasing hunger from her babies and her own was making her dizzy. The vicious queen that Loki referred to only as "that Black Court bitch" was thorough-not only incinerating the realm but rendering her daughter helpless to do anything about it. Frustrated, she turned to go inside, checking on her tiny patient. Gently holding the bird and humming to it, Ingrid tried to dribble more sugar water down its beak, but the creature simply spat it back out in a heave. "Little one," she sighed, "you must try. You cannot survive if you do not take nourishment." Trying to ignore the parallels to her own situation, Ingrid settled the bundle of feathers back into its box and left.

The war council waged well into the early morning hours when Loki abruptly ordered his wife to go rest. He was still struck with that curious mix of pride and possessiveness when Ingrid spoke intelligently about what that miserable cunt of a mother would do. A small smile played around his mouth to watch the Ljósálfar King watching Ingrid hungrily- knowing the Elf was desperate to know more about Ingrid. The Jötunn contingent was already out into the country sides that were ablaze, sending howling sweeps of ice and snow through the fires and rendering them into sullen ash. But there were so many infernos in so many sections of the three realms, and it seemed as fast as one was quenched, another sprang up. Troops from every realm but Midgard were massing to strike against the Black Court and the Muspelheim demons. But the king dreaded the next thing he had to do- nearly as much as he anticipated it. "Why are you still awake?" he frowned, watching Ingrid pace the floor. "You need the rest darling, as do our children."

Ingrid bit back a cross retort. As if she didn't know this? As if the lack of the sun and the moon was not affecting their twins already? And- and what would she do when Loki left for battle? How would she survive the heat without him?

What would they all do without him? Unbidden, tears filled her eyes and the elf turned her face away, humiliated to show weakness when there could not be a more important time to be strong.

"Little one…" Loki's exquisite voice purred into her ear, enjoying the responding shiver, "where are these tears coming from? You were magnificent in council today."

Forcing a smile, Ingrid turned to look up at him, "I'm with child, my husband. According to the Ljósálfar midwives, tears and babies are both to be expected."

The king knew there was more, but he appreciated her courage in trying to be strong for him. "There will be sunlight this morning," he soothed, "the Earth Magic is bound to clear the skies very soon." He ran a roughened hand up Ingrid's cheek. "But as for now, you and I have other concerns." Drawing her toward their bed, Loki grinned wickedly.

"Concerns?" Ingrid smiled, "In the middle of preparation for war?"

"Oh, yes," he assured her, lifting his wife by the waist and setting her on the tall mattress. "You must be clear-minded to complete the daily responsibilities of the Crown in my absence." Unlacing the top of her gown, Loki paused a moment to admire the new fullness of her breasts- always bountiful, they could now be characterized as decadently voluptuous. Placing one in each broad palm, his train of thought derailed briefly to toy with them, idly squeezing each breast, admiring how her pink nipples turned rosy under a few flicks of his thumb.

Pausing to slide his tongue around one bud and then the other, Loki leaned back to admire the results of his chilly caress, teasingly squeezing each taut nipple. "Where was I? Ah, yes, darling. Clear-minded. This delightful- but exasperating- heat of yours has been a most pleasant task for me as an expectant father, but for a queen?"

Ingrid was trying to pay attention to his words, couched as always in that silky tone he adopted when he stripped her bare. But those big hands squeezing her sensitive breasts and the electrical sparks that shot to her pelvis when his cool tongue landed on her nipples instantly took precedence over rational thought. "Clear... ah... clear-minded. Yes..."

Loki's hard chest against hers rumbled in the most enticing way as he laughed. "Poor darling," he soothed, "I'm going to teach you how to give yourself pleasure. You must take care of your heat alone when I'm away." Seeing the anxiety shoot into her upturned face, he squeezed her tender skin again. "Ah- ah!" he said sternly, "You can do this- in fact, I suspect you'll master the skill with great enthusiasm." Loki's knowing grin made Ingrid flush and cover his hands with hers, trying to pry them off her breasts. He simply up-ended the girl and sent her sprawling farther back on the bed. Ingrid raised her head to see her husband already naked and crawling up the bed to her like a wolf- head lowered, only those glittering green eyes watching her.

"But- " Ingrid pushed his wandering hands away from her breasts again, "You know I cannot! Your seidr..." His wide hand landed on her center, and she yelped in spite of herself. The same cooling green mist as before spread over her lower and half and sank into her skin. The elf felt like taking a deep breath was suddenly easier- as if a weight was gone from her chest.

"Put your hands on these beautiful breasts," was all Loki said, but it came out closer to a growl, and Ingrid did as she was told. Those same electric sparks began sizzling up and down her spine as the girl obediently tugged and pulled at her nipples as he directed her. Waving his hand to remove her gown, Loki settled her against the pillows at the headboard and drew her knees up. Spreading them, he groaned, "Look at yourself." Ingrid's gaze widened to see a large mirror suddenly propped against the footboard of the bed, lending her an uncomfortably intimate view of that part of her that was always private, hidden away.

The king wanted to grin at her violent blush, but he merely brought her chin back up. "Darling..." he paused for a moment; head tilted curiously. "I've done you a terrible disservice! You've never gazed inside this perfect little quim, have you?" Ingrid flushed again at his deliberately crude words, but Loki held her knees open as she tried to close them. "Look at yourself, my filthy, divine angel- so pink, those juicy lips already swollen- like petals on a flower. Now, put a finger on your little button." He reached out to take her hand, placing a finger on her clitoris. "Now, tap it gently..." Loki smiled darkly at his wife's startled gasp. "Such an apt pupil!" he teased gently. "Keep tapping and stroking yourself, and bring your other hand down here, like so-" he urged, sliding her slim fingers along her slippery lips. "Good girl," he purred, loving how she would always shiver happily when he praised her. "Dip your fingers inside, sweetness. Bring out some of that slick to play with, bring it up to your delicate button..."

Ingrid felt as if she was in the center of one of those raging wildfires, incinerating her own nerve endings with the scorching blood racing through her. Even the embarrassment of having to watch herself added to the heat, Loki's simmering eyes storing away every movement. "Oh,

Lokiiii..." she drew the words out slowly, "it's so..."

"Just so, my dirty little darling," he approved. "Take one of your fingers and put it inside you." Another gasp came from Ingrid. "Now, add another." Loki watched as his wife's hips began to move and swirl, as they did when he was thrusting inside her. "Move them as if they were my cock fucking up into you." Watching her fingers slide faster, the king hummed his approval. Ingrid loved his filthy talk almost as much as it embarrassed her. "You're so close now, aren't you, my pretty quim? Faster now..."

Loki's voice was suddenly strained as if the words were slipping through gritted teeth. Ingrid opened her eyes to see him across the bed from her, eyes intent on her wet center and stroking his painfully hard erection, long legs lewdly spread. The sight was so outrageously, unexpectedly erotic that she gasped, "Please! Please, Loki may I come?"

He answered with a laugh mixed with a groan. "You may, my delicious little whore." The filthy words sent Ingrid into a blazing orgasm, letting out a shriek as Loki's thick cock was suddenly inside her, surging upwards against her convulsing walls. "Now, again," he managed as he pinched her overstimulated clitoris. He growled as the divine press of her second orgasm forced him into his own finish. "My good girl," Loki managed, panting against Ingrid's shaking form. "My sweet, good girl." The two fell asleep nearly instantly, his cock still inside her.

It took every shred of Ingrid's courage to stiffen her spine and bid farewell to her husband's platoon that afternoon. Dressed proudly in a dress similar in style and color to Loki's armor, she stood with him as the horses passed by them, nodding as the men saluted sharply. When it was time for the king to join them, she pressed her full lips together, forcing back a sob. "Come now, darling," he whispered, "send me off with a smile." They'd already bid farewell in a more intimate fashion earlier, but Ingrid's chin raised and she smiled radiantly, trying to express her love and faith in him. With a brush of his cool lips, he was gone. Over the Bifrost and away.

Taking a deep breath and turning back, the queen returned with her entourage to the palace. Refugees from outlying towns were flooding into Asgard, and she was consumed with thoughts on where to place everyone. As she entered the massive dining hall, Ingrid's steps slowed to see the sheer volume of women and children. Most were high-born and insisted on their place in the palace as their due, but Ingrid opened the doors to everyone she couldn't fit in the city's inns. She was proud to see that many families in the city had opened their homes to those displaced by the Black Queen's malice. Ingrid began directing servants back and forth, issuing rooms and space by family and need. When a group of well-dressed women stepped forward, she sighed and braced for their protests.

"My husband is mayor of our village; I will not be placed next to a peasant family-"

"It is my due as the wife of a general in the King's army to be placed in a larger suite than-"

"My, my." Ingrid's eyes narrowed, hearing that poisonously sweet tone again. "We are so very happy to be here in the palace again..." after an insultingly long pause, the woman added, "Your Majesty." It was the witch Runa, malice glittering in those narrow eyes.

Chapter 31

*In which Ingrid takes charge...
and she's surprisingly good at it.
In more ways than one.*

Ingrid felt as if her spine was on fire. Gone was her grief over Loki's departure, her anxiety over handling so many lives- all sent into ash by the fury blazing through her with that- that BITCH- that WITCH'S appearance. One light brow rose as she fixed her lavender glare on the smirking Runa. "I'm astonished to see you here, Runa," Ingrid spoke clearly, not concerned about being overheard, nor using the witch's title. "Your ridiculous antics and your unpleasant behavior will not be tolerated here... as I believe I demonstrated last time?"

Runa's face paled, she'd never once thought the mouse would scold her publicly- even after the extremely uncomfortable day the witch had spent dangling upside down from her own whip.

Angrily calling on a spell to make herself seem larger and more frightening, she answered back. "But Majesty, I felt certain you would need my help- since I ran the castle for King Loki for many years. I only wished to offer my services to assist with your inexperience."

The witch's new threatening demeanor made several of the high-born ladies around them draw back nervously. No one in the group of women expected a confrontation in the middle of their grievances. Queen Ingrid's face suddenly seemed darker too, sharper. "We will not turn away any who fled from the affected towns," she was cold, but her words were firm. "But you are here under my indulgence, and at the slightest hint of mischief, I will be delighted to have you escorted outside the city walls." Turning as an anxious murmur ran through the crowd around her, Ingrid fixed a hard stare at them all. "We will shelter you all. But everyone must aid in saving the lives of as many as we can. This means you will not have the luxurious surroundings you may be accustomed to. We will keep you safe- but I will not hear complaints about your station or what you feel is your due. If you cannot agree to this, you are welcome to leave." The nervous buzz turned shrill, feet shuffling, women whispering complaints until Ingrid's suddenly amplified voice shot through the room like a lightning strike. "Do you all understand?"

With the subdued chorus of "Yes, Your Majesty," and "Of course, my Queen," Ingrid gave a final cold look to Runa and walked away with the palace steward, deep in discussion.

To say the queen felt utterly unprepared for this role was an understatement. A life spent in a cell with her only forays in court used to kill and maim was not adequate preparation for running an entire city under siege. But the palace steward and the captain in charge of her guard were invaluable. Surprised to see her taking their counsel- since the king never asked for, or accepted anyone's suggestions- the two worked tirelessly to assist her. The only issue the queen would not back down on was refugees within the palace. "Your Majesty, we cannot effectively guard you with thousands of strangers within arm's reach of you! Any of these people could be a spy from the Black Court." Captain Asgeir was attempting- for the fifth time that day- to convince Ingrid to clear the palace.

"I am truly sorry for the additional strain this puts on the Royal Guard," the queen paused outside her rooms, desperate for a quiet moment to sit down. "But I will not send these people away. The city is stuffed full of refugees, there is nowhere else for them to go." Putting up her hand as his mouth opened again, she forced a smile and shut the tall door in his face. Heading for the terrace, Ingrid looked to the soot-filled skies, searching for the sun- any glimmer of light to nourish the babies inside her. Finding none, she turned away on defeat. Walking back to her dressing room, Ingrid lifted the little bird from his box. "Little one," she crooned, "you must drink, please. You can be well again, I know it." As if hearing her, the tiny hummingbird lifted his scarlet throat and took a few drops of sugar water before pulling away, struggling to swallow. Tears rose in the elf's eyes as she stroked his feathers delicately. Why couldn't her power heal? The feared executioner of the Unseelie Court fought tears as she looked at the limp little creature. "I can do nothing but hurt, and kill..." she whispered, placing the hummingbird back in its temporary nest.

Ingrid paced her terrace that night, eagerly waiting for the time where she would be able to speak with Loki in the scrying pool. Feeling the light mental tug that she associated with her husband's thoughts, the elf hurried to the huge dish of shimmering liquid, carefully pouring in the sacred oils and reciting the seidr her husband had taught her. When her husband's image appeared in the reflection, Ingrid forced down a gasp, making herself smile warmly.

"Is your Guard attending you?" Loki's pale

skin was smeared with blood and ash.

"Quite well, my husband. But you look as if you've just walked off the battlefield!"

"Darling, I am fine," he promised, waving his hand dismissively.

The queen noticed more cuts on his long fingers, but she held her tongue and nodded. "Captain Asgeir has been overly attentive, I assure you," she leaned closer to the murky pool, "the addition of so many refugees seeking asylum within the palace walls has him convinced there is the spy there somewhere."

The angry expression on her husband's face told Ingrid she should have guarded her tongue. "In the PALACE? There are unidentified civilians within the palace walls? Where you are? And my children?"

"Loki," she pleaded, "you must not be upset. Everything here has been handled- everyone has their place and my Guard has not left my side. I'm fortunate to simply bathe alone."

Ingrid's little joke passed unnoticed as Loki struggled to conceal his fury. "You will not risk my sons!" he snapped, "Any of these pathetic creatures could actually be an assassin!"

The queen shook her head firmly. "No. I would know instantly if an agent of the Black Court was near me. There is a... signature, for lack of a better word, for a Dark Elf. And no other race in the Nine Realms can attempt to hurt me. I assure you; we are quite safe." Her pale hand smoothed over the small swell on her abdomen, and Loki's eyes followed the movement. "Your *daughters* are quite well, my husband, I assure you," she teased.

Taking a long drink of wine, Loki leaned back and sighed, looking at the reflection of his wife's smiling face in the scrying pool. "What concerns you, darling? Are there any serious problems within the palace?" Ingrid thought briefly about telling him that his former mistress had resurfaced, but decided against it. She could handle the witch.

"No," Ingrid shook her head with a smile. "The palace steward and Captain Asgeir have been exceptionally helpful. Even with the city flooded with refugees, there has been no violence. Nearly every home has opened their doors to the displaced. You would be proud of your people."

"I am-" Loki stopped, he'd been about to say that he was proud of her- and he was. But somehow, the words couldn't pass his lips. How could this sheltered, untrustworthy little girl have accomplished so much within the space of a day? Instead, he leaned forward with a slow examination of his lovely wife's body in her thin robe, the lines of her face, those damning lavender eyes. "And you, darling..." he purred, "have you remembered everything I taught you last night?" Grinning with pleasure at her sudden blush, the king pressed further. "Have you taken matters into your own hands today, little one?"

Ingrid flushed even redder, but she dropped her eyes and nodded.

"Use your words, darling," her tortuous husband drawled, taking another gulp of wine. Ingrid's flush made her pale cheeks blush pink, the color heading down her neck and over those milky breasts he so enjoyed. Feeling his cock begin to stir, even after the exhaustion of the day, Loki loosened the lacing on his leather armor.

"Yes, my King..." she whispered, head still down.

"Look at me."

Ingrid groaned, the authority in her beloved's voice was too strong to deny. Taking a deep breath and meeting his gaze, she felt goosebumps rise on her neck, remembering how those cool lips felt against her. Loki leaned forward, blatantly rubbing one hand over the swell of his crotch. "Lower your robe, little one. Let me see those lovely breasts and your sweet, swollen belly." Watching her husband deliberately spread his legs and display his thick cock, already being stroked by one hand as he held the goblet with the other. "Show your King your luscious quim."

The heat in Ingrid's face traveled down her chest to settle between her legs as she shyly opened her silk robe and bared herself to her husband's emerald gaze.

"So beautiful..." Loki almost groaned, seeing all that smooth flesh and the swell of his children within her. "Run your hands over your breasts, sweetness. Wet the tips of your fingers, then touch your nipples with them." He grinned at the involuntary shudder that went through the Elf, but she obeyed him. "So lovely, those taut pink nipples. Do you like that, little one?"

"Mmmmm... yes, my King," Ingrid managed to gasp, still moving her hand and imagining it was one of his. Looking down at his long fingers, clasped around his generous cock and idly stroking it to full girth, she moaned before pressing her lips together.

"Open that mouth, Ingrid," Loki warned, "those are my moans, my whimpers to own. Not yours to hide from me. When did you touch yourself today?"

"Be-before the evening meal," she whispered, "I sent everyone away to help with the dinner, and came into our bedroom."

"Really..." Ingrid groaned internally. She knew that tone, the greedy pitch that meant Loki would be relentless in his questions and orders until he got everything he wanted. "Show me, little one."

"H-here?" his Queen asked, nervously looking around the great room.

"Yes," Loki said in that deep, avaricious tone he employed when intending to seduce her. "Put one leg of the arm of the chair, and the other leg on the opposite. I want to see everything."

Ingrid obeyed, placing one leg, then the other over the arms of his favorite leather chair, shifting in embarrassment. "Yes, Loki? How may I please you?"

Those beautiful, incandescent eyes closed for a moment as a shudder of arousal went through him. To have this delicious, deadly creature splayed before him- Loki gripped his shaft harder to stop himself from coming. "Touch yourself, little girl. Just as you did this evening. Was it quick, perhaps in a hurry to return to your duties?"

"I- I ah, I had a little time. I got into our bed, against the pillows," she admitted, "I tried to remember everything you taught me."

"Where that tender little bud is, at the top of your cleft?" Loki inquired, his hand moving faster.

"Yes," Ingrid barely breathed, "I was very um. I was quite wet and I used it to play with my, uh, my spot." Her fingers were sliding up and down that pink slit, unconsciously mimicking her earlier behavior.

Loki groaned internally. By the Nornir! The little tart was going to make him come like a schoolboy! "Then, after tickling that lovely ah, 'spot,' did you slide your fingers inside that warm channel? Hmm, darling? Did you try to pretend your fingers were mine?"

The elf's eyes were closed, head thrown back as her clever hand worked against herself. "I tried, but they weren't good. Not like yours. I- I tried, but I couldn't..."

"Oh, my poor darling," Loki soothed, "what did my little one do?" He had to grip his rebellious cock again firmly, reminding it who was in charge.

Her eyes opened wide again, and Ingrid flushed miserably. "Please don't make me say it!"

Leaning forward, it was all Loki could do to not try plunging into the scrying pool in his desperation to reach his Queen. "I command you. As your King and your husband." She was cringing miserably, her hand slowing its ministrations against her cleft. "Tell me, Ingrid."

"I- I wanted something bigger, like you, so I- Oh, please Loki! Please don't make me say it!" He looked down to see the slick glistening along her thighs and on the hand she tried to use to hide her eyes from him.

Clearing his throat before managing his commanding tone, the king huffed, "You will tell me now, little one, or I will blister your bottom for your disobedience. I assure you, you will not be able to sit for a week-"

"I used a candle!" Ingrid's voice was louder than she meant it, and she cringed as her husband nearly toppled into his end of the magical connection.

"Show me." Loki's voice was beyond human, almost a lupine-like growl as his eyes turned nearly black as his pupils exploded from the hormonal surge.

His wife left the circle of the scrying view, but returned with a candle about half the size of the king's cock, forcing him to squeeze the head of his painfully erect shaft. Spreading her legs again as ordered, Ingrid looked at him pleadingly. "I didn't know if it was allowed! I just- my fingers didn't feel like yours and-"

Loki's silky black hair fell over his face as he shuddered in pleasure. "You clever, clever darling girl. I am so very pleased with you! Show me, show me how you reached your end."

Watching his wife's teeth bite into that plump lower lip, Loki growled again as Ingrid slid the candle down and gingerly inserted it from the bottom inside her. He could see the streaks of her moisture slide along the candle's slick surface, see the white taper split her lips and slide inside. Her back arched, one hand gently playing with her clitoris as Ingrid used the other to slide the candle in and out of her channel. "Loki! Oh... I wish this was you- that you were inside me..."

"It is-" Loki managed to stutter out the words, "it is, darling. Now move me in and out of your lovely quim faster. I want to feel you clench against me. Are you close, my filthy little one?"

"Yes," Ingrid managed, "yes! Please, will you come with me? Please?"

Watching her hand speed up, moving the poor substitute for her husband's shaft inside her, the elf didn't even see his hips move up and down helplessly as if fucking her instead of the candle. "Now!" Loki grunted, "You will come now, my precious, filthy slut! NOW!"

With an obedient scream, Ingrid did so, keeping her knees spread wide on the chair so Loki could watch the desperate clamp of her cunt on the waxy pillar, shaking and moaning as her thighs glistened wetly. The king spurted all over his clenching hand, unable to stop coming even after the first powerful surge. When the growls and the moans finally stilled, the husband and wife shaking together, he chuckled. "Every day, my darling, I am surprised anew at the exquisite, carnal treasure I stole from the dungeons of the Dark Elves. I will never let you go, my beautiful Ingrid."

Trying to control her wildly exploding nerve endings, Ingrid shivered and smiled back, giggling a little.

Seeing the shiver, Loki frowned and said, "Go and draw a warm bath, my precious girl. I am sorry I am not there to care for you."

Closing her legs and drawing her robe around her again, his wife smiled. "Just... please come back safely, my King. Come home to us."

To Loki's shock, he could actually feel tears prick behind his eyes. Swallowing angrily against the lump in his throat, he managed, "The scrying pool is closing, darling. Go care for yourself. I will see you very soon, my strong, lovely Queen." The sight of her joyful, surprised smile was the last thing he saw as Loki closed their connection.

"It's as if the elf wants to die!" Captain Asgeir was on his back still sweaty and panting a little in post-coital pleasure. "I spend nearly every waking moment trying to keep Queen Ingrid alive!"

A slim hand slid across his glistening chest as a soft voice soothed him. "How very frustrating, my darling captain. I know you must be aching to be at your king's side in battle."

Groaning as he turned over, the man looked at the soft, warm body of his lover next to him. "Perhaps you can help me free myself from my frustrations?"

His chuckle turned into a groan as the woman slid underneath him, long nails idly scratching his back, a noxious black liquid still seeping from the scratches left from their last furious coupling.

Chapter 32

In which Ingrid terrifies the snooty bitches at court, and comes to a realization that might turn the tides of the Black Court war.

Ingrid fought the next day against many things. Against snapping at the endless whining of the high-born who thought they deserved better accommodations, against the exhaustion brought on by the lack of light, and the most heartrending battle against the desire to free her friends in the lowest circle of the dungeon. Not Freya. In fact, in her heart of hearts, the queen felt a deep satisfaction about keeping the goddess there forever.

Pausing for a moment to rub her brow, Ingrid frowned. Satisfaction at another's suffering? Other than simply being rude, Freya had never done anything to her. But those oily, black curls of rage and spite began twining up her spine like a particularly malignant ivy, sliding into her brain stem with whispers of hate and suspicion. *'She fucked your husband. She laughs in your face about it. The others... there's so many, all mocking you.'* Struggling to push the hateful thoughts down, Ingrid ordered the noisiest group of elite complainers to her massive reception room. Truth be told, it was the first time she'd used the Allmother's room, admiring the shimmering green drapes that let in what would ordinarily be sunshine. Huge, cushioned seating areas and a massive fireplace carved with scenes from Asgard's history created an elegant and comfortable space. Ingrid smiled, it was the closest she'd felt to the late Queen Frigg, walking among her collections of art in that beautiful room. Sitting down on the majestic chair meant for her, Ingrid shifted. She was no queen. This all belonged to Frigg, even to her memory. But as the first ladies began filtering in, the new Queen of Asgard stiffened her spine and greeted them graciously. She had to be the Allmother now. For Loki.

"Ladies, I thank you all for joining me today," she smiled benignly, watching them all nod back. "I fear life here in the palace is more... understated than you might be used to-"

"Indeed!" Runa was the first one to agree loudly. "More room must be made for the delicate nature of so many of the high born here-" she broke off quickly as a rumble rolled through the enormous room, but like a tidal wave, instead of an earthquake. A small bout of fearful chatter went through the women as they felt shifted back and forth.

"As I was saying," Ingrid continued on as if nothing had happened, "while I know you struggle daily with the challenges of living on less, I fear there are thousands here in our capital city surviving on nearly nothing." The queen's face was briefly in shadow, cast by the endless clouds of boiling smoke on the horizon. It was fortunate that no one could see her eyes too closely, which now glowed blacker than the skies outside. "I'm sure women of your grace and nobility," she nearly sneered but caught herself, "would love to tend to the needs of so many of our countrymen. I will be taking you all with me to the city to hand out supplies and offer comfort." It was a brittle moment, but even the most stupid and self-absorbed of the nobility present knew better than to utter a word of dissent. Rising from Frigg's elegant chair, Ingrid swept from the room, leaving the palace steward and his assistants to herd the women behind her.

"If I may be allowed to speak freely, Majesty?" Her Guard's captain leaned closer as they strolled through the streets in the middle of the city, stuffed to bursting with the displaced.

"Of course, Captain Asgeir," Ingrid agreed, smiling as she offered more face masks to a big family, the mother exhausted and sweating.

"This is a brilliant plan," he grinned, "I'd wager this is the first time most of the... nobility here," his tone wavered on sarcasm, watching his queen press her lips together to keep from smiling, "have ever met the common folk, much less been required to care for them."

Smiling at the mother and raising her arms in a wordless request to hold her baby, Ingrid gave him a sly look. "It seems to be working, at least for a few," she said. It was true. Some of the haughtiest creatures were chastened at what they saw, so different from the gilded life they usually led. The queen bounced the baby as she watched in satisfaction as many of the women in their elegant gowns ventured in further, looking for those not well enough to come out and greet them. Others were still huddled around the witch Runa, having grudgingly given out the contents from the baskets thrust into their hands and glad to escape any further duties.

"That one's going to be a problem," Asgeir said bluntly, both their gazes on Runa, her red-painted mouth speaking rapidly to the other aggrieved women.

"Then I will send her elsewhere," Ingrid said calmly, but the captain looked at her uneasily, uncertain if she might be joking. Everyone knew about the witch's ignominious day dangling from the palace's highest tower. Looking down at the baby, she smiled and stroked his soft cheek. "I would have thought your first words to me would be a scolding for being required to accompany me into such a crowded place."

The man shrugged under his armor. "We have a protected circle, and there's likely not a soul here who wouldn't defend you with their own life after this day's work."

Ingrid's brow raised. "Why Captain, you never fail to surprise me!"

Asgeir chuckled, guiding his Queen in a safer direction as she returned the baby with a kiss. "That is what a sound military strategy is meant to do, Majesty."

He nearly bumped into Ingrid, stopped dead in the middle of the street. "Of course. Of course, she would..." Whirling on the captain, she hissed, "We must contact King Loki! At once! I know what my mother is doing!"

Summoning Loki to the scrying pool took some time. Ingrid poured the sacred oils over the water and chanted the words carefully, trying to be certain it was done correctly. Her husband was usually the one to contact her. As added insurance, Captain Asgeir sent a messenger through the Bifrost to reach the king as quickly as possible. When his exhausted face finally shimmered into view, Ingrid was so grateful to see him that she nearly toppled into the pool. "My King!"

"Darling, it is always a reprieve from the muddy horrors of the battlefield to see you, but we are at a rather crucial moment." Loki swiped a gauntleted arm across his forehead, unaware that he'd just smeared more mud on his pale face.

Ingrid frowned, knowing that her normally fastidious husband would be openly revolted by the muck on his perfect skin. "I- I know you are very busy, my King, but this is very important. You know I would not have bothered you other-wise-"

"Kindly cease apologizing and speak plainly!" Loki snapped, exhaustion and stress spreading his patience thin. "My mother is coming here, Loki! She's using your distraction to fight else-where in order to attack Asgard directly!"

This finally caught the king's decisive atten-tion. "How do you know?" he snarled.

Ingrid started pacing anxiously, careful to keep within view of the scrying pool. "I'd for-gotten the Black Queen's trick during the Svar-talfheim Offensive- 600 years ago? The Dwarves held off her warriors on three fronts- she was attempting to annex their precious metal stores. She held back her best warriors and waited for their troops to be spread so thin that there was only a skeleton crew to guard the gates of the Great Mines."

"I remember!" Loki agreed, absently rubbing at the dried mud on his cheek. "The Dökkálfar battalions made their way into the heart of the main mine before Odin sent in reinforcements."

"The timing was perfection," nodded Ingrid, "any later and the Demon contingent would have held the rare earth mining for all the weapons-grade materials." Watching the subtle shift of emotion of her husband's face, the elf's head turned curiously. There was an expression of pained reminiscence on Loki's perfect face, rapidly altered by resentment and cold fury. "You... were you the one who sent in the troops, my King? I remember my mother was shocked, she didn't expect the response from the Allfather- "

Even through the murk of the sacred oils and water, Ingrid could see the furious storm of rage and pain convulse the perfection of Loki's features into something darker, uglier. "You were too young to hear of my disgrace?" he hissed, "How Odin broke every bone in my body and nailed me to a cliff for the carrion to torment? My punishment for disobeying the sacred orders of the Allfather." Ingrid turned her face away from Loki's tortured face as he remembered the agony of his punishment for saving the Dwarves from the Black Court.

'Look back!' she furiously ordered herself, *'You will share your husband's torment, just as he shared yours.'* The realization that the Trickster had indeed felt her misery as he'd rescued her from the dank pit of the Niflheim dungeons stiffened Ingrid's back, her head rising to look him in the eye. The hate and heartbreak in those jade depths made her heart twist miserably, but Ingrid forced herself to keep his gaze. No matter how painful his injustice, the least she could do was bear witness to it. "But... you saved all of Svartalfheim- all the Nine Realms, really. If Queen Alfhild had gained control of the weapons minerals- "

"She would have conquered us all, most likely," agreed Loki. Turning restlessly, he circled the cauldron. "But dear Odin..." he spat the word like poison from his mouth, "the Allfather brokered a deal with your psychotic whore of a mother- to gloss over her attempts to overthrow his rule for an agreement of peace."

Ingrid shook her head, frustrated that this was all unknown to her. "But- if you saved everyone by defying Odin's order- "

"I was STILL defying his order," Loki snarled.

His pale face was twisted with hate, looking almost inhuman in his rage. The elf watched the tell-tale indigo of his Jötunn heritage stain his neck and cheeks. "He agreed to punish me- his dear, dear friend! He'd called me that so many times... He agreed to chain me to the cave that hid Máni during the day. While my old friend slept, Odin would send Veðrfölnir to tear at my entrails- ripping them from me as I screamed, bound to the rock..." He stopped abruptly, watching the tears stream down his wife's reddened cheeks. "Don't you dare pity me!" he shouted, disgusted with both of them.

"I don't." Ingrid's voice was soft, carrying to him as her husband's back was to the scrying pool. "I don't," her assurance gained strength. "I don't," she repeated more decisively. "I only wonder why you didn't kill the false king sooner."

Loki's suddenly sharp eyes met her steady lavender gaze. He could have seen her conviction, even if he didn't already know of her burden of speaking the truth. "Truly?" He hated how his voice wavered the slightest bit.

"Truly." Ingrid nodded vehemently, "Truly! He tortured another God of Asgard to smooth the ruffled feathers of the evilest creature in the Nine Realms. I never thought I could feel greater disgust for someone more than my own mother.

But Odin? He was destined to be right- to be good! He was not." She angrily dashed away a tear from sliding down one cheek. Loki didn't need her tears. He needed her outrage. "How dare he- it wasn't diplomacy! He was punishing you for being right, my King."

Loki was utterly still. Not in his long life- not even Frigg ever saw the truth as clearly as this girl, trying to hold back her tears of rage.

"Will you come home, husband?" Ingrid pleaded, "Will you come home to me? We shall crush her here. You will have your revenge. And I will watch it. Gladly." Her last word came out in a whisper, and even from thousands of miles away, Loki could hear the dull rumble of the earth move beneath her.

Leaning close, he murmured, "If I do, Pet, would you be so kind as to not level the palace in your rage in the meantime?" Watching her furious expression clear with a grateful laugh, Loki smiled at his little wife.

"I promise, my King. Just... come home, please. We shall finish her here." Ingrid pleaded.

Dropping his dark head with a sigh, her husband relaxed his grip on the edge of the scrying pool. "I will be there by sunset, little one. Make ready for me." As his eyes rose to hers, the queen shivered at the savage need there, echoing desperately by her own hormones. Watching her nipples harden instantly, Loki chuckled. "Be naked. In our bed. I have much time owed to me from your lovely body."

Ingrid shuddered with arousal. "My arms and my legs will be open to receive you, my King." Enjoying his shocked and vaguely lustful expression, she waved the connection closed.

Notes: I spent a fascinating summer with a group of close friends who are Quakers. They had a practice they called "bearing witness," where they would watch and remember the evils of the world. The Quakers make it their role to witness and repeat these stories to be certain the crimes and cruelty against the weak and helpless are not forgotten or swept away. It began during the abolitionist effort when the Quakers would help the escaped slaves on the Underground Railroad. They felt it was their sacred duty to recount the wickedness of enslaving your fellow man so it could not be forgotten. During our time, we were helping refugees from the Sudan, displaced by the cruel war waged on women and children there with rape and murder. I heard terrible stories that summer, but I tried to be strong and listen to them and to bear witness to what they told me. It sucked. It really did, but if they were strong enough and brave enough to endure it, then I had to be strong enough and brave enough to bear witness. And in Ingrid's own way, she is trying to bear witness to the suffering of Loki in this chapter.

Máni - the old Norsk moon

Veðrfölnir - the giant hawk who lives in the branches of Yggdrasil.

Chapter 33

*In which Loki finds a homecoming
can be especially sweet.*

The warmth Ingrid felt from Loki's promise to return lasted through the rest of the day as she plotted with the palace steward, trying to find one more space to fit another refugee family. Even the palace servants were sharing beds to make room. It moved the queen to see how willing the Asgardians were to help- even if it meant giving up their own beds.

But when she was finally alone, the doors to their rooms closed and locked, Ingrid leaned against them with an exhausted sigh. There was no sun to take that day for nourishment for her little ones, no moon showing in the night sky, no matter where she looked. Just more of the hellish soot and smoke from her mother's vicious curse. Running her hand over the small swell on her stomach, Ingrid found herself apologizing to their little ones. "Tomorrow, my darlings," she murmured, "tomorrow, I'll find the sun for you. Your father will clear the skies, you'll see."

After irritably bathing and trying to remove the soot from her skin and hair, Ingrid hovered by the door to their terrace, looking to the giant gates of the city for activity. Her unbearably sensitive center twinged when she thought of her King, riding arrogantly through the gates and coming home to her. Gods… she *needed* Loki. She needed his long, clever fingers and his knowing hands, his wicked grin. He could always make her come- a command and his mouth or cock and she would tip over the edge and into the abyss, moaning and crying for more.

Finally placing herself on a soft divan near the fire, Ingrid hesitantly drew up the diaphanous skirt of her night-dress and ran her hand over her center- it was hot, swollen and felt tender- the slightest touch sparking nerves alight, eagerly awaiting more. But the feel of her own fingers wasn't enough, causing more frustration than pleasure. She groaned. Where was her husband? Why could she not do this for herself? Perversely, knowing that Loki was only scant miles away made her need worse. Ingrid was so focused on her attempt to bank the fire inside her that she missed the calls of the watchmen at the gate and the clatter of hooves. There was a sound of boots briskly striding through the marble hall and the doors to their suite slammed open.

"My King," Ingrid sighed, "I need you; I need you to-"

Emerald eyes traveling over his wife's shamelessly splayed legs and the position of her hand cupping herself, Loki groaned. Dropping his horned helmet and stalking over to her, he dropped to his knees, wedging her thighs wider by pushing his broad shoulders between them. "Such a delightful homecoming, my pet," he grinned lasciviously. Running his tongue along his lower lip as he watched Ingrid blush, Loki chuckled as her hips still rose, arching up for his touch. He was already carelessly stripping away his armor, one hand pulling at stubborn buckles and ripping straps away to free himself while his other hand stroked along the soft flesh of his Queen's inner thigh.

"Darling girl, I am disappointed. What has happened between that rather delightful display last night with the aid of a candle and your helplessness tonight?" Loki chuckled softly as Ingrid growled a little, grasping his wrist and trying to pull his hand closer to where she needed him. "Have you already forgotten what I've taught you, little one?" Her eyes widened hopefully as his beautiful face drew closer to her center, long fingers spreading her lips as he shamelessly enjoyed the sight of her pink and swollen center. She gasped when Loki drew one rough fingertip from her channel to her clitoris, glistening wet and hard. "You've been so very delightfully... self-sufficient in my absence. And now, begging me like a greedy little thing? What shall I do with you?"

"Please," Ingrid's hand was still pulling at his wrist, and he laughed unsympathetically. "Please, husband. I need you; I can't make it stop- I feel like I'm on fire." She'd worked so hard to appear regal and the queen the city needed while Loki was gone, but he was here now. "I've... been waiting for you," she finished lamely, not sure how to ask for what she needed.

Perhaps the Trickster fooled himself into thinking he'd teased his sweet girl long enough, but the truth was, he'd reached the end of his legendary self-control and dove into her quim, lips and tongue and teeth working against her. Ingrid's back instantly snapped into a tight arch and she let out a breathy scream as she came. Rubbing his stubbled chin into the sore entrance to her channel, he diabolically blew the frigid breath of his Jötunn self against her heated tissue and her hands grabbed thick fistfuls of his hair.

"Be my good girl," he admonished, "you must come again. Show me you missed me, sweetness."

"OH! Oh…" Ingrid couldn't seem to make any other sound, even as she felt her wicked husband laugh, shoulders shaking under her knees and his cool fingers spreading her wider for his tongue. Her hands were still stroking through the thick silk of his hair and she couldn't seem to stop, skin on fire and hips twitching as Loki continued to torment her. He was blowing chilly breaths and rolling that frigid tongue around and around her clitoris until his knowing gaze rose to hers and then he pulled the little bud between his lips and sucked hard. Any poise or polish Ingrid had managed to develop as Queen of Asgard was gone, and she screamed blissfully, like a banshee and the world went dark.

When she regained consciousness, Ingrid was lying in their vast bed, her husband's sculpted, lean body lying against hers. Loki's head was resting on his hand, looking her over as his fingers trailed along her cooling skin. "There you are," he praised, smiling slightly as her drowsy eyes fluttered open. She smiled back sweetly until her gaze roved over his soot-stained skin, cuts, and bruises littering his torso.

"My dear husband," Ingrid said, "I'm so selfish! You're filthy and exhausted and this is how I greeted you?"

Loki could see she was building up to a remorseful round of crying. He lifted her from the bed swiftly, enjoying her startled squeal as he strode toward their bathing chamber. "You may attend to your King's bath, lovely. No tears, be my good girl now." Ingrid nodded eagerly, and as she started the water, he summoned a servant, ordering a truly impressive amount of food.

His sweet bride was already nude and half submerged, waiting for him to return. Something twisted in Loki's chest at the sight, and he dropped the last of his clothes and seated himself in the hot water with a groan. He felt Ingrid wind herself around him like a particularly succulent octopus, long limbs stroking along his as she carefully washed him, making small, concerned noises as she found each wound and bruise. "Wife, I am fine," Loki soothed, "I shall be completely healed by morning." But when he took her hips and attempted to pull her onto his lap, Ingrid balked.

"Loki, you are so..." her pretty face was clouded with concern, and she tried to pull away, worried about opening a cut or scrape even wider.

The king pulled her to sit astride him more forcefully than he'd intended, but the feel of her slick skin against his was what he needed. "Shhh..." he soothed, "give me what I need, darling. This will help me." His sly smile made Ingrid's eyes narrow, but she obediently rose over his cock, already hard and held in place for her to slide down. Gently rotating her hips so the throbbing head of his shaft stroked against her opening, she dared to enjoy his growl for a moment before sinking down over him. From there, her husband took over, fingers squeezing tightly into the soft skin of her waist and forcing the girl up and down almost violently, forcing a shuddering orgasm from her, his following shortly after. But Loki had been away from his Queen for far too long, and he was a god, not a man. His cock was instantly hard again and he chuckled malevolently as Ingrid gave a startled shriek, bouncing again on his shaft. When they'd both found their end enough times to actually be sore, Loki pulled his bride off his cock, feeling the warm rush from their spend dissipate into the water. "Come and feed me, darling," he groaned, "and then we'll rest."

Ingrid happily nodded, carefully drying his sleek body with a soft towel and wrapping Loki's robe over his shoulders. Pouring him a glass of very strong wine, she piled his plate high with roasted meat, cheese, and grapes, crusty bread spread with butter. Watching him with a small smile, she admired her beautiful husband as he finally ate enough, leaning back with an exhausted sigh- a weakness she knew he would never show to another. Warmed by the subtle show of trust, she kissed him gently, then leaned back to rub his feet with oil as he talked about the campaign. "We captured just enough of the Muspelheim scum to get information on the Black Court's troop movements. You are quite correct, my angel. They seemed to be in a holding pattern, sending Surtur's soldiers against us as a distraction." Watching as she placed a little kiss on his big toe, Loki's thin lips curved fondly. "Come now, to bed. Tomorrow should be quite entertaining."

A shadow passed over her face, but his bride forced a smile and nodded, drawing him to the bed and snuggling her back against his front. Loki's cool hand slid over her stomach, stroking the skin there softly. "And our sons? Have they moved for you?"

Giggling sleepily, Ingrid's hand covered his. "Our daughters have been quite strong, my Lord."

Chapter 34

In which Ingrid and Loki are betrayed.

I t seemed that the sated and exhausted couple had been asleep for only a few short moments when the alarm sounded from the Royal Watch. Both Loki and Ingrid woke instantly to the sounds of screaming and explosions. They looked at each other in instant, horrified understanding.

The Dark Queen was attacking Asgard.

Waving a hand to dress them instantly, Loki was already half out the door- mentally with the defense already. "Stay here," he ordered, looking back to Ingrid. "Your Guard is just outside."

The queen looked back at him in astonished fury. "No," she said simply as she pushed past Loki.

"You will hear me, wife!" he snarled, furious that Ingrid would waste even a moment with arguing at such a crucial time.

His Queen caught his hand and started walking faster, their Guard falling in behind them, trying to debrief Loki as they hastened down the corridor. "You need me," Ingrid's voice was low, knowing her husband would never forgive her for an open show of defiance. "I can best protect our children by stopping my- my mother. If you allow me, my powers will be useful to you now."

Running one long arm behind her and lifting his wife to his hip like a child, Loki moved even faster as he spoke into her ear. "You haven't taken the sun or moon for days, Ingrid! You need your strength for the three of you."

Irrationally overjoyed that Loki thought to include her well-being along with his progeny, she smiled reassuringly. "I am well, and anger lends me strength-" An explosion just outside the window they were racing past nearly knocked the group off their feet, but Ingrid furiously thrust out one hand, palm flat. A huge wave of gravity shifted, shoving a pulse through the courtyard of the palace and knocking the invading Niðavellir forces into the stone walls, crushing limbs and pulping Elven bodies into mush. Ingrid felt a painful twist tear through her arm, but she gripped her hand into a fist and moved on, hearing the cheers from the defensive troops outside.

Loki's head shot up, looking startlingly like a wolf's, scenting the air. "I can feel a portal has been opened. Where would that murderous cunt most likely seek out?"

Ingrid rapidly changed course, sending the soldiers stumbling after her. "The Treasure Chamber. She has spoken often of all the powerful artifacts you hold there. She will seek everything that offers her an advantage against us." The king longed to pick her up and simply transport them there, but the group was close and he was unwilling to separate Ingrid from her Guard. When he tore that vicious Black Court psychopath into shreds, his Ingrid must be protected. "Here-" she gasped, one hand cradling her swelling stomach, "She is here. The Black Queen will be well-guarded, we must wait for more troops."

The King of Asgard waited for no one. The vision of the torture Ingrid had endured clouded his judgment. He could taste the flesh of that loathsome excuse for a mother- practically see her blood flow over the granite floor of the chamber. Anxiously watching the set, intent expression on Loki's face, Ingrid knew he would not wait. The smoke that poisoned their atmosphere finally breached the walls of the palace when the Black Queen did. Clouds of choking pitch fouled their lungs and dimmed their vision. But sound still carried.

Ingrid shuddered as she heard the low, crooning pitch of her mother's voice, vigorously breaking the protective wards over Asgard's most powerful treasures. The clash and howls of weapons against flesh sounded the last of the Treasure Chamber's Guard, valiantly struggling against the horde of Demons greedily swarming them, taking chunks of Asgardian flesh with fangs and claws. Bracing one shaking hand against the scorched wall, Ingrid closed her eyes and "saw" the monstrous black claws of her mother stroke the artifacts, seeking the power within them. A huge gout of flame shot out between the titanium stands holding the precious items and the grasping hands of the Unseelie Queen, searing her and the Black Court's Guard. Her daughter smiled in a slightly guilty way, enjoying the screeches of rage and pain from the monstrous creature that gave her life. Biting her lip till it bled, the girl braced against the searing pain that shot up her spine, curling an arm around the babies inside her as if to protect them from her suffering. Her defense was eating at her body- savaging tissue and muscle to replace the psychic toll of her powers. Ingrid knew it was a matter of time before the precious souls inside her would be next to face the damage. Slumping against the cold stone of the wall and helplessly sliding down to the floor, she managed to croak, "Loki- I- I have nothing left. I'm so sor-"

Turning to hear Ingrid's desperate moan, the king growled in rage and horror to see the trail of blood following her descent. "Sweetness - just - be still. GUARD!" Loki suddenly roared, "Attend your Queen!" Turning to ward off a brutal strike from two of the Dökkálfar warriors, he viciously slashed against them, decapitating both with a single stroke as he forced himself to concentrate on the threat before him. He could see the singed, but grinning visage of the Black Queen behind her forces, multiple waves of armored monsters trying to tear their way through the wall of flame to get to the paltry defense assembled with Loki. Ingrid knew her King's forces would reach their site in minutes, but she was terrified it wouldn't be soon enough. Drawing up her knees, the queen coughed painfully and slammed down her feet, sending another shockwave through her mother's forces and spraying the walls with blood. The move gave Loki precious time to slaughter multiple demons with the few soldiers backing him.

"Majesty- come, we need to take you to safety!" Dimly, Ingrid could hear the urgent tone of Captain Asgeir above her as he picked her up, carrying her limp form towards the door. The elf stiffened suddenly, something was wrong here- it was wrong and-

Ingrid's lips formed the words "No!" and "Stop!" but nothing came from her mouth, her body remained stubbornly still despite her brain screaming at it to struggle free of the captain's grip. Behind her, the soothing voice of her maid urged, "Be still, monster. Do not make this harder than it needs to be."

Loki glanced back to make sure his wife was being carried to safety, only to be met with her horrified gaze. Captain Asgeir was holding her tightly as her maid - what was she doing here? - her maid lifted a heavy iron mask and slammed it shut over Ingrid's head. Loki could hear her scream of agony inside his head, one hand still furiously spraying sparks and pulses meant to kill those his troops were fighting. But as he fought, the king struggled to reach his wife. *'Why would they put that horrible thing on her? Ingrid's an Elf- you imbecile! You're torturing her-'* his thoughts were disjointed as his Queen's guard began taking her to a searing sliver of blacklight- a rift opening against the chamber wall close to the Dökkálfar forces. *'Why isn't Ingrid fighting?'* Loki groaned internally, *'Why-'* he suddenly remembered that he'd angrily commanded his wife that she must "Obey your Royal Guard as you do me!" He'd created the means of her capture.

A high, shrieking laugh came from behind

him, and he whirled to see the Black Queen cackle madly as she headed for the rift, her guard closing in around her. One of his treasures was gripped in her scorched hand. He groaned; it was the most powerful stone Asgard held: Oppløsningsstenen. It could dissolve life into dust, cities into rubble. Everything humanity had built for centuries could be reduced to nothing in a matter of moments. Black eyes dancing with malice, Queen Alfhild raised it mockingly to Loki, calling out gleefully, "Thank you for the return of my daughter and your most gracious gift of the Oppløsningsstenen! I assure you; I shall put both to good use." Blue fire shot from Loki's long fingers, desperately pushing for the rift as his wife was shoved through it, followed by her laughing mother. The demon troops howled with rage as they realized they'd been left behind as the Dark Elves raced through the portal and it sealed with a blinding flare of blacklight.

Several things happened at once: new Æsir troops poured into the room, ripping apart the abandoned demons. Loki threw bolt after bolt of magic against the wall where the rift had appeared, trying desperately to open it again. And the fires across the country suddenly died down to ash, the skies clearing of the pitch and soot, their part in the destruction accomplished. A howl of rage tore from the King of Asgard's throat- so inhuman in its desperation that people across the crowded city shuddered in horror as they heard it.

Their Queen was taken.

Ingrid felt herself thrown to the floor of the Throne Room at the Black Court. Instinctively curling to protect the tiny souls inside her, she fell awkwardly on her side, moaning in pain before gritting her teeth. Ingrid would not feed her mother's murky soul with her daughter's suffering. She could barely see around her through tiny slits in the hideous iron mask clamped over her head- the cruel metal causing the skin touching it to sizzle, burn, heal, and burn again. Painfully turning her head, Ingrid could see the curiously blank face of Captain Asgeir and the fearful expression on the last person she would expect to see here. "Gundrun?" Ingrid gasped, "Why? Why would you betray your king?"

"Because you are a monster!" the girl shrieked, her pretty face contorting with fear and disgust. "You are an abomination! To sit on the throne of Asgard? You belong here! I knew it the night you praised those filthy Jötunn! When you showed how you could move the earth? A monster should not be among good people-"

The Black Queen began chuckling harshly, her throat raw from breathing in the inferno sent to stop her. "Have a care, you worthless cunt. You speak of your betters. In fact..." One black tipped hand reached up negligently, and the Dark Elf behind Gundrun stabbed the girl through the heart. Ingrid wept in dismay, her hand still blindly seeking that of her little maid, trying to comfort Gundrun as her life's blood poured from her still body.

Shuddering, Ingrid rose to a seated position, one hand still guarding her fragile abdomen. Her cruel iron hood slowly rotated as she sought her vicious parent. "Mother," she finally managed, "can you do nothing but cause suffering and destruction? You are a disease! A blight!" A booted foot rose to kick into her side as the elf managed to roll enough to catch the blow on her spine. The man sworn to protect her stood above Ingrid, still staring down with that oddly blank face.

The girl could hear the metallic click of her mother's pace come closer, until the Black Queen stood over her, nudging Ingrid's side to roll her daughter on to her back. "Hmmm..." her raspy voice mocked, "who would have imagined? A child from the God of Lies and the Black Court Executioner? Genius. Had I thought of it first, child, I would have petitioned for your betrothal. This spawn will be a god above all others- and under my control! You've outdone yourself."

"Never!" Ingrid hissed, grateful that her mother was not fully aware of the secret she carried. "You will never touch my child! My husband will tear this court apart first!" She gritted her teeth, waiting for a blow from the monster who'd given her life. Instead, Queen Alfhild knelt gracefully and ran her black-tipped nails over Ingrid's belly.

"Stupid girl," she said almost fondly. "You will obey me eagerly. Gratefully. Or I shall tear this child from you and you will watch it die. Now, obey your mother, and-"

"You are not my mother!" the Queen of Asgard suddenly screamed, "And my name is Ingrid!" The pain overwhelmed her, and the elf sank gratefully into the dark waters that seemed to close over her ironbound head.

Chapter 35

*In which some enemies are reunited,
and some enemies are destroyed.*

Though he sat in the center of dozens of shouting military men and women, Loki may as well have been alone. Hands flat on the table, he stared ahead blankly. None of the promises, questions or speculation from the warrior elite around him penetrated the silence. Finally, he looked up, and every voice silenced. "Leave me." There was a scraping of chairs and hasty steps to the door as everyone scrambled to obey him. When the King's face was frozen in rage- as it was now- nothing good could come of being in his presence.

How could it have come to this? Loki suddenly waved one hand and every chair flew against the stone walls, the heavy furniture shattering with the force of the impact. How could he have allowed the wards around the castle to weaken? How did the Dökkálfar bitch know where to invade? There were traitors among his men. And when he found them, their suffering would eclipse anything Ingrid had ever endured at the hands of her psychotic parent.

The king's heart ran cold as he stood and began pacing the room, angrily kicking aside broken chunks of wood left over from his tantrum. His pregnant wife weakened from a lack of sun or moonlight. In the cruel hands of the thing that called itself her mother. With his children. His helpless babies. This time it was the huge silver and wood table that exploded, guards outside the room ducking instinctively from the detonation within.

"Wake, Executioner!" The guard's sword clashed loudly against the heavy door of Ingrid's prison.

Ingrid's heavy eyes dragged open, struggling to see through the narrow slit in the iron mask still enclosing her head. She'd forced herself to step aside from the agony of the metal against her skin, trying to sleep and give the babies rest as well. The elf could feel the little ones inside her, twisting this way and that in an agitated way. Placing one tender hand over the swell of her belly, she sent every bit of love and comfort she could muster inside to her tiny cargo.

"Sweet ones," she whispered, "Mama is here. I will not let anything happen to you, no matter what I must do. Have calm. Mama is here." Tears rose to Ingrid's eyes. Where had she even found those words to say to her babies? They'd certainly never been spoken to her. But these were Loki's children as well. She must return them home safely. Forcing herself to stand as the door slammed open, Ingrid clenched her fists. If she could find the strength, she would break her vow to never take another life. She would kill them all if she had to. But her babies were returning home to Asgard. To their father, and safety.

"Ah, there she is." The Queen of the Dark Elves lounged on her obsidian throne, her black-tipped nails clicking aimlessly against the armrest. Behind her throne, General Gorum hovered like a diseased vulture, his pale face alight with excitement. "Have you come to beg my forgiveness, you disgusting creature? Throwing all my love and care back into my face, ungrateful cunt!" Her shrill voice rose in pitch and volume as her rage at her disobedient daughter began to spill over the narrow restraints of the Unseelie Queen's tenuous self-control.

As Queen Alfhild rose from her chair to strike Ingrid, a rumble moved through the room, the heavy granite floor shifting as if disturbed by an earthquake, knocking her back onto her throne. The general behind her steadied himself, staring at the girl before them with growing alarm. Ingrid was perfectly still, one hand placed lightly over her belly, the other flicking carelessly at the floor. Another upheaval rolled through the ground, swaying furniture and knocking over priceless decor and artifacts.

The vicious Queen of the Black Court stared at the blank expanse of the iron mask eclipsing her daughter's features. The brutal cage should have weakened Ingrid to the point where she could barely stand, yet the monster stood tall and silent- the only thing in the room not affected by the violent tremors. Finally making her way down the polished stone of her steps, she stalked over to Ingrid. "You're causing this, you miserable thing. Do you think I will allow your pitiful attempts at defiance?" Shoving her face close to the mask, Ingrid's mother suddenly screamed, "I OWN YOU, you pathetic bitch! Everything you are IS MINE! And you WILL obey me, or your vile spawn will suffer-"

Ingrid viciously slammed her heavy trap of iron into the face of her mother, smiling in the middle of her own agony to hear the woman scream in pain and rage as the contact with the heavy mask broke her nose, the vicious metal burning the left side of her face. Still shrieking in shock, the queen thrust out one hand and Ingrid flew halfway across the cracked floor, still managing to land on her side, rather than her stomach. "Get her out of here!" the Dökkálfar Queen yowled, more like an animal than elf. "Let us see how another day in her cell improves her behavior!" The uneasy Royal Guard poked and prodded a still silent Ingrid with their swords, not daring to lay a hand on her.

Without quite realizing where his booted feet were taking him, Loki walked mindlessly to his Throne Room. The light was dimmer there, and as he approached the steps to the throne, the king stopped at the glass case holding the symbol of his triumph over the idiot he had called brother for so many centuries. Mjölnir rested motionless on its elaborate stand, the gold surface gleaming dully. His eyes were drawn to the jagged crack a distraught Ingrid had made the day she realized his treachery, discovering that she was with child. The case... Loki thought distractedly, the glass cover was spelled by himself to be impenetrable, and yet his Queen had easily caused the fissure. The thought of his courageous wife's stubborn sweetness in the face of all the horrors the Unseelie Court had forced her to endure... his dark head fell into his hands. He must save her. And now.

The next walk Loki took was a long one, down the countless flights of stairs that led to the dungeons of Asgard, then further still to where the vilest and most monstrous of beasts were imprisoned. Then, further still, 'till the air grew rank and the walls dripped impure water, growing mold and mottled lichen over the stained surface. And there were four heavily enchanted cages, holding the people the king despised the most.

Freyr looked up first, moving his lank hair aside from his eyes. "Majesty," he stumbled to his feet, sketching a low and elaborately insulting bow to an expressionless Loki. "You honor us with your regal presence. You must forgive me; I haven't tidied up today." The disgraced gods moved closer to their glowing force fields, gazing at the monster before them.

"What do you want?" Freya hissed. "What more can you do? Killing us would be a mercy."

"My wife..." Loki's deep voice died off for a moment as he struggled to gather his scattered thoughts, "Ingrid- she has been taken. The Black Court Queen created a temporal rift in the Artifacts Room. She made off with the Oppløsningsstenen, and far worse, with- with my wife and children."

Balder spoke first, trying to recover from his horror and shock. "Loki... what rescue efforts have been made?"

Loki angrily shook his head. "The troops are

massing now. The White Court is sending all their best soldiers. But - with that vicious cunt's powers and bolstered by the Oppløsningsstenen - the risk to Ingrid and the babies..."

Tyr sighed heavily, remembering the shy elf who brought him huge baskets of food every day, pretending it was nothing. "What can we do?"

Raising his head, Loki glared at them, his white face distorted in fury. "Help me."

King Leafstred nodded distractedly to Heimdall as he came through the Bifrost with a huge retinue of soldiers and advisers. "Gatekeeper. This is a dark day. I did not think this war could be worse."

The golden eyes of the huge man were sorrowful, even though Heimdall's face was expressionless. "King Loki awaits you, Majesty. He needs you now."

The bustle and noise from the White Court troops entering the courtyard of the castle sent grooms and servants in every direction, trying to accommodate the Ljósálfar as King Leafstred strode into the War Room. "Loki," he began, "how do we proceed-" He stopped in astonishment to see four familiar faces turn to him from their high position at the table, seated next to their King.

Freyr grinned with his old, rakish smile restored. "With all due haste, Your Majesty."

Shaking his head in relief and amusement, the Light Elf removed his gloves and seated himself. "Then what are we waiting for?"

Still expressionless, his pale face set and composed, Loki looked up as the doors slammed open again. "For him."

"BROTHER!" roared a familiar voice. "Where is Mjölnir?"

The Queen of the Dark Elves sat alone in her throne room, having not moved since she'd ordered her daughter forced back to her cell. She hummed, suddenly rocking back and forth on her monstrous throne as she raged against the change in her weapon of flesh. "All my magic," she snarled, "all my skills went into that bitch, and she defies me? How could it have gone so wrong?" she questioned, gripping her chair. "That Jötunn bastard! I should have disposed of him the day he murdered Odin." Her beautiful face was distorted by rage and fear. How could he have turned her spawn into such a rebellious creature in such a short time? After centuries of discipline? One clenched fist reached out to stroke the stone beside her, resting on a silk pillow and sparking with arcane magics. "Let them come," the Black Queen mumbled, "I have more than one unconquerable weapon at my disposal…"

There was a great deal of shouting and exclamations as the four formerly disgraced gods fell upon Thor, hugging him and slapping his back repeatedly. The Ljósálfar King simply stared, one brow raised as his gaze went from Loki's impassive face to Thor's grinning mug and back again. "The friends are united again, I see?" He leaned closer to murmur to Asgard's monarch. "It is a wise choice, friend. Truly."

Loki's lips thinned into a tight line, but he nodded. "It is what is best for us all at this time. The Black Court must fall." Glancing irritably to the thicket of admirers around Thor, his voice rose authoritatively. "If you're all quite finished fawning over the blond oaf, return to your seats. There are thousands of our people held captive by the Dökkálfar. Including your Queen. And my progeny." Everyone slipped into their chairs in abashed silence, ready to listen. "The plan of attack," he began, "is unusual. We shall strike from within to without in their Palace. The main thrust of the battle is holding off the Dökkálfar troops as the other group splits to recover my- my wife and the Oppløsningsstenen. Let us make no mistake. The Black Queen must die."

Leafstred felt a tug in his soul- no matter how evil the creature was who sat on that throne, the Seelie and Unseelie Courts had been aligned for thousands of years. To attack them seemed unimaginable. But there was no other choice. "You speak of attacking from within, Loki. How shall we accomplish this?"

Here, a dark smile finally graced the king's face. "That Black Court lunatic is not the only mage that knows how to create a temporal space rift. The finer details are selecting the location and not ending up inside a stone wall. She will have wards surrounding her palace. But I know where the Oppløsningsstenen is. The magical signature was bound to me when I first took the sacred stone from the Wandering Moons centuries ago. This is a crucial fact that murderous cunt does not know." After that, there was a cacophony of the clashing of arms, as the troops began leaving via the Bifrost, one huge group after another.

Walking down the hall to the Throne Room, Thor and Loki couldn't look at each other, both searching for what to say. The atmosphere thickened as the huge blond approached the stand holding his weapon. Looking down to see his fists tighten anxiously, Loki smiled sardonically.

"Do you fear to take the hammer?"

Thor's head dropped for a moment. "There was a time before my banishment that I could not. To not be able to help save your wife as you have saved mine-"

Loki broke into cold laughter. "Ingrid saved your Sif. Not me. And I punished her for her kind heart. I was cruel to my pregnant wife…" Feeling Thor's big paw land on his shoulder, it took every ounce of self-control the king had to not scornfully shove away Thor's attempt at comfort.

Thor's hand left him as he circled the stand. "How- the container has been fractured," he said, brow furrowed. "I know the spell you uttered would have made this cage impenetrable for…"

Another harsh chuckle from Loki. "It was Ingrid. She was quite angry at the time."

Thor whistled respectfully. "Angry at you? I would not have wished to be within two realms of the palace at such a time." Throat clearing, he straightened his bulky shoulders. "Let us… let us begin. Time is short."

Nodding, Loki's long fingers made a series of complicated movements, and seconds later it felt as if the vast hall had lightened somehow. He watched determination mix with fear on Thor's face and his dark brow rose. Somehow, he'd never imagined the arrogant God of Thunder afraid of anything, except perhaps, Loki himself when Thor was banished. But when his fist carefully closed around the handle of Mjölnir, the hammer rose from its glass prison easily, and the God of Thunder beamed with joy, swinging it this way and that. "Brother!" he roared happily, "Let us save your bride and my nieces or nephews!" Nodding, Loki walked in front of the bellowing god, rolling his eyes. The palace had been so restfully quiet for so long...

The final group of warriors met Heimdall, their horses snorting and shifting, eager to move. The Watchman pinned them all in his golden gaze. "The coordinates are ready. My King-" he turned to Loki, bowing slightly, "Queen Ingrid is in a chamber just off the Throne Room." The huge golden god hesitated for a moment and pressed on. "It is a torture chamber. You must hurry."

As the men swiftly apparated into the Throne Room of the Unseelie Court, they could already hear the battle outside, led by King Leafstred. No one Dark Elven battle strategy better than their Light counterparts. But the horrors before them seemed without end. Many of their soldiers were lying in pieces, torn apart by the Black Court troops and the savage cursing of Queen Alfhild, sending wave after wave of deadly magics in every direction. Loki could just see over the fray that she was wielding the Oppløsningsstenen. "Thor!" he roared, trying to catch the God of Thunder's eye. "You and the other four- you must hold against the Queen. I will find Ingrid!" Winding up to send Mjölnir smashing through another group of guards, Thor nodded cheerfully, grinning like a maniac at the sheer joy of wielding the hammer again. A small unit followed the king as he raced in the direction of the chamber where Ingrid was held. Suddenly, a haggard Captain Asgeir stepped in front of him, narrowly avoiding losing his head as Loki's sword slashed down.

"Majesty!" the captain shouted, "This way, quickly!" He barreled into General Gorum's antechamber, the site of many torturous hours for Ingrid during her life in the Unseelie Court. Loki's teeth ground with rage so tightly he could feel a molar crack. The Dökkálfar guards were attempting to stab at Ingrid under the general's shouted instructions, his voice shrill with rage and fear. Even under the monstrous iron mask that blinded her, Loki's brave Queen was sending one and then another smashing into the marble walls, crushing them to a pulp. He could feel her anguish and terror, and Loki's voice rose to a volume that made the walls shake.

"INGRID!"

Diving forward, he viciously thrust and stabbed through the guards, clearing a path to his wife. As he was within arm's reach, the repellent features of General Gorum appeared over her shoulder as he held a viciously sharp dagger to her neck. "Burning death from the poisoned blood of Jörmungandr- shall we see if your unborn creatures can withstand it?" The fury of Loki's attack knocked the general off his feet, seizing the poisoned blade from the elf's hand. He could see from the corner of his eye Captain Asgeir leading her quickly from the room. Satisfied Ingrid was safe for the moment, the king set himself to killing Gorum with a thousand lightning-quick, agonizing strikes from the knife intended for Ingrid, each one meant for a mark the foul Elf had placed upon his wife. Turning to race for the Throne Room his step faltered to see Asgeir pinned to the granite walls by invisible bonds, the captain's body struggling like a butterfly pinned to a board. Loki could see the agony and guilt in the man's eyes, but as he reached him, the captain managed to gasp, "Forgive me..."

Suddenly, there was silence, shocking after the pandemonium from the vicious fighting within the room. Ingrid was standing before her mother's throne, her horrible iron bonds shattered into pieces around her. The Black Queen grasped the Oppløsningsstenen stone in her fist, thrusting it at her daughter.

"You think to stand against ME?" The madness radiated from the Unseelie Queen's ebony eyes as she screamed, "I will strike you down, just as I did your pitiful excuse for a sire- then I will tear this child from your womb to create my new weapon of flesh!"

Ingrid never spoke, ascending the stairs to her mother's throne, her head cocked strangely to one side. Whatever magics the Oppløsningsstenen contained that were meant to stop her advance did nothing- Loki concentrating with every ounce of his power to hold the weapon inert. He watched, dumbfounded as did all the other warriors in the cavernous hall as Ingrid's monstrous mother staggered back and away from her daughter, falling against her throne and cowering, black blood pouring from her eyes and ears. Loki realized Ingrid was searching the woman's mind, casually ripping through her synapses as Alfhild howled and shrieked. Nodding briefly, one hand pressed to her pregnant belly, the other hand of his wife raised to point at the Black Queen, elevating her from her chair to dangle high above the stunned soldiers. "YOU WILL NOT kill your mother!" Alfhild screamed, black tipped claws clicking helplessly as they stabbed towards her daughter. "I MADE YOU! YOU ARE MINE!"

With a sudden, vicious thrust from her pale hand, Ingrid finally spoke. "Then I am more like you than I could have expected, Mother." The destruction of the most powerful creature in Niflheim was unspeakable- some portions of her body exploded, spraying bloody gobbets of flesh in every direction. But her trunk and head began to implode, the nauseating "crack!" of bones crushing into powder, flesh flattening as the last of the Queen of the Dark Elves was reduced to sinew and clotted blood, landing with a nauseating sloshing sound on the floor. One desperate ebony eye rolled free from the mangled lump. Loki somehow knew that some part of the monstrous queen's consciousness was there- staring up at her daughter with a horrible awareness. Reaching out one booted foot, Loki slowly crushed the eye, noxious fluids sizzling and sinking into the stone like acid. Ingrid suddenly wavered and would have fallen, but at once Loki was there, lifting her limp form in his arms and heading for the Rift.

"Thor!" Loki roared, "Can you-" Nodding as Mjölnir flew again, the god laughed boisterously.

"GO! We are merely tidying up! NOW! WHO IS NEXT!" A dozen or so of the hapless Unseelie guard fell like ninepins in the wake of the hammer's path. It was only moments as Loki raced for the opening and carried his wife safely through. Once inside Heimdall's chamber at the end of the Bifrost, he fell to his knees, brushing the tangled silver hair away from Ingrid's pale face.

"Wife-" he groaned, "-sweet wife! Speak to me, dear one-"

Ingrid moaned as she forced open her eyes. "Loki?" A sweet smile spread across her bruised face. "You came for us. I knew you would."

Her husband, the god known as Silvertongue, simply laughed and stuttered, trying to find something to say as he kissed her. "I do not believe you needed any help, my beautiful Valkyrie."

Her shaking hand slid into his hair as she smiled up into his bloodied face. "Loki. My King, I- what- what is happening?" Ingrid's appalled expression as she stared down at the gush of fluid erupting between her legs and staining her dress made Loki bite his lip to not laugh at her shock.

With the experience of a god accustomed to fathering monsters, he kissed her again. "Your body is telling us that our children are making their way into the world, my darling."

Chapter 36

In which something is lost, and something is gained.

Since becoming King of Asgard, Loki had never received the treatment he did as he carried a gasping Ingrid into their chambers. The Light Elf midwives were already there, eagerly preparing the bed for her. Once he placed her on the soft sheets, Loki smiled down at his wife, kissing her tenderly. "My lovely Ingrid. You honor me."

Smiling back, she placed a hot hand on his cheek, stroking along one sharp cheekbone. "We'll meet our children soon, my King. I am- oh!" Her words ended in a gasp as the next tremor of pain swept through her tired body. There was nothing left, she feared, all her strength and energy given to protect their babies by destroying her mother. Gritting her teeth, Ingrid shuddered through the labor pain and smiled again at his concerned expression. Pulling his dark head closer to hers, she whispered, "I hope they look just like you." Kissing her hand tenderly, Loki was about to reply when he was politely shoved aside by the head midwife.

"Your Majesty, the queen is well into labor, we must care for her. It's time for you to leave." Loki's mouth shaped into a snarl, but the concerned expression of the midwife before him made him stop. "We will take excellent care of your family," she soothed. "Allow us the privacy to help her prepare."

Reluctantly nodding his head, Loki bent to kiss his Queen one more time. "I will be close by, sweet girl." Forcing a resolute smile to her lips, Ingrid nodded and stared at him with love, trying to memorize his face, his rare expression of unguarded affection. Suddenly, Loki found himself in the hall and the huge doors to his rooms closed firmly behind him. Irritably shaking his head, he looked around him, how had this happened? The king realized he'd always planned to be by Ingrid's side during her labor, soothing her and being the first to witness the birth of his children. He nearly turned around and threw the doors open when the clamor in the courtyard caught his attention.

"VICTORY!!" Loki rolled his eyes, hearing

Thor's effusive bellow and the corresponding cheers as if the oaf had taken down the Dark Elves with only his ego and Mjölnir. Forcing himself to turn his back on the room where his wife was straining through her labor, he strode down to the returning warriors.

"The Black Court has fallen, Your Majesty," said Tyr, his face bloody but alight with the victory, "the hostages have been removed from their subspace prison and returned home."

Loki nodded curtly, looking at the group, then again at Thor. An uneasy silence fell over the gods, knowing that the moment was suddenly uncertain. Would Thor be sent back to Midgard? Would the four gods who supported his claim to the throne find themselves again in their cages? The king's thin lips twisted in a wry smile, knowing exactly what they were thinking. Jerking his head back to his palace steward, he ordered, "Open the dining hall and feed these soldiers. They have saved the day." A cheer went up from the exhausted troops and the poor steward made for the kitchens at a record clip. Loki hesitated, wanting to turn back to his chambers, concerned for Ingrid. His desire for complete control was battling with the midwife's warnings. Thor threw one gigantic arm around Loki in something just shy of a choke-hold, and dragged him into the hall with the others. "Where is Ingrid?" the blond asked, once he'd been provided with a massive tankard of ale. "Is she well?"

Sighing, Loki took a gulp of his own drink. "She is in labor. Her water broke just as we came through the Bifrost." He looked up to Thor's horrified countenance, and he burst into sardonic laughter. "Brother," he mocked, "is the God of Thunder- the man who fears nothing- afraid of a woman giving birth?"

Swallowing another mouthful of ale, Thor tried and failed, to stop a shudder. "It- ah- it is unseemly to speak of such things," he managed, his handsome countenance twisted with disgust. "To speak of a woman's er, waters..." He broke off into another shudder as Loki laughed and Freya looked on in disgust.

"Really?" the goddess snarled, "You buffoons fear childbirth? You should." Freya smiled malevolently at the suddenly uneasy soldiers. "The unimaginable pain of forcing a child through a channel you have all utilized for your own selfish pleasures? The agony of enduring the pain and blood, the-"

"Stop!!" Thor howled; his face already slightly green from Freya's highly descriptive narrative. "Stop! We hear you! The courage of women and the- the, uh..." He trailed off as the Goddess of Love and Fertility broke into spiteful laughter, but it ended the conversation and returned to the "glory" of battle.

Once Loki had patiently walked the five of them through the finish of the attack, he pulled aside two of his generals and gave them orders to hold Niflheim's defenses and to debrief the key hostages, such as the Vanir King. But his attention went back to Ingrid immediately, the concerned monologue he'd pushed to the back of his mind insistently trying to return to the forefront.

Twice, he rose to return to his chambers, only to have Thor or the others pull him back, insisting on another round of ale and more stories of battle. Suddenly, Loki felt a painful twist in his gut, a faint wail of, *"Loki! Please, I want my husband!"* in his mind, the soothing hisses of other women trying to silence Ingrid's pleas. Rising angrily, he strode from the room, ignoring the calls from the others. Pushing open the doors to the main area of his rooms, Loki was blocked by the determined Midwife Mistral again, shaking her head fiercely. "Your wife is in heavy labor! You must not distract her, Sire!"

"I heard her!" Loki was suddenly furious at the woman before him, "I heard her call for me!"

Mistral scoffed. "All women call for their husbands during labor, a wish to have them remove the pain somehow. This, you cannot do, Majesty. You must allow us to do our jobs." Loki angrily moved an arm to shove her aside, but the midwife was surprisingly strong. "Do you wish to endanger your wife? The lives of your children?"

He stopped dead, looking down at her in shock. "How dare you speak to me in such a way, midwife! Of course not, why do you think you are here? To give Ingrid- to give the Queen the best of care, and-"

"Then let us do our jobs!" Mistral nearly shouted, leaning closer to Loki's furious face. "Your wife is weak from her captivity; she must concentrate on giving birth. You must not distract her!"

The king stumbled backward, his natural grace deserting him for a moment. Distract? His presence could harm Ingrid? Pressing his lips together furiously, Loki snarled, "I expect reports upon the half hour. Promptly." Nodding, the elf pushed him to the door again, watching him flinch as he heard Ingrid's cry.

"Please, please find Loki! I need-" her sobs were hushed by the midwives, and feeling as if his heart was being torn from his chest, Loki reluctantly turned to leave.

Ingrid could feel her control over her body abruptly leave her, reassigning itself to the flesh and blood, an organism fighting to create life from suffering. She'd drained herself - and she feared the tiny bodies of her children inside her as well - and now there seemed nothing was left. She rode the waves of agony pulsing through her, trying to focus on freeing the tiny souls within her. Ingrid could feel them- sense their consciousness reach for hers. It seemed they'd awakened fully during their captivity at the Black Court, their minds moving along with hers in the desire to escape the sordid confines of the Dökkálfar stronghold. Between gasps and gritted teeth, Ingrid spoke to them soothingly, promising her babies that she and their father were so very happy to meet them, that their arms were open and ready- then, the tidal wave of agony would sweep over her again, sending her rolling and helpless under the force of it. "Is it-" Ingrid gasped, trying to regain her senses, "are elven births usually this- mmmmmm..." She bent double, eyes squinted shut as she tried to refocus against the anguish, "Is- is- is it usually this forceful?"

The Light Elf midwives bent over her, smoothing Ingrid's hair away from her sweating face and rubbing her clenched hands and feet. "Shhh..." soothed the eldest, "you are doing beautifully, my dear. I know this is difficult, but you must be brave." Ingrid laid her head back against the pillows, tears slipping from her eyes.

"Please let me have my husband," she wept, no longer ashamed to let them see her beg, "please? I need him- aaaah, GODS!" Back arched and twisting from the pain, Ingrid couldn't feel the charms the midwives were attempting to spell on her tortured body, trying to ease the way. She could vaguely hear the low murmurs around her.

"The babies are not moving down the birth canal-"

"I don't understand why this is not progressing-"

"We must contact Queen Soren..."

Ingrid wept with desperation. Was the only thing within her capacity destruction? Was she not worthy to create life? Perhaps her mother had been right, all along... "Loki," she whispered, turning her face away from the midwives, "please, please come..." Her emaciated body arched again.

"What do you MEAN, she's not progressing!" Loki shouted, his eyes blazing with fury as he advanced on the cowering midwife. "I trusted you with her care, with her LIFE!"

"Loki! Wait-" Thor attempted to hold back his enraged friend, who looked ready to tear the Light Elf's head from her body. "Listen to her, I am certain she has an answer!"

Loki's slitted gaze settled back on the midwife, her pale face betraying that really, she had no answers. "We have sent for Queen Soren," she said helplessly. "Perhaps there is medical knowledge passed down through the bloodline-" The elf's explanation was cut off the by the flurry of horses arriving at the palace, and Loki angrily pushed away from her to head for the stairs, trailed by an anxious Thor. King Leafstred peeled off from the arriving group to head for Loki, taking his cold hand in his.

"What news, my son?" The words slipped past the Ljósálfar King's lips without thinking, betraying how much he had come to view Loki and Ingrid as his own children.

The slip seemed to hit Loki like a blow, and he slumped back on his chair. "The- our babies, they are not progressing as they should. For some reason, they cannot make their way down the birth canal."

Thor swallowed as if trying to hold back a gag, but he was wise enough not to enrage Loki.

A shadow moved over Leafstred's beautiful face, but he nodded encouragingly.

"I am certain my wife can assist," he said stoutly, "she has attended many royal births, she will know how to help Ingrid." Loki's hand suddenly clenched on his, and the look of hope in those emerald eyes was heartrending. Of all the centuries of their acquaintance, the Light Elf could not remember a moment when the cold King of Asgard looked to him with such desperation. "It will be fine," he said, squeezing his icy hands again.

Ingrid was past understanding what the agonies of her body were meant to accomplish, but she felt the helpless tug and pull at the base of her spine as if her treacherous form refused to release her babies. She mindlessly hummed lullabies to them, whispered words of love and encouragement as she fought against her own body to free them. "Loki..." her voice was too cracked for the plea to emerge as more than a whisper, but suddenly a warm hand smoothing over Ingrid's sweaty face.

"What, my dear?" The voice was so kind, Ingrid thought distractedly. Perhaps if she'd been raised in her Ljósálfar family, she would be capable of delivering her little ones safely. Perhaps she wouldn't be such a monster. "What do you need?"

"L- Loki, please, I need..." Ingrid drifted into unconsciousness as the flurry around her rose to a fever pitch, the newcomer barking instructions with a furious, controlled voice.

After a few more minutes of silence, the Kind of Asgard had had enough. Furiously apparating inside his great room, he began to stride to the bedroom when he was stopped by the tiny cry of one, then two sweet voices. "What- are they-" he barely managed to whisper as the pale face of the Ljósálfar Queen emerged from the bedroom, two little bundles held tenderly in her arms. Stepping closer, she leaned in to show Loki what she carried.

"Your children, Loki. Welcome your son and daughter to the world."

He was suddenly so overcome with joy that Loki failed to see the tears gleaming in her eyes, and he carefully took one, then the other baby into his long arms. "They're perfect," he said reverently, gazing down at the tiny faces, the mouths opened in silent yawns. His daughter's head was covered in inky hair, while his son's soft cap of down was pale, like Ingrid's-

"How is my wife," Loki said suddenly, his voice cold and clipped, his focus suddenly searing into the droop of the elf's head. "How. Is. My. Wife?" he snarled, his pale face draining of what little color he had.

"Loki..." Queen Soren's face wore the expression Loki despised of all others. Pity. "We - were forced to take your children from her stomach by incision - they could not make their way down, and their life signs were weakening. They are well, wonderfully healthy."

"HOW IS MY WIFE!" Loki suddenly howled, making the babies startle and begin to cry. He shoved past the agitated women and into the bedroom, stopping short as he spotted Ingrid's pale form, her silver hair stained red with blood, the silk covers around her gone crimson. The woman seated beside her rose, turning to Loki with a look of infinite sorrow on her beautiful face.

The king was oblivious to the soft weeping of the servants around him, the grief on the midwife's face. "Frigg?" Loki slurred, staring at the Allmother, who was holding the hand of his wife. Stumbling to the bed, he gazed down at Ingrid's pale face, finally serene and at peace. "What?" he gasped, and then couldn't speak again.

"I came the moment Soren contacted me," the former Queen of Asgard took his limp hand. "I should not have sequestered myself on Vanaheim. I could have done more; I should have been here sooner."

Loki's mouth was trying to form words, ask questions, but nothing seemed to pass his lips.

"Ingrid was such a brave girl," Frigg's voice

was choked, "She survived so much. The midwives should have allowed you to stay, your seidr would have seen what blocked the babies from being born. But the labor... it took such a toll on her, and she was terribly depleted from her captivity. I had to remove your children by cutting them free from Ingrid. The procedure is very unusual. They are never performed here, so no one knew-"

"Get out." Loki wouldn't have recognized his own voice, and the room stilled, everyone staring at him. "GET OUT!"

A scramble for the door ensued, and even Queen Frigg withdrew, leaving him with a comforting squeeze on his arm. Sitting on the bed with suddenly numb legs, Loki stared at Ingrid. Carefully placing their son in one thin arm, and their daughter in her other, he shakily smoothed the hair from her pallid forehead. "They're-" his voice broke, and Loki swallowed, bending his head. "They're beautiful, my darling. Our babies are perfect. Just like their mother. My sweet girl-" His dark head dropped to her still chest, beginning to weep. "My love. I am sorry. Forgive me, this is my fault. I- I shouldn't have trapped you. I was no better than the monster who called herself your mother. I was no better, taking your bindings and holding them for myself. I could not imagine someone as perfect as you st- staying with me. I did this to you, love." One trembling hand moved to Ingrid's back, sliding down to the base of her spine where he knew the cruel chains tore through her delicate wings. "I will release you now, my sweet girl-" Loki choked on his sobs. There was never a time - not even the horror of discovering his origins - that had caused him such anguish. He could never have imagined his heart feeling as if it was torn open, bleeding. "You are free. Free in death. You deserved to be free for the rest of your life. I stole that from you. My Ingrid." Laying his head against her cool chest, he began to weep hopelessly, moving his hand over her spine with a seidr to sever the chain.

For an utterly still moment, there was nothing but the sound of his hoarse sobs, then a sudden "CRACK!" seemed to split the air, the smell of ozone and blood and- flowers? Loki thought dazedly as his head shot up. Then, a huge surge from his wife's chest, a gasping draw of oxygen that released in a shriek as Ingrid surged up on the bed, still managing to safely hold her sleeping babies. Looking around frantically, she took more heaving breaths, trying to understand what had happened. Gazing at Loki's shocked face, realization finally struck, and Ingrid's head tipped back in bliss. "You freed me..." she whispered.

With a sudden displacement of air, two exquisite white wings suddenly erupted from her arched back, an expression of incandescent joy on Ingrid's face. "I am free!" she laughed, sweeping the air with the iridescent feathers. The soft swoop of the wings suddenly closed gently around her shoulders, covering their children and smoothing along Loki's shaking arms. Tilting her head to rest against his, Ingrid kissed his wet cheeks, crying herself and laughing at the same time in a confused, hiccupping sound.

"You're alive!" Loki gasped, frantically running his hands over her face and hair, "You're... here," he finished lamely, unable to express more.

"I suppose I am," Ingrid stuttered, shaking her head with a smile. "You freed me, and you gave me life again." Those delicate wings slid gently against him, and Loki carefully, tenderly stroked the tip of one, smiling at the downy feel of it. Kissing her sweet mouth, the King of Asgard - and by default all the Nine Realms - dropped his head to his wife's shoulder, weeping in gratitude as her wings closed around her family, hiding them from the world.

Chapter 37

*In which love triumphs and a
family is reunited.*

L oki had spent the many centuries of his existence with a mind in constant motion- always calculating, manipulating- staying twenty or thirty steps ahead of his enemies. But at the moment, there was no room left for anything but the vision of his wife nursing their children, smiling down at their daughter while her thumb stroked the cheek of their son. He'd carefully placed pillows under her arms, supporting Ingrid as Frigg tactfully showed her how to nurse before leaving the room, and the family to themselves.

After the initial shock and tears, Loki allowed his Ljósálfar in-laws and Queen Frigg to hover over mother and twins before politely steering them out. He could dimly hear the clamor from the streets of Asgard, his people celebrating both the victory against the Dark Elves and the joy of the birth of the royal twins. Loki shook his head in irritation, knowing that Thor, that oaf- would be in the middle of it, drinking himself insensible with Freyr, Tyr, Balder, and Freya- still likely hoping she'd finally get a leg over the God of Thunder if he drank enough.

Turning back to Ingrid, he cupped her cheek briefly as she flushed, helping their daughter latch on before looking over to their son, who was beginning to cry hopefully for his share. "Husband, can you..." Loki nodded and nestled the boy in her other arm, moving her robe open to help guide him to her other breast.

"Such a delightful, accomplished mother you are already, my darling," he purred, enjoying the view of her cheeks growing even redder, the blush making its way down her neck. One big hand gently ran over the downy heads of his babies, watching their little starfish hands open and close contentedly. He'd been a little disappointed to see Ingrid's beautiful wings fold quickly away when the others had been admitted to the room, even though he knew this was a precious secret between them until it was time to be revealed. But the feel of those silky feathers against his wet cheek- it was a sensory memory that would never leave him. They'd carefully touched their babies, unwrapping their swaddling blankets to examine their backs- both little ones carried their mother's winged markings, and to Ingrid's delight and Loki's concern- their father's Jötunn patterns over their chest and legs, the spiral of design fluttering in and out of sight.

"Why do the markings not remain constant?" Ingrid asked.

Loki had forced a smile, securely bundling their twins in blankets again. "I'm a shapeshifter, my love. I suspect they are as well. There is a learning period before such things can be mastered." Looking up into his beautiful eyes, Ingrid frowned to see the darkness returning there.

Taking his hand and placing a kiss against the rough palm, she reminded him, "I told you that I hoped our babies would look just like you. My wish has been granted." A frown creased her forehead when Loki suddenly opened his other hand. Resting under his fingers was the bedraggled hummingbird she'd fought so hard to keep alive. A sob erupted from her throat when the tiny bird gave an irritable 'cheep!' while turning its head and back forth, looking for nourishment. "I thought this little one was dead," she admitted, "that the only thing I could do was destroy..." Her purple eyes traveled upward when the creature took flight, swirling happily over their heads.

Loki subtly moved his hand, finishing the

seidr that had healed the bird during her absence. "I think the end to your fears rests before you, my love."

When his family was sleeping peacefully in his huge bed, Loki pushed away his exhaustion by bathing quickly and putting on (slightly) less formidable armor before going in search of the Allmother- Asgard's Queen Frigg, thought by all to have passed away in grief after her husband Odin was killed. Loki found her, as he expected, in the Queen's chambers. "Your funeral was magnificent," he observed, bowing as she invited him in.

Frigg's full mouth curved into a secretive smile. "I would assume. You would have given me the finest of all ascensions to Valhalla."

"Because I loved you, despite your choice in husbands," Loki grinned, despite his best efforts to appear stern.

Inclining her blonde head, Frigg added, "And because you cannot resist all pomp and circumstance."

The king chuckled; a bit giddy after the most tumultuous day of his existence. "Of course." Sobering a bit, he fixed her with a stern glare. "And where have you been, Allmother? Such a disappearance- Heimdall could not find you-even I could not see through this ruse?"

Frigg was too elegant to actually roll her eyes, but it was close. "Vanaheim, of course. Home. It is quite easy to hide in the place of my birth, even from the all-seeing gaze of Heimdall."

Loki settled heavily on to a divan, absently accepting a glass of wine from the goddess he'd once viewed as closest to a mother as he'd had. "I would have thought that if not... dispatching the Allfather would earn your ire, that banishing one son to Midgard and sending the other to work in the Royal Stables might have caused you to seek your vengeance."

She still smiled at him fondly, the way Frigg always had before Loki had upended the Æsir gods and goddesses and taken the throne. "I am Vanir," the Allmother reminded him, and Loki rubbed his aching brow. Finally taking pity on the exhausted god, Frigg patted his hand. "One of my strongest gifts is that of Sight. I knew what was to come. And it was the correct course."

Whatever Loki might have expected to come from the lips of the Allmother, it was not that. Raising one dark brow, he managed, "You - masterfully, I might add - convinced us all that you had ascended to Valhalla and sought refuge in Vanaheim, even knowing what I would do to your sons?"

Frigg lounged back on her multitude of pillows, sipping her wine. "The Æsir - including Thor and Balder -" she added with a sigh, "were soft, arrogant. Nothing to challenge their perceived superiority. Until you took the throne, of course." She smiled, watching Loki's perplexed expression. "A good mother knows when to step back and let her children make their own decisions, even if they are wrong. Including you, Loki. You may not be a child from my body, Trickster. But I have known you all your life. You are a child of my spirit."

The King of Asgard was still, gripping his goblet of wine and pondering Frigg's startling approval. His Frost Giant origins didn't allow for weakness, Fárbauti and Laufey may have given him life, but they were not much interested in him from then on. The Jötunn were not sentimental. With an exhausted sigh, he said, "And now that you have returned, Allmother, does this signify approval of my reign or disappointment?"

Frowning thoughtfully, Frigg took his hand. "I would not have returned, had it not been for your queen- for Ingrid's plight. There is more to the girl than Elf, is there not?" She watched Loki's look of bland amusement- the expression he usually wore that gave nothing away. It faded then, and for a moment she could see the stark terror in his eyes.

"You saved her life. You saved our children." Loki swiped his hand through his hair, leaving it wildly disordered. "My sweet Ingrid nearly died because I was too selfish... I..." he stuttered to a stop, the legendary Silvertongue unable to speak.

Taking his hands, Frigg squeezed them reassuringly. "Oh, Loki..." she sighed, "you must always learn your lessons the hard way, mustn't you? But you did." Leaning in to catch his gaze, she nodded firmly. "You did. Now, go to your family and get some rest. We will speak more tomorrow."

As expected, Thor and his drunken following didn't return to the palace until late the next afternoon, still a little inebriated- yet managing to be hung over- a miserable combination that Loki was pleased to see on every pale face. Standing at the top of the granite stairs leading to the assembly hall, the king looked down his elegant nose at the ale-soaked group. "Ah," he drawled regally, "I see the 'Heroes of Asgard' have returned." Freya's eyes narrowed angrily, but the others- even the calm Balder, were childishly giddy. That emotion evaporated as Loki took one stately step down, then another, still gazing coldly. A stern gaze flicking over them, he controlled an urge to grin at the growing alarm on the faces of the most fearsome warriors in the Nine Realms. "After you have changed and bathed away the stink of a night at every bar in the capital city, Ingrid would like you to meet your niece and nephew." He stifled another chuckle at the uncertain expressions from his former stable hands. "She was most specific in requesting the three of you."

The gods all eagerly dispersed, anxious to clean up and meet the Crown Prince and Princess of Asgard. Freya was left standing alone, glaring at Loki. "Fortunately for you," he said, eyeing her thoughtfully, "the queen is more forgiving than you are. I would suggest you find a way to behave in a civil fashion to the one person in this kingdom who has the power to restore you to your former glory as a Goddess of Asgard." Loki watched Freya's fists clench. The stink of her rage and hate was usually a lovely perfume when he was in a spiteful mood, but he had no patience for it today. Irritably waving one hand, he dismissed the seething Freya as he returned to his chambers. There were better things to do.

Chapter 38

*In which Loki is a loving father,
a caring husband and powerful
king. But he's still Loki.*

Which means mischief.

F ifty years later...

"I'm telling Mother!" The outrage in Arne's voice was part of an often-repeated pattern between the twins, where one of his sister's schemes would somehow end up involving him- very much against his will.

"Tell Mother what?" Brynja's voice was a more delicate version of Ingrid's- a sweet, light tone that melted the hearts of everyone around her. It was not matched by the diabolical gleam in her lavender eyes- something most people failed to notice. At their peril. "That we flew in Queen Frigg's garden? The thing we are expressly forbidden to do? Imagine our punishment."

"Our? OUR?" Poor Arne's increasing frustration was suddenly drowned out by the splintering of a marble statue by the twins. "You- you said we should practice! It was your idea!"

Brynja strolled over to the statue, tilting her head to examine the damage from her brother's agitation. "You didn't have to," she observed in an infuriatingly calm tone. The truth was, she was jealous of Arne's power to alter the natural world, even if he had trouble controlling it. He worked with their mother every day, while she would stroll down to her father's potion's garden.

Loki- with patience never seen before- would explain the properties of a root or blossom, showing her how drying the substance or crushing it into a powder could affect the spell. Under the sun and the vague drone of the Valerian smudge bees, Loki would remember doing the same with Frigg. Re-creating the timeworn pattern with his daughter finally gave him some peace over his past. And sometimes, the All-mother would return from Vanaheim to join them. Listening to their banter now, his broad shoulders shook with a silent chuckle. His son's wide green eyes- so like his own- were filled with an innocence that Loki's had never been. For that reason, perhaps, he often found himself siding with the boy in his innate and stubborn decency- even when Loki secretly praised his daughter's guile.

Finally deciding to end the argument, the king stepped out from behind the flowering Dryad Nettles who were hopefully humming a tender little tune to draw the unwary closer to their black-tipped thorns. "Yes, children. Tell your mother what? Do explain."

His twins whirled as one to face him, little hands reaching for each other unconsciously. "Explain, Father?" Arne's face radiated innocence. "We don't know what you mean."

Pursing his lips against a grin, Loki looked sternly at the two, instantly aligned against him. "And how did this sculpture crack?" He ran his hand over the rigid marble, secretly impressed at his son's power.

Brynja shook her inky curls, a sincere confusion on her sweet face. "We have no idea, Father."

"Now, now, my darling children." Loki bent his tall frame, looking his children right in the eye. "You do realize you're attempting to deceive the God of Lies, do you not?" He knew the twins were scant seconds from crumbling, but looking at their tightly entwined hands, their father shook his head and stood. "No more flying in your Godmother's garden. Your mother's ban is for a very good reason, is it not?"

Both heads, blonde and dark, lowered. "Yes, Father," they repeated together.

"Good," Loki attempted to sound stern. "Now, Hannah is waiting to take you to your astronomy lessons. If I find your professor 'accidentally' hanging upside down from the balcony again, you will not leave your rooms for a month. Am I clear?" Smiling at their instant nods, he kissed them both on the head and handed them over to a now grey-haired Hannah, who nodded apologetically as she herded Arne and Brynja off to the tower.

"Hurry now, little ones," she urged, taking one small hand in each of hers, "Prince Thor is to arrive in time for dinner with Princess Sif. You don't want to miss that, do you?" The delighted shrieking of his offspring made Loki shake his head. Thor. Of course.

Ingrid was on the massive balcony outside their chambers when Loki let himself in. He leaned against the doors for a moment, watching his wife's head, circled by radiant jade and silver butterflies, swirling in unison as she hummed to them. If he looked closely, he could just see the outline of her wings fluttering lightly under her silk robe. "Your children are quite mendacious, darling," he finally said, straightening from his position as she whirled to greet him.

"My children?" Ingrid was laughing as she turned her face up for a kiss. "Mine? I do believe there is no question, my King, that when our twins are naughty, they are your children."

Kissing one soft hand and then the other, Loki held them to his chest. "They were flying in Frigg's garden again."

Ingrid's pale brows drew together in concern. She and Loki had shared the precious secret of her Fairie gift- passed on to their children- with Frigg and the King and Queen of the White Court, but no one else knew. They both had a powerful, almost unreasoning desperation to keep this secret from the Nine Realms. It wasn't time to reveal something this precious. They were both certain, feeling the same shudder of fear and discontent every time the subject rose again with Arne and Brynja. "I know the Allmother's garden is shielded, but how do we explain the danger to such young children? Other than binding them- I- I just-"

Loki leaned down, tilting her head for a long kiss. "Despite disobeying us, they did do so only in Frigg's sacred space, where they knew they couldn't be detected. But I will decide on a magnificently creative punishment for them tomorrow."

Ingrid burst into laughter, knowing that her husband's disciplinary actions with his off-spring were varied and brilliant. "I bow to your original and diabolical plans, my King."

"Really..." Oh, she knew that tone, and his wife smiled nervously as she edged away from Loki, who glided after her with the sinuous grace of a cobra, head down and gazing at her greedily. "Come here, darling. Listen to your King, now."

A small yelp burst from Ingrid's lips as Loki suddenly reappeared behind her, sliding one firm arm around her midsection.

"My King? Your- ah!" She broke off as he bit sharply into her neck, licking the sore spot before moving on to another. "Thor and um... Sif are..." He grinned against her skin as Ingrid's protests died off.

"Yes, my darling?" Loki purred as he wound her long silky length of hair around his fist. "You were saying?"

"I... hmmm..."

Looking down, he could see Ingrid's pink lips part, even though she was helpless to answer him. Running one big hand down her abdomen, he enjoyed the way her muscles twitched against the press of his palm. "Does my little one require something... does she need something from her husband?" Grinning against her neck as she shuddered, he urged, "Use your words, darling."

Shyly, Ingrid grasped his hand and slid it down to her wet pelvis, pushing against his fingers. "Please?"

Loki's silky black hair tickled her cheek as he shook his head, chuckling darkly. "After all this time, lovely- after all the delicious, filthy things we've done together- things you've let me do to you- you're still shy?" Two of his long fingers slid into her wet center, moving into her channel easily. Ingrid's hips thrust against his hand helplessly, gasping in pleasure. "Darling," he hissed, "you're so wet, you dirty little girl. What am I to do with such a filthy creature? Hmmm?"

Putting her hand over his and pushing him harder inside her, Ingrid moaned, "Take care of me, my King. I'm... um... I'm needing you. Please?"

Loki's hips were moving against his wife's now, and he turned them to brace her hands on the stone balustrade that blocked them from view from below. Sliding her silk robe open, he played idly with her breasts, swelling harder when he remembered them full with milk. They'd gone against every royal tradition by refusing a wet nurse, Ingrid happily nourishing her own children. The king would spend hours watching the contentment on the beautiful faces of his family as his babies suckled from their mother. And when Ingrid finished caring for them, she'd often feel the cool, devious mouth of her husband on one peaked nipple or another. "My darling, I remember these sweet breasts, so full of milk..." he squeezed them harshly and she moaned, arching against him. "But I did so enjoy taking ownership back from our children. The only one to touch them-" Ingrid moaned again, louder this time as his hard fingers twisted her hardened nipples between them. "-to play with them, to suckle them..."

Suddenly impatient, he ripped open his leather trousers, grateful that he wasn't in full armor. Yanking her silk robe to the side, Loki began sliding his swollen cock against her, sliding up and down against his wife's wet center. He could feel Ingrid brace her long legs, pushing back against him eagerly. Sliding two fingers around her clit, he pulled sharply, forcing the little nub against the cold stone of the wall. Her startled yelp made him grin. "Oh, little one..." he soothed, "does that feel uncomfortable? Your sweet clit rubbing against that chilly granite?" Loki thrust into Ingrid, enjoying her little shriek as he shoved her sensitive center against the wall again. He began pounding up into her channel brutally, knowing she could bear the force of him inside her, watching her hands grasp and slide against the balcony. "There's my good girl," he growled, hips snapping painfully against her soft ass, forcing her into a faster rhythm.

Putting both hands hard on Ingrid's hips, Loki lifted her off his cock and higher, resting her hip bones against the rock. Looking down at his slick cock, he ran his hand along it, adding more lubricant with a complex movement of fingers. Sliding himself against the little pucker of her bottom, he leaned closer, whispering into her ear. "Does my little one want me in her tender bottom? Would you like my cock up inside you? Hmmm?" Hearing her answering whimper was enough, and Loki began slowly sliding himself inside her. Despite his filthy urging, he was exceptionally cautious with the tender bits of his wife's body, enjoying the sudden clench against his burrowing shaft. Halting reluctantly, he licked her ear. "Let me in, now. Open for me. Let me in." Pulling her chin around to capture her mouth, Loki quickly stifled a shriek from his wife with a kiss as he began pushing forcefully against her resistant channel, enjoying the tightening and relaxing of her little ass. The squeeze against his shaft was almost painful, but he gritted his teeth and pushed forward another inch, then another, smoothly sliding two fingers back inside her clenching pussy, shoving the heel of his hand against that swollen clit. Finally opening her to the point his cock could slide smoothly in and out, Loki increased his pace against his wife, moving harder and deeper until he felt Ingrid's body begin to shake. "It's time. Give me what belongs to me- to your King. Now. NOW!"

With a shriek that could be heard in the farthest reaches of the courtyard, Ingrid obediently came, writhing against the hard flesh spearing through her bottom as his fingers pressed brutally down on her clit, forcing her finish, and then another one before he groaned, flooding her back channel with his come. Leaning over her, enjoying the feel of her heaving back against his chest, Loki groaned, carefully removing his fingers from her cleft, then his cock from her squeezing bottom, feeling the cool slide of his come seeping from his wife. Suddenly, Ingrid began to giggle. Loki's brow creased with confusion, even as he kissed her neck and her mouth, smoothing her sweaty silvery-blonde hair away from her face. "You must leave yourself in the other channel, if you wish to have those children you keep mentioning, my King."

Her giggle cut off in a yelp as Loki slapped his wife's ass, but he held her against him as he carried her back into their bedroom. "Then perhaps I should tidy us both, my Queen, and then you can show me the correct, ah, channel?" Feeling Ingrid's arms wrap around him as she burst into laughter, the King of Asgard - and by default all the Nine Realms - could not have dreamt of anything more.

The laughter rang against the soaring ceilings of the Royal dining room that night- a more intimate seating than the massive banquet hall. Looking around, Loki watched Ingrid gently place her hand on Sif's swelling stomach, smiling with happiness for her as Frigg squeezed her hand. "Your lovely Sif looks well," he observed to Thor.

The god he once again called 'brother' smiled proudly. "She is so tiny... I was not sure such a thing could be done, even after Sif was restored to immortality. Fortunately, Ingrid has some experience with being impregnated by a Frost Giant, so she was of great assistance, along with Mother, of course."

Loki shuddered, "Please do not mention my beautiful wife in conjunction with anything having to do with your awkward couplings." Thor drank from his cup, laughing and refusing to take offense. King Leafstred and his wife chatted with their grandchildren, laughing uproariously at something that Ingrid was quite certain was blatant misbehavior.

"You must not encourage the twins!" she laughed, half-scolding the Light Elves.

"I'm sorry, my dear," the Ljósálfar King chuckled. "It's just... they remind me so much of Ulbricht- of your father. The same mischievous faces." His expression sobered. "I wish he were alive to see them. He would be so very proud of you."

There was the faintest breeze that passed through the group as if the air was displaced by the wings of a bird. "My father is alive," Ingrid said casually, taking another slice of bread.

There was dead silence around the room, every face turned in shock to her. "What did you just... say, my Queen?" Loki leaned in; certain he had not heard his wife correctly.

"He lives," said the former Black Court Princess, who could only speak the truth. "My father lives, and he will return here, along with more of the Fairie." Her lovely face clouded for a moment, "There is... something more. Something terrible. It will be coming for us, too."

Thank you for reading *"I Love the Way You Lie*

Thank you for reading "I Love the Way You Lie."

The sequel to this story will be out in winter of 2020. Until then, please enjoy the first chapter of: *"Jólablót: The Night of Sacrifice."*

Part two of the *"Loki, God of Mischief and Lies"* series.

Chapter One

In which Loki and Ingrid celebrate the Jól of the Old Gods. Where a sacrifice is demanded to bring an end to the darkness of winter.

"**G**od Jól!!" The toast went up from Thor, who bellowed at the top of his substantial lungs, making the king's eyes roll slightly as the great hall shook with the returning cheers of "God Jól!" in return. The God of Thunder was deep in his cups and had been for the last three days. But tonight's feast was the culmination of Jól, which began on the day of the Solstice, and Loki, King of Asgard - and by default all the Nine Realms - was prepared to tolerate his friend's antics. The reason for Loki's new leniency was seated next to him- Queen Ingrid, his beloved wife, and mother to his twins. Who despite overseeing three weeks of celebration at the palace - which was flooded with dignitaries and nobility from across the Universe - was still flushed prettily and laughing at Thor's exuberance.

But because he could not resist instilling awe and fear, the king spoke next. "Ah, yes Thor. This day we celebrate the return of the Sun with the Night of Sacrifice- the Jólablót." Loki's voice had deepened ominously, and a hush fell across the huge hall as his magically amplified voice carried to the farthest reaches. "The nights and days of darkness now begin to shorten, as the Goddess brings her sun chariot across the sky again." These stories were mainly myth, crafted for the mortals who still feared and worshipped the Æsir, not just on Midgard, but on several Realms who still clung to the superstitions of their elders. So, Loki's dramatic retelling was really just self-aggrandizement since the myths and legends focused mainly on him - and Thor - who was busy raising his gigantic goblet and gesturing for more mead. "But first, we must offer Jólablót."

Hundreds of guests shifted in their seats, murmuring anxiously and feeling the primitive, atavistic fear rise within them at their king's words. Loki paused, a splendid and terrifying figure in his dark armor- such a dark green as to be nearly black- his silver weaponry and magnificent crown. "But for that, it is not yet time. So, celebrate, our good friends! Eat and drink!" A huge and somewhat relieved roar of applause rose, and everyone got back to the business at hand: eating, drinking until they passed out, then reviving themselves to do it all over again.

Seating himself and kissing Ingrid's hand, Loki winked at her faint smirk.

"Really, my husband? You could not let Thor's silly toast go unanswered?" His Queen's voice was low and teasing, and her eyes shone with love for him, something Loki sometimes still could not believe had been gifted to him.

"Of course not, my darling," he murmured, deliberately adding a purr under his tone, knowing it would make Ingrid shiver a little, "we cannot allow the unwashed masses to believe that my idiot friend brings the new year, when it is clear that the end of the darkness comes from the All-father."

"Of course not..." Ingrid's eyes sparkled before she leaned in, clearly asking for a kiss, which Loki gladly granted.

A light, lovely voice spoke up next. "What is a Jólablót, Father?" Brynja, of course, was the one to lean forward eagerly, hoping for all the gory details. Her lavender eyes and her sweet voice came from her mother- but the conniving brain under that pitch-black hair was all her sire.

"Where a sacrifice is demanded from the Gods

- a Jólablót," Loki smiled indulgently at his daughter.

"Wh- what kind of sacrifice, Father?" The concerned question came from his son Arne, his jade green eyes wide and with an earnestness never seen in Loki's matching ones.

"The Goddess does not bring the sun again without an appropriate sacrifice, my son," he answered, "an offering is required."

Ingrid, picturing several weeks of nightmares to come, gracefully stepped in. "And something best explained when you are older, my darlings-"

"I'm old enough!" protested Brynja immediately, but her mother laughed and shook her head.

"It is very late, and time for you to sleep. We must bid farewell to all our guests tomorrow. Please go and tell your grandparents goodnight before retiring." Ignoring their half-hearted protests, Ingrid tenderly kissed their children, who went to their father for the same before heading off with their nurse Hannah, long gone grey from looking after the offspring of the God of Mischief, who insisted on living up to their sire's name.

Watching them reach the Light Elf contingent, Ingrid's eyes misted to see them enthusiastically hug and kiss King and Queen Leafstred, their Ljósálfar grandparents who were alight with love for the twins. Loki leaned in close to kiss her just under her ear, then whispering, "I am sorry your father is not here tonight, my love."

She blinked back the moisture in her eyes and smiled firmly. "All things in their time, husband."

She never knew how a stab of fear went through Loki's hardened heart when Ingrid spoke of her father- the brother of King Leafstred and unwilling consort to the vicious Queen of the Dark Elves. Ingrid - who could only speak the truth - possessed incalculable power and was the last of the Fairie in this universe. And how she had predicted her father and the Fairie would return, followed by a Something unspeakable.

Forcing a smile back to his mobile lips, Loki kissed her again before leaning back to survey the great hall, not noticing that his Queen continued to watch him, smiling lovingly. Loki was her king, her husband, the father of her children. Her savior. Thinking back on their beautiful, tumultuous history, Ingrid didn't realize the exhaustion of creating the massive celebration of the past three weeks was finally catching up with her as she dozed off.

Ingrid woke with a start, sitting up abruptly and anxiously rubbing her eyes as she looked around her. She'd fallen asleep at the banquet... but this was not her bedchamber. She was alone on a massive snowy field, stretching as far as she could see under a night sky so black that not a sliver of light could be seen- no moon, no stars, nothing. Rising to her feet, she walked for a moment, flicking a charm with one hand to keep her feet from sinking into the deep snow. Her heavy ceremonial gown trailed after her as Ingrid turned in one direction, then the other, trying to spot any kind of a structure, the smoke from a fire, perhaps. Whatever brought her here was powerful magic. Her own should have grounded her in the great hall- or Loki would have surely blocked any attempt at abduction. With a sigh, she closed her eyes, sending her senses soaring in all directions, trying to discover where she'd been brought. The answer was not a comforting one.

This was a hunting ground.

The baying of hounds and distant shouts galvanized Ingrid into moving, racing across the snow. Another flick of her fingers changed her useless gown into heavy boots and leather pants, a thick coat. With a grim smile, she kept moving. She didn't need to conjure weapons, because she did not need them. Whoever was hunting her would discover that soon enough. Still, the Queen of Asgard had taken the vow a century before to no longer take life if she could avoid it. But returning home to her family was paramount. The sounds of the animals hunting her and their masters grew closer, and Ingrid gritted her teeth, feet flying over the snow. How could any animal run this fast? She knew her speed could be nearly supernatural if required, but the heavy beat of hooves and paws grew closer still.

"There she is!" The roar went up, making the hounds howl and the shouts of the other hunters were cruel, eager. "Do not let her slip away! The king will tear us to pieces for animal fodder!"

Ingrid groaned. A king. Who else would be insane enough to challenge her husband? Loki would dismantle this place down to the last molecule when he discovered her disappearance. As she squinted, she could just make out a line of trees, if she could make it into the woods, she could-

"We have her!"

She heard the wild singing shrill of the noose before she felt it, a loop of shining energy that landed over her head and wrapped instantly down her body, binding her arms to her sides and legs together, making Ingrid fall ignominiously face-first into the snow. A string of harshly growled words- something from one of the Dead Languages stole her consciousness before she even hit the ground.

It was the heat of the fire Ingrid felt first as she forced herself back into awareness. She was still bound in the glittering bindings, but she was naked underneath it. 'At least I'm comfortable and warm,' Ingrid thought bitterly. Shielding her from the cold stone floor was a massive white fur from some unimaginably huge creature. It was thick and soft. Forcing herself upright, she looked around her. The fur was in the middle of a towering throne room, lined with fireplaces large enough to roast several oxen at once. There were hundreds of torches battling away the darkness outside.

"Ah. Awake at last, my prize." The voice was beautiful, sonorous like her husband's but with a jagged edge of cruelty. "I've been waiting for you, and patience is not a virtue I possess. You will pay for that."

Whirling, awkward in her bindings, Ingrid's jaw dropped. *"Loki?"*

The man on the throne was Jötunn. Soaring black horns with delicate silver chains adorning them rose from his forehead. Luxuriously thick ebony hair, braided with beads and jewels and- were those bones? Long blue limbs stretched on from broad shoulders and a narrow waist. And the markings... Ingrid had only seen her husband's beautiful display on his cobalt skin once when he had changed for her, just before their wedding. He'd refused to show her his Jötunn form again, no matter how many times she'd begged him. But the dots and lines along this giant's body were exquisite, spiraling and sailing along his limbs in a pattern of unspeakable elegance. This exotic creature wore silver-plated Schynbald -armor covering his shins and heavy boots, a jeweled chest-plate and some kind of leather kilt or loincloth. When her eyes finally rose to his ruby red ones, the Jötunn grinned, showing the tips of razor-sharp fangs. "Do you like what you see, slave?"

Ingrid leaned forward with a snarl, still managing to look dangerous while securely bound. "I am no slave. I am Her Majesty of Asgard, Her Royal Highness of Alfheim and Niflheim and you will *die* for this. How dare you-"

With a growl, the Frost Giant cut her off. "You will be silent! Slaves do not speak and believe me. You are a slave," he leaned forward with a cruel grin, "mine, in fact. To do with what I please. And oh, pretty thing, I have so many things planned for you." He rose then, and Ingrid looked up, and up and up until her neck cracked as he strolled down the steps of his dais and stood before her, legs arrogantly apart in just the way her Loki would. "You blurted out a name," he hissed, "my brother's. Do not utter it again. I am the rightful King of Jötunnheim."

Ingrid ground her teeth in fury. What madness was this? Loki ruled the frozen world of the Frost Giants. He had no siblings. No one to aspire to the throne. No one certainly, powerful enough in magic to abduct her from Asgard and to here. Was she in a parallel universe? What could possibly be happening here? She shook her head, eyes narrowed. "You do not silence me, pretender. My husband rules Jötunnheim. Loki," she emphasized tauntingly, "rules the Frost Giants."

This time the Jötunn answered her with a roar, arms stretching towards her as if to throttle the life from her. But Ingrid had no reason to hide her gifts any longer. With a resounding "crack!" that felt like the air in the massive room was somehow displaced, magnificent, snowy white wings shot from between her shoulder blades, exploding her enchanted bonds as she flew at the Frost Giant with a hiss that made the several ton slabs of stone beneath them rumble and shift. They crashed together with a fury, twisting and turning in mid-air as they tore at each other, both attempting to land a blow that would incapacitate the other. The blue King smashed into a wall, leaving a sizeable dent and a shower of granite chips and dust cascading down as he shot out with a howl, leaping at Ingrid and squeezing her between his impossibly long arms, folding her wings back inwards. But she laughed breathlessly, slamming her forehead brutally into his and stunning him briefly as she twisted loose, one wing slamming him sideways and halfway across the room. He groaned, having smashed head first into his own ice and ebony throne, exploding it into pieces. But the Jötunn was already up and thrusting one cobalt fist towards her and shouting, "Slaven blir straffet!"

Ingrid screamed, in rage, pain, and frustration. Lightning blue streaks of fire shot out from his fingers and encircled her, humming and sparking ominously and she twisted and writhed, trying to break free from the net of energy that was racing up her body, slithering along her skin and spiking nerve endings. To her horror, she could feel her center begin to warm as the enchanted fire moved along it, making her lower lips swell and eagerly moisten. She was furious. How could her body betray her like this? To an enemy?

That enemy was strolling towards Ingrid, absently smoothing back his hair in an unconsciously sensual move. One she'd seen her husband use many times and it never failed to arouse her. "Pretty little Fairie. You did not think I knew? Your kind are meant to be subjugated. Under my foot. Writhing on my cock. And you will be, slave."

"Skitten dyr! Monster! Feil ting!" Ingrid shouted, focusing her power in a way that should have torn her assailant into a thousand pieces. It did not, and he continued his inexorable stroll towards her, crimson eyes examining her beautiful, wiggling form.

Instead, he raised one huge hand and made an almost negligent gesture. "Åpne nå for din konge, lille fugl." To her horror, Ingrid found herself on her back on the massive fur again, and her legs- as directed by this arrogant blue bastard, were indeed spreading wide for him. And then he was standing above her, loosening his chest plate and armor and tossing them away carelessly. Ingrid's breath caught in her throat. Even shielded by his heavy leather coverings, she could see his cock begin to rise. It was suitably- and terrifyingly enormous. The Jötunn knew where her gaze was caught, and he grinned insolently. "I begin to think mounting you will not be such a battle, Fairie."

This time, Ingrid's foot broke loose and shot up viciously, heading for the gigantic bulge in his kilt and the Frost Giant turned enough to catch the blow on his thigh. Still, it was clearly painful and he growled, showing his sharp canines in warning and pounced on her, shoving his knees between hers and blocking the elf's furious attempt to close them. "Off me, beast!" she hissed, "Or I swear I will tear you limb from limb. I do not need the true king to destroy you!"

Ingrid's taunt hit home, and his eyes lit with an unholy fire. Yanking his leathers loose, he pulled his cock from them and arched his hips at her, stroking the massive organ. It was glimmering cobalt and like the rest of him covered with swirling marks of his clan, ridged lines...

"...That will rub along the tender silk of your cunt, slave. Adding to your pleasure until you beg me to come." Chuckling unkindly at the look of fury on Ingrid's lovely face, he continued, "Yes, I can hear your thoughts, slave. And I will sink into you to the root. Shoving my spear through your body until you feel skewered upon my cock. Hmmm... even wetter, slave. You want this, don't you?"

She couldn't speak- why? Ingrid grappled with the rising arousal and confusion. She should be screaming at this filthy bastard, using her powers to dissolve his brain and make it drip from his ears as he howled in agony, so why-? "AAAH! You do not dare!" The rest of her protest was cut off as the Jötunn fastened his frozen mouth against her heated quim. His shoulders moved in laughter but his tongue was occupied in tracing along her clitoris and tickling the entrance to her cunt. His hugely broad shoulders shoved her thighs wider, painfully wide and held them open as his frigid lips closed over her cunt in a filthy, carnal kiss. Ingrid was shaking and writhing, trying to move and dislodge this bastard, this invader from her body but he didn't even twitch. And oh, by the Nornir, his long, chilly tongue was sliding up her fiery channel, stroking in a terrible, knowing way that told her he was quite familiar with Elven physiology and knew exactly what he was doing to her. Ingrid continued to try to fight, to move away but her eyes closed, unable to look at him. Because this Jötunn was beautiful. Thick black lashes in a fan on those cruel cheekbones, and his hair-so wonderfully thick and silky stroking along her sensitive belly and tickling her breasts. His detailed musculature under that smooth cerulean skin begged to be traced, and his hips were mindlessly thrusting against her knees. Without thinking, just trying to shove him away from her somehow, Ingrid flailed out, grabbing one of his horns.

This was a mistake. With a long, shuddering growl, his head rose from her quim, chin wet with her slick and a snarl on his face. The Jötunn's huge chest was heaving and he moved swiftly up her body, his cock trailing surprisingly hot lines of the moisture oozing from it along her thighs. Ingrid's gaze was wide and startled. His horns, his long, shining ebony horns were blazing with heat in complete contrast to the rest of his polar-cold body. The Frost Giant was desperately trying to keep a hold on his sanity. The infuriating little Fairie had touched the one thing that made him vulnerable- his horns. The strokes of her soft hands and her initial, desperate grasp of it had stiffened his cock to an impossible length and it was everything he could do to not simply shove it up inside her as hard as he could, hammering himself into that sweet quim until she-

Groaning, his head dropped between her breasts, those long horns bracketing her face and holding her immobile. With a muttered curse under his breath, the Jötunn magicked her hands over her head and drew in a breath. Leaning over her, he grinned insolently. "I'm going to take you now, Queen of Asgard. Elf. Fairie. I'm going to force my cock inside your heated little body and split you wide. And when I am done, you will beg me to take you again." He laughed when she hissed at him, baring her teeth. Angling his beautiful, chilly body over hers, he took his indigo cock in hand, sliding it up and down her wet lips, enjoying the conflict in her expression as Ingrid tried to close her thighs against him.

"Open up, little slave, I own you, and I own this." He plunged into her as he finished his taunts and Ingrid bit back a scream, ending in more of a strangled shriek. "There we are..." he crooned in that deeply sonorous voice, so deep that it rumbled in her bones like a bass drum, playing along her spine and making her arch helplessly against his frigid chest.

Ingrid was gasping and moaning, so over-whelmed that she couldn't speak, couldn't fight. There had been no one for her but her husband, no cock that invaded her narrow channel but his. But this! The Jötunn's shaft was cool, cool as well water and so wide, splitting her just as he'd threatened and then those lovely, raised markings rubbing against her wildly sensitive channel, making her stomach muscles tighten, her toes point helplessly, her nails sink into the tough skin of the Frost Giant's biceps. He growled, thrusting up into her harder, enjoying the quivering silk of her, her sweet-smelling slick flowing to help him drive in deeper. Reaching one black taloned finger down, he slid it around the strained entrance to her cunt, enjoying the feel of it stretched so tightly around him. Holding the blue digit up to her eyes, he laughed tauntingly. "Protest all you like, sweet slave. You want this. You want me."

Bracing his feet, the Jötunn pushed and slid, moving deeper inside her, deeper than Ingrid

imagined her channel could possibly accommodate. The force of his thrusts was pushing her
backward against the fur, and as her silver hair
flowed dangerously close to the fireplace, he
growled and went back on his long haunches,
pressed against his heels as he hauled Ingrid upright, balancing her in front of him as her hands
grasped blindly at his shoulders. The huge hands
slid up her waist and behind her to cradle Ingrid
by her shoulder blades, leaning her back as his
glacial mouth landed on one pink nipple, pulling it with his lips, enjoying her startled squeal.
As he moved to her other breast, the Jötunn
chuckled low in his throat. "Such bounteous
breasts..." he rumbled, "so full and soft."

"My- my mother hated them, she said I had
'the teats of a peasant,'" Ingrid suddenly volunteered, shocked at the words coming out of her
mouth, confiding to this- this bastard, this arrogant blue villain who was vigorously hauling her
up and down on that thick staff of his.

He looked up suddenly, his eyes glowing a vicious crimson again. "Fortunate the monstrous
bitch is dead and gone. It would have pleased
me to end her myself." He arched his hips up ag-
gressively as he brought her down against him,
bringing himself to the hilt inside her, the coarse
hair at his pelvis rubbing against her swollen
clitoris. The Jötunn suckled at her breasts again,
growling low like an animal, a wolf perhaps.

At some point, Ingrid found one hand gripping tight to a handful of his thick hair as the other one slid gently along one of his horns, enjoying his snarl of pleasure and feeling the heat of it against her fingers. The hard ebony of it was smooth, sleek and boiling hot- warming her as the rest of him chilled her flushed skin and smoldering center. Ingrid was half out of her mind, horrified to realize she was about to come around his invading shaft, and there was nothing she could do to stop it. The Jötunn must have felt it, because his hands went to her hips, pulling her down more tightly as his thrusts shortened, sharpened inside her. "And now delicious, perfect slave it is time. On the Night of Sacrifice, you are my Jólablót. I will not impale you on my dagger but upon my cock. Come now, soak me with your come, Ingrid. Your pleasure is mine to own, and I will have it from you. NOW!"

Wide, mesmerized lavender eyes met glowing vermilion, and Ingrid, the Queen of Asgard and the last of the Fairie, found herself obeying this pillaging Frost Giant and came. Screaming, writhing, clutching his horns and ignoring his groans as she arched and shrieked through an orgasm so powerful that the heavy stone walls shifted and cracked, and the flames roared out from the fireplaces, sending wild shadows against the stone walls and nearly setting the fur beneath them ablaze. And he came too, so powerfully that Ingrid could feel it warm her belly, her chest as she fell against him, panting and moaning, still coming as his finish seeped from her flooded channel. The two wrapped their arms around each other tightly, still attached and rocking slightly.

"You were perfection, my beautiful, exquisite wife," Loki finally managed to croak.

Head still resting on his shoulder, Ingrid giggled weakly. "You were far too convincing, husband. I nearly brought the stones of this hall down on top of you before I realized it was indeed, Loki, the God of Mischief."

Groaning as he gently disengaged from her and watching the flood of his slick and hers pour from his wife's somewhat battered quim, Loki kissed Ingrid. "And the Night of Sacrifice is finished, Jólablót has been made." Waving a hand to tidy his wife and dress her again, the King of Asgard lifted her in his arms. "I have used you roughly, my darling. I shall make amends with great tenderness when we are alone in our bed."

Ingrid laughed, hiding her face in his neck. "I would do it again, every Jól. God Jól, indeed!" Loki shook his head at his wife's little dirty joke and the Frost Giant's throne room disappeared.

Later in their shadowy bedroom, Loki kept his promise, luring his wife to bed with sweet words. He kissed her over and over, whispering of the loveliness of her face, reflected in the firelight, the perfection of her body, the tightness of her quim, and they finished together with sighs and moans. Loki murmured, "I love you, wife," falling asleep still inside his beloved Ingrid as she whispered her love in return.

"Slaven blir straffet!" - "The slave is punished."

"Skitten dyr! Monster! Feil ting!" - "Filthy animal! Monster! Foul thing!"

"Åpne nå for din konge, lille fugl." - "Now open for your king, little bird."

Notes:

While it might almost be sacrilegious to compare Loki to a goat, there are certain breeds that have blood vessels in their horns, rather than just cartilage, and their horns are surprisingly, startlingly hot.